FLUX

PAM & OATES   PART ONE

MW00415822

M.J. WOODS

©2019. All rights reserved. No part of this book may be reproduced or transmitted in any form or by any means, electronic or mechanical, including photocopying, recording, or by any information storage and retrieval system, without permission in writing from the publisher.

This book is intended for a mature audience.

Flux

Copyright ©2019 M.J. Woods

Cover design by M.J. Woods Books

Cover photo licensed by Adobe Stock

www.mjwoodsbooks.com

First published by Perfect Balance Publishing
901 James Street
Syracuse, NY 13203

ISBN 978-0-9994741-2-9 (PAPERBACK)

This is a work of fiction. Names, characters, places and incidents either are the product of the author's imagination or are used fictitiously, and any resemblance to actual persons, living or dead, businss establishments, events or locales is entirely coincidental. The publisher does not have any control over and does not assume any responsibility for author or third party websites or their content.

Printed in the United States of America

9 8 7 6 5 4 3 2 1

"Every part of your life has unfolded just right."
- Esther Hicks

"Sometimes life's going to hit you in the head with a brick.
Don't lose faith."
-Steve Jobs

For Mom, In Loving Memory
Thank you for giving me a chance at the perfectly unfolded life,
bricks and all.

Acknowledgments

After publishing *The Amped Series* trilogy in one year, it pained me to take an entire year to complete a single book. Although this manuscript was complete in early 2018, my editing and publishing schedules had to be pushed back when life intervened. Just like the heroine in this story, I found myself in a state of flux that I could never have predicted. (Except maybe I did predict it, because I named this book long before Fate threw me all these curveballs. If life continues to imitate my 'art', my next book may be about winning the lottery.)

My sincerest gratitude to the following kind, generous, and talented souls who make my work and my life better:

Cheryl Meany and Sue Ames, for your tireless efforts in editing this work and for sharing your enthusiasm for these characters. I could not do this without you!

To Bree Weber, for loving this story and for steering it off my desk and into reality.

To my author friend Ron Bagliere and his longstanding writers critique group, for welcoming me into such a unique bunch of souls with extraordinary imaginations and talent, for challenging me, and for helping me improve.

To author Sandra Jackson, for your guidance about all things relating to Ontario, Canada and for triggering my memories of epic times spent in the "friendliest country ever!" on the St. Lawrence River.

To James, my girls, Dad, and my sister Jill, for your unselfish and boundless support, even when I feel unworthy of it.

Lastly, to all of my family, friends and readers, for putting up with me when I stumbled through the stages of grief, for encouraging me to step back when I needed to, and for cheering me on when I picked it up into a jog and pretended I knew what the hell I was doing.

Thank you to all of you, especially on those days when multiple bricks were tossed at my head.

1

Pam

June 20, 2016
Monday, 12:00 p.m.

Toronto, Ontario
Canada

I am royally screwed.

I run my thumb across my signature in disbelief. It all comes down to three words in blue ink, in the best penmanship I could manage with a shaking left hand.

Pamela Jean Clayton.

Summer session is in full swing here at OCAD U, but I'm not here for a class. I'm off this semester, sitting in the Student Advising Centre as my knees bounce.

Edwin Fedders called me last night from his personal cell phone — *on a Sunday* — and I've been on edge ever since. My student advisor's insistence that we talk in person today was a super-sized red flag.

Tomorrow, I'm headed for the States to visit my sister-in-law Alexis, though she's completely unaware of this. Her gorgeous billionaire boyfriend let me in on his plans this morning, which absolutely floored me.

He's arranged a grand, selfless gesture to honor the brother I lost: the man Alexis made a life with before she'd ever met the infamous Aidan Pierce. Somehow, the guy arranged the whole ceremony without Alexis finding out. No small feat given she's a savvy New York lawyer who isn't easy to surprise. She's going to be totally awestruck by what he's done.

Just like I am.

I shared the information about travel plans with my parents, thankful for something happy to offset my nerves after my conversation with Fedders. Still, I haven't been able to give Mr. Pierce's exciting news the attention it deserves.

By eight a.m., I left my tiny hometown in Bay Falls, Ontario, grabbed my caffeine fix and started driving the three plus hours to Toronto, all so Fedders could spend ten minutes with me in his cramped and cluttered office. He offered a donut which I declined, insisting he get to the point of our chat.

That's when he said it.

He's completely screwed up my fourth year plans.

Being the upstanding guy he is, he wanted to break the news in person that my fall semester options have changed. I'm left with two evils, my signature the single thing confirming my choice: stay in Canada — which I absolutely do *not* want to do — or uproot myself all the way to freaking California.

In my head, I cursed him up and down. I wished a click of my heels would land me in New York *Wizard of Oz* style to start my visit with Alexis one day early. I don't want to face a long drive home after this crushing blow only to end it by sharing the news with my parents.

This decision to stay in Canada or move to the Golden State will put a damper on tomorrow's happy occasion for all of us.

Total buzzkill.

I did manage not to ugly-cry in front of Fedders. And because this is how backwards my brain is, I actually feel bad for *him*. He's disorganized, but not incompetent. He excels at his job so much that his nickname is 'Lottery'. Any student assigned to him feels like they've won a grand prize. Though my path is now a question mark, I'd never have options in the first place if it weren't for him.

This also tends to be the way things go for me, so it may not be his fault. It's not the first time Fate has tripped on a rock, doing a face-plant in dirt just when I needed her most.

Fedders just sent me to the waiting area to think about the whole mess so he could meet briefly with another student. We'll talk again before his next appointment and, if I'm not ready to decide now, I can take one additional week. With my strong academic record, I can have my pick of internship programs here in Toronto — ones my peers would kill for.

The problem is I've dreamed of leaving Canada since I was twelve. If I hand in the form attached to this silly plastic clipboard, I won't have to stay. I can complete my studies in the States as planned, though it will send me farther away than I wanted to be.

Of course I signed my name as soon as I sat down. This is my only ticket out of here. But I've been a bundle of nerves ever since. I stare at my signature, realizing my own handwriting looks foreign.

Am I sure this is what I want?

Another student comes in and sits across from me. I tuck my feet beneath my chair so I'm not invading his personal space.

I'm tall 'for a girl', or so I'm constantly told. My eyes are brown to match my long, too thick hair. (You can add my thighs to the 'too thick' column, too, as far as I'm concerned.) Adding fuel to that fire is the fact that I'm a self-proclaimed nerd.

Yes, I actually like math and video games. I recognize the guy that just crash landed across from me because we take a lot of the same classes. We're both majoring in Digital Futures.

I'm a girl competing and excelling in a class dominated by guys.

Sure, some of them are guys I'd call friends. We can debate game consoles of the past or dating apps of the future over coffee. The rest treat me like a delicate flower or use their weak skills to pry into my head (for ideas) or into my pants (for the virginity they presume I still have).

Guys at home aren't much better, but there are fewer of them. My artsy university bustling with unique and creative souls is another dimension compared to Bay Falls. Home is only minutes north of the U.S. border, a rural and picturesque spot on the St. Lawrence River where the population is statistically outnumbered by livestock.

Dating has never been a priority for me, but more like an experiment conducted for a few weeks at max. My focus easily remained on my studies through the conclusion of my third year at

University. Any guy I had an ounce of feelings for turned out to be a straight-up jerk anyway. I swore off serious relationships and focused on my goal of moving to the States for my final year as an undergrad.

I truly am proud to be from the friendliest North American country, but I've always been full of wanderlust. Everyone close to me is aware of this fact, just as everyone knows to call me Pam, not Pamela.

Well, except for one guy.

Mr. Daryl Oates calls me Princess and, as lame or condescending as that may sound, he's totally allowed to do so.

I laughed the first time the nickname was coined by my best friend Carly. When Daryl said it to me, he had no idea I'd heard it before. I love it now, especially since he's the guy who made it stick.

Oates, as his friends call him, is one-of-a-kind man-candy. There is simply no substitute for him. He's a Geek Charming wrapped in a damn fine physique with a heart of gold at his gooey center. His brain is worthy of examination by science when he's done with it because he's definitely smarter than I am (which I both admire and envy). He can make a girl swoon without knowing he's doing it.

The icing on his cupcake is a mess of ink-black, curly hair that falls just so when it's wet.

He's someone I never thought I'd find until I left my quaint hometown and moved to the States. But then Fate intervened, showing up drunk and confused about the natural order of things.

Mr. Oates traveled all the way from his native California for a brief visit to Canada, and Fate planted him (literally) right in front of me. He's one reason for my current state of utter shit, and Fedders' screw-up is the other. The venue for my fourth year is now a choice that has my head battling my heart, and I have no idea if I'm doing the right thing.

This is infuriating for a girl who swore she'd never allow anything — especially a guy — to cause her to lose focus.

You'd think my brother's death just a year and a half ago would have disrupted my life and thrown me into orbit more than this. Without question, losing Ben was a catastrophic event for my family and the most devastating moment of my twenty-one years on this planet.

What I could never have predicted was his death becoming the moment my trajectory changed, the point in time when I began careening off my plotted course.

Because without that tragic loss, I never would have met Daryl Oates.

Twelve Days Earlier...

2

Oates

June 8, 2016
Wednesday, 7:00 a.m.

Palo Alto, California

"Next!"

In desperate need of caffeine, I step forward in line. It's seven a.m., I've been working twenty solid, and my self-imposed deadline is looming.

Before I can get out the words Iced Mocha Tesora to the barista, my phone vibrates in the pocket of my shorts. I ignore the call, keeping my eyes on the menu board. While I'm upright and out of the house, I should probably eat.

And the cupboards at our bachelor pad are currently bare.

"Sir?" the girl asks in a pleasant tone. Her blonde ponytail bounces as she tilts her head in wait. All the girls wear ponytails here, but I know this chick's new. Unfortunately, my favored barista is nowhere in sight.

My phone buzzes again, and I check the display. If the ringer volume was up, Fort Minor's "Remember the Name" would sound off in Philz Coffee right now. My closest friend on Earth must have something urgent to discuss.

"Shit." I pocket the phone.

Either at my cursing or at my lack of action, Friendly New Barista flips her switch to Irritated New Barista.

Real smooth, Oates.

"Sorry, not you," I say, waving a hand in the air. "I meant it for the guy blowing up my phone while I'm trying to order."

She doesn't seem receptive to my apology. She looks past me to the next guy in line, so I tell him to go ahead, then step away without my fix while my friend's call rolls to voicemail.

Typical shitty timing in the World of Oates.

Eleven days ago, my friend's call was welcomed. I answered eagerly and asked how he was faring some three thousand miles away in New York. But, surprise-surprise, he wasn't calling from New York. He was temporarily back in California for Memorial Day, insisting he would fly me down to LA so we could finally begin my project.

The tech baby kicking around in my head for years has been granted a chance at life by my best friend Aidan Pierce. What my sister calls one of my 'hare-brained nerd ideas' has now made Pierce an investor in me, Mr. Daryl Oates.

Okay, so he's my *only* investor.

But I'm not greedy. I just need the aid of one fantastically rich guy to get things moving.

My brainchild is a music sharing app he believes could be a household name, and Pierce's offer to help birth it is the best I could ever hope for. Our fifteen year friendship aside, he's hella-smart when it comes to business. If there's anyone you want in your corner on this kind of endeavor, it's Pierce. I don't even care that he's the cause of my current state: sleep deprived and stressed-the-hell-out.

I hit the button to return his call as I climb onto a stool and rest an elbow on the counter. I have to push my hair out of the way as I lift the phone to my ear, realizing I'm long overdue for a haircut.

"Oates!" he answers.

What the hell? "Pierce?" He almost sounds cheerful. Highly unusual.

"Yeah," he says, "it's me."

"Speak then, and tell me what can I do for you at this unholy hour."

But I have to wait while he excuses himself, interrupted by something urgent from his staff.

Pierce recently abandoned California for a small city smack in the center of New York State. He wanted to elude attention and pursue charity rather than stay on the left coast to idly rake in more dough. I watched him crush his goals to prepare for the move, which in turn motivated me to finally begin my project.

Pierce has a way of doing that. He can convince a stormy day to retreat and leave behind blue skies and rainbows just by looking up.

Before leaving the Golden State, he sold an extensive list of properties, dismantled several businesses, and oversaw renovation of an entire four-story building in his new home city of Stanton, New York. Meanwhile, his celebrity, attention-seeking ex-girlfriend refused to accept their break-up or the fact that he was leaving. She made ridiculous attempts to hold him back, which he did his best to ignore.

Despite the hurdles, every task he assigned himself was completed quickly. When progress at the building housing his new residence and charity headquarters slowed, he pulled up stakes and left for the East Coast earlier than planned.

Pierce doesn't do waiting.

He was out of here in early May but unexpectedly called back to California over Memorial Day weekend thanks to said ex-girlfriend and her shit-show. During our impromptu meeting about my music app, I knew he was feeling the pressure from trying to juggle everything on two coasts.

But, ya gotta know Pierce. He's one of those guys that turns any Everest-like climb into an idle day in Santa Cruz, all while looking good. He could land a side gig as a Calvin Klein underwear model if he damn well felt like it.

Not that he would *ever* do that.

"Sorry, had to put out a fire." He still sounds upbeat despite the interruption. "You holding up?"

"Dude, it's fucking seven a.m. I'm trying to caffeinate and you're java-blocking me."

"Sorry, it's ten here. I'm way past coffee." He lets go a subdued laugh, and now I'm completely puzzled. Aidan Pierce isn't usually one for outbursts of amusement. "I'm calling because I need a favor."

I exhale in relief that he's not pushing for our next meeting, and my mood lifts further when my regular barista Jenny waltzes in and gives me a nod.

Thank you, sweet baby Jesus.

"Sorry, one sec again," Pierce says.

"Take your time." I'm used to this. He's often interrupted multiple times while on a personal call.

Jenny keeps her voice low as she comes over, realizing I'm on the phone. "The usual?"

I'm still seated as she reaches me. She's barely five-two while I'm six foot. Her irises are a pretty shade of blue, a striking contrast to her dark hair. While my mop of black curls is a mess, Jenny's hair is straight, cut short enough that her neck is exposed. She's the only barista working here that doesn't need to wear a ponytail.

I smile at her and mute my phone. "I'd kill baby bunnies for a burrito. Haven't eaten since lunch yesterday."

"Spicy Sausage and a large Iced Mocha Tesora, right?"

"Please," I say with a grateful smile, "and your recall is astounding, Jenny."

She beams at my compliment. "I'll bring it over for you, but you really need to stop pulling those all-nighters. And don't kill any bunnies, please." She heads behind the counter to start my order, saving me from the line that's now twice as long.

I considered asking the sweet brunette out once but decided against it. I rarely have time to date, and my last brief relationship was a horrific crash and burn. Jenny's also younger than girls I go for. I know she's a sophomore at Stanford, and I turned the dreaded three-oh this spring. The milestone somehow made it feel weird to ask out a young college student.

I unmute the phone just as Pierce comes back to the line.

"Sorry," he says, "busy morning."

"What's this about a favor?" I say, pretending to seriously consider his request. "Don't know if I'm inclined to accommodate."

"Funny, Oates."

"Just name it, man. I'm on a deadline."

"Don't you want to know what it is before you agree?"

"Not necessary," I say. "You're my brother-from-another. Ask and ye shall receive."

After everything he's done for me, I'd drop everything for him — especially given it's a rare occasion that I can be the one to help him out. He's been my mentor since the day my parents enrolled me at Cal Tech and waved goodbye as I checked into a freshman dorm, as though this was a normal thing for a fifteen-year-old kid.

I knew better.

I was the exceptional student who graduated high school early, only to be thrown into college life with guys at least three years older than me. I would've been an easy target if Pierce hadn't looked out for me, even with my dad being a professor on campus then.

I learned Pierce had seen his share of tragedy, far more than I ever have. I'm just a geek from the Bay with regular working class parents and one flighty sister. My friend's façade is smooth as silk despite his past, or maybe because of it. When faced with a shit sandwich, he'll turn it into the finest chocolate cake.

Lucky for me, he's happy to share his magical conversion recipe with his closest friends.

"Are you busy the next few days?" he says, still sounding distracted.

"Back to the work grind tomorrow. Trying to finish up the business plan tonight, so I'm ready for our next meeting on Project Oates. Been working on it for five solid days, but I'm not quite there."

"Yeah, about that..."

"Is that what you're calling about?" I interrupt. "You need to back out?"

"Actually, the opposite."

Oh, shit.

Since Pierce agreed to go all-in, I've spent every spare minute on this. I worked through the weekend, then hit pause on my rat race job as a VP of Engineering at Soft-Cell for the last three days, hell bent on finishing my first set of tasks by five p.m. today. I planned to go back to work tomorrow and still be ready when Pierce wants to meet up again.

But I wasn't expecting him to call for a second meeting until next week.

"It's part of the favor," he says. "I have some time to dig in this weekend."

"Dude, I'm not ready."

"How much time you need?"

"I've given myself until five p.m. today for Phase One. I've got twelve hours of work to squeeze into the next ten. But then I need time to review."

His voice is muffled as he gives more instructions to his staff before responding. "So you will have Phase One ready today?"

"I'll be done with my initial business plan as discussed, yeah. But I have work tomorrow, and I might be heading to Vegas with the guys this weekend. Are you back in town already?"

"Oates, I'm telling you, take Thursday and Friday off."

"Have you lost your hearing, man? I said today makes three days off already. I don't know if—"

"Tell Caruthers it's important," he interrupts. "Do you have the time available?"

"Yeah, but—"

"Then call in. And you'll need to cancel any weekend plans with the twins. I'll handle those guys."

My roommates (also known as YouTube sensations The Hawthorne Brothers) came up with the last-minute plan to head to Vegas this weekend. We're celebrating our recent migration across the Bay to Palo and the sale of software I helped them develop, which made it all possible.

A successful sale also meant I won our gentleman's bet. The guys had to quit making YouTube videos of themselves cooking shirtless. Chicks on social media have been begging for the return of the channel, but they swear they've given it up for good. Their channel's new stage would've been our shared kitchen, and I wasn't having that.

Their prominent parents never found out about their sons' Internet popularity, and the twins decided to quit while they were ahead. Another catalyst for their caution is the fact they're turning thirty this weekend. The guys have been evaluating everything about their lives for the last month in some responsibility-focused, reverse mid-life crisis.

Their Vegas trip seems like a last hurrah, and I declined their invite initially. Chasing women and partying round the clock aren't really my gig.

"I'm not committed to plans, but it is their birthday Saturday."

"Cancel."

"Aside from Project Oates, I've been dividing time between day job, packing, and moving. It's been three sleepless weeks. I told Zach I was changing my 'no thanks' to a 'why not' as of this morning."

"I'm more concerned with your job than disappointing those guys," he says. "I think Caruthers will allow it though."

"Work's another story."

"Can't hurt to ask if you can take the rest of the week, right?"

"Why?" I say. "What's so important?"

He ignores my question. "This is going to work out great. I'm glad you took my advice and jumped on that position at Soft-Cell."

"That was three years ago. What's that got to do with anything?"

"Because the last asshole you worked for never would've let you take time off with such short notice."

"Touché."

My day job's solid, and I never would've made the move without his advice. And Pierce is right. My last boss was a complete dick.

Bryson Chalmers made the covers of trade mags when he sold his start-up for three times its original value a few years ago. To his credit, he grew his business from a side-hustle headquartered in his basement to a cash cow. He's next-level smart, and he earned that sale. Most people in Silicon Valley thinks he's the second coming of Christ.

But I worked for the guy for six months at his new company. I know first-hand Chalmers is young and irresponsible, not to mention a pompous asshole. When I left, rumors were becoming more frequent that his interactions with female employees bordered on harassment — sometimes on his company campus, sometimes elsewhere.

I was happy to abandon any ship he was running.

I'm still in the Valley, but I earn a decent buck at Soft-Cell now. I lead a good team, and my boss Gerry Caruthers is older, wiser, and genuine. The downside is it's still a rat race. Ten-hour days on the hamster wheel with no escape are the norm, and that doesn't include the work I put in outside the office.

"Typical misfire in the World of Oates," I say. "This is the only time you've got for the foreseeable future?"

"Shit." He speaks to his assistant Samira and apologizes again for the distraction. "One sec."

"No problem. I'm not going anywhere."

Timing wouldn't be such a huge issue if I hadn't just inked my deal with the twins to buy our new house here in Palo Alto. My liquid funds are nearly tapped out. As solid as my ideas are, I can't afford to act on them without help. With the poor timing for my bank account and the ripeness of the market, Pierce is stepping up to propel me forward.

And of course he's now ready to dive in while I'm burning the candle at both ends.

"Sorry, again," he says. "So, you won't need to be at the airport until five a.m. tomorrow. That should give you plenty of time to prep."

What? "You need me to pick you up at the airport? Why can't one of your henchmen do it?"

"I'm not flying to California. You're coming out here."

"Whoa, wait a sec. Back up the private plane. No can do, bruh. We found a Wednesday night game in our new 'hood. At five a.m., the only place I intend to be is flat in my bed, which is a long way from New York. And by seven-thirty a.m., I'm due at my desk."

"Trivia with the Wonder Twins tonight?" he laughs.

"We're set to slay. Finn's been scoping this place out for two weeks. Maybe we can virtual conference?"

"I really need you here, Oates. You know I wouldn't normally insist, but there is a method to my madness. I can get you out here tomorrow and back Sunday night, I think. I'll have solid plans once I confirm Dad can fly out."

"I'd have to fly to New York and back with your rentals?"

"You're going to complain about a free ride?" he fires back.

"No, of course not. I mean, Reggie and Mamasita are better company than most, but I thought your mom wouldn't set foot in Stanton?"

"She's not coming here. Neither are you."

"Stop confusing me, Pierce. I know I'm suffering from a lack of caffeine, which is also your fault by the way, but you lost me." As if on cue, Jenny comes to save the day. Pierce rambles in my ear as she sets down my coffee and burrito, and I mouth a 'thank you'.

A customer I've seen here on the regular comes up behind her, carelessly tossing his dishes into a plastic tub. Jenny startles as metal silverware clangs against an acrylic plate, then flushes in embarrassment.

"Jerk," she mumbles as the guy heads for the exit.

I give her a sympathetic smile, then hand her a twenty and wave her off. She smiles back, hands me a folded napkin, and returns to her duties.

I figure the napkin is because she's seen me scarf down one of these bad boys before. Then I notice ink bleeding through the recycled brown paper. Inside, there's a phone number penned in skinny black marker.

As much of a tech nerd as I am, this old-school gesture is not lost on me. She must've had her number ready to hand me before I tipped her.

I half expect she's written "867-5309" under 'Jenny', then realize she wouldn't be old enough to make the joke, unless by some chance she's into eighties music. (For me, an add to the 'date-worthy' column.) But the number looks legit. I recognize the area code and the exchange.

Well played, Jenny.

But I'm not currently looking.

"Oates, did you hear me?"

"Sorry, man. I was getting hit upon. Please repeat."

"I said you can still take your time with Phase One. No need to cram it all in today. I won't be available to see you until Friday."

"I can already see where this is going. If I don't call Caruthers and beg for two more days, you'll do it."

"I promise not to interfere. But I'd need you on that plane tomorrow morning if we're doing this."

I let out a groan.

"Unless you want to delay yourself a month, this weekend is the only time I can fit you in. There's a lot going on here."

"This timing blows, man."

"Isn't that the first Rule of Oates?" he asks through a short laugh. "You're used to it."

"I just don't want to piss Caruthers off. He's been on a tear since the Carolyn incident."

"If you want to put it off, that's okay by me. It's your project. But you said yourself—"

"Market conditions are ripe, and we shouldn't wait another day. I know, I know. Don't use my words against me."

"I also have a surprise once you get out here."

"What kind of surprise?"

He dodges my question, instead asking me if I'm in or out.

Something is definitely up with him.

"All right, I give. As long as my boss is cool with it. My absence won't change the guys' MO in Vegas anyway."

"I'll take care of the twins. Shoot me an address, and I'll send them something to make it up to them."

"Like a birthday gift?"

"More like a consolation prize," he says. "They're losing the battle over who gets the pleasure of your company this weekend."

"Oh shit, bruh. This must be serious. You've been reduced to ass-kissing."

"Negative. You want your ass kissed, you better take up yoga and figure out how to do it yourself."

"Whatever. Send the Hawthornes what you will, but it's not legal to ship blondes with big tits via U.S. mail. That's all they'd want."

"Noted. I'll email or text you the flight details later, probably after seven tonight."

"Seven your time?"

"Pacific time. I have to talk with Dad. Just plan to be at the airport by dawn tomorrow."

"Got it. That means I can still make trivia. I'll just call it an early night."

"Do what you gotta do. Just be on that plane. We'll go over your business plan Friday or Saturday. You have my word we'll make time to put you in vacation mode too."

"Thank God. I'm about tapped out of brain cells."

"Trust me, I need a break, too. And don't forget your passport."

"What the hell for? Last I checked traveling to New York did not require one."

"Weren't you listening? I told you we're not staying here."

"And I told *you* I was getting hit on."

"Oh," he says, "I thought you were kidding."

I lower my voice and tell him to fuck off.

"Anyway," he says once his laughter subsides, "you'll be driving to Canada after you land north of Lake County tomorrow. I'll meet up with you guys late Friday morning."

"Get the fuck out," I mutter in disbelief. "We're going to The Gables?"

No wonder he wants me to show up.

I haven't been to the Pierce family's impressive island compound in Canada since our college days. The pristine spot on the St. Lawrence River left such an impression that guests always begged to be invited back, including yours truly. But the Pierce family hasn't visited the St. Lawrence in years, not since Aidan's brother Thad passed away.

"Yes, we're going back." His voice turns solemn. "I think you should be there for the occasion."

This explains Pierce's insistence, and now I know why he wouldn't elaborate.

Being back at The Gables will be a trigger for him, a reminder of the devastating loss his family suffered. I'd never let him face that without backup.

"I'm definitely in. But uh…can I ask the obvious?"

"Ask away."

"What's the occasion?"

"You'll see, my man." I can tell his smile has returned. "You'll see."

3

Pam

June 8, 2016
Wednesday, 8:00 p.m.

Bay Falls, Ontario
Canada

"You must film this for me," Carly insists. "I'm going to drink these assholes under the table."

"Not again."

"Yes again," she says, grabbing a hair clip from her purse. "I want evidence this time."

My best friend hops off her barstool and sheds the teal and gray flannel she's wearing, psyching herself up like a boxer for a fight. She ties the shirt around the waist of her jeans, revealing the tight purple tank top she decided on before we left her apartment. Her blonde mane is pulled up in seconds. Despite the speed of her style change, she doesn't need a mirror to know she looks great.

She always looks great.

While we wait for her two friends to cross the room and accept her challenge, I grab my phone to check email.

"You know how they say no epic story about a night of partying starts with 'so I was eating a salad'?"

"We're eating fried food in a pub," I say dismissively. I look up when I feel a nudge from Carly's elbow. "Yeah, I've heard that."

She eyes me in scolding. "Well, same goes for the phrase, 'so I was staring at my phone'."

We're at a pub in our hometown to celebrate her 24th birthday and she's right. My head is elsewhere. I don't mind she's called me out for being distracted, though. Carly's been like a big sister to me since childhood. A beautiful, brutally honest, life-of-the-party-girl that looks nothing like me — but still. She's my sister-by-choice and she's allowed to scold me.

"Maybe you have a point, but— "

"Of course I do," she interrupts. "I need your undivided attention."

"*But*, in my defense," I say, "this is my future we're talking about. You've already got yours all figured out. And you're the one who's always on YouTube drooling over videos of the Hawthorne Brothers."

"I watch those videos to improve my skills. It's research."

"Ogling hot guys on your phone is not research."

"It is when it's them," she says. "I've learned a ton from that channel. They're talented foodies."

"They're twenty-something twins from California who cook in the nude. Watching them while we're trying to have a conversation is most certainly *not* research."

"Half-nude," she corrects. "They're always wearing bottoms. Totally nude would be foolish while standing in front of a gas stove." She waves Dave and Connor over to us. "C'mon, let's do this!" she shouts to them before turning back to me. "Just ask these two what they think of the Hawthorne twins' skills," she whispers. "They'll back me up."

"They're gay, Carly. I wouldn't be surprised if Dave and Connor were two of the first subscribers. And for your information, I was checking for that email from Fedders. It should've come by now."

"It'll come," she insists, "when it's meant to. Now, eat up. We have drinking to do. And nothing's going to happen while you're hovering over your phone. You've been staring at it for the last hour."

I turn to her, smile a sarcastic grin, then take a bite of a fried pickle. "Happy?"

"Yes." She takes a bite of her fish, which looks amazing. "It's the Law of the Universe, Pam. A watched pot never boils. Same-same."

Carly often shares her enlightened thoughts with anyone who will listen. She's only three years older than me, but she's wise beyond her years. My brother Ben thought her wisdom was a load of B.S. and teased her to no end, but I've seen her approach to life work in her favor. I can't dismiss her point entirely, especially when my gut tells me she's right.

Then again, for all of Carly's intuition, sometimes she can't summon enough willpower to keep her cheating ex-boyfriend out of her bed, and that seems like a no-brainer to me.

"Besides," she says, "your advisor is definitely not going to email you at nine o'clock on a Wednesday night." She dusts the crumbs off her hands and takes my phone away before pulling hers from her back pocket. "Take the video with mine. The clarity is better. And for *your* information, the Hawthorne twins took down their channel."

"No more videos?" I don't subscribe to the twins' channel, but I can't help voice an 'aw' of regret. She hears me and shoots an 'I told you so' glare my way. "What?" I shrug in defense. "I can admit watching those guys flip pancakes shirtless doesn't suck."

"I knew you'd be bummed." She plucks a fried pickle off my plate. "Remember that time they demonstrated how to properly cut up a pineapple? Good Lord," she says, fanning herself. "*So* hot."

"One or both of them is probably off the market," I say. "Getting ready to marry royalty would be my guess."

"Or an American Senator's daughter," she says with a disappointed sigh. "Anyway, the channel disappeared a few weeks ago. Now, get ready! Here come the guys."

Carly bellies up to the bar of Duke & Earl's Pub along with her friends Dave and Connor, and I stand up to join them. A few others are celebrating with us, too, but they're wrapped up in their game of darts across the room.

Dave and Connor are both single, openly gay, and entertaining as hell. They're already razzing her about who is going to win this race.

"There's no way you're going to finish first. See this?" Connor points to his red hair. "You're not outdoing an Irishman in a pub."

"At least not this time," Dave digs.

"That was when we were still in school,"Connor defends. "We tried five different beef entrees that night. I had no room for multiple shots."

"Thanks for confirming you'll have no excuse when I kick your ass *this* time." Carly smiles as the bartender pours three shots of whiskey for each participant. "Not only will I finish first, but I will walk out of here tonight under my own power and without stumbling."

"I've been priming for this for two weeks." Dave shakes out his hands before he turns them to fists, then lets them fall at his sides. "Bring it, Carlsbad."

As the birthday girl tries to pay, the guys insist it's their treat.

"Thanks, loves, but I don't take bribes to throw a contest."

"It's not a bribe. It's your birthday gift," Connor shrugs. "We didn't get you anything else."

"You're both pricks," Carly says, pointing from one friend to the other. "And I'm going to kick both of your asses while Pam gets it all on film."

"Fine," Connor says, laying his palms flat on the bar top. He turns to me. "Make sure you only get my good side."

"Which side's that?" I ask.

"Oh, any side." He winks. "They're all good."

I laugh as I click the camera off selfie mode. I have no doubt Carly (a.k.a. Carlsbad, Carly Cakes, and reigning Shot Queen) is going to win this challenge. Her tolerance is and always has been unbelievable, but the guys are well aware. The three friends graduated from a prestigious cooking school in Montreal last year (another celebratory occasion still talked about to this day). Admittedly, that epic night didn't start out with eating salad or staring at phones either.

"Ready?" she asks me.

I peek around the phone and give her a nod as I start recording. "On three, guys."

Carly counts to three, and each of them knocks back their first shot of whiskey. As the guys catch their breath and tip back their second, my best friend is already on her final.

"Shit yeah!" Carly slams her third glass on the bar, arms thrown above her head in victory. She pops a chip in her mouth just as Dave and Connor finish the race. Dave shakes his head, his face twisted in repugnance while Connor grimaces but quickly recovers, chasing his whiskey with a sip of his beer.

"Cut!" I say as a laugh escapes me. "Sorry for the shaky camera work. You guys are too much."

"I don't see what's so funny," Connor says. "Your bestie had the advantage by calling for the start."

"You're better than that, Connor. She beat you fair and square." While Carly is distracted, I drop her phone in my purse. *She can't drunk-text her ex if she doesn't have her phone.* I lift my vodka cranberry to her in a toast. "You win as usual."

"Lord Byron have mercy," Dave mutters. "That's some strong shit. You're supposed to sip and savor whiskey, not slug it."

"Suck it up," Carly says as she elbows him. "Stretch here isn't complaining."

"Of course I'm not," Connor says. "It's your birthday, love. Tonight, I am your bitch." He bows to her and smiles.

"What else is new?" Dave says. "Princess always gets her way."

"I'm no princess, am I Pam?"

"Nope. You're the Shot Queen," I correct, "and the coolest chef that ever lived."

"Damn straight." She picks up another chip, considering as she chews. "Am I as cool as that chef who travels the world and eats bugs?"

Dave's quick-fire answer is a deadpanned 'no'.

"I wasn't asking you," Carly says to him. "And P.S., you're the one that always gets your way."

Connor chimes in to agree and Dave looks at the two of them, his expression sheer disbelief.

"Why?" he asks. "Because I always pick the restaurants we go to?"

"Or the watering hole we'll end up in," Connor says, "or the movies we see, or the recipes we try."

"Well," he says, his tone feigning superiority, "can I help it that I always have the best taste?"

"I suppose not," Carly says. "But I'm still the reigning Shot Queen. Pam, you can be my princess."

"Oh, can I?" I gesture with praying hands. "Please?"

Carly rolls her eyes at me, then looks to the dance floor. Someone among our party of seven has just started up the new music system that replaced the old jukebox last winter. Justin Bieber pours out to us, and two older men sitting nearby grumble into their draft beers.

"The Biebs!"Carly shouts as she does a half-assed pirouette.

"Easy, killer," Connor says, stealing a bite from her plate. "You look like a fish on a line. And speaking of, I told you this fish would be excellent. Their breading is perfection."

"Agreed," she says. "Can we dance after I finish my *ah-maz-ing* meal?"

"I'll sit this one out." Dave straightens his white button down shirt over his jeans as he seats himself on a stool.

"I'll hang with you," I say, sitting next to him. "Not a fan of Bieber, hmm?"

"No," he feigns a shudder. "He scares me."

Carly laughs at the irony of his statement.

Dave's a big guy with bulky arms and several tattoos. He's certainly not scared of a featherweight pop star. He has a dry wit and a slightly protruding belly (either from his taste for craft beer or his line of work), and his personality is not warm and fuzzy. As he tells it, his no-BS style and his famous *coq au vin* are what earned him the job as head chef at Layla's, the one and only upscale restaurant in our town.

Despite this, he reminds me of a giant teddy bear you'd win at a carnival.

In contrast, Connor is a waif in Levis. He's six-foot-four and looks like he could be knocked over by a gust of wind. His red hair is buzzed tight to his head. Necessary, he says, unless he wants to resemble Orphan Annie. He's an amazing pastry chef, though he's currently unemployed. When he left his job at a bakery in Montreal, he put the word out in Toronto that he was available and had three offers within a week. As of tonight, he hasn't yet decided which one to accept.

Besides me, these two guys are my best friend's closest confidants, which I could've predicted. Other girls tend to have their guard up around Carly. They envy her looks, presuming she's a bitch or worse, a boyfriend thief. I've known her since she was nine and can attest she's neither of those things.

Carly polishes off her meal and asks for a sip of Connor's pint.

He obliges just as the music gets louder, and Carly dances in place, eager to hit the floor.

"You're a phenomenon, woman," Connor hollers to her over the music. "Marry me."

"Never." She grabs the fabric of his Beatles t-shirt to pull him close, planting a kiss on his cheek. "The minute you put a ring on it, you'd stop taking me out dancing. You ready?"

"Bieber beats country," he sighs. "I'm in."

Carly squeals with delight and attempts another dance move as Dave and I cringe from our barstools. I love my girl, but dancing is the one kingdom where she does not reign. It's one of the few talents I possess that she was not blessed with.

"I'm gonna miss you so fucking much, Carly Cakes," Connor laughs. "No one moves like you do."

"Back 'atcha, Stretch." She reaches up to rake a hand over Connor's buzz cut. "Now let's hit the floor."

Connor is still twirling my best friend around the small patch of open hardwood in the back of the bar. The English-style pub has capacity for a hundred people, but after the dinner rush, weeknights are usually dead. Except for a couple of regulars, our group of seven are the only patrons.

While Carly's occupied, I check the email app on my phone every few minutes until Dave leans over to me. "Please show me the video you took."

I pull my friend's phone from my purse and hit play.

"Oh," he smiles, "that's definitely share-worthy."

"Even though you lost?" I tease.

"Even though," he smiles. "You got my number?"

"It's Carly's phone. I'm sure you're in here." I scroll through her contacts and find Dave. "Remember this?" I turn the screen to show him the photo Carly assigned to him.

"Wow. We were as wrecked as her kitchen last year." He smiles at the selfie he snapped of himself and Carly covered in cake flour. "That was the day I first met you in person, Princess Pammy. A year ago tonight. I'd never forget that."

I don't know Dave well, but we developed an instant rapport that night. From the stories Carly shared, I knew she had a blast with Dave in class. Their friendship distracted her from problems with Mick, her hockey-playing, skirt-chasing ex. I offered all the help I could when it came to her rocky relationship, but history proved that sometimes it was better to hold my tongue.

Distance was also a factor. I was at University in Toronto, so quality time with my BFF was limited while she was in Montreal. Last fall, after some frank, unsolicited advice from Dave that turned into a true heart-to-heart, my friend found the courage to dump Mick the Prick.

"Is she ready for this move?" he asks. "It's a big step bugging out for the States."

"She's pumped, I think. She isn't taking much, so that part was easy. She's moving in with her cousin Kate."

"I told her to pack a two piece and a smile," he says with a mischievous grin. "The douchebag still leaving her alone?"

"Far as I know, Mick's still a tool of the past."

"Good. Now pass me her phone."

I raise an eyebrow in question.

"I wanna load it with hook-up apps. That girl needs to let loose in Florida."

"I was never involved." I hand him the phone and turn an eye to Carly, making sure she's not watching. I know she'll think it's hilarious when she discovers it, and she can delete the apps once she finds them. If she can't figure it out, I can talk her through it.

No harm done.

Dave works his magic and sets the phone back on the bar a few minutes later. "I've got three of them downloading."

"Don't you have to set up profiles for her? What's her handle going to be?"

"Head Chef KU," he says with a smirk.

"Okay, call me confused. That's not the name of the resort she'll be working in. What's KU stand for?"

"Kate Upton," he says through a chortle.

"What's funny about that?"

"I've always told Carly that's her celebrity doppelgänger." But his smile stays so wide, I know he's leaving something out. I narrow my eyes at him until he confesses. "I'm going to put the word 'head' in quotation marks. To give it a different meaning, if you will."

"Dave!" My hand flies to my mouth as I try not to burst into laughter. "She'll kill us."

"No," he says, laying a hand on my shoulder. "She'll *thank* us. She'll have more dates in a week than we'll see in six months. We're looking out for her. You have to admit her taste in guys is subpar."

"Yeah, but— "

"But, nothing. She needs a palate cleanse."

Confusion spreads across my face again.

"Listen, sweetie. Here's the reality. Ten Palms is going to run her ragged. I predict she won't last there long term. This way, she can hook up with random surfer dudes while she gets sick of grilling seafood."

"And then?"

"And then she'll move back home to us, settle down with someone worthy — a nice Canadian boy who doesn't play hockey — and come to work with me."

"That's very selfish of you. Or of us?"

"Maybe," he grins, "but my evil plans always work, Emmy."

"I don't think— wait, what did you call me?"

"Emmy," he says, all nonchalant like that's my name.

"Who is Emmy?"

"Your celebrity doppelgänger."

"Emmy who?"

"Rossum," he scoffs. "*Obviously.*"

My mouth hangs open until I find words. "You're not serious."

"Completely. But not the strung-out, Fiona-from-Shameless Emmy Rossum. Voluptuous, magazine-spread Emmy Rossum."

"Oh my God, Dave," I say through an outburst of laughter. "I don't see that. Like, at all."

"Your skin is better, though. She's vampire-pale compared to you. Can you sing?" he asks. "She was amazing in *Phantom of the Opera.*"

"That's my all-time favorite show," I sigh. "I never saw the movie, though."

"Did you see it on Broadway?"

I shake my head. "But I did see it in Toronto when I was little."

"See the movie," he insists. "She was incredible."

"Deal. But that just confirms you're way off." I stare up at the TV.

"I have no desire to act and I can't sing the jingle to that tire commercial, never mind opera."

"Do you deny I pegged Carly right with Kate Upton? Not with personality," he emphasizes, "just her appearance."

When I don't agree, he pulls up a side-by-side photo of Carly and the famous Kate.

"Okay, yeah," I admit. "They could be related. But you'll have to keep trying on mine. And P.S., I don't think surfers are Carly's type."

He purses his lips, deep in thought. "I guess I don't really know her type. Other than the fact that he's effing gorgeous, I never understood what she saw in that puck-pusher."

"Me neither." I drain my glass, praying that my best friend doesn't shoot me when she finds out I granted Dave phone access.

"You've been nursing that drink all night," he says. "Let me buy you another."

"Thanks, but I promised to drive."

Dave checks Carly's phone then taps away, making quick work of establishing her dating profiles. "Done," he says. "Put this back in your bag."

I do as he asks and make sure my friend isn't watching. She's slow dancing with Connor, completely unaware. "I'm *so* going to hell for letting you do that."

"That's not a thing," he insists.

I roll my eyes.

"Also, I just looked at her recent calls. Mick's number comes up twice today."

Damn. "You're a devious man, Dave."

"Know it and own it," he says. "Let me ask you something. Do you think Mick's really that good of a lay?"

"I wouldn't know."

"Oh, good one," he says through a chuckle. "But riddle me this, girlfriend."

I slide my empty glass away and look at him. "Shoot."

"Why did she give him a chance to redeem himself? Even if the sex with him is amazing, once she knew Mick was having the sex with other chicks, why would the Queen ever let him into the palace again?"

"Don't know," I shrug. "Maybe he is just that good."

"Well," he says, turning his attention to the TV, "that's the only thing I can think of."

"There's one thing I do know. When Carly wants something, there's no stopping her."

Dave swings his head back to me. "That sounds like a story."

"Oh, I have tons of them."

He leans against the back of his stool, grabs his pint and sips. "I've got time."

"After the dating app thing, this definitely feels like a betrayal."

"Nah," he says, "trust me. It's for her own good. Besides, she's told me a shit ton of embarrassing stories about you."

"I don't even want to know."

"C'mon," he nudges, "tell me."

"Fine," I say after a deep sigh. "When she was ten, she insisted we could make a fortune selling homemade muffins to the little grocer. You know, the shop around the corner?"

"There's only one store in this town. Of course I know it. I don't shop there for the restaurant, but I go in for myself. Otherwise I'm hitting up Metro in Ganonoque."

"Welcome to our world. You can probably walk to the little store from your new apartment, right?"

"Mm," he nods, "they have great farm fresh eggs."

"Well, Carly was relentless, convincing me of her plan to make money by selling them her muffins. She roped me in as her baking assistant."

"Was she right?"

"Sort of. She made a killing, and I came away with a new bell for my bike, just like she promised."

"O-M-G. The little tycoon. And how old were you?"

"Seven. I also came away with a minor burn on my wrist," I say, showing him the one-inch scar. "But the bell was worth it."

"What if the goal she's trying to reach isn't good for her?" he asks. "Is she still that determined?"

"That would be more like the winter she insisted she could learn how to ice skate in a week."

He looks at me with raised eyebrows. "Please tell me you're kidding."

"I'm not."

"That girl is dangerous in a pair of sneakers, never mind having two sharp blades strapped to her feet."

"You're not wrong," I say through my laughter.

"Please tell me you stopped her."

"I told her to rethink it, which only fueled her to speed the wrong way down that one-way street."

"And how old was she then?"

"Thirteen. It was the year the winter Olympics were held in Italy, and she was obsessed with figure skating. She ended up with a broken ankle during her second lesson."

"At least no one else got hurt, eh?" Dave chuckles as he nods towards the dance floor. "I'm worried about Connor's safety about now."

I look over in time to see her step on Connor's toes. "We've been friends for fifteen years, and I've learned two things. One, let her dance alone."

He laughs again. "And two?"

"Don't try to talk her out of a guy. Mick's permanently on my Asshole List, but I've never told her that."

"You have an Asshole List?"

I smile coyly. "Only one drink and I'm spilling all my secrets to you."

"Then let's definitely get you another." He signals for the bartender. "Who's on this list?" He acts excited, as though he's about to hear gossip straight from a Hollywood insider.

"Any jerk I've dated since I started college."

"That's it?" He raises a brow and curls his upper lip. "Carly says that's a short list."

"Oh, there's more."

"Do tell."

"The kid I tutor during the summer, for one."

"What's his damage?"

"Let's see. He squanders his tech talent, he's a total spaz, he lacks manners most toddlers have mastered, and because his parents are wealthy, he acts like he's above everyone else."

"He definitely sounds like Asshole Numero Uno. Who else?"

"The guy at Canadian Tire who tried to sell me a vacuum cleaner for my dorm room when all I wanted was a Keurig. The boy who stole my lunch everyday for a month in grade three. And Mick."

"Did you ever retaliate against the lunch thief?"

"Didn't have to," I grin with pride. "My brother took care of it as soon as he found out."

"Ha, that's awesome." He ponders while he sips some more. "I think I'll start an Asshole List, too."

"It's very therapeutic. I knew Mick was a jerk, but I had to keep that to myself. This was a way to let it out."

"Well, I certainly didn't hold back about him," he says. "I'm just glad I didn't accidentally make her stay with him."

"Without your no-holds-barred advice, Carly never would've left him." I briefly lay my hand on Dave's shoulder. "So thank you."

"Hey, I just said what was on my mind. But she's still taking his calls, so she's having a harder time letting go than I thought."

"Sometimes. Especially after three shots," I say pointedly. "That's why I held onto her phone."

"Good call. Carly always brags to me about your intelligence." The bartender arrives, and Dave asks for a glass of water and another drink for me.

"She's just as smart," I say. "Usually."

Carly confessed she'd ended up in Mick's bed a couple times since they broke up. She was still as attracted to him as the day they met, and I couldn't blame her for a relapse. If I found a guy who had my engine firing on all cylinders, I might not want to give him up either.

"Well," he says, "that's what the palate cleanse is for. It'll get Mick out of her system for good. And what about you?"

"What about me?"

"You're not seeing anyone? I can download those apps to your phone, too. You guys can compare notes."

"No, thanks. I'm better off single."

"Guys at OCAD-U aren't as bad as Mick, I hope."

"Not really. I'm just focused on school, and the guys there aren't my thing, I guess. They're either uber-intellectual—"

"And boring," Dave interjects.

I shake my head. "It's more like there's no happy medium. There are a lot of creative types there, and they're all super cool. Guys I talk to on the regular are techy, smart. But they don't interest me to date. A lot of them don't find humor in much of anything."

"Like fart jokes."

I chuckle. "Exactly. So if it's not that, then they're really creative, and every conversation is about art or something highbrow. Or, they're super good looking, but lacking in the personality department."

He grins at me. "Like, all they do is make fart jokes?"

"A broad generalization, but not entirely inaccurate."

"That sucks."

"Yep. And if they don't fit that cross-section of categories, they're treating me like a dumb girl or just trying to get laid."

"Hold out for a prince that rocks your world," Dave says with a wink. "You'll find one."

"That'd be a miracle."

"Why? You're gorgeous and intelligent." He finishes his pint and slides it away. "Do you have a problem getting dates?"

"Um," I pause feeling my face flush. "Not really. I guess I just see myself as the kind of girl a guy asks to make him a snack before he'd ask her for a date."

"That's supreme nonsense. A guy would ask *me* for a snack before he'd ask you."

"Ah, good point."

"Seriously, though. You're a hot chick, Pam."

"That's not how I see myself. And guys that do show an interest have never moved the needle for me."

He leans closer and whispers. "Maybe you're batting for the wrong team?"

"No!" I giggle at his insinuation. "It's not that. I know who I play for. I think I'm just meant to ride the pine. At least for now."

"Okay then, prove your devotion to the male species. Has Carly made you watch the Hawthorne Brothers' cooking channel on YouTube?"

"Repeatedly."

"Great. So, the Hawthorne Brothers. Hot or not?"

Oh, God. "Yes?" I bury my head. My cheeks are definitely crimson now.

"Was that 'yes' a question?"

"No," I laugh. "I meant it as a definite yes. They're extremely hot."

"Well then, your judgment is spot on far as I can tell. When you find the right guy, you'll be lunging for him at every turn."

"We'll see," I say as the bartender delivers Dave's water and my cocktail. "I'm unconvinced."

"You just need more than a one-night-stand kind of guy. It's not what does it for you."

"Right?" I sigh. "I'm the lamest college girl ever."

"No," he says, waving his hands. "There's nothing wrong with you. You just need a smart, interesting, and attractive guy," he pauses, "who just wants to get laid."

"Of course!" I say through my laughter. "Why didn't I think of that?"

"Oh, I was just describing myself. Unfortunately, I'm not an option for you, being I fuck dudes."

My laughter is so loud and uninhibited that it draws Carly's attention. I give her a thumbs up and she beams back at me. "Well damn," I finally say, "guess we're not a match then."

"No one's a match for me." He lifts his chin in regal fashion.

"Mick's free now," I tease. "Maybe he'd take you out." Dave laughs as I raise my hand to order him another pale ale. "On my tab," I insist to the bartender. "I'm not drinking alone. But two is my limit tonight, so do not order me another."

"Understood." He thanks me and glances over at Carly. "This move is going to be good for her."

"Agreed. She'll be far away from Mick, and she'll have no trouble making new friends."

"Or outdrinking them."

"Hellz yeah," I say. "She puts me to shame."

"She puts me to bed," he says with a smirk, "and more often than I care to admit. Then I come down from Montreal to live in this one-horse town, and my only drinking buddy up and leaves."

"That does suck. I'll miss her, too, but I'm leaving soon myself."

"Where you off to?"

"Hopefully New York for my fourth year."

"Not California?" he asks. "I thought that's where all the tech nerds ended up."

I shrug. "I don't think I'd fit in with the California lifestyle."

"It'd be an adjustment, but you could learn to surf. Or like, roller blade or some shit."

"No thanks," I say with an involuntary grimace. "Besides, I don't want to abandon my parents entirely. When my brother studied in the States, the drive to the middle of New York State was manageable to get home. I'd like to have that option. But I'm still waiting to hear from my advisor to confirm my placement."

"I would've loved a semester in Italy or France." Dave slides his glass of water closer and expertly squeezes a lemon into it. "I did one trip to New York City. Some of our classmates snagged good contacts there. We had a blast, but it isn't my scene long-term."

"I've always wanted to go there," I sigh. "I told Carly when she's there this weekend, she has to send me pics every day."

"You should just go with her. No boyfriend, you're off from school." Dave nods in appreciation at the bartender as she sets down his fresh beer and departs. "What else have you got to do?"

"Can't," I say with a head shake. "My sister-in-law is coming up to visit this weekend. I haven't seen her in forever." *Mental note: text sister-in-law tomorrow to check in about her arrival.* "What about you?" I ask. "Can you travel abroad now that you're done with school?"

"Nah," he says. "I haven't been at Layla's long enough. I'd need at least two weeks off."

"How's it going there? Your first night seemed pretty intense."

"It's gotten better. I just wish the management had the brass to change things up. Tradition, expectations of patrons," he rolls his eyes. "They won't let the new guy mix things up with the menu."

"You'll turn them around." I nudge him and smile. "You have a way with people."

"Right? I'm good at convincing people of shit. I could be a politician."

"You got Carly to see Mick for what he really was. Anyone who can do that can make a difference at Layla's. I see it happening."

"You're right. Carly's always touting that power of positive thinking baloney." He raises his glass of water in a toast. "Thank you."

"No!" I quickly lay a hand on his arm. "Never toast with water. It's bad luck."

"You're into affirmations *and* you're superstitious?" He sets down the glass and grabs his fresh pint instead.

"Yes, I know. I'm weird."

"An enigma you are, Princess Pammy." He smiles and puts a hand on my shoulder. "An incredibly pretty enigma. Here's to you." He lifts his beer this time, and we clink glasses.

"Thanks." I lean in to kiss his puffy cheek, and he scoffs to shirk my attention.

"I mean, obviously you're pretty." He pretends to fuss with his well-styled sandy brown hair. "Otherwise, I wouldn't let you sit anywhere near me."

I tilt my head, considering him for a quiet moment. "I just figured out who you remind me of."

"Is it a celebrity?"

"No, better." I smile at the realization. "My brother's friend Charlie."

"Is he half as handsome as me?"

"About. And you're both straight shooters armed with constant sarcasm."

"Well then, I should get to know this Charlie person."

I pull up a photo of my sister-in-law Alexis and her right-hand-gay-man, Charlie Young.

"Wow," Dave says with big eyes. "Who's the knockout?"

"That's Alexis, the one coming up this weekend. She was married to my brother before he," I pause. *It's still so difficult to say.* "Before he passed away."

"That's nice. I was referring to the guy."

"Ah," I smirk. "I walked right into that one."

"J-K," he says with a nudge. "She's smokin' too. She was your brother's wife?"

I nod.

"His name was Ben," Dave says, lost in recollection. "He died at the end of oh-fourteen, right? Around Christmas?"

I swallow the lump in my throat as I nod again. I didn't think he'd remember.

"Carly talked about him a lot," Dave says. "Said he was like a brother to her, too. She was pretty broken up about his sudden passing."

"We all were." I turn away, relying on my rehearsed method to force down the ache. One deep breath in, one out. I turn back to

Dave and smile. "The guy in the photo is Charlie. He, um..." *Shit. Don't cry.* "He was friends with my brother through work. They met while Ben was in New York City on assignment."

"Assignment for what?"

"He was a television reporter."

"Ah, I could see that. He looked like a TV personality." Dave eyes the regulars getting up to leave as an upbeat Cher song comes on, then turns his attention back to my screen. "Your guy Charlie and your sister-in-law look happy there," he comments. "What was the occasion?"

"Alexis was celebrating her first year at her solo law practice. She oversaw the rehab of her dad's old building, and, with Charlie's help, they renovated the interior. This was taken in her office."

"He's dressed pretty nice for a laborer."

"Oh, he's not in construction. He helped her hire a designer and used his eye to assist. He's her paralegal and also became her best friend." I smile at the photo, at how proud they both are. Charlie stands behind Alexis wearing an enthusiastic grin, his hands resting on her shoulders.

"Does she divorce people?" he asks. "Or does she handle like, traffic tickets and slip-and-fall cases?"

"None of the above. She's into real estate mostly. Some estate planning too, I think."

"Well, she's a lucky girl. He's effing gorgeous. But I can't see how I remind you of him. He's built and bald, and far more tan than I am."

I laugh at his wisecrack. Charlie is African American, his skin a gorgeous milk chocolate color. Anyone can see Charlie is one buff guy (even through his designer clothes). "The comparison might not seem obvious, but you share a few traits."

"Does he happen to be gay?"

"Actually, yes. And," I say, leaning closer, "he's the only one that's ever called me Pammy, like you did."

"You'll have to introduce me to Chuck if we're ever in the same country."

"I definitely will. But here's a tip: never, ever call him Chuck."

Squeals erupt from the dance floor (mostly from Connor) as Kelly Clarkson sings about what she's done since he's been gone.

Carly is feeling it, mouthing the words while she tries to move to the beat. She catches sight of us and crooks her finger in a 'come here' motion.

"How about Kelly?" I ask Dave. "Does Kelly do it for ya?"

"You did not just ask me that." He looks down his nose at me as he stands up. "I F-love her."

"Then let's go put Carly's dance moves to shame."

"Sure," he says, offering his arm. "It's the least I can do, and what I'm best at."

4

Oates

June 8, 2016
Wednesday, 7:00 p.m.

Palo Alto, California

Zach Hawthorne bumps me with his strong shoulder. "Put down your phone and drink the hell up."

My roommates waltzed into The Tap Room all of five minutes ago. One of them is already giving me shit, and I haven't even broken the news about skipping Vegas. My boss gave me the go ahead to take the rest of the week off, but I'm waiting to hear from Pierce to confirm travel plans.

"Settle, aright?" I adjust my glasses and set down my phone. Zach's twin brother Finn is seated next to me, not paying either of us any attention. He snagged the only open stool left in the place, and his eyes have been fixed on the flat screen hovering above the shelves of brightly colored liquor bottles.

Wednesday Night Trivia draws a big crowd here. Still, it's a chill vibe. The noise isn't so loud that we have to shout to be heard. Beyond the bar area, weathered whiskey barrels serve as high-top tables where people are eating, drinking or gearing up for game time.

I gesture a hand up in accusation at Finn. "He's watching TV.

What's it to you if I'm checking email? I finished a beer before you assholes even got here."

"Damn. Chill," Zach says, palms thrown up in defense. "What's eating you, Oates? We've just moved to the Promised Land, and you're all cramped up like we've landed in Purgatory. You hit a wall on the app plans today?"

I ignore his question and keep my opinion to myself.

True, Palo Alto (a.k.a. The Promised Land to Zach) was our goal a year ago. We couldn't wait to abandon Fremont and put an end to our long commutes. Finn and Zach left behind their shared walls in Ardenwood, surrendering their modern townhouse to a supermodel who could afford it.

The single-family we now call home crowns a cul-de-sac in Greenmeadow. We dropped close to three mill on our five-bedroom 1950's ranch, which is mid-century modern by design but remodeled to include luxuries the guys insisted on. We split the down payment, the twins mortgaged the balance owed, and my attorney made sure my rental agreement says they'll buy out my equity if I ever decide to bail.

The Hawthorne Brothers have promising side hustle plans, and both are gainfully employed. Their parents' fortune will eventually be theirs.

In short, they don't really need me.

The guys spent their mid-twenties working hard and occasionally smoking pot and playing video games. They never get into the hard stuff, though. This went into the 'pro' column when deciding whether to share a house with them. I watched Pierce's brother Thad go down a dark road of addiction only to meet his demise. Seeing it once was more than enough.

Zach and Finn are just chill guys who happened to be born rich.

And good looking.

And really fucking smart.

As twins.

Sometimes I consider punching them both in the snot-locker, just to even the playing field and take away one of their super powers.

"I'm adjusting to the upheaval," I say. "I'll snap out of it."

"Hope so," Zach says. His eyes follow a few more people entering the bar. "You need to beg off paying rent for a month so you can invest in more R&D for your app?"

"Nah, I'm all set. And day job isn't going anywhere."

"Long as you're sure." Zach looks to his brother to be certain he's heard this.

"I'm cool with whatever," Finn says without looking at us. "Just let us know if things change."

As much as this move has been a dream realized, I've been half regretting it for the last week. I used to rent a place from a retired B-list actress. Her two-bedroom house in the Glenmoor neighborhood was small, but it had easy access to Dumbarton Bridge.

I may not miss the commute, but I do miss my guaranteed privacy. I spent late nights brainstorming my app, blaring music and forgetting to eat. That phase is easy to romanticize compared to the reality of a launch. I came here to live in a place where realized tech dreams can skyrocket a guy to comfortable wealth or notoriety.

Of course, said guy could just as easily end up in tremendous debt or suffer epic humiliation when his ideas flop.

My app has been through multiple revamps since I thought of it, given the ebbs and flows of my field. Pierce agrees I'm onto something unique, but competition is hyper-fierce. Ideas are pinging off people like invisible pinballs, and developers can move faster than the twins in a room full of hotties.

It's also not beneath some shady characters to steal ideas. I saw it firsthand during the crash-and-burn relationship I had with a former coworker ('Crazy Carolyn', as the twins call her). I never predicted she'd pull the shit she did, but that's what I get for dating someone...well, crazy.

I pull my phone out again.

"Can you believe this guy?" Zach smacks Finn's shoulder so hard it makes a loud clap, but his twin doesn't flinch. "We're supposed to be celebrating."

"I'm expecting an email from Pierce."

"You need to stop stressing," Finn says. "It'll happen when it happens. He's a busy man."

"Actually, he's already set our next meeting. I talked to him this morning."

"Get the fuck out." Zach looks at me in genuine shock. "When are you meeting?"

"Friday. Heading to Canada by way of New York tomorrow."

"Wait," Zach says, "we're leaving for the Strip on Friday. You sure you want to miss that?"

"He's practically your brother. He wouldn't want you to miss our thirtieth birthday shenanigans," Finn says. "MML would understand if you put him off a week."

I met the Hawthorne Brothers almost four years ago during a trivia event put on for charity. As well as I've come to know them, they don't fully understand my best friend Aidan Pierce.

They know he was my mentor and roommate at Cal Tech, but their overall impression of him comes from tabloid headlines or articles in Forbes. They assigned him the nickname MML, short for 'The Man, the Myth, the Legend', which he would find absurd.

"It's the only chance Pierce has to see me for a month. His family is heading to their place in Canada this weekend. We used to hang out there on summer breaks, before his brother Thad died. Going back is a milestone for Pierce. But it's business, too. You guys know he takes that shit seriously regardless of who I am to him."

"I get it." Zach's expression changes to understanding as he lays a hand on my shoulder. "You need to go."

I remove my glasses, huff on my lenses and wipe them clean. "I'm sorry for missing Vegas, but I'd never disrespect him by taking this on with anything less than everything I've got."

"Your app's gonna kill," Finn says without averting his eyes from the television. "Still, sorry we'll be partying without you."

Zach agrees. "Just get yourself some R&R too."

I laugh. Our ideas of R&R don't always align. For me, partying and chicks are never priority number one. I tucked Jenny's phone number away in a drawer this morning and forgot about it. My goals will never be realized if I'm distracted by a cute brunette just because she passes me her number.

I finished my work, intending to review it again on my flight to the East Coast tomorrow. My weekend will be spent with my best friend, sitting around a campfire having a couple beers while surrounded by tall pines and the serene waters of the St. Lawrence River. This is more the 'Speed of Oates' than Vegas could ever be.

"It's all good," I say. "I'll present my plans to Pierce on Friday, discuss our next steps and still have time for feet-up relaxation at the island."

"An island, huh?" Finn says. "Why am I not surprised MML has his own island?"

"It belongs to his parents. I'm hitching a ride with them."

"Whoa," Zach chides. "Lame."

"His parents are chill, and it's amazing there. Massive main house, other quarters scattered across the property. There's plenty of space for guests to spread out. I'll get to soak up some nature 'n shit."

"Still say you could've unwound by the pool with a sweet honey at your side," Zach says. "I doubt you'll find any scantily clad babes on Pierce's arctic island in Canada."

"It's June, dumbass. It's not cold there. And I don't need to be finding any babes, scantily clad or otherwise."

Finn laughs. "Even if you did, they'd all flock to him."

Like I don't know this already. I went to college with the guy. "Pierce is in all-biz mode right now," I say. "Neither of us has time for women."

While the twins see Pierce as formidable, profitable and all-business, they also think he's got extremely flawed taste in women. Or, one woman.

Stella Ireland is Pierce's former girlfriend, and she's the only reason he's ever wound up in tabloids. The twins think she's nuts, and they've never even had the displeasure of meeting the celebrity in person.

They're right about Stella being *loco*, though I disagree with their assessment that she's a 'High Maintenance Monica'. According to their ridiculous category system, this means she's still "fuck-able", because she's that hot. According to the World of Oates, she's a 'No-Fucking-Thanks-Even-If-The-World-Is-Ending'.

The guys are closer to the mark on their assumption that Pierce is reserved and professionally focused, but that's only one side of him. He's Ivy League smart and finds my nerdity an asset, but he also possesses a great sense of humor. He just doesn't show it off to a lot of people.

In college, Pierce helped me and our Third Musketeer, Nate Edwards, build a robot to prank one of Nate's academic rivals who also happened to be a campus track sensation. We programmed the robot to mow a depiction of a lady part onto South Field and planted evidence that his rival had done the damage. Our behavior during the rivalry was semi-regrettable, but in our defense, it was in retaliation. And the crass humor was not lost on my serious friend Aidan Pierce.

"How's he doing in New York?" Finn asks. "Has he already conquered the drug dependence and rampant despair of that small city?"

"Far as I know he's just getting started," I say. "He seemed different though."

"Different how?" Zach asks. He turns his head to eye a girl that's just come through the door.

"I couldn't pinpoint, but he almost seemed—"

"Bored?" Finn says.

"No," I shake my head. "He sort of sounded— "

"Pissed?" Zach asks.

"Nah. More like happy."

"Whoa, that doesn't sound like MML." Finn finally gives us his full attention. "That's not good."

"Why?" I'm curious why Finn would have an opinion one way or the other.

"Because Pierce is like Batman," Zach says.

"Right," his twin agrees.

"You guys lost me."

In true Finnegan Hawthorne fashion he leans back, arms crossed over his chest. I suppose it's his birthright to act all-knowing, given he's the older twin. To me, he's always been the more philosophical and self-assured brother. I sometimes joke his confidence is due to the eight minutes of life experience he has over Zach.

"Batman is the alter ego of Bruce Wayne," he says. "Wayne is loaded beyond comprehension, has a butler and a bad-ass collection of tech to rid his city of the scum of humanity. But," he adds, raising his gin and tonic, "Batman doesn't get *happy*. Batman gets shit *done*."

I laugh because in a way, he's right.

Pierce's good intentions are as plentiful as his keen instincts and the cash in his bank accounts. Like Batman, he does have a guy at his beck and call. But his lead security agent Byron isn't a thousand-year old, white-haired dude. He's ex-military and just as badass as Batman.

Pierce can be short-tempered, but he does get shit done. He's the only person I trust on this planet as much as myself, and he puts heart into everything. Since his move, I haven't talked to him much for that reason. All his efforts are going towards his ambitious charity project.

But he also has something Batman doesn't, and that's his ex-girlfriend Stella. She complicates everything. When I hung out with him briefly last month, he was in a sour mood. I guess escorting your ex to rehab is no trip to Disneyland.

"I don't know much about Batman," I finally say, "other than the fact that Michael Keaton played him best in any of the movies." Zach huffs aloud to indicate his disagreement, but I put a hand up. "We are *not* debating that now. I'm just saying, Pierce was pretty maxed out when I saw him last. His upbeat mood today surprised me."

The bartender clangs the iron bell mounted to the wall signaling trivia begins in five minutes.

"Happy usually means a business conquest or a woman," Zach says. "Given he's all into charity now, I'm guessing it's the latter."

"Which means his whole world is fucked," Finn says.

I shake my head. "It's something else. Or I'm misreading him."

"Mark my words," Zach says. "I'm calling it. It's a chick."

"I'll take that bet," I say. "What are we wagering?"

Zach looks to Finn. "If I win, you owe me a bottle of thirty-year-old Scotch. My choice of distillery."

"And," Finn adds, "we get to bring back the show."

"There's no way you're right about Pierce, but I can't agree to that. I don't want to see you guys get third degree burns on your nipples while flipping flapjacks in our kitchen. I will agree to buy you the booze," I smirk at them, "*if* you're right. And that's a pretty big if."

"What's the prize if you win?" Finn asks. "And for the record, I'm siding with Team Zach. Batman has a woman."

"If I'm right, you owe me a pair of tickets to two concerts of my choice. Front row, with backstage passes. You may have to pull strings with your parents' contacts."

"Done," Finn says without batting an eye. "I'll even throw in two tickets to a Broadway show."

Zach and I shake hands to solidify the wager. "I'll decide which events while I'm flying to New York. And I am sorry for missing your birthday festivities," I say, "but I'd probably just bring down the party. My brain is fried."

"We're fried, too," Zach smiles. My friend shrugs his broad shoulders and nods towards the parking lot. "I got a one-hitter in the Beemer if you're interested."

"Thanks anyway, Z-man. I'm good."

Zach laughs and smacks me on the back. "That's our Oates, always the straight and narrow. You're forgiven for missing Vegas, bruh. You know what that means, though." His smile widens into a wicked grin as he lets a pretty girl in a short skirt squeeze by him. "We'll be making the most of tonight."

Forty minutes later, round one of trivia ends. Our three-man team is in the lead. The host calls for a ten-minute break, and we head for the bar. We snag a spot closer to the kitchen this time, and Finn strikes up a conversation with the trivia master.

The smell of chicken wings wafts to us from the pass-through window as hunger rumbles in my gut. I haven't eaten since my burrito this morning.

"Should we order food, guys?" I grab for a peanut as the trivia master walks away.

"We ate on the way over," Finn says. "You go ahead."

I discard a hollow tan shell to the floor and look up at the television. The sound is muted and a baseball game airs to the backdrop of Tom Petty and Stevie Nicks singing about hearts being dragged around.

"I'm starving and tired," I mutter. "It's been a long seventy-two of being focused. I need to go home."

"I can tell you're not focused," Finn says. "There's a trifecta staring at us from the corner and you missed it." He turns his attention to Zach. "You too, handsome brother."

I smirk at his last comment.

Finn often compliments his brother's looks in an indirect effort to brag about his own. It's credit where credit is due, though. Either of them can pick up a chick in under thirty minutes post-introduction, while I'm stumbling over words or staring at my shoelaces, unsure how to act when a girl just complimented my hair.

The twins do have a few tells to set them apart if you know them well, but they're a dead ringer for one another. Each was born with the noticeable combination of blue eyes and dark hair, and both earn their ripped physiques by spending as much time at the gym now as they did when they were college athletes.

Zach covertly scans for the women of mention, zeroing in on them before turning back to us. "I saw them when they walked in earlier."

"How did *you* see them?" I ask Finn. "You were staring up at the TV the whole time."

"He's been watching their reflections," Zach says flatly. "But they've been checking us out all night. He didn't need to use that tired move. Oates, didn't you see them look our way when Finn answered the question about the Cameron Diaz movie?"

"I did not. But I'm glad as ever we have your bro's insight for the chick-flick category."

I swivel on my barstool to look around. The dim tavern is full of people. The three young women huddled in the corner smile at me, then turn inward to whisper to each other.

Their dresses progress in levels of indecency, yet they appear uniformed. Glossed lips curved in flirtatious smiles, white dresses, strappy sandals. Even their martinis appear to be the same. The only thing setting them apart is their hair color – one brunette, one blonde, one redhead.

They're a 'three-girls-walked-into-a-bar' joke waiting for a punchline.

"All yours, guys," I mutter. "They look a little too basic for me."

Finn chimes in. "Looking around, it seems basic is all that's showing up tonight. If I'm looking for a no-strings attached fling, a random 'basic' girl is usually agreeable with these terms. Afterwards, we go our separate ways."

"Yeah, like before daylight," I mutter.

"So what?" he says. "I make it clear up front that attachments aren't my thing. Let's not pretend some chicks don't want one night stands as badly as guys do. Case in point, there's a girl over there staring at me like I'm dinner."

"Exactly," Zach says. "That look certainly doesn't convey that her goal is marriage and matching cemetery plots."

I turn and, sure as shit, they're right. Brunette is hurling a come-hither stare at Finn. He winks at her, and she smiles coyly before conversing with her two pals again.

Zach pulls his phone from the pocket of his jeans, not realizing the redhead is now eyeballing his t-shirt. It's one of his favorites and declares "I Got a Dig Bick" in large black letters. The small print beneath it says, "You Read That Wrong".

The guys never dress exactly alike, thank God, because two grown men would look ridiculous doing that. The guys have money to spare and dress accordingly. Their jeans probably set them back more than I'd pay for a one-year supply of coffee. High-end everything complements their looks, from their belts to the cars they drive. Still, each has his own unique style.

Finn's the more conservative brother. The sleeves of his button-down shirt are rolled up to the elbows, revealing his expensive watch. Unlike Zach, Finn's blue t-shirt declares nothing.

My roommates spent years apart during college and grad school, distancing themselves from the twin stigma they were born with. Their bond is unmistakable, though. Odd coincidences dominate their behavior even while apart. Often the two of them are unaware they've sent me the same verbiage in a text.

Simultaneously.

While they're not even in the same state.

"Speaking of no attachments," Zach says, scrolling through his phone, "don't we have something this fall that we need dates for? We may have to break those rules soon. Lay some groundwork for that formal function."

Finn cracks open a peanut shell and pops the reward in his mouth. "Seems like, yeah. Family wedding in November maybe? We'll need women who can pull off temporarily convincing the folks that we *might* think about settling down."

Martin and Iris Hawthorne are successful, upstanding members of society who parent from a distance. They love their sons, but they provided the guys with more opportunities than affection and their sole heirs are expected to live up to a certain standard.

The Hawthorne name doesn't make the guys so famous that they're hassled just walking down the street. They're able to fly under the radar in most social circles. But in the presence of their parents, the surname's standard is to be upheld.

Zach also reaches for a peanut. "You know how our parental units are," he says to me. "Gotta placate them sometimes. Especially Mom. If not, she'll start introducing us to every unattached female over twenty-five that she's ever met."

"Our dates will need to be independent and smart," Finn goes on. "Able to have an intelligent conversation."

"And most of all," they say at once, "*not bat-shit crazy.*"

"Never forget that, Oates." Finn raises his drink as the two share a laugh. "Absolutely no Toxic Tinas."

I join in their amusement, recalling a girl Finn briefly dated right after I met the guys.

Dated isn't fitting, actually. For two weeks, 'Tina' veered into the realm of stalker after just one date with Finn. None of us could recall her actual name, just that it started with a 'T'. Tina has been the *loco* girl's assigned moniker during any retelling of the stalker story.

"So, what do you say, Oates?" Finn asks as he eyeballs the ladies.

"I think I might head out before round two starts. I gotta pack."

"Suit yourself." He slides his glass across the mahogany. "Bombay and tonic, please," he says to the bartender. "I'll be back in under five minutes." Finn heads for the corner where the three chicks wait to be formally noticed. Zach takes his brother's empty seat.

"You're not joining him?" I ask.

He shakes his head. "I'll wait here to see if brother strikes out."

Like that would ever be a possibility. I gesture to my near empty pint. "I'm leaving after I finish this."

"Probably not the worst idea if you're flying early. You haven't been flat in days." Zach nods across the room to Finn, who's holding up a finger suggesting he'll just be a minute. "We're about to have some company."

"Yeah, well. Don't offer *my* company to any of them."

"C'mon, Oates. That's a rare Neapolitan trifecta over there. You should give it a go with Vanilla." He shares a smile with the redhead then swerves his stool back to me. "Hands off Strawberry, though."

"She looks kind of sweet," I comment. "Doesn't seem your type."

"Sweet my ass. Gingers are wild behind closed doors. Any woman fitting that description is my type."

"You can have them all," I mutter. "They're definitely not my preferred company."

"A hook-up is just what we need. Don't take it all so seriously, man."

When I don't reply, he opens his mouth, then snaps it shut again. "What?"

"Nothing," he says. "Just wondering if you're still spacing out about Crazy Carolyn."

"No." I shudder at the mention of her name. "She was a Toxic Tina I've put behind me."

"That she was. If you'd been paying attention, you would've called that one early on."

"What can I say?" I shrug. "I was focused on work. I dated Carolyn on auto-pilot."

My former girlfriend was attractive. Conversation flowed easily enough when we were introduced at the office. As it turned out, working together was all we had in common. From choosing date night films to what time of day is most ideal to launch an app, we never agreed on anything.

Not that I care to date someone who always shares my opinion, but Carolyn had a way of turning even a minor conflict into a dramatic argument. Finn only met her once and was convinced she'd be capable of starting a fight while standing alone in an empty room.

Those were the first red flags I ignored.

"Anyway, when I said *sayonara* to her, I meant it. That was three months ago. She ended up shit canned shortly after. Haven't seen her since."

"Glad to hear it." He eyes me closely. "Dude, you look like you could sleep for a week."

"Agreed. That's precisely why I'm leaving. You guys can fight over the third *chica* and close the bar without me."

I have to admit a sexy, sweet-scented woman would be nice company. But one night rolls in the hay aren't my thing.

If looks and a smile snag my attention, great. But my ideal girl would have to converse about more than the weather and be able to laugh at ridiculous or juvenile shit, like Zach's t-shirt. Bonus if she doesn't compliment my eyes, or my dark curls, or how she can't believe what a toned body I hide under my clothes. I've ridden on that compliment train multiple times round-trip, always the uncomfortable passenger unable to make eye contact.

Most girls who compliment me that way lack substance. My home state of California hasn't proven to be a deep well of dating material — at least not for me.

I've met a lot of intelligent, beautiful girls living here as a grown man, but most are focused on killing it in their career. These chicks put in triple the effort at work because they're competing with a guy one cube over who may have worked on an AI robot-nanny for Mark Zuckerberg's kid.

The last thing on the minds of all these ambitious ladies is dating. The climate of career-driven females greatly narrows the dating field, and the girls Finn's chatting up in the corner are classic examples of what's left to choose from. I'd bet at least one of them has auditioned for a commercial, unless they're tourists. With the eyes they're making at the twins, I'm inclined to agree they're looking for a hook-up.

I'd rather *date* a girl, one I can talk to about anything.

Eighties movies. Music spanning eras and genres. Scientific nerd shit. How much of a pain in the ass my nomadic, flighty sister is. Someone who gets that a relationship shouldn't be about finding someone to fill a void. Maybe this dream girl could show up for a relationship already responsible for her own happiness.

Crazy Carolyn couldn't get happy watching kitten videos, even if there was a cameo of a unicorn blowing rainbows out its ass.

"Here they come," Zach says. "Be cool."

I glance behind me, watching Finn approach with his new fan club. Chocolate Brunette has her arm linked in his.

"Ladies," he says with his effortless charm, "I'd like you to meet the only guys I'd take a bullet for."

Zach stands up for introductions and I spin around on my stool to face the group.

"This is my brother Zach and our friend Daryl Oates. Guys, this is Rachel." He gestures to the woman on his arm. "She's a math teacher. And these are her friends who are visiting from Virginia. My sincerest apologies ladies, I didn't catch your names." He ignores the friends from Virginia to lock eyes with Rachel.

He's doing what every kid does with Neapolitan — ignore strawberry and vanilla and dig right into the chocolate.

"I'm Linda," Strawberry Redhead says, gently palming my hand and then Zach's. "We're from D.C."

"Near the White House," Vanilla Blonde smiles proudly.

"Charmed." I can't help my sarcasm. I'm not feeling capable of making small talk.

Zach speaks up. "Any of you ladies need a fresh cocktail?"

Strawberry beams up at Zach, then does a double take as she looks to Finn. "Wait," she says, studying my friends intently. "No. *Way.* Are you guys twins?"

I stare at Finn to see if he's pissed. This a trigger for him, a question they constantly field that he has no patience for. Zach is usually more indifferent when asked. In the interest of getting laid tonight, neither of them says anything, instead smiling in recognition.

"Duh, Linda," Chocolate Rachel says with an eye roll.

"Actually," I say, "we're triplets."

This brings a giggle from all the girls, and I smile before I turn back to the bar. Zach strikes up a conversation with 'Duh-Linda' as Vanilla Blonde seats herself next to me.

"Hey," I offer.

"Hey yourself."

I look over and she smiles at me in that way girls sometimes have, with an inviting hint in her eye. She's cute and smells nice, but my gut tells me she'll fall short in the captivating intelligence department.

Before I can say anything, she carries on without taking a breath. *It's unreal the coffee is as expensive here as it is inside the Beltway! Is the weather here always this perfect? Do you even realize how ah-mazing your brown eyes are?*

Weather small talk, check. Compliment my eyes, check. *Strikes one and two!*

On she rambles. This chick's either on coke or incredibly nervous.

As I hear the words Kardashian and DVR tumble out of Vanilla's mouth, my phone vibrates in my pocket. I pull it out in time to see Nate Edwards' name zoom across the screen. A rare text from the Third Musketeer has saved me from this nightmare.

Nate's the only friend from Cal Tech Pierce and I still keep tabs on. He roomed with us during our undergrad years, and we bonded over the pranks we dreamed up. He's undoubtedly the smartest of the three of us. If he had any idea I was allowing myself to suffer through this conversation, his NASA-contracted ass would crucify me.

I mutter an apology to Vanilla Blonde and quickly read his two-word message.

Call me.

Nate doesn't have time to contact his friends on the regular, and hearing from Nate and Pierce in the same day is like witnessing the Hawthornes strike out with a pretty girl. It just doesn't happen.

"I don't mean to be rude," I smile at the blonde, "but I need to call my buddy Nate. I think it's urgent."

I'll call him on my way home, right after I hit In-N-Out for a cheeseburger and a milkshake.

"Aww," she says. "I haven't had a chance to ask you about your work in Silicone Valley. Your friend said you're a pretty big deal."

Oh, holy shit. Did she really just say *Silicone*?

"Your glasses are kinda hot, too. A shame you're hiding beneath those gorgeous dark curls, though."

Ladies and germs, she mentioned the curls. *Strike three!*

I offer a polite thank you and get up from my seat.

"I was hoping we might join forces for the rest of the game?" she coos. "Something tells me you're a smart guy, Darren."

Darren?

Jesus. How many martinis has she had?

"Sorry, but it's usually frowned upon to mix up teams once play has begun. Wish I could though." I pocket my phone, then throw a twenty on the bar. "Have yourself a drink on me tonight. Save your money for the expensive California coffee instead."

She beams at my gesture just as my phone rings. Elton John's "Rocket Man" soars over the din. *A follow-up call from Nate?* Definitely important.

"That's him again. I really must go." I turn away to answer. "One second, Nate. I'm just heading for the car." I mute the phone and turn back to her. "I'm sorry, I don't think Finn mentioned your name?"

I'll at least ask that much before I make a run for it.

I nod to the twins as they charm their new friends nearby. I know Vanilla just answered me, but I missed it over the crowd noise and the clang of the bell. Trivia teams are reassembling.

"Sorry, say again?" Scattered peanut shells crunch under my sneakers as I tilt my head to listen.

She smiles while batting her lashes. "It's Tina."

It's damn hard not to laugh given the irony. We haven't crossed paths with any girl named Tina since we re-named Finn's stalker. If there is a God, He or She has a killer sense of humor. Maybe this girl's not the stalker type, but she'd likely dot her 'i's with a fat heart instead of an intelligent, understated dot.

"Tina, it's been a pleasure." I shake her hand and walk away, closing in on Finn and Zach. "Important call." I hold up my screen to show them Nate's name and they lift their chins in unison, recognizing the rarity. Finn excuses himself and his brother, and the ladies join Tina at the bar as we step towards the door.

"What's up?" Zach asks. "Nate never calls."

"I'm about to find out."

"I call bullshit," Finn says. "You probably called him."

"I didn't respond to his text post-haste. He followed up with a call."

"Whoa," he concedes. "I hear that, bro. Serious."

"Definitely. Also, Vanilla is not for me. Maybe you're in luck and Chocolate's into threesomes."

Finn cocks his head to the side and looks toward the ladies, contemplating the notion.

"I'll text when my plans with Pierce are final, but I think I bug out for New York at five a.m.," I say. "Should be back Sunday or Monday."

"Rachel has a condo nearby," Finn says. "We'll be out for the night. Lock up when you go."

He offers up our typical bro-handshake, and I put the gesture on repeat with Zach. I wave goodbye to my new blonde friend at the bar. As I move closer to the exit, the twins stare at all three ladies, probably having a subliminal war about who will be savoring an additional flavor tonight.

"Oh, and guys?"

"What?" they ask in unison, still fixated on the women.

"Get moving," I say over my shoulder. "You shouldn't keep a Tina waiting."

5

Pam

June 8, 2016
Wednesday, 11:00 p.m.
Bay Falls, Ontario
Canada

My friend is pretty lit, though she burned off some of her alcohol attempting to dance. She's debating whether to order a nightcap.

I can tell from the bartender's expression she's ready to end her shift. We kept her busy the last couple of hours, but our party died down fifteen minutes ago, given most people have to work tomorrow. Carly and I are the only ones left.

"Ready to close out?" the bartender asks.

"Yes, thank you." I smile at her and sign off on my tab, which is next to nothing. Given Carly is gainfully employed and I'm on a shoestring budget, she only allowed me to buy one round. The rest of her drinks were bought by others in our party. "We gotta go, girl. Dave's waiting for us out front."

"I thought he walked home already."

"No," I say, "I told him I didn't want him to walk."

"We've got to go find some food," she mumbles.

"You ate dinner earlier."

"That was hours ago. I'm *starving*."

"No, you're drunk." I smirk at her as she sits on a stool, resting her head on the bar over her crossed arms.

"No, I'm hangry." She perks up. "Or, I guess if I'm drunk too, I'm...what am I? *Hankry*? *Drunk-gry*?" She cracks up at her own joke, and I can't help laugh at her foolishness. She's not typically this far gone.

"Anything you want," I tell her. "Let's go find food."

She snaps to attention and hops off the stool, suddenly in complete control. She's ahead of me, beelining for the door. I'm not looking up as I search my purse for the key to my Mini Cooper. When she halts in her tracks, I bump into her.

"Shit, sorry," I mumble. "You okay?"

"Pam."

"Yeah, what?" I notice her phone is lighting up the bottom of my purse as I dig. "Who is calling you at this hour?"

She tugs on the strap of my dress to get my attention. "Pam, what in the actual fuck?"

I palm my key and look up, following her gaze out the front window. Dave is holding his phone to his ear while he blows out a drag of smoke. I check the display of Carly's phone and realize he was the person calling.

"So?" I say. "Even I know Dave occasionally smokes. And that was him calling. He's probably tired of waiting."

"No, it's not that. Did you see who he's talking to?"

I take a step forward. Dave's pocketed his phone, but he wasn't calling to hurry us up. He's listening to Carly's ex blather on about something and must've been calling to warn us away. Mick's tone is borderline irate. Dave doesn't seem bothered and uses well-timed eye rolls as his response.

"Did you tell Mick we were coming here?" I ask Carly.

"I may have."

I scold her with a look.

"What?" she says defensively. "I said I may have. In passing. I really don't remember."

"We'll call Dave and tell him there's a new plan," I grumble as I link arms with her. "Let's go out the back."

"No." My friend removes her arm from mine and grabs me by the shoulders. "I refuse to scurry out of here because of him."

"Fine." My shoulders sink in defeat. "But we do not engage."

She turns away and stares at the door, and I can tell her resolve is wavering.

"*Carly.*"

"Yes, I hear you."

"No matter what he says, whether he compliments your sweet tits or calls you something awful, promise me you will say nothing. We do not acknowledge him. We walk to the car, and that's it."

"I will put him on ignore," she says, crossing a finger over her heart. "Promise."

"I can't believe I let you talk me into this," Carly says with a mouthful of food. "This is a bad idea."

"Relax," Dave chides. "Pam's sober. Shut up and hold onto your hash browns." He removes the wrapper from his sausage sandwich and tosses it into the empty Tim Horton's bag. "Where are we going again?"

"The usual," Carly says. "Where we always go."

This means nothing to Dave. He's never traveled by boat with us before. It's nearly midnight and too dark to see much. I can't blame him if he's a little uncomfortable or at least curious. We're floating on the river across the road from Carly's dad's place. Their river frontage has a dock and a small boathouse where her dad keeps his pontoon. We've just boarded the vessel, and the only light is cast by a couple of cobweb-covered bulbs overhead.

"You'll see," I say. "Are you comfortable on boats, Dave?"

"Enough to come along for a moonlit cruise. If this boat was one of them speedy versions with racing stripes, I'd pass."

"We'll be fine," I insist as I start the engine. "And this will sober you guys up a little before you pass out tonight. Carls, your Dad doesn't care if we take a ride as long as the driver is sober, right?"

"Yeah, I'm not worried about that. He's on the road until morning, anyway," Carly says between bites of her bacon and egg sandwich. "I just want my bed."

"I'll get us all back to shore in less than thirty minutes. Dave, can you get the lines?"

"That much I can do." He steps off and unties both nylon ropes from the cleats and tosses them in the boat. "Carly, you're off to

N-Y-C tomorrow, then on to Florida from there. Your bed can wait until we have one last Goonie adventure."

"You're right as usual," she says, only slightly more enthused. "Let's motor."

I pull away from the dock and we glide up the main channel of the St. Lawrence River with the headlamps on. Cool air whooshes past, and I'm grateful for Carly's insistence that we stop at her apartment over her Dad's garage before our voyage. She insisted I swap my sundress for jeans and a hoodie.

A sliver of moonlight reflects off the green channel markers that guide us. Navigating this river in the dark isn't easy, but Carly and I are lifelong river rats. We travel only in the areas of the river we know with certainty, especially if it's dark.

I have this particular route memorized.

"Pass the coffee," Dave says. "The breeze is giving me a chill."

Carly pulls a paper cup from the cardboard holder and passes it to Dave.

"You want yours now?" she asks me.

"You know I do." I take the cup and sip, then place it in the holder next to the wheel.

"My God, this is the worst breakfast sandwich ever," Dave says after a few bites. "Why does it taste so *fucking* good?"

"Because you're even more shitfaced than I am," Carly throws back.

"How's your hand?" I ask Dave over the engine noise as I pick up speed to cross the channel.

"Better than Mick's face."

Carly laughs and nearly chokes.

"I still can't believe you did that," I say.

"Last guy that spoke to me like that walked away in worse shape," Dave insists. "I held back out of respect for Carly, so Mick's mama wouldn't vomit the next time she sees him."

"Thank you." Carly scoots closer to Dave on the bench seat. "I'm not mad that you defended my honor. We just can't believe it."

"So, the truth now. Did you ask Mick to meet up with you?" I ask as we arrive on the opposite side of the channel. "I mean, I kind of hope so, because otherwise he's stalking you."

"I knew he was going to be at Town Tavern with his hockey

buddies. I may have mentioned Duke and Earl's, but I didn't say for sure where we'd end up. And I definitely didn't extend an invite."

Carly tried to chill Mick out when we left the bar, but there was no talking him down. It only took a minute for her to throw up her hands and walk away. Dave walked us across the street to my car, but before we could even open the doors, Mick was hurling insults so vulgar my mum would pass out if she heard them.

Dave popped Mick in the mouth so fast, her ex was recoiling long enough that we could speed away in my car before things got worse.

"I about died when you huffed it back across the street like that," Carly says to Dave. "That's an impressive right hook, big guy. He never saw it coming."

"I agree, Dave. Remind me to bring you along anytime I think there might be trouble."

"And you can be my getaway driver any time," he says to me. "You peeled that Mini out of there like we were in a *Fast and Furious* sequel. Thank God Carly fit in the backseat. I sure as hell couldn't."

I laugh recalling our escape. Once our adrenaline wore off and we stopped repeating 'holy shit' to each other, Carly was again insistent on food. I drove us to Tim's. She and Dave went in to use the bathroom and order, and when they returned to my car, Carly said she wanted to retreat to her apartment and wallow. Instead, I came up with the river cruise idea. I had to insist, telling her the universe would rather we end the evening on a high note than let Mick ruin it.

That convinced her.

I wind around a few small islands on our short ride, careful to avoid the shoals until we come upon the property Carly knows I'm obsessed with.

"It's so beautiful," she admits with a sigh. "Never gets old."

We slow down as we begin to circle the white Colonial-style house perched on a cliff of granite. The main house peeks out from leaves that would appear lush and green in the daylight. The island's tall trees disguise the property from full view, but a sliver of moonlight shines on my favorite part of the home.

"You're still as mad about that veranda as ever, aren't you?"

"Obviously," I say. "Just look at it." We're all admiring the Southern style, wrap-around porch accented with several large pillars. "I've always imagined sitting on a rocker up there, passing the afternoon sipping lemonade and reading a book. Such a shame it's hardly used."

"I bet it's a great spot to watch boats drive up and down the channel, too," Carly says. "That's gotta be some view."

The Gables is infamous around here and aptly named with too many gables to count at first pass. (There are eleven.) There are three access points around the property.

The main home we're currently admiring sits on the bigger of two islands. It's accessed by docking at the main slips off the back side of the island, then by the walking paths leading to either side of the porch.

A rustic cottage sits on a second, smaller island. That's accessed by parking at a different dock, the one hidden in a small bay between the two islands. A wooden bridge connects them if you're on foot, which I know because my brother and I crossed it countless times when I was younger. The bridge isn't visible from the main channel, though. You have to dock first, then take the paths to find it.

Though we never had the guts to go up to the porch of the main house, my brother Ben and I often docked our family's small boat in the hidden bay, sneaking off to explore the compound.

A third point on the larger island is home to a boathouse and a dock along the shoreline (technically more like a wharf). We've already blown by that so we could scope out the impressive main house.

"I think someone rented the place for the U.S. holiday," Carly says. "The weekend after Victoria Day, the sounds of partying carried all the way to Dad's house."

"Good." I smile over at her and turn my gaze back to the porch. "It deserves more attention."

Mum always told Ben and me stories about the famous people that had come and gone from The Gables years ago, from the time she was a little girl and even before that, when her mum was little. The Americans who now own it no longer come here, though. Countless rumors circulate about why, but I've never heard one that was believable.

When Ben moved to the States permanently, I came here less often. My brother and his wife Alexis were rarely up here during the warmer months, especially once he began taking out-of-town assignments for the TV station. I stopped coming at all after I left for University, only driving by with Carly during summer breaks.

"So the owners rent it out?" Dave asks. "They must make a killing."

"Yeah," Carly says, "they rent to rich people in the summer and button it up in the off season."

"You guys ever see the inside?" he asks.

"No," we say in unison.

"The rental periods aren't on a predictable schedule," Carly says while chewing. The crinkling sound of her sandwich wrapper echoes across the water as she discards her trash. "I'd never want to be caught trespassing there."

"Me either." *Though it would be so worth it.*

"Let's dock and snoop around," Dave says, as though reading my mind.

"I thought I was the drunk one with poor decision making skills?" Carly says. "Even I know that's a worse idea than this midnight cruise."

"It's not entirely bad," I whisper.

"Some of the lampposts are on." She points to the interior of the island and the thick groupings of trees that are lit up. "Someone is probably renting it this week. When no one's here, it's totally dark."

Carly knows what she's talking about. Her dad's house isn't far away, and she's been by here more than I have, especially the last few years. I look back at Dave and see his mischievous expression. Usually, I would second Carly's position that we don't risk getting caught doing something kind of wrong.

Okay, illegal.

But my curiosity about this property trumps everything. It always has. Something has always drawn me to it.

"I'm with Dave." I drive us out of the main channel, closer to the island, then cut the engine.

"Did you just turn the boat off?" Dave asks.

"Yes. The current will drag us around to the back side without any noise. It's really strong here."

"You're sure?" he asks.

"I'm sure. I've done it tons of times. We'll end up over by the main dock slips. If it looks like there's any activity, we'll drive away. But if not—"

"If not, we park and explore!" Dave crouches down, staring at the island as we circle it. "We're going *incognito!*"

I laugh at his enthusiasm.

"I've never seen you this excited about something other than food." Carly lets out a belch and excuses herself before sipping her coffee.

"Queen my ass," Dave says. "Nice out. And this property is Sotheby's-worthy. I wouldn't mind peeking in the windows."

"What's the plan if we get caught?" I ask.

He points a thumb at our mutual friend. "We say she's drunk and confused. She told us to drop her off at home, and we didn't know this was the wrong house."

"Ha!" Carly hoots with laughter. "Like that's a common mistake."

We arrive at the back side of the island and look towards the main house. "It's totally dark," I say. "Even if someone was here, they're gone now."

"Or sleeping," Carly says.

"There's no other boats," Dave points out. "There can't be anyone here unless they can walk on water."

"Okay, okay," Carly agrees. "Dock this vessel. You only live once, right?"

"Last Goonie adventure," Dave says, lifting his coffee. "What about coffee, Pam? Is it okay to cheers with coffee?"

I shoot him a dirty look.

"Tried to cheers with water?" Carly asks him as she rolls her eyes.

"Yup," he says. "I was quickly schooled."

"Hey," I say, "both of you can kiss my ass."

Dave throws a hand to his mouth feigning shock. "Such talk for a princess."

I flip him the bird, then turn the engine on to motor us out of the current. At the dock, Carly hops out to tie off the lines. "C'mon," she whispers to Dave. "This was your idea. Get off your ass."

He follows her command, and I step out after them. "Anyone have a flashlight?"

"On my phone," he says. "My battery's low, though."

"I should be fully charged. I haven't used mine all night." Carly pats the back pocket of her jeans. "Shit. Where is my phone?"

"I told you, I have it." I hop back on the boat, grab her device out of my purse, and hand it to her.

"Were you purposely hiding it from me?"

"Drunk dialing is a thing," I shrug. "I was saving you from yourself."

"I see you don't trust me as much as I trust you." She shines the light up the dirt path between two rows of tall pines, and I stifle a nervous laugh. *Wait until she finds those dating apps on her phone.* "Where first?" she asks once we reach the split in the path. When we stop, so does the sound of dry pine needles rustling beneath our feet. "Main house?"

"Yeah, definitely. I have to see the view from the porch."

"You go first," Carly says, pushing Dave ahead of us. "This was your idea."

Dave leaves the path and, as well as a guy his size can, tiptoes up the steps on the west side of the house. He leaves the two of us standing there as my heart pounds. Carly lets out a giggle like we're teenagers prowling outside the home of our boy crush. Despite my feet being firmly planted on solid granite, my knees feel weak.

"Well?" I whisper up in Dave's direction. "You're killing me here!"

He responds at full volume, waving enthusiastically. "It's pitch black in there. Bring that light." We climb the steps in time to see him pull out his Zippo and light a cigarette. "Point it in that room," he says, courteously exhaling a drag of smoke away from us. "Looks like it's the kitchen."

Carly points her phone at the window and we see Dave's guessed correctly. I can't make out all the room's details, but light bounces off stainless steel appliances.

"That kitchen's fucking huge," my friend mutters. "It's as big as my apartment."

Dave puts an arm around her. "Imagine what damage we could do in there, babe."

"For reals." Carly wonders aloud how many ovens there are and whether there's a prep area just for baking, and how big is that island?

I hear her voice but I'm lost in my own holy-shit moment as I walk the length of the porch, enjoying the creaking of wide boards beneath my feet. The view is more incredible than I ever imagined. I pull out my phone, snap a shot of the moonlit water far below, then turn the camera around to take a photo of myself with the grand porch and my two friends in the shadows behind me.

As Dave comments about something on the kitchen counter, there's rustling in the distance.

Carly shrieks.

"Shut up!" Dave throws his hand over her mouth, pulls her down to crouch beside him and nods towards the path. "Someone's here."

"Where?" I whisper. "No boats pulled up." I walk back to join them, checking that the house next to us is still dark.

"We just heard voices down there." Dave points in the direction of the boathouse on the opposite end of the main island.

"Fuck," Carly blurts. "I wasn't paying attention when we went past. Was a boat docked there?"

"I don't know," I whisper. "I didn't look either."

She points the flashlight into the kitchen again. "There's grocery bags on the counter. Someone must be here delivering and getting the place ready for renters."

"You better hope they leave going up river," Dave says. "Otherwise they'll see our boat."

Carly turns off the flashlight and looks at me in disbelief. "How are you not panicking at a time like this?"

"What good would that do? If we're caught, we're caught, and we go with the plan that you can't remember where you live."

"Not on my watch," Dave says. "C'mon ladies."

"C'mon where?" Carly asks in her too-loud drunk voice.

"Shh," he says. He tosses his cigarette over the porch railing and we all watch it fall to the river below as though we've got nothing better to do. "We'll scope out the boathouse. If they leave headed east and find our boat, they'll dock and come up to see who's here. That will give us time to sneak back down the path and make a run for the boat before they can catch us."

"As long as they don't think to snap a picture of our boat's numbers before they come up here," Carly says.

He ignores her pessimism. "If they drive away up the channel, they'll never know we were here, and we can get a look at the boat-house and the cabin before we go."

"I may not be panicking," I say, "but I don't know if we should hang around and roll the dice, either."

Before we can object further, Dave leads the charge. He stalks along the porch and follows the trail as it splits to the left, meandering downhill toward the boathouse. We're walking in the opposite direction of the main docks where our boat (and only means of escape) is tied up.

As the boathouse comes into view, memories of my brother and I venturing up to its second story play through my head. We'd been surprised to find living space up there, too. Ben had wondered aloud how many guests the owners needed to accommodate.

"The main house, a guest cottage, and bedrooms above the boathouse too?" he'd said. *"They can host an entire hockey league for hell's sake."*

As a thirteen year old girl, I'd been impressed, too. All we could see when peering through the second floor of the boathouse were an open living area and kitchenette, but with the late afternoon sun pouring in that day, we could tell it was fancier than our modest home.

Dave stops abruptly a few paces ahead, halting behind a pine tree at another fork in the path. The footbridge crosses to the right, leading to the bay and the smaller island where the guest cabin is.

As Carly and I get closer, he turns and gestures with flailing hands. "Get down!"

We do, crouching behind him in time to see a woman climb into a Boston Whaler and start the engine. A man unties the lines and climbs into the boat after her, and Dave leans forward, trying to make out what they're saying.

Carly's phone sounds off at full volume. Eminem is rapping from the palm of her hands.

Mick's ringtone.

Crap.

She shoves the phone into her bra to stifle the sound, but the noise startles Dave and he loses his balance, thrown into a forward tumble. He somersaults down the path towards the boathouse.

Double crap.

I cover my mouth and cross my legs, trying not to panic or

laugh so hard I'll wet my pants. My eyes are fixed on the couple down below, making sure they haven't heard us or looked up to see us trespassing.

Carly lets out a whoosh of breath as the couple's boat leaves the island. The motor noise gets louder at first, then trails off as the boat heads up river to the west.

"Are we fucked?" Dave hollers.

"They're gone," I say, finally allowing myself a sigh of relief. "It looks dark down there."

We walk towards Dave, who is sprawled out on his back and laughing his face off from where he landed, midway down the path between us and the boathouse.

"You ass," Carly says as we reach him. "We cut that way too close."

"We?" he huffs. "Your prick of an ex is what almost gave us away. I recognized the ringtone." Still lying down, he pulls his smokes out of his shirt's front pocket and lights one up. "And by the way, that's an incredible insult to Eminem."

"You're the one that almost gave us away," she sneers.

"I'm laying in dirt, humiliated after tumbling down a hill while trying to save your ass and you're giving me shit?" He darts up from the waist into a sit, brushing pine needles and dirt off his formerly white shirt. "Federico will never be able to get these stains out."

"Piss off," my friend says, but now she can't contain her laughter. "I told you I just wanted a breakfast sandwich and my bed."

"Hey, at least we didn't get caught." The filter of Dave's cigarette is stuck to his bottom lip as he talks. "And you know what this means."

"That you have less wilderness skills than even I could fathom?" Carly asks. She taps away at her phone to silence it.

"No, Backwoods Barbie." He brushes off the knees of his jeans, still firmly planted on his ass in the dirt. "It means we know for sure we're alone. They're getting ready for renters, but no one's here now." He smiles a Cheshire cat grin and puffs on his cigarette without lifting a single finger.

Carly removes the flannel shirt from her waist, puts it on, and throws her hands on her hips. "Let's not push our luck."

"He does have a point," I offer. "Maybe we could peek in the other two buildings real quick."

"Dumb idea, guys," she says. "Plus, I'm still hungry. I left my hash browns on the boat."

"This will be the last time we come here for possibly *ever*," I plead. "Who knows when you'll get back from Florida, and when you do—"

"We won't have time for these kinds of shenanigans," Dave finishes. "You'll probably come back knocked up and married."

"Shut your mouth," Carly says. "That will never happen."

"C'mon, Carls," Dave says. "Live up to the badass within."

"Fine," she sighs. "I'll give you guys ten minutes."

"That'll do." Dave high fives me from the ground, and I turn to look at the giant house looming over us while Carly helps him to his feet.

"'Scuse me, ladies," he deadpans. "After all the liquor and coffee, I gotta piss." He steps off the path into the woods.

"Not fair," I mumble to Carly as she sidles up to me. "Guys have it so easy."

"No shit." She puts an arm around my waist and rests her head on my shoulder. "You think you'll ever see inside?"

"Maybe, if it's meant to be." I lean in and stare up at the stars. "Like you always say, you never know."

6

Oates

June 8, 2016
Wednesday, 10:00 p.m.

Palo Alto, California

Nate calls me back as I pull into my driveway. I put him on speaker as I shift my relic Jeep Wrangler in park.

"Well?" I ask.

"Plans made. You better make sure all my ingredients are there."

"I shall do my best, man." I hop out with my coveted dinner — a cheeseburger animal style and fries. In honor of Tina, my milkshake is vanilla. I'm unlocking my front door, the food bag clenched in my teeth while Nate rambles on about his Best-Fucking-Cake-You-Will-Ever-Fucking-Taste. "Yessir, boss. I know how important your baking is to you."

"Fuck off," he says. He falls silent for a few seconds. "And thanks. I didn't anticipate a trip to The Gables when I got three days off. I'm really looking forward."

Nate's earlier call wasn't due to an urgent disaster, thank God. I was paranoid he was warning me about an impending deadly earthquake or asteroid hit, but he called to report an event twice as rare. He has this weekend off and wants to hang if I'm available.

Nate likes to bake on his time off and yeah, he's been picked on about it repeatedly. Chicks used to ask me and Aidan if he was gay. (He's not.)

But when you break it down, baking is ingrained in him. His focus during the process is as concentrated as it'd be calibrating settings for a missile. To him, a recipe is just a far less complicated math formula with a sweet reward at the end. And, for whatever reason, the act itself chills our Third Musketeer out better than yoga would.

"Organic flour and real maple syrup," he insists.

"I know, I know. I got your list. I already sent it to Mamasita via text."

"Wow. Tori texts?"

"She does."

"Huh. Never would've pictured that. Anyway, no offense about your capabilities of securing groceries, man. Force of habit."

"No offense taken. Still overseeing highly educated people who outrank you but can't tie a shoelace?"

"Something like that."

"Where are you again?"

"Still in the Midwest," he says with a frustrated sigh. "I'm due back in Florida by Monday morning, but I can sneak in a stop over in Canada for the weekend."

"Awesome. The island awaits, man. Beats staying here."

"I could've made it to California or New York with equal travel time, but I had to get cleared to cross the border into Canada. Avoids causing an international incident."

"Good call. We wouldn't want a repeat of 2012 when you were detained in Dubai."

"Precisely." He shouts an instruction away from the phone. "Sorry, I gotta let you go. Did you tell Pierce?"

"Haven't breathed a word."

Nate admitted earlier he hadn't considered calling Aidan. The two of them are like brothers, too — but they're too busy to connect without planning ahead. I'm always the more available one, and when Nate realized he had free time, he called me first.

"So you said he called and wants to work on your app, but he sounded not like himself? He's not," Nate pauses, "I mean, you don't think he's getting into old habits?"

"No, nothing like that. He actually sounded upbeat. It was weird."

"Maybe excited to get up to the island again?"

"That could be. But he said he has some sort of surprise. The twins swear he's got a woman. They're so convinced they took me up on a bet."

He laughs maniacally. "They're about to lose."

"Right? I should've asked for something huge. All I could come up with on the spot were concert tickets. They upped it to include a Broadway show."

"That's a pretty good haul. Can't imagine what Pierce would surprise you with. Unless Stella's joining him in New York."

"Gag, and *hell* no. He shit-canned her months ago."

"Can't say I'm heartbroken. I've watched the tabloid headlines everywhere I've been for the last three months."

"She's a hot mess." I sip my shake and fire up my laptop at the kitchen island to look at the trip itinerary Pierce sent. "Forever glad he's done with that."

"Agreed."

"I didn't tell him you're coming. You're a surprise that can't be outdone no matter what he has up his sleeve. By Friday afternoon, I have no doubt Musketeers Two and Three will be getting one over on Number One."

"He's going to hate that."

"Of course he is. That's why it's awesome."

Nate exhales a heavy sigh. "You realize Thad's funeral was the last time we were all in the same room together?"

"Yeah." I let a moment of silence pass before I turn the topic around. "I'll make sure you have everything you need for your baking, Betty Crocker."

"Blow me, Zuckerberg."

"Can't you build yourself a robot for that?" I dig.

"Whatever. See you Friday, *Fucker*berg."

"Looking forward to it, *NASA*hole."

By six a.m. Pacific time, my flight to New York is well underway. I expected Aidan's father to be our pilot, but he chartered a small private plane to get us there instead.

Well, small for the Pierces, anyway. We're cruising through the sky in a Challenger 350, and we're not traveling alone. Two other couples have joined us — the Hamiltons and the Reeds. I've only met them in person a few times over the last ten years, usually at a social event Aidan invited me to. They're wealthy and accomplished people, but thankfully not snobby.

They've also kept Aidan's parents occupied, so forced small talk hasn't been required. I've been in my own little corner of the cabin, reviewing data on my laptop. I hear Tori excuse herself from conversation with the other ladies before she seats herself in the chair closest to me.

"Work?" she asks.

I nod.

Tori is like a second mom to me, though I haven't seen her in almost a year. She's as pretty as ever. Her outfit is tailored, but casual. Long 'mom' style shorts, white boat shoes, and a navy t-shirt that looks soft. She radiates that Bacall-esque elegance I've never recognized in another lady.

Victoria Pierce carries herself as proudly as any dignitary, but somehow does it modestly. I always assumed her rocky start in life accounted for this.

Regardless of the how or why, Tori is just Tori, and everyone loves her.

"So how is Mr. Oates?"

"Can't complain, Mrs. P. Not sure you knew I moved to Palo Alto a couple weeks ago."

I'm graced with her proud-mom grin. "Aidan said that was your goal. Are you renting or did you invest in property?"

"Went in on a sweet house with the Hawthornes. Technically I'm renting and have an out, if I need it. So far, it's working out okay."

She dips her chin in doubt. "You don't sound convinced."

"I guess I'm not."

"The roommates or the location?"

"I've been toying with the idea of getting out of California. Eventually."

"That would be a big change for you, Daryl. Have you ever lived anywhere else?"

"No. That's why I've been thinking about it."

"Mm," she says. "You like the house though?"

"The house itself is great. Work's busy. And I have roommates that I don't have to parent or clean up after."

"Thank goodness," she laughs. "Better than my son when you two were undergrads, I presume?"

"No contest." I push my glasses up. "The Hawthorne twins don't do messy."

"Well, neither does my son. He just hires someone else to clean. And the girl situation?" she asks. "Seeing anyone?"

"Single and searching." I return her smile and change the subject. "So, Mr. Pierce doesn't fly anymore?"

"It's silly for you to call him Mr. Pierce. You're a grown man. And no, Reggie doesn't fly as much anymore. Blames it on his eyesight. He flies with Mr. Reed every once in a while, but he didn't feel comfortable going this distance. It's been years, as you know."

She looks out the window, and I join her in watching clouds float by, knowing she's likely thinking about the son she lost. Her next question pulls my attention.

"Did Aidan tell you why he asked us to come out here on such short notice?"

"Just that we had to get to work because he could afford the time this weekend. He also said he has a surprise. Do you know what it is?"

"Maybe," she says, this time with a conspiratory smile. "But I won't be the one to tell you."

"Come on, Mamasita. I'll owe you big."

"Tell me why you're still single. You'd be a catch for any girl."

"Please don't try and distract me with false flattery. I've been so busy with work and the move, I haven't even had time for a haircut. My looks are not on point this trip."

She laughs. "To me, you look like the same young man I met all those years ago. And any girl worth your time won't be so shallow to worry about the timing of your haircuts. Have you been dating much?"

"My last dip in the dating pool turned into a frantic swim for sanity."

"Well, you can't let that dissuade you. We all have our relationship horror stories." She looks off into space a moment, then recovers with a polite smile. "Did you have anything in common with the last girl?"

"Just our employer. We met at work. I never should've gone out with her, given she was on my team."

"So you were her boss?"

"Technically no, but sort of a supervisor. Anyway, she turned out to be kind of crazy."

"Crazy how? Did she push for marriage and babies on your second date?"

"Crazy, like she tried to steal my app plans, and when I caught her, she tried to sabotage a fellow employee and blame it on him. Then HR called her in for a meeting and she got fired for reasons I'm still unaware of."

"Wow," she says, taken aback.

"I know. They escorted her off property and everything."

"That's awful. I can see why you're gun-shy. But I'm sure she's a rarity you won't run into again."

"From your lips," I say with a chuckle.

"May I make a suggestion though?"

"Of course," I say. "You're like my second mom. And my mom's about given up on me."

"Stop," she laughs. "I'm sure she's done no such thing." She folds her hands in her lap and looks me dead in the eye. "But maybe work should be the last thing you consider when you meet someone."

"I find that ironic coming from you."

She furrows her brow, her regal features conveying confusion. "How do you mean?"

"The way you met Mr. Pierce. You were working at the time."

"Oh," she swats the air with her hand, "that was different."

"He fell under your Florence Nightingale spell, and the rest is history, right? It's not all that different. You met him at the hospital on a shift. While you were *working*."

"Nonsense," she laughs. "It was fate we met the way we did. Hang on." She gets up to move about the cabin and returns with a magazine. "Here. I think you should read this."

"What is it?" I keep the article she's chosen marked with my thumb and close the cover. "*L.A. Ladies' Luxury*?" Despite my mountain of respect for her, I can't help laughing. "No offense, but I don't think I'm the target market for this mag."

"Don't be a chauvinist, Daryl. It's just an article. I promise reading it won't cause you to grow breasts." She grabs it from me and shows me the article again. "See? It's all about how Americans are constantly focused on our employment status, and how the question 'what do you do' is second nature when we meet people."

"What's that got to do with dating?"

"In other parts of the world, that's the last thing you would ask someone when you're introduced. We tend to define ourselves by our careers, while many others don't. You said that was the only thing you had in common with this last girl?"

"Right."

"And that relationship was disastrous?"

"Yeah, but I don't see the connection." I remove my glasses, wipe off a smudge and hold them away to inspect them.

"Maybe the next time you meet someone you're interested in, don't ask what she does for a living. Or don't lead off with that, if you're talking about yourself. Try to find some common ground outside of your careers and see where that leads."

"Huh. You may have a point, Mrs. P. I never thought of it like that."

"Of course, it does help if you learn she's gainfully employed at some point," she says. "You want a strong and independent woman."

"Absolutely." I close the cover again and put my glasses back on to look at the publication date. *Summer 2016.* "Isn't this the magazine Aidan bought when you retired from nursing?"

"Yes," she admits, "and I'm still completely addicted to it. I wish we'd followed through on making it a monthly, but I didn't have time to carry out such a sweeping change. I encouraged him to sell it, to help fund his cause in New York. Then the sale went through so fast, I didn't have time to execute all of my ideas."

"You should be writing for them now."

"No," she shakes her head. "I could never. And I passed my editorial duties on when he sold the company."

"You could," I insist. "Aidan always said even your birthday cards were poignant."

Knowing how much she loved the magazine — and writing — Aidan bought the publication for her as a retirement gift. Tori always voiced the magazine should bring more attention to social issues. She wanted to use the platform to appeal to the target market of wealthy women and support a greater good, not just sell them luxury products.

Aidan and his mom always touted this mantra, taking on projects in the name of 'the greater good'. She spent a year improving the content and bringing in new writers. Subscribers increased tenfold, Aidan said. But she never published her own column.

"I still think it would be good for you, and for all the women who read this. Give them some motivation to do something good with their lives."

"I think I did help that cause," she says. "Plus, there are so many young writers who do it better. I'm proud of the people I brought on during my time there. The magazine is doing well."

"Thanks to you."

"In part, maybe. Regardless, I'm certain this article was meant to be read by you. Take it from the former Senior Editor of Ladies' Luxury."

"I'll give it a read as soon as I'm done with this last report. Did you tell Aidan that Nate's on his way tomorrow?"

"Didn't you ask me not to?" she fires back.

I lower my head and look up through the top of my glasses. "You know I did, Mrs. P. I'm just making sure there wasn't a slip."

"Your secret's safe, Daryl. Also I think Nancy Lonergan picked up the groceries for him. We'll double check when we arrive."

"Great. And since you won't tell me what your son is up to behind my back, I'm going to call him."

"Go ahead," she says. "I'll bet he won't tell you."

"Oh, definitely not. But I can gloat that I have my own surprise."

"He'll absolutely hate that."

"Yeah," I say, grinning up at her as she rises to rejoin her friends. "I know."

7

Pam

June 9, 2016
Thursday, 8:00 a.m.

Bay Falls, Ontario
Canada

"I cannot believe it," Carly groans. "I feel awful."

In Carly's tiny apartment above the garage, I sip my iced coffee and kick back in her dad's old recliner. I ran out to Tim Horton's a half hour ago for my usual while Carly was still asleep. When I called from the drive-thru, her answer was a groan. She said she couldn't even stomach coffee. By the time I returned, she managed to migrate from her bed to the couch.

"I'd bet my life the liquor had nothing to do with it." I bring her a glass of water and two ibuprofen and flip on the TV. She's snuggled under a blanket though it's an incredibly warm June day. "Definitely had to be the twelve a.m. breakfast sandwich."

"Ugh," she says, "that was a bad choice."

"You should've stopped at the hash browns and left well enough alone."

"Never again. You know it's only when I'm inebriated that I can't make good choices about food."

"That's wasn't even food. You of all people should know this."

"Let's not talk about it anymore," she says. "I'll barf. Can I see the clicker?"

"Yeah, sure." I toss the worn remote to her, and she flips to Food Network. "I thought you couldn't stomach food?"

"This is a cake decorating challenge. I think I'll be okay."

We watch the show in comfortable silence and when it's over, I glance around the apartment. "You don't have a single thing to pack?"

"I shipped the one box of stuff I can't live without to Kate. I'll have my laptop on the plane with me. And I already sent down some cute framed pics of us, of course."

I smile over at her. "Of course."

"I'm starting from scratch. Dad will keep the apartment available for me, just in case. You're absolutely sure you don't want it?"

"I shouldn't need it if I get into this program. We'll both be in the U.S. How awesome is that?"

"Pretty awesome. Is Fedders' email still MIA, though?"

"Yeah." I don't elaborate about my fourth year plans hanging in the balance. Nerves have me so wound that if we get into it, I might barf myself. By now, I should've heard *something* about where in New York I'll end up next semester.

"It'll come," she says to reassure me. "Anyway, Kate says I don't even need to bring clothes. We can share stuff until I get an idea of Florida weather and buy my own. All my hoodies are yours for the taking."

"Well, thank you. I am jealous you'll be living in your new bikini when you're not wearing an apron. But can we talk about your other poor choices now, beyond your twelve a.m. sandwich?"

She pulls her attention away from a frying pan infomercial to look at me. My best friend is a sucker for infomercials.

"Going to The Gables was your idea," she says, "and we didn't get caught."

"Not that," I say with a scolding stare. "Mick."

"It wasn't my fault. I can't control him." She unmutes the TV and turns her attention back to the screen.

"I told you we should've gone out the back."

"I know," she shrugs. "But it turned around. Can you even believe our night?"

"If you mean can I believe Dave decked your ex, then no. I cannot."

"Told you he always has my back," she grins.

"I never doubted that. I just can't believe how it all went down."

"Or that Mick didn't rearrange Dave's face." She chugs some of her water and curls up again. "Mick never holds back if he's confronted."

"We sped out of there before he had a chance. I'm just hoping Mick doesn't retaliate at a later date. Besides," I huff in frustration, "that's not the big money question for me."

"Okay, I give up." She scrunches up her face and mutes the TV again. "What's the big question?"

"Why the hell was Mick even there?"

She ignores my words and eyeballs my drink, asking for a sip with a grabby hand.

"I thought you felt like vomiting?"

"I think the ibuprofen kicked in. I'm feeling better."

I pass her my plastic cup. "You're happy Dave did that to Mick, aren't you?"

She takes a sip and hands my coffee back, shaking her head. "No, I'm not *happy* about it. But I like that a friend stood up for me. He did the same thing you would if it came down to it."

"I don't think I'd ever punch Mick. I'd be too afraid his hockey pals would track me down and pummel me."

She lets out a half-hearted laugh as she flips to her list of recorded television. I know what she's going to put on, even before the theme music of our favorite eighties movie of all time begins.

Besides *Top Gun*, *Cocktail* is the only Tom Cruise movie we've ever agreed on. My best friend takes him any way she can get him, while I typically pass. She likes that kind of clean cut guy in her movie crushes, though she admits that clean cut is the complete opposite of any guy she's actually dated.

But this movie is one of my guilty pleasures. I'd never say no to it.

"Can you stay for the whole thing?" she asks.

I give her a look that says 'obviously', and she smiles in satisfaction. "Thought you had to fix up Ben's old room for Alexis this weekend?"

"I told Mum I'd take care of it later. I don't think Alexis will leave Stanton until after work tomorrow night, given it's not a holiday weekend."

"Most it needs is a dusting and some clean sheets, right?"

"Yeah. Mum won't let anyone touch anything in his old room anyway."

"Why didn't Alexis come up for Ben's birthday? I thought that was the plan. Then I could've seen her, too."

"She had to go visit her sister in Arizona — an emergency with her brother-in-law, I guess — and she was still recovering from that trip."

"I didn't even know she had a sister."

"Half-sister. Her name's Jill. They aren't really close, but I met Jill at Ben's funeral. She seemed nice."

"Well, I'm bummed to miss your *sistah-by-love*'s visit."

"I'm psyched she's finally coming up, but I'm also wrecked I can't come with you to Manhattan. You know I've always wanted to go."

"I'll be slammed with work anyway. From what Mr. Cruz said, this is going to be an intense weekend of training before I head to Ten Palms. And you'll get a chance to go to the Big Apple when your study program comes through."

Hopefully. A sad sigh escapes me. "I can't believe you'll be flying far, far away on Monday."

"Me either. But Florida isn't that far, especially if you're in New York."

"If Fedders comes through," I mumble.

"He will. And if you're staying to hang, then I'm going to pause the movie." She points the remote at the television. "I need coffee."

"Let me guess. You have none?"

"I know," she groans. "I'm sorry I'm so unprepared. Dad's cleaning out what's left in my cupboards after I leave. He said it was one less thing I'd need to worry about. But I know I ran out of coffee two days ago."

"I was just at Tim's," I say. "Even I'm not there every hour. They're going to think I have a serious caffeine problem."

"Please?" She gives me a hopeful grin. "I'll grab a shower while you're gone."

"How can I say no when you beg so sweetly?"

"Like a princess to her sugar daddy," she laughs. "Thank you, babes."

"I thought I was the princess?" I stand up and grab for my purse. "And I'm only doing this because you're leaving me forevs."

"It's not forever." She adds a but, then lowers her voice so much, it's inaudible.

"What was that?"

"I said you're not the first to impose the guilt trip on me."

I step into my flip flops and look over at her, my eyebrows scrunched up in question.

"If I tell you something, do you promise not to judge?"

"You're kidding, right?" I sip from my straw. "It's me, Carly. I love you no matter what."

"Yeah, but this is bad."

"How bad?"

"Very bad."

"Did you sneak out of here to meet up with Mick last night? Or were you the one that told him to come to the bar in the first place?"

"No," she waves a hand in the air. "Nothing like that. Remember when Connor was joking around with me last night after I did those shots?"

"I guess, yeah."

"Do you remember when he asked me to marry him?" She toys with the threads on the blanket in her lap, her eyes avoiding mine.

"I didn't think it was out of line, really. Did his comment bother you?"

"No, of course not. I adore Connor."

"Me too, so I have no idea where you're going with this." I lean against the half wall by the door, waiting for her to elaborate. She finally looks at me, her shoulders scrunched and eyes squinting.

She's been dreading this admission.

"What if I told you that wasn't the only proposal I received yesterday?"

My purse lands with a thud on her tile floor. "What?"

She bows her head and extends a hand to borrow off my coffee again.

"I'm not sharing until I get an answer, Carly. Did Mick ask you to *marry* him yesterday?"

"You say that like he's someone I just met. We were together for almost five years."

"I know that. But he cheated on you for two of them. Not to mention his verbal diarrhea last night, which your non-violent, gay friend from cooking school thought deserved a punch in the mouth. Why didn't you tell me this yesterday?"

"I guess I already knew what you'd say. And then after last night, I knew it would sound awful."

I take a deep breath.

Carly may have crawled into bed with Mick for post-break-up sex on a couple of occasions, but I know she'd never consider marrying him. Getting angry is not the reaction my friend needs, and it's not her I'm upset with anyway.

She has more than enough self-respect to realize she's been proposed to by someone who hasn't shown her an ounce of it.

But damn him for even asking.

"So," I use the calmest voice I can muster, "you're not considering his proposal, right?"

Her head whips up as she looks at me like I've sprouted an extra eyeball. "Please tell me you know better. I would *never*."

Whew.

"That's what I thought. So what's the deal?"

"The deal is that I still love him." She takes one huge deep breath, her eyes cast down to her bare feet as they poke out from her favorite fleece blanket. "Even though he's a complete asshole and a cheating bastard, I still love him."

"Aw, girl." I approach and hand over my coffee as a peace offering. "That's not so bad."

She looks up, tears forming in the corner of her blue eyes. "So you're not mad?"

"Well, not at you. I'm upset that he makes you feel this way. But you're probably going to love him forever, at least a little." I wrap her up in a hug. "On the bright side, you're still the reigning Shot Queen."

"Some queen I am. I've got no king, and I'm leaving the only kingdom I've ever known to live in a place I've only visited twice."

"You're going to be fine."

"Pam," she sniffles into my shoulder, "I'm scared to death."

I pull back from our hug to look at her. "Okay, so you're scared. But what positive outlook crap would you tell me, if it was me saying all this? Something about fate and everything for a reason, right?"

"Yeah," she says through another sniffle. "I guess. I'd sound off some quotes and you'd call it BS."

"Stop. It's not BS. And you already know the most important thing, at least in this scenario." She eyes me and holds her breath, waiting. "You know you never want to be that jerk's wife."

"That is the cold, hard truth." She manages a smile, using the back of her hand to wipe her nose.

"You're emotional about leaving here, and it's affecting your judgment. Next week, you'll be footloose and fancy free in Key West and settled in with Kate. You won't even give him much thought. I promise."

"What if I'm a wreck once I get there? My only American cousin does not need a basket case slowing down her party train. She's a personal trainer with high paying clients, and she's single. She's got guys falling at her feet everywhere she goes. I don't want her to feel like she has to 'deal' with me."

"Are you kidding?" I hand her a box of tissues so she can wipe her face. "You two are going to rip it up. Together. You're a gorgeous young blonde headed for Florida. You're starting out your foodie career in your choice of dream jobs. Don't let Mick's last ditch effort of proposing make you forget how amazing this is going to be."

"He doesn't understand how I can just up and leave him," she says with an eye roll. "We were supposed to have a future," she emphasizes with air quotes. "The jerk actually bought a ring."

I start in about how crazy he is given they broke up months ago, but she interrupts me.

"It hasn't exactly been a clean break."

"I'll give you that, but he's clearly desperate. If he didn't want to lose you, he shouldn't have screwed a different girl everywhere he went. This is the same guy that guaranteed you had to be tested for every STD known to man."

"Point made, okay?" She throws off her blanket and stands up, shuddering at the recollection. "I just...it's not easy."

"If he loved you, he'd not be selfish. He'd encourage you to do this, not try to trap you or talk you into staying here. He knows what a great opportunity this is for you."

She's silent, considering my words.

"This is the perfect chance for both of you to move on." I step closer and take her by the shoulders. When she looks at me, I level her with a stare only best friends can. "If there was any chance Mick could treat you the way you deserve, I'd phone Kate myself and tell her you don't need her spare room, just so you could stay and try again."

"But you're not going to do that, are you?" She grabs for the blanket, drops herself into the recliner I'd been sitting in, and throws the fleece over her head.

"No freakin' way." I pull the blanket off and kneel in front of her. "Don't waste this opportunity by wondering what might've been if you stayed."

"I know what might've been," she says softly. "Mick's not going to change for anyone. I'm doing what I need to do. This is just... when he asked me, it was the moment of clarity I needed. I just had to get through telling you about it."

"Good." I smile at her as I stand up. "You deserve the moon and stars, champagne and filet mignon." I wave my hand in the air with a flourish. "Only the finest will do for my queen!"

"Thanks princess, but haven't we already figured out that all the good ones are married or gay?"

"Maybe. But," I say with two thumbs down, "that doesn't change the fact that you deserve gourmet, and all Mick can offer you is a shitty Tim's breakfast sandwich."

"Facts," she laughs. "Thanks for reminding me."

"Your head knows this, Carly. It's your heart that needs to do the catching up. I promise you it will. The distance will help."

"How'd you get so good at giving relationship advice? I'm older, dammit. And you've never dated a guy longer than a month."

"Three-weeks-and-two-days," I correct. "And it's because I know what's best for my friend. And I'm going to tell Alexis the same thing this weekend."

She blows her nose and grabs for more tissues. "Well, that's ballsy."

"I was thinking about it last night while I was kept awake by your snoring. She needs to move on from my brother."

"Uh, her situation was a bit different. He died."

I slide my foot out of my flip-flop and stare down at the newly formed tan line. "Kind of aware."

"Oh, shit. *Shit*," she says to herself in scolding. "I'm sorry. That was cold."

"It's okay," I smile. "You didn't mean it to be. And speaking of cold, that's how Charlie describes Alexis' bed. She's gotta start dating at least. It's been a year and a half."

"I thought she was busy running her own law office now? Maybe she just doesn't have time."

"Trust me, she's not that busy. Charlie says her friend Gloria set her up on one blind date, and I guess it went horribly. She hasn't tried since."

"I love that Charlie," Carly muses. "I wish he was still living in Manhattan so I could meet him in person this weekend. Hey," she says, her eyes opening wide, "we should *totally* introduce him to Dave."

"Funny you say that. I showed Dave his picture last night. He made me promise to introduce them if they're ever in the same country."

"Which is unlikely," she laughs.

"Yeah, I don't think Charlie's coming farther north than Stanton. It kills him to be away from Manhattan as it is, but he wanted to be near Alexis."

"And her cold and empty bed."

I laugh. "Right."

"Well," Carly spouts, "I'd point out that your bed is suffering the same fate."

I ignore her comment and grab for my keys. "Maybe I'll try to set Alexis up while she's here."

"Yeah, because a long-distance relationship with a Canadian is just what she needs," she says with an exaggerated head-back eye roll. "Don't change the subject. What happened with that guy Steve?"

"I never dated Steve. He's just a friend. I helped him get through our business elective when he ended up in my 'Understanding Trends' class."

"That's the problem with you. They're all just friends."

"No, you misunderstand. I couldn't date him if I wanted to. Steve's gay."

"Ah. Figures. He's hot and he's a sweetheart. Married or gay," she says, "had to be one of the two. Oh, except what's his name, the guy you tutor." She snaps her fingers as though that will help her remember.

"Jay?" I'm mid-sip and almost lose a mouthful of coffee. "Carly, you know I don't go for guys my age. Or any guy that's shorter than me. And Jay's on my asshole list."

"Not him," she says with a wave of her hand. "I meant his brother. I can't remember his name either."

"Kyle?" I look at her, bewildered. "He wouldn't give me the time of day." Kyle Tremblay is ten years older than me. He's the stunningly handsome, older brother of the classmate I tutor every summer. "He only dates girls his own age. Or much older. Jay's told me so himself."

"Excuses."

"He's a successful young lawyer who would want nothing to do with a fourth year student."

"Unproven."

"And his family has a crap-ton of money," I conclude. "Our worlds just don't mix."

"That's funny, because he was making eyes at you when we ran into him at Layla's that night. And he was there with his parents and Jay. He didn't have a date."

"You mean the night we went to visit Dave during his first shift?"

She nods and beams a coy smile at me.

"Oh, please. I'm not the type of girl who guys 'make eyes at', Carly. I am okay with this. You don't have to try and make me feel better."

"Correction. You don't *think* you're that type. So you had some awkward high school years? So what? We all go through an awkward phase. You need to take charge of your love life and get out there."

I flip her off because if she ever had an awkward phase, it lasted about a week.

I was cursed with thick thighs and braces all through high school, and my nose was always stuck in books. I read everything from sweet romances to biographies of famous mathematicians and didn't pay boys much attention until college.

Even then, I was fed up with dating in a hurry. Guys my age proved to be harder to understand than quantum physics. I'd seen plenty of girls lose focus academically because of drama with a guy she'd only known for a matter of weeks.

I refuse to fall into that trap.

Sure, I received more attention once I got to University, but I wasn't happy about it. Guys suddenly made it a point to tell me I was 'sexy' or 'alluring'. I could never be sure whether to believe them when their goal was either to get inside my head or separate me from my clothes.

In my mind, I'm still the smart girl who isn't sure what kind of guy she's looking for or what she might do with him once she finds him.

"Point is," she insists, "you're definitely a head-turner now. I've witnessed it with my own eyes. Like a couple months ago while you were leaning over the bar to talk to Dave, and Kyle Tremblay was checking out your ass."

"He *so* wasn't."

"So *was*. And since you're stuck tutoring Jay again this summer, I'm sure you can find plenty of opportunities to flirt with Kyle. I bet he'll ask you out on day one."

"Stop," I scold. "Tutoring Jay is my job. It's *work*. The only work I have, besides an occasional shift at Aunt Lil's diner when one of her waitresses flakes."

"Exactly. He would've failed out without you," Carly scoffs. "You'd think he'd be a little more grateful."

"Jay can be a handful, but his parents pay me well enough. That paycheck takes the pressure off my parents when my tuition bills come. I can handle him for one more summer. Plus, we aren't starting for a couple weeks yet, so I have some time to relax."

"Well, if opportunity knocks—"

"Maybe it already has. I'm going to introduce Kyle to Alexis while she's here. That'll be an excuse to escape my parents Saturday night. I can take her to Layla's, introduce her to Dave. I'll ask Kyle and Jay to meet us there for drinks. Maybe Alexis and I will crash here."

"You're welcome to, but like I already told you, Kyle has the hots for you. Maybe I was wrong about you being good at relationship advice."

"He doesn't know I exist, Carly. All I am to him is some girl that passes through his parents' huge house during the summer months to tutor Jay. He and Alexis would have something in common. They're both lawyers."

"You are so blind, girl. But, you are right about Mick." She stretches up from the recliner for a hug. "Thank you for always being here."

"Like I ever had a choice," I tease as I let her go. "I live down the road. I'm bolting for your coffee now. You feeling up for food?"

"I'll make some scrambled eggs in a bit."

"Or," I say with a hint of longing. I gesture with praying hands as she looks up at me. "I know something that takes an hour to cook. You'll be hungry by then, right?"

"You want me to make my world-famous quiche?"

"God, yes."

She doesn't answer, her expression indicating she's not sure she wants to bother.

"Please," I beg, "it'll be forever before I get to have it again."

"I have just enough eggs. Grab some fresh cream and the Swiss while you're out."

"Yes!" I pump a fist in the air as she gets up to head for the bathroom.

"Only for you, girl. And for coffee. Make mine hot, please."

"This is why our friendship works," I say as I move for the door. "You feed me, I'll do whatever you want."

"Keep Mick out of my sight for the rest of forever, and I'll feed you every day."

"You'll feed me from Florida?"

"Dry ice and shipping can't be that expensive."

I laugh. "I wish. And distance is all you need." I open the door, take a deep breath and let the sun warm me as I step out onto her second floor landing. "Once you're on that plane, you'll forget all about Mick."

8

Oates

June 9, 2016
Thursday, 12:45 p.m.

NY to Bay Falls, Ontario

Before one in the afternoon local time, we've landed in northern New York. I reached my best friend by phone while in the air, able to brag that I had a surprise of my own. He responded by asking me if I was bringing a girl with me, and I instinctively replied with a smart ass remark.

Given Finn and Zach's guess about his relationship status, the comment threw me off. *Why would he ask me that?*

I can only hope the twins are wrong about Batman's current source of happiness being a female.

Our party of seven stops for lunch in Watertown before continuing north in a rented white Cadillac SUV outfitted with all the bells and whistles. By three o'clock, we've made our way through customs and have arrived via executive-luxury-pontoon boat at the island.

The Reeds and Hamiltons haven't been here before, so my hosts are busy showing their friends around Brat Cottage — the rustic two-bedroom cabin the Pierces built a few years after they bought the island. Aidan and his brother shared the cabin from the time he turned seventeen.

I assume Aidan will want to crash there this weekend. Tori offers me a guest room up at the main house, but I prefer to stay in the boathouse for old times' sake.

"It should be ready," Tori says as the three couples make their way up to the main house. "The Lonergans said they had all the bedrooms made up. Go get settled and come on up for drinks by five?"

"Sounds great, thanks." I wave and excuse myself from the group as they take off up the trail. I follow the path in the opposite direction, where it splits off from the main docks and criss-crosses the island toward the boathouse. I climb the metal steps to the cozy studio two stories above the water. With my bag and laptop in tow, I open the door and inhale.

Ah.

Faint odor of campfire, either from previous guests or neighboring island parties. It's a little stuffy from being closed up for an unknown amount of time, but the predominant smell is the same as ever.

Refreshing, smogless air.

I take a step into the small kitchen and let the screen door close behind me. The appliances are apartment-size, and the sink sits under an octagon window that provides a view up to the main house.

The only bathroom is off the kitchen. It has a toilet and sink, but the only shower for these quarters is an open-air version outside. It's behind the boathouse, walled off and private, but it's downstairs on the dock near the hot tub.

After traveling all day, the outdoor shower sounds like a killer idea.

Across the room, the same tube TV and leather pull-out couch I remember from years back welcome me. Even the old Sega game console still sits in the cabinet below the TV. The pull-out is where Nate always slept, and given he won't arrive until tomorrow, I head down the short hall to claim the bedroom. I toss my duffel bag on the dresser and leave my laptop on the double bed. The room is only big enough for these two pieces of furniture.

The place smells freshly cleaned, even though no one stays here on the regular. Back in the living room, a squat vase of lilacs is on the coffee table, also acting as a paperweight. A laminated sheet of guest information is pinned beneath the vase and I'm thankful to find it lists a Wi-Fi password.

This has to be the tiniest guest home the Pierce family owns but, to me, it's off the charts comfortable. The kitchen and living area are open to each other, so the place feels plenty big enough for two guests, and everything is homey and familiar.

I inhale the fresh air coming through the screen door before I'm drawn to the large picture window that overlooks the river. In the distance, boats zoom by each other to navigate the main channel. It may be a warm and lazy late afternoon for me, but the river rats are cruising around, going about their everyday lives in this extraordinary place.

A yawn overtakes me. I sprawl out on the couch and pass out cold, only roused from sleep by the sound of my phone ringing.

"Daryl?" Tori says when I answer. "You okay? I sent you three messages. I wasn't sure you had reception up there."

"So sorry." I shake off the mental cobwebs. "I fell asleep. What time is it?"

"It's nearly six. You going to come up? We're holding up cocktail hour for you."

"Just gonna grab a shower first," I say through another yawn I can't stifle. "I'll be right up."

I grab a quick shower down on the dock. Nothing tops standing out in the middle of nature under hot running water with only blue sky and tree limbs overhead.

I've missed this place.

By the time I'm dressed and arrive at the main house, it's six on the dot. Mr. Reed and Mr. Hamilton are relaxing in rockers on the enormous front porch as I climb the steps. They look over the dark waters of the St. Lawrence River from where they sit, discussing what hopes the Mets have this season.

"Gentlemen." I nod to them as I open the creaky screen door and walk into the foyer.

The Gables has not changed a bit in all these years, save the fresh flower arrangement on the entry table. If memory serves, the last time I was here they were white roses. Today they're lilacs, just like in the boathouse.

"I love the sound of that screen door." Aidan's mom hands me a beer as I come into the kitchen. "I've missed that so much."

"Agreed," I say, lifting the bottle. "And thanks for saving me one of these soldiers. Can I help with anything?"

She nods to a silver tray of snacks on the kitchen island as she selects a bottle of wine from the wine chiller. "You can pass those off to the gentlemen out front."

"Oh, I'll do that," Mrs. Hamilton says as she exits the powder room. "I'm going out anyway."

"Thank you," Tori says with her charming hostess smile. "Daryl, I guess you can go through Nate's groceries then, make sure we have everything he needs?" She gestures to a canvas bag sitting on the counter next to the stove.

"Sure thing." I cross the room and sort through the groceries. "Where's Reggie?"

"He's been down in the boathouse tinkering with the Whaler since we got here. Mr. Lonergan said he had it going at midnight last night, but it quit on the way here this afternoon."

"No way. Is that the same boat Aidan had when we used to come up?"

"It is," she beams with pride.

"Probably the fuel line. That was a recurring problem with that boat back in the day."

"I think that's what Reggie said, too. Mr. Lonergan and his wife came to say hello and deliver it after we arrived. Mr. Lonergan was driving their boat and Mrs. Lonergan was driving the Whaler when it up and quit right in the middle of the channel. What a production," she sighs. "They had to tow the poor woman to the dock."

"I'm sure she handled it fine. They're river rats, aren't they?"

"Oh, yes. They both sell high-end real estate up and down the St. Lawrence. It didn't phase them a bit, but I felt terrible. Their service stocked the bar and cleaned, they delivered the groceries and helped get boats situated until nearly midnight last night. I invited them to dinner Saturday to thank them for all they did on such short notice."

"Sweet. Sounds like a party to me. And I can't believe you guys still have the Whaler and the Garwood. I saw the Victoria is in the boathouse."

"I wouldn't let Reggie sell either one," she smiles. "Too many fond memories. They were in storage until last year."

"I have some great memories of them myself." My back is to Tori, and I realize she's gone quiet. "You okay, Mrs. P.?"

"Fine," she says, seeming wistful. "I'm going to run upstairs and freshen up before dinner." She pats me on the shoulder and heads for the front stairs.

I check Nate's list against the contents of the bag and realize I'm short three items. "Shit," I mutter, "he's gonna be pissed."

"Who?" Reggie asks as he comes into the kitchen. He moves to the island to wash his grease-stained hands.

"Ah, just a few things missing for brother Nate. Maybe I should check the pantry?"

"I doubt there's anything in there," he says over the sound of the running faucet. "We've only rented the place out once this season. But it's worth a shot, I guess. What are you looking for?"

"Flour and maple syrup. Organic flour and real maple syrup to be exact."

"Well," he says with a good-natured laugh, "your odds just went down."

"Picky bastard asked for farm fresh eggs, too."

"I saw eggs in the refrigerator. I'm sure they were on a farm at one point in time."

"Good one, Redge. We'll take them out of the carton and put them in a bowl. He'll never know. Which means now I'm only missing two things."

"Still the evil genius, hmm?" He dries his hands with a fancy dish towel and hangs it over the stove handle to dry. "I won't tell if you won't."

"Even if we sneak the eggs by him, you can't make a cake from scratch without flour. I'm not Paula Deen, but even I know that."

"Check in there," he nods to the oversize oak door that leads to the walk-in pantry. "If you don't find what you're looking for, I can run you over to the mainland. Store's open until nine, I think. It'll give me a chance to make sure the Whaler is seaworthy after I tinkered with her."

I open the door and walk in, remembering the days when the shelves were stacked to capacity with ingredients for S'mores, fancy crackers for the 'adults', and enough different kinds of cereal to feed an army of guys.

Those were the days.

"There's a canister labeled flour," I shout through the open door, "but it's empty."

"Looks like we'll be heading out," Reggie says. "I don't need someone with Nate's capabilities angry with me."

"I don't mind going, if you want to drop me at the Town Dock. I'll take the SUV."

"You remember your way around? Know where the store is?"

"I think so. Plus you've got nav, right?"

"Yeah, I do. Funny, I never thought of that."

"Right?" I say. "Wasn't an option the last time we were here."

"I'll drop you off at the marina and send you on your mission right after dinner. The main grocery store is about a ten minute drive. I doubt the small grocer in Bay Falls will have what you need. They may already be closed up for the day."

"I can even take the boat out myself," I offer. "I think I remember how she operates."

"It's been years since you've navigated these waters in the dark. You remember to stay within the markers to avoid the shoals?"

"Of course."

He considers this scenario a moment in the serious way he has. I've always respected Aidan's father as much as my own, but I couldn't imagine growing up with him as my dad.

Reginald Pierce and his son share an interest in The Wall Street Journal and the stock market, among other things. The only thing my dad and I trade are our favorite albums on vinyl or, before the digital age, the occasional eighties movie on DVD.

"I guess that works," he finally says. "That'll give me a chance to take Tori out in the Garwood for a sunset cruise."

"Good for you, ol' chap, keeping the romance alive."

"Says the guy who's forever single."

"By choice," I qualify, "and I'll remind you to pass me the car keys before you leave. I'm sure your memory hasn't improved. You've nearly graduated to a Super Creaker now."

Even ten years ago, Reggie was famous for getting to the mainland and forgetting the vehicle keys. During our weeks-long stays, he got out of the habit of carrying them around, and I got into the habit of razzing him about his forgetfulness (among other things).

"Have I mentioned how I missed your clever insults, Daryl?" He takes the cap off a bottle of water and hurls it at me.

"No."

"Take note of that," he says through a sarcastic grin. "And you better hope you're wrong about my memory, given I'm the last one to fix that boat. Unless your upper arm strength has improved."

"I'm ripped, Mr. P. I've taken advantage of my company's gym for the last few years. See these guns?" I pull back the sleeve of my t-shirt and flex my right arm just as Aidan's mom and Mrs. Reed descend the stairs.

Ah, shit.

The two ladies politely stifle their laughter and make their way to the porch without saying a word. I turn to Reggie, who finally speaks up once his belly laugh recedes.

"Smooth, Mr. Oates. At least we know if the Whaler breaks down again, you can rely on those pythons to paddle to shore."

9

Pam

June 9, 2016
Thursday, 9:00 p.m.

Ganonoque, Ontario
Canada

I'm fifteen minutes from home, browsing the aisles of groceries at Metro to find the last item on Mum's list.

Since I parted ways with Carly early this afternoon, my mother had me running all over the place to fetch whatever she forgot when she did the shopping yesterday. She insists on having a cake to celebrate Ben's belated birthday while Alexis is here, since my *sistah-by-love* didn't make it up here for our family celebration at my aunt's diner last weekend.

In keeping with tradition, I used Carly's recipe to make Ben's favorite three layer chocolate cake before I left the house. As I was icing it, Mum realized she forgot to pick up birthday candles.

Music blares in my earbuds as I seek out the jumbo number candles to garnish the top. I finally get my hands on a zero, but I can only find the number three in pink. I search the bins more intently, determined to find the three in any other color. My brother wouldn't be happy with a pink candle.

My music is interrupted by an incoming call. I'm muttering

aloud about what else Mum could possibly have forgotten, but the call is from Carly. I tap the button to answer.

"We've been away from each other seven hours," I laugh. "You miss me already?"

"Desperately. I'm hiding out in the bathroom of our hotel room."

"So you're not calling from the top of the Empire State Building?" My friend lets out a half-hearted laugh. "You don't sound like yourself. What's up?"

"It's been a long afternoon. We just got to the hotel. Dad and I were ready to kill each other an hour ago."

"That doesn't sound like my BFF."

Carly's dad works an insane amount of hours. To them, any free time they spend together is more precious than gold.

"It only took a couple hours to cross into New York and get to the airport," she says. "Then we hopped the plane out of Stanton. But you know how Dad hates being cooped up like that. The flight made him miserable."

"Yeah, I get it." Carly's dad sits still enough while he drives truck, but his cab is like his second home. Being crammed in an airplane cabin with strangers is outside his comfort zone. "Are things okay now?"

"Now that we're settled and he canceled his flight home, yeah, he's fine."

"Wait, what? How's he getting home?"

"He said he couldn't endure another flight, even if it was under an hour. He rented a car so he can drive home on Monday. But now, he's ready to go explore the city."

"And you're irritable and tired."

"Exactly," she says. "I've got a crazy day tomorrow that starts at six a.m., and I'm still exhausted from being up late trespassing on Fawn Island."

"Sorry not sorry, girl. It was so worth it. That place is bonkers."

"Truth," she mumbles through a yawn.

"You're going to miss your dad like crazy soon enough. Grab a beer with him and then you can go to bed."

"Yeah, you're right," she sighs. "I need to suck it up. It's my last weekend with him for awhile."

"I had the *Cocktail* soundtrack blaring in my ears in your honor. Does that cheer you up?"

"Maybe a little. Guess what?"

"Um, you saw the Naked Cowboy already."

"No," she says through a giggle. "I may not be on the observation deck, but I can actually see the Empire State Building from my room."

"That's so amazing! I hope you get to see it in person."

"Doubtful," she says. "Maybe next time, though. Where are you?"

"I'm at Metro. Must be the day for parents irritating the crap out of us 'cause Mum keeps remembering something else she forgot when she shopped yesterday."

"How many stores have you been to since you left my place?"

"This makes three."

"Oh, damn."

"Right?" I blow a wayward piece of hair out of my face while my hands are busy digging through the display of candles. "Once to the little grocer for fresh bread, the second time to the LCBO for rum."

"You're adding rum to Ben's triple threat chocolate cake? That may not turn out so well."

"Please. I'd never mess with your recipe. The rum was for my mother."

She laughs. "Mum's the best. And you better hurry up. Metro closes at nine."

I look at the time on my screen. "Shoot, that's in ten minutes. I've gotta check out. Send me pics of the Empire State Building, please. And call me tomorrow night. I want to hear all about your first day."

"I'll do you one better. Hang up."

"What?"

"Just do it."

I disconnect, expecting she'll text me pics of the landmark outside her windows, but nothing comes through. I'm back on task, pawing through the bin when I find the elusive 'three' candle in blue. I toss it in my basket and check my phone again, but nothing from Carly. While I have it on my brain, I compose a text to Alexis asking about her arrival tomorrow. As I hit send, my phone rings.

"Girl," I say as I answer. "Why didn't I think of that?" Carly's video call provides a live view of the few floors of the Empire State Building visible from her hotel window. "That is so cool!"

"Isn't it amazing?" Her voice echoes in the background. "Dad went downstairs to wait for me in the hotel bar. I guess that's as far as we're making it tonight. And by the way, you're going to be blown away when you come here. Everything is so...I don't know. Alive, I guess. It's true what they say. The city does have a pulse."

"Do you feel better now?"

"Somewhat."

I still can't see her, but she sounds a little perkier. I spot something in the next bin over and grab for it. "This will cheer you up all the way." I'm giggling to myself as I put the item on my head. "I found something fit for my queen!"

Before she pans the camera back to herself, I extend my arm so the camera captures my shiny accessory. "Ta-dah!" I say when she comes into view.

"O-M-G," she says through her laughter. "It's perfect! You need to buy it."

"You really think so?" I tilt my head side to side, trying to get a better look at myself wearing the silly plastic crown.

"If the tiara fits, princess," she laughs. "And that tiara definitely fits. You can wear it next time we go out with Dave. He'll die."

"I found it in the birthday party aisle. Mum forgot candles for the cake." I start to rant about the irritations of parental units when Carly interrupts me.

"Pam!" she says in a loud whisper.

"What?"

"Who's the stud behind you?" She's still whispering, even though I'm the only one that can hear her through my earbuds.

I turn around in time to drink in the profile of a six-foot-something, amazing specimen of male. He has to be at least six foot because even from a distance, I see he's taller than me. He's looking at a display on the end of the aisle I'm standing in.

"He's gorgeous," she mumbles, and I swear I hear her lick her lips. "Come this way, dude," she says a little louder. "Over here!"

As though he can hear what she's saying, he turns and walks right toward me.

"Shh," I tell her. "I don't want him to hear you." I turn back to the shelves so I can cast a more discreet glance as he gets closer.

Jeans. Converse sneakers. Faded green t-shirt.

Glasses with black frames that are somehow *hot*.

"Nerd alert," Carly whispers. "Check out those specs! He's adorbs."

Be still my heart. I'm being sucked into the orbit of a gorgeous geek.

I can feel it from the heat spreading across my bare neck to the zing between my—

Whoa.

My eyes stray from his biceps long enough to read the front of his shirt, which says "Talk Nerdy To Me".

Holy. Crap.

Insta-swoon.

Carly's right. He is noticeably attractive, resembling a Greek God with that dark hair. He stops before he gets so close to me that it's awkward, then turns to look at the display of spices. His plastic shopping basket is empty.

"What's in his basket?" she asks. "Move the camera to your right."

I turn away from him so I can whisper into the microphone hanging around my neck. "Nothing."

"Ohhh, *shit!*" she squeals. "He's *single*! Talk to him!"

I look down at the phone display, hoping with video she can read my lips if she can't hear me. "You don't know that from the contents of a person's basket," I whisper, "especially if it's empty."

"The hell I don't. No attached guy braving the market after eight p.m. will risk coming home empty handed if he was sent out by his lady. The store's about to close. Mark my words, he's shopping for himself."

"Crap. Is it nine?"

"Who cares?" she says. "Go *talk* to him."

I turn again, now blatantly staring at the back of him as he squats to look at something on a low shelf. His hair is a gorgeous shade of black and falls in loose curls just past his shoulders. He's close enough that I can smell a hint of cologne, and he appears freshly showered. His hair is slightly damp.

"Hold the phone to your left now," she says. "I want a better look."

I do so as discreetly as possible. He's definitely not from around here, given the golden skin on his arms. That's a year-round tan we Canadians can't manage.

"Damn," she says. "His biceps are screaming to break free of that shirt." She lets out a low whistle.

"Shh," I blurt. "Get a *grip*, girl."

His head turns slightly in my direction, then he turns his attention back to the spices.

Crap! He heard me. I just know it.

"I saw that!" she whisper-screams in my ears. "Ditch your crown and go talk to him! I'm hanging up."

Double crap.

I totally forgot I was wearing that stupid thing.

"Don't hang up," I mumble to her. "I don't know what to say."

I hear the click as she disconnects, then the *Cocktail* soundtrack blares in my ears. "All Shook Up" takes off from the second chorus.

How appropriate.

The stranger looks my way and smiles, revealing perfect white teeth if only for a split second. He recovers his smile into a sly grin, then looks away as though he's trying not to notice me.

Like he could miss the girl wearing a dress and a hot pink tiara covered in fake gems.

Thanks a bunch, Fate. One of the few guys ever to move the needle for me, and I must look like a very tall ten-year-old shopping for her own birthday party.

I remove the crown, drop it back into the bin, and pray my hair isn't completely out of whack. My heart's beating as fast as it was while sneaking around at the Gables. I hope a smile will be enough to start a conversation. I feel too short of breath to speak, and the only thing I can think to say is "nice shirt".

I take a deep breath to compose myself, then turn around.

And, as Fate would have it, he's gone.

I look up the aisle to the front of the store and see there's only one cashier open.

Wonderful.

I text Carly that our sighting of the Nerd Prince ended up a bust when he disappeared into thin air. Fate knocks me back with another punch as I realize the store is going to close any second and someone on my Asshole List is already in queue. My chin reflexively lifts to the ceiling as I curse my luck. Carly's ex is the last person I want to run into, especially after Dave clocked him one last night.

I rush for the checkout to meet my doomed position in line behind Mick when I accidentally kick something, sending it skidding up the aisle.

What the hell?

I follow the noise and reach down for a key fob to a Cadillac. I presume (and hope) it belongs to the stranger I'd been drooling over. I didn't hear him drop anything, but I had my earbuds in. He could've lost it when he stood up from browsing that low shelf.

I reach the checkout as some of Mick's items are being bagged. Hopefully we can keep this conversation short. I'm sure the stranger is out in the lot wondering how the hell he's getting home without his key.

I set my candles on the belt and give Mick a once over as I wait for him to realize I'm standing here. He's dressed in a white polo shirt and expensive jeans, his usual good-looking self. I suppose it's one reason girls throw themselves at him twenty-four seven. He's like a chameleon that can change his colors to appeal to any sort of prey. Uniformed on the ice or standing in line at the store, he's pretty attractive on the outside.

He's also a lesson in 'looks aren't everything'.

I'm surprised at his expression when he sees me. He's got a busted lip and some minor bruising (which I did expect), but I thought he'd be angry with me right off. Instead, he looks at me forlorn, like a kid who's lost his puppy.

"Hey," I say.

"Hey." He grabs for a pack of gum and tosses it on the belt next to a bag of frozen peas.

I'm sure I shouldn't ask, but I'm feeling a little gutsy. "Those frozen veggies for your lip?"

"No, for my mom."

"Ah," I nod in understanding. "I'm here for my mum, too."

Maybe that's the end of it, then.

Please, for once, let me have some well-timed good fortune. I've got a Nerd Prince to find!

A young girl with curly red hair hands Mick his change. Instead of greeting me, her gaze follows him as he walks off. As she starts scanning my items, she finally says hello, but now I'm staring at him, too. He stops in his tracks just as the automatic glass doors open ahead of him.

He turns back to me, his eyes cast to the floor.

Yep, here it comes.

"Look, Pam, I know I said some shit." He looks out the window, then back to the floor before looking up at me. "I know you hate me. But—"

"I don't hate you, Mick." He nods slowly and turns away, but I don't stop there. Maybe I want to out him for the jerk he really is, so gullible women everywhere (like the cashier) can be saved from a heartache like Carly's. Or maybe it's because I've not given him a piece of my mind yet. Whatever the reason, I open my big mouth again. "I do hate what you did to her."

He spins around to face me. "I know this. I've apologized to her over and over again. Can't it ever be enough?"

I just shake my head as I pay the clerk and thank her, smiling politely before I make a move for the doors. I have no desire to exchange words with Mick, especially in public.

Why didn't I keep my mouth shut?

As I walk by, he grabs my bare arm and spins me around.

Oh, he did *not*.

"I am not about to let you cause a scene in here." I glare up at him, then down at where he has a grip on me. "Let. *Go*."

"Shit." He removes his hand in a hurry and throws palms up, taking a step back in obvious frustration with himself. "I'm sorry. I just...I wish I could get a second chance here. I don't know what to do."

"Play hockey," I say. "That's what you love, and *that's* what you need to do." I exhale a deep breath as I step out into the warm night, hoping he'll head for his vehicle.

Instead, he follows me. "Pam, wait."

"Wait for what?" My small plastic grocery bag swings along with my dress as I whip around to face him. "I have nothing more to say to you."

"I love her." He stares down at the blacktop, then shifts his weight from one leg to the other as he looks into the distance. "It's gutting me that she's leaving."

"You mean that she left," I correct. "She's gone, Mick. Get over it."

"I'm serious," he says. "Like, I don't want to live without her. It's killing me."

"And it killed her when you screwed a woman in every town you ended up in long enough to buy a pack of gum." I wait for his full attention, hoping he'll finally get the freaking message when he looks up. "Leave. Her. Alone."

"She still calls me," he says boastfully. He follows me as I head for the Mini. "I don't ask her to."

I say nothing as I arrive at my car and unlock it.

"I never thought you'd be so cold," he says. "You of all people know what it's like to lose someone."

"I'm not cold," I say to him across the roof. He's standing next to my passenger door, staring at me. "I just care about her more than you do."

"You have no idea how I feel about her. The distance is going to kill me."

"She was your first love, Mick. I get that." I toss my tiny grocery bag in the passenger seat. "But for you, she wasn't enough. For someone else, she'll be far more than enough."

"Not if I have something to say about it." He smacks my roof with a firm hand and walks away as I climb in behind the wheel.

What an asshole. *And he better not touch my Mini again!*

I roll down the passenger window, in no hurry to drive off now that he's got me all ticked off. I'm thankful there's no one else out here to overhear our arguing, because I can't help myself as I refuse to let an asshole get the last word.

"I get it," I call after him. He looks back at me, stopping before he reaches his restored muscle car. "Now that she's gone, you realize what you had. But it is over, Mick," I say loud enough so I'm sure he's heard me. "Leave her the hell alone."

10

Oates

June 9, 2016
Thursday, 9:00 p.m.

Ganonoque, Ontario
Canada

This evening has been an epic cluster fuck.

Reggie and Tori dropped me off at the town dock in the Victoria before setting off for their sunset cruise. The Whaler was having issues, and I only made it as far as the opposite side of the island before she quit again. After I paddled the short distance back to the dock, I was so busy razzing Reggie for not being able to fix her that it took me until we reached the mainland to realize I failed to grab the Cadillac SUV key from the dash of the broken down boat.

That meant a trip back to the island for the key, and once the Pierces dropped me off on the mainland, it was after eight-thirty. I was left with less than thirty minutes to drive to the store and find what I needed before it closed. This would have been plenty of time, until I was distracted by something unexpected — a circumstance entirely beyond my control.

An absolutely gorgeous girl was in the same aisle I needed to be in.

She was impossible to miss. Brown hair flowed in silky waves around bare shoulders as she held her phone out in front of her, talking to someone on video chat. Her voice floated to me along with her giggle. It was a complicated mix of sounds that were sexy and cute all at once.

And she was wearing a bright pink tiara on her head.

I immediately wanted to be closer to her, though I wasn't sure what the hell I'd ever say to a girl like that. I was almost certain we'd have nothing in common.

But something drew me in, and I spent nearly five minutes staring at the spices just to be next to her. I knew the cinnamon Nate required was already purchased and sitting on the counter back at the Gables, but my position allowed me to steal a quick glimpse of her across the aisle.

She was tall, even in flip flops. Her toes were polished pink, the same color as the fake gems on her crown and the tiny flowers on her otherwise white dress.

When I realized she was looking at my basket, it dawned on me the damn thing was still empty and the store was about to close. I raced out of the baking aisle to find Nate's real maple syrup, only to recall that I'm in freaking Canada. There were too many choices, making my decision that much harder.

I checked out just before the staff closed the doors for the night.

As I approached the cashier, I couldn't help wondering where the mystery princess had gone to. Adrenaline spiked when I spotted her near the exit talking to some douche who grabbed her by the arm. For a split second I was amped up and ready to come to her aid, but before I could do that, she gave him what must've been a stern warning and he backed off.

I stood there as Nate's syrup was scanned three times, watching the guy follow my mystery princess outside. The redheaded cashier graciously knocked a couple bucks off the syrup, and it was only then it dawned on me that she had delayed my check-out so she could check *me* out.

I thank her and rush out of the store, scanning the lot to make sure the creep isn't out here harassing the beautiful brunette. I don't see either of them.

It's then I realize I'm standing outside a closed store and that I've forgotten one of the two items I came for — Nate's flour.

I tap the handle of the SUV to auto-unlock the doors, frustrated and wondering how I'm going to explain this to anyone. It'd be an obvious lie to claim the grocery store in Ganonoque didn't have flour.

I try the handle, but the door won't open. It's still locked.

What the hell?

I pat the back pocket of my jeans to pull out the fob and realize it's no longer there. "You've got to be kidding me."

I set down my one grocery bag, pull out my phone and look up the store's phone number. If I can call inside and get a staff member to pick up the phone, they'll have to let me in to look for my keys. Maybe they'd let me grab a bag of flour while I'm at it.

I copy and paste the phone number into the keypad, ready to hit call when someone in the distance catches my attention.

Mystery Princess.

She's without tiara this time, leaned up against a Mini Cooper (Lightning Blue convertible, if my eyes aren't playing tricks on me as the blinding sun sets). She's parked in the next aisle over and a few spaces down, staring at me with an incredibly beautiful yet knowing smile. I tilt my head in question, unsure what the hell that's all about.

Is this some weird Canadian flirting game?

She looks at something in her hand and extends her arm in my direction. I throw my head back in realization as I hear the locks of the SUV click.

Mystery Princess has my key.

She glances at the fob again, points it once more, and the SUV starts.

Oh, she's sassy this one.

I cross the lot to talk to her, dodging one eager employee speeding away from the store in his pickup truck.

"Did you lose this?" she asks as I cross the last empty parking space between us.

"Indeed, I did." As I approach, my eyes dart around the lot tentatively, hoping the jerk that was manhandling her isn't lurking nearby. She has no passenger in her front seat, only a small grocery bag from the store. "I was going to call inside and ask if they found it." I take the key from her and an odd sensation of warmth spreads up my arm as our hands touch. "Thank you."

"No problem," she says. "I think you dropped it near the spices."

"Ah, yes. Where I saw you with the tiara."

"Yeah." She looks away in a brief moment of embarrassment, then turns back to me and shrugs. "Lame attempt to cheer up my best friend."

"I hope you bought it. It suits you."

"Oh no," she smiles, a sudden air of confidence about her. "There was no need. The one I have at home is much nicer."

I can't help but smile. Sarcastic and cute. *A one-two punch.*

"Well, you should definitely wear it out more. And thanks again." I hold up the key. "At least this solves one of my problems."

"That's me, Princess Problem Solver," she says as she opens her door. "Bye, now." She minds the bottom of her dress as she gracefully climbs in.

God, she's gorgeous. Almost regal, with or without a plastic tiara.

And she's leaving.

As much as I want to stop her, ask her anything and everything about herself, I don't want to weird her out. It's a warm summer night, and she's a young woman alone in a parking lot at dusk. Plus she's already had a creep trying to manhandle her tonight.

If I were her, I probably would've sped away from me already.

I take a couple of steps back from her car to give her some space. "I don't suppose you'd want to help a tourist solve another problem?"

"I can try." She smiles as she shuts her car door and rolls down her window. "Do you need directions?"

"No, but I forgot the one other thing I was sent here for. My friend's going to kill me if I don't come back with flour. Are there any other stores close by? Preferably stores that are open after nine?"

"No, sorry," she says with genuine sympathy. "I think you're out of luck there. At least until tomorrow."

"Thanks anyway," I smile. "Have a good night, princess."

I head for the SUV, toss the one item I purchased inside and climb in, figuring I've completely blown it.

Not that it matters. I'm here for all of three days. You can't really blow it in another country around girls you're never going to see again. Chalk it up as one random interaction with a stranger, one of those cool but weird stories to tell around the campfire.

So what if my attraction to her is off the charts, immeasurable by any scientific gauge? She's young and beautiful, so she probably has a boyfriend. I'm either turning into a weird creeper or I'm incredibly hard up. Maybe I should've taken Vanilla Blonde up on her flirtations after all.

As I put on my seatbelt, I realize Mystery Princess has pulled up next to me, faced in the opposite direction. We both roll down our windows. "Did I drop something else?"

"No," she says through that pretty laugh I first heard in the store. "I may regret this later if someone finds me chopped up in little pieces in the back of my car, but there's a Tim Horton's a few minutes up the road. I was just wondering..." She looks straight ahead for a moment, as if having second thoughts. The tapping of her right thumb on the steering wheel halts as she looks up at me. "Do you like coffee?"

I'm shocked at how my luck has turned around tonight. What started out as a complete mess has turned into an accidental date with a gorgeous Canadian princess. Once we got to the local Tim's, I insisted I would buy. First, because I'm a gentleman. Second, it was the least I could do to thank her for finding the key to my borrowed ride.

She agreed and wandered off to find us a seat while I was in line. I order her an iced double-double (as she requested), and a hot mocha latte for myself, then find her in a quiet corner by an unlit fireplace. I take a seat in the empty swivel chair next to her.

"Double-double, hmm?" I set down her beverage on the squat table between us. "Been a long time since I've heard that."

"You've spent time in Canada before?"

"It's been several years, but yeah. Used to come up here a lot in the summers when I was an undergrad."

"And you're from where?" she asks.

"California." I reach for my drink, but I can tell through the paper cup it's too hot to sip. I leave it sitting there and open the lip so heat can escape. "Born and raised and currently residing."

"You're a long way from home. Are you here for business?"

"Sort of." I can't help a smug smile, recalling Tori's advice on the plane today as stats from the *Ladies' Luxury* article flash through my head.

The pretty girl sips from her straw and watches me as she shifts to get comfortable. Her dress falls a few inches past her knees, preventing her from baring much even as she crosses one long leg over the other. Looking down, the only glimpse of skin I see is slightly above her feet. A delicate chain graces her right ankle.

There's nothing risque about the way she dresses. The straps of her dress are skinny enough to show off the sexy bronzed shoulders I noticed in the store, but she doesn't reveal even a hint of cleavage. Her neck is complemented by a simple silver chain that matches the one on her ankle.

And I realize, despite this, I find her sexy as hell.

She's nothing like the girls I've met in California.

Apparently, leaving more to the imagination is my gig.

"That smile is a bit conspiring," she says. "Are you trying to figure out if I'm worth kidnapping?"

"No," I say, raising a palm. "Swear."

"Okay. Let's see then. Are you here directing a movie?"

"No." A genuine laugh escapes me. "Why? Do I look like a film director?"

"You have a director-esque quality about you. Studious. Hip, yet unsuspecting. Like a Hollywood newbie whose first film lands him an Oscar nod."

"Studious?" I say through my grin. "I think you meant nerd."

"No, I meant studious. Nerd would be a huge compliment coming from me. I hardly know you well enough to bestow such an honor, despite your shirt."

"Well thank you, I think." I don't hide my amusement. "And I'm smiling because I'm in good company."

"And I'm thinking maybe there's more."

"Okay," I say, palms up again. "You got me. A conversation I recently had popped into my head just now."

"And?"

"And now explaining it out loud seems ridiculous."

"Maybe I like ridiculous," she says. "Try me."

"Okay," I say, exhaling to feign defeat. "On my flight in, I had this conversation with a woman who's kind of like a second mom to me. She took it upon herself to give me some advice. At the time, I thought it was without merit and now—"

"Now you're wondering if she was right?"

"Exactly."

"Definitely sounds like a mum tactic. What kind of advice?"

"God, this is going to sound so lame." I run a hand through my hair and lean back, watching her as I answer. "It was dating advice."

"So you're single," she says, matching my relaxed posture.

"I am. You?"

"Yes, by choice," she says. "I'm not, like crazy or anything. Just focused on my fourth year at University."

"I'm not crazy either. And I was the same way about school." As she sips from her straw, I find myself insanely curious about what it would be like to kiss her.

"May I ask what her advice was?"

"She recommended an article to me. Said next time I meet someone I'm interested in that I shouldn't lead off talking about work or asking a woman about hers. It's all the rage in Europe," I kid her. "Only Americans focus on work constantly, even when they're on a date."

"Hmm." She leans forward, an elbow resting on her knee as her chin hits her palm. "I think there may be something to that. So, if you were to meet someone you were interested in, what would you talk about instead?"

"That's an excellent question, and I have no idea. She gave me this advice...oh," I pause and glance at my watch, "less than twelve hours ago." I take a sip of extremely hot coffee and set the cup down again.

"Well, here's your chance to practice," she says in a serious tone. "Pretend I'm someone you're interested in."

My grin returns. "I think I can manage that."

"So work is off the table as a topic. And we can't talk about education either. You know I'm in school, and I'll tell you I'm 21. That way you have an age reference, because you'd probably know that about a girl you were interested in."

"Noted." *Thank you, Jesus. Twenty-one isn't a deal breaker.* "And you're from here?"

She nods. "Born and raised and currently residing."

"There is a flaw in your plan, though," I tell her. "I don't know what to talk about at all because I don't know anything about you, other than the fact that you're royalty who's left her proper crown at home. I don't even know your name."

"True." She uncrosses her right leg and sits up straight, arms resting in her lap as she grips her cup and thinks on our issue.

Stop daydreaming about laying her down, Oates. Damn.

"Okay, I got it," she says. "No names, no work, no school. The only facts are that neither of us is a serial killer or crazy, I'm 21 and you're?" She gestures with a hand up in wait.

"Thirty," I say. "This past March."

"Okay, so we're just two people having coffee who will probably never see each other again. And," she says, pulling out her phone, "we're limited on time, because if my best friend doesn't hear from me soon, she'll call the police. Or worse, my dad."

"I'm glad someone knows where you are." *Especially after I saw that jerk grab you in the store.*

She dips one sexy shoulder towards me. "I don't think you're a serial killer, but I'm not stupid. I told a couple people where I'd be. Carly wants to be sure you haven't murdered me."

"I promise not to disappoint her. So, how much time do you have?"

"About twenty minutes."

I check my watch again. Reggie said he'd meet me back at the marina around ten, so we're on the same clock.

That should be enough time to conduct this experiment.

"You like games?" I ask.

"Usually, yes."

"Are you competitive?"

"Extremely."

"Okay, so the game is Love It or Hate It. We take turns naming something that interests us. Could be anything — person, place or thing — and the other person has to say if they love it or hate it. If you hate it, you can say why, but you only get one sentence to explain."

"Deal. You can go first."

"Oh, ladies and royalty first. I absolutely insist." I lean forward and rest my elbows on my knees to show her I'm listening intently.

"Okay," she sighs, "here we go. Eighties music?"

"Love it. Fanatically. Math and science?"

She grins ear to ear. "Love, also fanatically."

A mumbled wow escapes me. *Seriously?*

"Okay, um…" she thinks a minute. "My brain's malfunctioning. All I can come up with is Justin Bieber, but I can't really say I'm interested in him."

"That's sneaky. Is this a test because he's Canadian?"

"Ah," she says, waving a finger at me. "Isn't that cheating? You didn't say we could ask questions. Auto-response only, is my understanding of the rules."

"Touché. Auto-response would be hate it — musically speaking — but not personally or because he's Canadian. My turn." I squint with one eye as I think. "Video games?"

"Love."

No. Way. "Fanatically?"

"Depends on the gaming system and stop cheating," she teases. "Dancing?"

"Love it. Fishing?"

"Love it," she says. "Yoga?"

"Crap. I'm in a quandary." She tilts her head, indicating she wants to know why. "Uh, I've never tried it."

"Well, that is unfair, then. We need a new rule. How about we can pass if we don't have enough knowledge about the topic?"

"Deal," I say. "And since I passed, you should get another turn."

"Reading?" she asks.

"Love it. Beer?"

"Hate it," she says through a laugh. "Um…this song."

I tilt my ear to listen. Huey Lewis is singing about feeling the power of love.

"Love it. Star Wars?"

"Love it," she says, "and Star Trek, too. Dogs?"

"Love them. Snow?"

She shrugs. "I'd say love before I'd say hate. The cold is another story. Meat?"

"Hmm. That's a tough one. I think that's too general. Would you agree?"

"Okay, then. Bacon?"

I smile. "Love it," I say. "But not peameal bacon like you might find up here."

"I totally agree," she says with a smile.

Damn, that smile is dazzling.

"Okay, here's one like Bieber was for you. Not necessarily something I like, but I'm curious about your answer."

"Shoot," she says.

"Internet dating." I take off my glasses, and when I look back at her, I realize she's staring at me. She stalls for a second, then says she hates it. "Reason being?" I clean my lenses with my shirt.

"I can justify the compatibility aspect of it, statistics and algorithms bringing like-minded people together with the common goal of dating."

"But?"

"But, I have a hard time believing that something extraordinary, like meeting someone you have a real connection with, can result from filling out a form online. Sort of takes away the exciting part, at least to me."

"So your judgment isn't soured by a bad experience then?"

"No, I've never done it," she admits. "In fact, maybe I should've said pass."

"Interesting."

"Interesting in a good way, or?"

"Interesting as in unexpected. I'd like a sidebar." She looks bewildered for a minute, then nods in agreement as she sips from her straw again. "The guy that grabbed you in the store back there. He wasn't a boyfriend you met online or elsewhere?"

She throws a hand to her mouth as though she's trying to keep the liquid in. Her eyes go wide. "Mick?" she says, trying to regain her composure. "God, no. That's my best friend's ex. I'd never date him. He's a jerk. One hell of a hockey player, but a jerk nonetheless."

"Good to know."

"I'm sorry you saw that," she says, a hand waving in the air. "He's all clenched up because Carly's moving to the States. He royally screwed up their relationship. He's kinda kicking himself now is all."

"And you told him tough luck?"

"Essentially," she smiles. "Maybe with more colorful words thrown in."

She's got a backbone.

She doesn't date tough guys that play hockey and manhandle her.

Just a couple more for the plus column.

I remind her that it's her turn.

"Right. Um, New York City?"

"I'd have to pass on that one."

She seems surprised. "You've never been there?"

"Oh," I say with a scolding *tsk*, "I believe you just cheated, your highness."

"I'd like to quit then. Tell me why you passed."

"I've only been there a few times out of necessity. Can't really speak to whether I love it or hate it. Have you ever been?"

She shakes her head. "That's where my best friend is now, the one I was trying to cheer up in the store. I've always wanted to go."

"Does she live there?"

"Nope. She's just passing through. She's training for her new position in Florida."

"Well, there's no rule saying we can't talk about someone else's work. What's she do?"

"She'll be the head chef at some fancy Key West resort. So I understand your dilemma," she says, setting down her cup, which I notice is down to just ice. "If Carly asked me to bring her flour and I failed that mission, she'd be pissed."

I glance at my watch, regretful that we've already killed over ten minutes.

"Do you need to go?" she asks.

"Not yet, but I'm hitching a ride from the town dock in Bay Falls. I don't want to hold anyone up."

She looks away, glancing out the front windows of the restaurant. *Shit, did that upset her?*

I clear my throat to get her attention. She looks back at me, and I smile in reassurance.

"After playing this game though?" I smile as I grab for my paper cup. "I definitely wish I didn't have anywhere to be."

11

Pam

June 9, 2016
Thursday, 9:45 p.m.

Ganonoque, Ontario
Canada

I'm not sure where the hell I got the audacity to ask a hot stranger to come have coffee with me but am I ever-loving glad I did.

In the moment I asked him, it felt like an outside force had taken over my mouth.

My mouth, my lady parts, everything.

When he headed for his SUV, something inside me screamed *'Don't let him walk away'.*

So I didn't.

And already, I know this guy is a gentleman through and through.

He held my door open when I got out of my car, again when we walked into Tim's, and then he stood in line for our coffee, which he insisted he pay for. Not because I was some sort of damsel in distress, but as a genuine thank you for finding his key.

My mother's scary 'watch out for crazies' voice interjects. *Even serial killers can be gentlemen.* But my gut tells me this guy is for reals (and most likely *not* a serial killer). Once I handed over his car key, he was ready to drive away from me forever, when he could've easily tried to abduct me in the empty parking lot on the first go.

After my run-in with Mick, I was surprised I made it outside ahead of the stranger. I had the privilege of watching him saunter out of the store to an extravagant white Cadillac, and all I could picture was a prince walking up to his trusty thoroughbred.

Being up close and in person with him for the last fifteen minutes has only solidified Carly's hunch about his looks.

He's *effing* off-the-charts handsome.

Before I got here, I sent Carly a text to thank her for pointing him out.

Then I told her I asked the stranger for coffee because some intense force told me to.

She wrote back with a shocked face emoji, said she was half asleep, but would set her alarm. If she hasn't heard from me again by ten p.m., she'll call my dad (who will then call the police and start a search and rescue mission). In the meantime, I called Mum on my way here to tell her I have the candles but ran into a friend so I'd be a little while longer.

Stranger turned Friend is now waiting in our cozy spot because, much as it pained me to halt our conversation, I desperately needed to pee. In the washroom, I do what's necessary as quickly as possible, knowing both of us have to get going soon. Thankfully, there was no wait as the washroom was empty. We're the only two nuts grabbing coffee and a chat after nine p.m. on a Thursday.

I paint a coat of gloss on my lips and head back to the handsome stranger. He stands to greet me as I return.

See, Mum? He is a gentleman!

"Oh good," he says with a charming grin. "I thought maybe you were ditching me."

We both sit. "Not a chance," I smile back at him. "Feel like another game?"

He relaxes into his chair and rests an ankle on his opposite knee.

I notice his jeans have a few tatters in them, leaving skin exposed in random places. They don't look grungy, though. More like ripped by design. He's wearing an Apple watch. Somehow he makes 'sexy' and 'casually-hip nerd' seem like they're always a package deal.

"Sure," he says. "Your choice this time."

"Okay, quick-fire question and answer."

"Sounds simple enough. Rules?"

"Five questions at a time. Yes or no answers only. You go first."

"Okay." He feigns an effort to gear up, fingers laced as he stretches his arms. He tilts his head side to side, then sits up straight. "I'm ready. You?"

"Fire away."

"Aright, Princess. Would you consider yourself a nerd?"

"That's a big yes."

"Have you ever done hard drugs?"

"Emphatic no."

"Ever drank so much you ended up vomiting?"

"Yes," I say through a giggle. "Twice. And p.s., that's a gross ask."

"Do you have any siblings?"

"Um..." I fidget with my dress. "No. Not anymore."

He swears under his breath. I expect him to excuse himself in a hurry or at the very least look away. No one wants to hear about a girl's tragedies, especially if she's a stranger. I feel a gentle hand rest briefly on my knee. When I look up his hand is back in his own lap. "Did you have to bump off your evil sister so you could wear the crown?"

An outburst of laughter escapes me before I answer.

Dammit.

He's funny. Off-the-charts cute.

And from California.

Figures.

"A good guess, but no," I say. "I had a brother. He passed away in 2014."

He nods, letting a moment of silence pass. "I had a close friend lose a sibling. I get it. And I'm sorry for your loss."

"You couldn't have known, but thank you."

This guy is a different breed. Am I freaking dreaming this? If I could order up a guy from a menu, it'd be this one (with the exception that he not live light years away). He'd be American, he'd definitely look and sound like this guy. But I'd meet him while studying in the States next year, not now.

Stupid, drunk and confused Fate.

"I think that was four questions, Stranger," I say. "You get one more."

"Do you always look this nice when you go to the grocery store?"

"Um...pass?"

He lets go a short laugh, then leans back in his chair again. "Yes or no only, please."

"I don't know how to answer that. Except to say this is how I always look, I guess? My turn now. Are you a nerd?"

"Obviously," he says, pointing to his t-shirt. "A big one."

"Do you have any younger brothers who are also single nerds and who might happen to live in Canada?" I swoon at the smile that lights up his brown eyes.

"Let's just say if I did, I certainly wouldn't let on." He adds that he does have one wild sister, but she lives in Arizona.

"Do you get along with your parents?"

"Yes."

"Have you ever been engaged or married?"

"No and no," he says, "and that's technically two questions."

I turn my amused expression into an exaggerated pout.

"I'll let it slide." He smiles back at me as he dips his chin. "This time, anyway. You still get one more."

I blurt the next question before I lose my courage. "Are you gay?"

"Damn," he laughs, "usually it's my flour-seeking, cake-baking friend Nate that has to field that one."

"That's not an answer."

His lower lip disappears for a second as he bites it. "Tell me why you're asking."

"You really seem to be dodging this one, mister. Are you not sure? I mean, what happened to yes or no answers?"

"Consider it paying the price for your extra question last time."

"Well," I exhale and draw a fresh breath, embarrassed that I asked. I forge ahead anyway. "You never did say if your friend's mum was giving you advice about dating men or women."

"True."

I ramble on, each word tumbling out faster than the last. "And my best friend and I were having a conversation about dating, about the guys we adore being married or gay, as the saying goes. So I'm trying to work up the courage to ask guys up front. Just in case I meet someone. You know," I shrug, unable to stop my cheeks from turning red, "someday."

"Well in that case, I'll tell you. No, I'm not gay. And that's your last question, your highness."

My phone pings, and I glance at it to see simultaneous texts from Alexis and Carly. *Crap.* "Before I go, can I ask one last question?"

He furrows his brows at my additional rule-breaking, then softens. "I'll allow it," he says, then adds, "if you will."

"Deal."

"You first," he says.

"Are you still going to be here tomorrow?"

"Define here."

"In Canada."

"Yes," he says. "I'm here until—"

"Ah," I say, holding up a finger. "Don't say any more."

He's visibly confused. "Why not?"

"Because." I stand up, grab for my purse and toss it over my shoulder. "This way, I can imagine for one full day that I might run into you — or your car keys — again in Metro, and we could try this experiment all over again."

He rests a hand on his exposed knee, his elbow cocked out as he looks up at me. "Yeah, I'm not, I mean, I head back—"

I hold a finger to my lips in a 'shh' motion. "If you don't say it out loud, it makes our parting a little less sad."

For a second he just stares at me, and I can't tell if he's put off by my superstitious nonsense or at my admission that I'd love to have this spontaneous chat all over again. Then that sexy grin comes back, and he nods.

He knows exactly what I mean.

"Thanks for the coffee, Stranger." I start for the door, my heart a lump in my throat. "I hope you find the flour you're looking for."

"Wait," he says as he stands, "I get one last question too, remember?"

I'm at the exit. I rest my hands on the cool glass and turn around to face him, waiting for him to ask what he will.

"What's your name?"

I bite my lower lip, debating whether to tell him. *But what's the point?* As much of a dream guy as he might seem, I won't know him beyond this day, beyond this perfect moment in time.

"Princess works fine," I say.

"Accepted, but evasive. I get one more question." He sets down his cup and stares at me so intently I feel chills radiate down my bare arms. He closes the distance between us, and my breath catches. My heart pounds as he looks me in the eye. "If your name was really Princess, would you dot the "i" with a heart, a fat circle, or a regular dot?"

"Um…" I scrunch up my face, caught off guard by his silly ask. "What?"

He lowers his head, his eyebrows raised. "Just an answer, please."

I purse my lips, then answer seriously. "A regular dot," I say. "No question."

His grin widens, and just when I'm wondering if he's going to kiss me, he leans back while pushing the door open for me. The smell of donuts and coffee collides with fresh air as I step out.

"Good night, Princess."

"Good night, Stranger," I call over my shoulder. "Enjoy your time in Canada."

I dial Carly from the car.

"What the hell," she mutters. "I'm sleeping, girl."

"It's 9:59. Just wanted to let you know I'm headed home."

"Oh, right. The geeky stranger." I hear her fumbling around in her hotel room. "Hang on, I've gotta turn off my alarm."

"Is your dad still up?"

"Uh," she pauses, "looks like he's still downstairs. So how was it? Is he amazing?"

"Yes. And he's from California."

"Shitballs."

"Tell me about it. There's one other thing I have to tell you before you hear it from someone else. Then you can go to sleep."

"Yeah, go," she says over the sound of a toilet flushing.

"Seriously? Tell me you did not just take me to the bathroom."

"Okay," she says, then yawns. "I did not just take you to the bathroom."

"Lies."

"Obviously. Now spill it, so I can go back to bed."

"I ran into Mick."

"Ugh," she groans, "I don't want to talk about him. Tell me about the cutie from Metro. He looked a little too smart for my taste. Then again, with those guns he was sporting, I could overlook it."

"He is even hotter in person," I sigh. "I mean, seriously. A charming geek in a stud's body."

"But?"

"But I'll never see him again. He was wandering around Metro looking for flour for his friend, and he totally spaced and forgot to buy it. Probably because he saw me arguing with Mick."

"About what?"

"He's sorry, he loves you. Yadda, yadda. Same shit as always. I told him his actions were deplorable, except I was super pissed when I said it."

"Thanks for defending my honor, love. Did Dave's right hook leave a mark?"

"Kinda, yeah. And Mick nearly left a mark on me."

"What?" She suddenly sounds alert.

"It was nothing, really. He just grabbed me to stop me from leaving. He's lost without you, hates that you're going away."

"Oh, Jesus," she mutters. "He acts like we never broke up. I'm sorry he hassled you."

"He was looking for some direction. I gave him some."

"As in, you gave him a road map to hell?"

"No, I told him to focus on his sport and leave you alone. I think he got the message."

"He ever lays a hand on my best friend again, he'll get more than a message. I'll sic Dave on him. Next time, take your own advice and do not engage."

"Agreed. You should go get some rest."

"Yeah," she sighs. "I'm sorry your stranger lives in Cali. Did he ever get his flour?"

"No, he spent the last half hour with me and nothing's open."

"I've got a canister in the apartment. Help yourself," she says through another yawn. "I'm back in bed now. I'll be asleep in thirty seconds. Love you."

"Love you most," I laugh. "Good night."

In twenty minutes, I've raced to Carly's apartment, let myself in to grab what I need, and continued on to the marina. As I pull into the parking lot next to the Bay Falls Town Dock, I exhale in relief.

I know I've beaten him here. The white Cadillac isn't in the lot.

Thanks to the nine p.m. caffeine and the leftover adrenaline rush after meeting my Perfect Stranger, this mission's going to be executed at turbo speed.

I walk down the concrete to the dock carrying a canvas tote that has everything I need: the container of organic flour from Carly's otherwise bare cupboard, the note I wrote standing at her kitchen counter, and the packing tape I confiscated from her overflowing junk drawer. I stop on the dock at the first lamppost I come to, the one closest to shore that has the official "Welcome To Bay Falls" sign screwed to it. I peel some tape off the roll, attach my note to the metal sign, and leave the canvas tote with the flour on the dock.

There's no way he can miss that.

And if he's any kind of nerd at all, today might not be the last time I speak to my Perfect Stranger.

12

Oates

June 9, 2016
Thursday, 11:59 p.m.

Fawn Island

I'm in the small bedroom two stories up in the boathouse, stripped down to boxers and lying under a surprisingly soft sheet. Relaxed as my body should be just before midnight, sleep is evading me. Back home on Pacific time it's only nine p.m.

The room isn't exactly quiet, either. A few islands away, someone is having a rager of a party that won't quit. The sound of music, laughter, and fireworks easily reaches me across the water. Pierce will show up in a matter of hours. Project Oates will be in progress, and we're going to reunite with brother Nate as a trio after ten long years.

But none of these factors is the catalyst for me lying here wide-eyed with a stupefied grin that won't quit.

I arrived at the town's public marina less than two hours ago, parked the SUV and found a note taped to the town's welcome sign. Sitting below it on the dock was a small canvas bag with a container of flour inside it.

straNger,
welComE tO the friendLiest countrY EVAH!
We aim to please here in Canada.

I happened to know someone with a container of flour who no longer needs it. I hope all of your problems are now solved.
Cheers,
Princess Problem Solver (<==== See? Regular dot.)

I stood there dumbfounded.

First, by the fact that she'd been so thoughtful.

Second, at what an impression she made on me (again).

And third, at the weird capitalizations in her note.

I looked around the dark marina searching for her or her car but found neither. I was still staring at the note when Reggie pulled up a few minutes later. Before he could see it, I tucked the note away in the bag and tossed my purchased syrup in along with it.

After mystery princess left the coffee shop, I killed five minutes in the parking lot, sipping my finally-cool-enough-to-drink coffee in the SUV with the same expression I've been wearing since. I spent the most amazing half hour with a girl ever, and she up and left just when things were getting good.

Not that I had hours to spare. I couldn't spend the rest of the evening sitting in that Canadian coffee chain talking her ear off.

But I wished like hell I could've.

Then she left without telling me her name, so I have no way to find her now. On the drive back to the marina parking lot, I resolved that's just how things were meant to be. But then I found the note and her friendly flour offering (also the one thing that would save me from being shot off into space by Nate Edwards), and it left me blown away once more.

On our way back to the island, Reggie informed me he'd already dropped his wife at the house so she could go to bed. The other couples had turned in, too. He took the groceries up to the main house, and there was nothing left for me to do but plod up to the boathouse alone. I fired up the old TV and Sega console to distract myself.

The girl must live somewhere near here. If I were home, I'd hack into whatever systems I had to, track down all 21-year-old female drivers who own a Mini Cooper in a twenty mile radius, then knock on every door until I found her. She's definitely worth all that. But in a foreign country, I can't take the risk. I don't have enough horsepower with me to accomplish such a goal anyway.

I gave up trying to make sense of it all and went to bed thirty minutes ago, my eyes blurry from staring at a cartoon hedgehog. Now I'm lying here awake, unable to stop thinking about her.

My phone startles me as it vibrates from its temporary home on the dresser. I throw off the sheet and grab it, then head to the kitchen to get a bottle of water.

The text is from Zach.

Dude. Did you get to Canada?
Finn is playing big brother.
Keeps asking me if I've heard
from you.

All is well in Canada. Sleep well, gents.

Does MML have a girl or what?
I'm running low on Scotch.

We'll find out when he arrives tomorrow.

Shit, that's right. Forgot you said Friday.

I can't sleep. I'm gonna pick out tickets. What Broadway show is hot right now?

We will win this one. I feel it.
But waste your time any way you want.

And then one minute later:

P.S. Tina was phenomenal.

Congrats. Does this mean Bat Shit Crazy Toxic girls need a new "T" moniker?

Already done. 'Tinas' are henceforth Tantalizing. 'Tonyas' are Toxic. Mark it down.

Noted and filed. Adios.

I set my water on the coffee table and sit on the edge of the couch, thinking about the note from the mystery princess. I'm not sure what the deal was with those oddly placed caps. Those letters reminded me of a ransom note spelled out with letters clipped from magazines. Maybe she was more loony and less princess?

If so, my gut is *way* off, because she didn't seem like a Crazy Carolyn.

I exit out of Zach's text messages so I can look up Broadway shows, and the screen to dial out pops up. I'd left it open earlier, intending to call inside the grocery store looking for the SUV fob. I close out of it, then immediately open it again, staring at the black numbers on the screen as it hits me.

No. Fucking. Way.

"It's a code," I mutter.

That would just be...I mean the kind of girl that does that...

Would she actually think to do that?

I jump up and run to the bedroom to search through my pants, but the note isn't there.

Duh, Oates. You left it in the canvas bag with Nate's cake-making shit.

This fucking figures.

I consider running up to the main house to get it, but I'd startle everyone out of their skin just by opening the creaky screen door. I close my eyes and recall the note, but memory fails me as to which letters were capitalized. I need the note in my hands to figure it out.

And my hands aren't getting anywhere near it until the sun comes up.

Friday morning I'm up at dawn. I spent the night falling in and out of a restless sleep, but it's a new day now. I grab a hot shower down on the dock, watching the sun rise in all its glory as I wet my head.

It's gonna be a magnificent day.

I'm confident there's a pot of strong-ass coffee up in the kitchen with my name on it. And, better still, the princess has left me a mystery to solve.

I dress and head up to the main house. The front door is open, only the screen between me and the smell of coffee. The porch is quiet. As I enter the house, Reggie comes down the front stairs.

"You're up early." He's wearing navy pajamas, but they have

white pinstripes and look tailored to fit. Mr. and Mrs. Pierce always look put together, even right out of bed. "Sleep well?" he asks.

"As well as can be expected."

"Ah, right. I understand you and Aidan have business to discuss."

"Uh, yeah." *Sure, that's it.*

"I'm sure you're well prepared. Don't give it another thought." He heads for the kitchen and I follow.

"Thanks. And you're dapper as ever in your PJs. Sleeping in these days?" He shoots me a scolding stare. "It is after six, Redge. I thought you'd be putting on the coffee."

"I'll have you know I'm typically up at five. The wife thought I could use some extra sleep on this vacation. And believe it or not, Tori is capable of making coffee."

"Yes, somehow I've managed it, Daryl," Tori calls from the pantry. "Just had to put the stuff away you bought for Nate." She enters the kitchen beautiful as always, dressed and ready for the day ahead. She's also carrying the item my brain has obsessed over so much in the last six hours, it made its way into my dreams.

I reach for the canvas tote I covet. "Can I put that away for you?"

"Sure." She smiles, folds the bag in half and hands it to me. "Go ahead and put it in the front closet, if you wouldn't mind?" As soon as my back is turned, she adds, "That's a nice bag the grocery store gave out. Were they having a promotion?"

"Uh, yeah." It's killing me not to rummage to the bottom of the bag this very second, but I turn around to answer her. "I guess they must've been."

"And you found everything okay?"

Jeez, what's with the third degree, Mrs. P.?

"Yep, scored Nate's flour and maple syrup. He owes me one. Have you seen the syrup choices in Canada?" I shake my head in disbelief. "*Bonkers.* Took up almost an entire aisle," I exaggerate. "Had to spend five minutes choosing one. Let's hope I didn't botch the job."

"Don't worry." She smiles a conspiratory grin and winks. "I'm sure you picked the right one."

Breakfast is great, as always. Something about the air up here always makes me especially hungry. Everyday food tastes better than usual. After a full plate of a hot breakfast, I polish off a raspberry danish and a second cup of coffee with the Pierces and their friends in the breakfast room off the kitchen.

Even the view is worth writing home about. From where we sit in the back of the grand home, I snap a picture of the beautiful St. Lawrence below and send it to my sister Annie. Who knows where she'll be when she opens it, but it's my brotherly way to let her know that I give a shit about her, and also that I'm up here for the weekend.

Despite a good meal, pleasant conversation, and the peaceful setting, my mood's turned sour.

The canvas bag I tucked into the front closet for Mrs. P. was empty. Tori and Reggie refused my help to prepare breakfast, which meant I had no reason to lurk in the kitchen. That would've allowed me to turn the room upside down for the solitary item in this country that might help me find my mystery princess.

I excuse myself as the rest of our party lingers around the table, scouring the pantry in a frantic hunt for the note. But my search (and a discreet picking through of the trash bin) nets zero results.

No note means no code to decipher.

Which means no girl.

I sit on the porch with my third cup of strong coffee pondering every moment of last night, especially the ten minutes between leaving the marina and arriving back at the boathouse.

I know I dropped the note into the bag next to the flour before Reggie could see it. It didn't occur to me Reggie would take everything up to the house when he turned in. Then again, the paper could've easily blown out of the bag before that when the ol' man picked up speed to cross the main channel. I'd been talking to Reggie as he navigated in the dark, focused on the waters ahead and not paying the bag any attention on the ride over.

I head down to the boathouse to grab my laptop, intending to shift my focus to work and put this girl out of my head for good. By eleven, I'm enjoying the breeze on the porch, ready for the weekend to officially start. Aidan messaged to say he's less than an hour out, and Nate's plane has just taken off for the last leg of his journey through Canada. He's due here by 1:30.

The Pierces' friends just took off to explore the mainland by car and find a place on the river to have lunch. Aidan's parents are somewhere. I haven't seen them since breakfast.

I set up at the iron patio table planning to prep for this business meeting, but instead I'm searching for universities in the area where a beautiful nerd might go to learn. I've come to the conclusion she must be enrolled somewhere in Toronto or Oshawa, but even that much information is useless without a name.

If Aidan and Nate would hurry up and get here, I could put the girl out of my mind and get down to bro-time. I'm concentrating on my screen when Tori walks out of the house, the door creaking until it gently shuts behind her.

She takes a seat across from me. "Working again?"

"Sort of."

"Did you read that article yet?"

"I did, actually." I pull the magazine from my laptop bag and hand it to her. "And I have to thank you. Your advice paid off."

"Oh?" She tilts her head. "Already, hmm?"

"Yeah." I can't help my smile. I duck behind my screen so Tori won't see it, but she peeks around to talk to me.

"Did you meet someone online?"

"No, I uh...sort of met someone last night. It was just a trial run though. Kind of an experiment."

"How do you experiment with another human being?"

"I just mean I'll never see her again, so I can't really say how it would work in the real world. But it gave me a chance to try your suggestion."

"And?"

"It was interesting."

"All told you were only gone, what, an hour and a half? What did you learn about this girl in such a short time?"

"I only spent thirty minutes with her. But I learned a lot. And we didn't talk about work at all."

I expect her to brag (with signature Tori class, of course), but she doesn't. She's just looking at me like she did this morning, only she's not saying anything.

"What's with the smug mug, Mrs. P.?"

"You really liked her."

"Like I said, I'll never see her again," I shrug. "I really should get down to work. Aidan's due here any minute."

"Yes, about that," she says, leaning back in her chair. "You may not get a chance to deal with business right away. Just so you know."

"Why?" Now it's me peering around my screen. "Does this have something to do with his surprise?"

"I can't say." She picks up the copy of *Ladies' Luxury* and starts reading.

"Spill it, Mamasita."

"You'll just have to wait and see, Daryl."

Reggie comes up the path and onto the porch, once again filthy up to his elbows. "Got 'er going this time," he says. "The Whaler is ready for you guys to do your worst."

"Great. I can pick up your son when he gets here."

"Not necessary," Tori says. "The Reeds drove themselves and the Hamiltons over with the pontoon, so it's already at the marina. I sent Aidan a text to let him know he can use that boat to get over here."

"Cool. I can keep working then. And by the way," I say to her, "Nate can't believe you're texting."

"He'd be shocked if he knew I can make coffee, too," she laughs.

"Right?" I chuckle. "I told him you were a modern woman."

"What time's he getting here?"

"By 1:30. This is gonna be an epic reunion."

"It'll be interesting for sure," Reggie says. He winks at his wife.

"Honey, please get cleaned up," Tori urges. "Aidan will be here soon."

"Relax, dear. I'm sure this girl doesn't care if I happen to be dirty from fixing my son's old boat."

I narrow my eyes at Tori. "What girl?"

"*Reggie.*" Tori shoots him a scolding look. "Go up and shower please? You should have just enough time."

He nods to me and hurries off, fully aware he's in the husband doghouse.

"Please." I close my laptop and look her in the eye. "You've gotta level with me, Mama. Tell me he's not bringing a girl."

"I'm not sure what you mean." She ignores me, staring into her magazine.

"Aidan. He's not...I mean, is he bringing like...a date up here?"

She shrugs as she flips pages. "Wouldn't you love it if he found a nice, normal girlfriend?"

"It's not that. I just..." *I don't want him to cost me the bet with the Hawthorne twins.* "Is that his surprise?"

She says nothing.

"Just tell me it's a business thing. A guest he wants to show some charity. Please, just confirm the surprise is not a chick."

Batman doesn't get happy! He gets shit done, damn it!

But she reveals nothing, and her only acknowledgment that I've said anything is a sly wink.

Son of a bitch.

I excuse myself from conversation with Tori to put my laptop in the kitchen while trying to put my thoughts together about Pierce.

If he's bringing a girl up here, I have no idea how this weekend's going to go. He must want me to meet her, which is a first. Back in college, I knew a couple of the girls he dated only by sight. Of course I'd met his nightmare of an ex Stella Ireland on several occasions the last couple of years, but Pierce blazed through a lot of women between those two phases of his life. I'd never been introduced to any of them.

If he's coming up here with a girl to introduce her to his parents and to me...

Fuck.

I may as well text Zach and admit defeat now.

I arrive back on the porch to find Reggie has followed orders from HQ. He's cleaned up and sitting at the patio table across from his wife. They're deep in conversation about which area of the river they'll head to next with the Garwood when we hear the pontoon come tooling around the island from the direction of the boathouse.

"They're here," Reggie nods, waving to the slow-moving vessel far below. Tori waves too, and I move to the railing as my friend comes into view.

Or I should say, my friend and his *date*. He's not alone.

"Pierce, you fucker!" *You just cost me at least ten Benjamins!* Tori nudges me for swearing, same as she's done since I was fifteen. "Get the hell up here!" I lean over the railing, waving with crossed arms like I need rescuing. "It's time for cocktails and these old people are killin' me!"

Aidan's parents laugh as their son yells back, "We're coming! Stand down, you ugly bastard!"

The boat cruises away headed for the other side of the island, and I look over at Tori. "I do believe he said 'we,'" I scold her, "and I'm pretty sure that brown-haired beauty on the boat is not Aidan's secretary or a Thousand Islands tour guide."

"I told you it wasn't my place to say. I didn't say you were wrong."

"Behave yourself, kid," Reggie chimes in. "I'm sure she's nervous enough having to meet us."

"I promise to be on my best behavior." I raise a hand in dedication to my oath. "As long as you promise not to mess up my surprise. No one says anything about Nate's impending arrival." I throw a glance in Reggie's direction. "Deal, blabbermouth?"

"Mum's the word," he says, looking across the table at Tori. I follow his gaze as it shifts to the path leading up from Brat Cottage, and he nods at his wife so she'll turn around. "Here they come."

"Oh, you're here!" Tori tosses her magazine aside and beelines for Aidan as he climbs the steps with his girl. Reggie pulls me into a distracting conversation about the problems he's having with his new phone as we wait our turn to be introduced.

The girl standing next to my best friend has that unassumingly gorgeous look about her, like the girl-next-door that surprises her entire high school by winding up a famous model. I hear Tori compliment her, and she blushes while Tori makes small talk post-introduction.

She's dressed the opposite of Aidan's last girlfriend Stella. That High Maintenance Monica would sooner show up here in an evening gown than what this girl's wearing: colorful t-shirt, cropped jeans, sandals. She's not frumpy by any means, but she's not over the top styled either.

She's also not a whole lot shorter than Aidan. She seems to carry herself well, sort of polite and conservative despite her casual dress code. I suppose that doesn't mean shit for her personality, though. She could be a crazy bitch just after his money and still be polite.

Tori gives orders and asks Reggie to come over for introductions. He leaves me to greet his son and the pretty girl.

Or is it girlfriend?

Either way, I'm out at least a cool grand for a bottle of liquor I won't get to drink. And I have to admit, pretty is an understatement for this blue-eyed woman with chestnut hair.

Unless I'm comparing her to the mystery princess from last night, who qualifies as an incomparable beauty.

"Mr. Oates," Reggie says, "would you like to come and meet this young lady?"

"I'm tryin'," I say, pushing off the railing. "All you old timers are keepin' a brother down." I cross the porch and throw a friendly smile in her direction as she reaches out her hand.

"Alexis Greene," she says. Her smile is friendly, but I can tell she's not sure what to make of me.

I make no eye contact with my best friend, deciding to pull off an Oates grandstand as payback for his little surprise. Rather than shake her extended hand, I lift it to my lips. "Bonjour, Mademoiselle," I say with my incredibly goofy grin. "Welcome to the Thousand Islands."

Just as I hoped she would, Ms. Greene bursts into laughter, and everyone follows suit.

"You must be Oates," she says once she regains her composure.

"The one and only." Before I focus on Ms. Greene, my eyes dart to Aidan, and I notice he's genuinely amused. "Daryl Oates, at your service. And apparently the ice breaker for the welcome wagon."

"Well, it's very good to meet you, Daryl Oates." She leans closer to me, as though she's sharing a secret. "And thank you for breaking the ice."

"My pleasure. So you're putting up with this pain in the ass, huh?" I throw up a hand to my brother-from-another and he pulls me in, slapping me on the back as I return the gesture.

"I am," Alexis says. Now she's beaming too.

Jesus.

These guys are *done-zo*. Goose cooked. Game over.

Tori breaks up the love fest by going Mom on us, asking her son and his girl if they've eaten.

"Yeah, we had breakfast on the way up," Aidan says. "We're good."

Reggie pipes up that maybe Bloody Marys are in order.

"Great idea. I'll help you old man." He gives me shit about giving him shit as we head inside. "I'll grab the liquor from the bar," I say. "Meet you in the kitchen."

He puts a hand on my shoulder to stop me. "She seems great, huh?"

"I suppose," I shrug. "They're both glowing, that's for damn sure."

"Someday you'll get it," he laughs. "In the meantime, once Nate gets here, you'll have someone to commiserate with."

"Aw shit." I look at my watch. "We'll have to go pick him up soon. Get on those drinks, Mr. P. I'll be right back."

I pop my head out the porch door to find Tori sitting down with her son and pretty Ms. Greene.

"Pierce!" Tori startles, a hand thrown to her chest as the other two look my way. "Can I get a ride to the mainland at one-thirty?"

"For what?"

"I gotta pick up my surprise, bro. Can you do it, or do I have to swim for it?"

"Sure, you can ride over with us," he says. "I have to take Alexis over around one."

"Thanks, shithead."

"*Daryl*," Tori scolds through her polite smile, "language."

I salute Tori by way of apology, then head inside to grab the liquor from the library bar and meet up with Reggie in the kitchen.

"The big pitcher is in the cupboard there," he says with a nod, "above the refrigerator."

I pull the pitcher down and set it next to the prep sink, where he washes stalks of celery and lays them out on a cutting board.

"Mr. P., how much do you know about this girl?" I ask. "You think it's serious? 'Cause I think it's serious."

He shrugs. "I'd say it's probably a little serious, given the number of times my son has introduced me to someone he's dating."

"My thoughts exactly. Any idea how long he's known her?" I grab for a celery stick and munch on it.

"Just since he's moved to New York, I think. So a few weeks maybe?"

I shake my head. "I just don't get it."

He trims up a stalk and puts it in a glass to showcase the flowery end, then grabs for another. "Get what?"

"Does it really happen that fast?"

He looks up, knife still in hand, considering me. "You want the truth, or do you want me to sugar coat it?"

"The truth," I say. "Always the truth."

"Yes, it does. And I can prove it to you."

Proof? Now he's speaking my language. "Hit me with the facts, ol' man." I lean forward and narrow my eyes at him, the granite counter sending chills up my arms. "Does this have to do with how you met Tori?"

"No," he waves a hand dismissively. "You've already heard that story a thousand times over the years."

"Then what proof could you possibly provide?"

"If I told you Tori found something in your bag of purchases from last night, would you have the faintest idea what I was talking about?"

"Uh..." My eyes go wide, then dart around the room. "Maybe."

"And if that was the case, you would've received that item, what, twelve hours ago?"

"Hypothetically," I say with a shrug.

"And by your frantic search through the trash this morning, maybe this is something you'd like to have back?"

Shit. "You saw that?"

He laughs in the maniacal way he's always had when we're in a battle of wits and he's winning. "Tori and I both saw you, actually. She gave me an elbow, and after you retreated to the porch she let me in on her little secret."

"Mr. P.," I lean in close and lower my voice, "please do not *eff* with me about this. Do you know where the note is?"

"Maybe." Another chuckle. "Hypothetically, if I did, what kind of scratch would you give me for it?"

"Dude." I walk around the island to the prep sink and stand in front of him. "I'm gonna level with you right now. If I can find that note, it's possible I can find this girl. I'd probably drop a Benjamin without blinking twice."

"Left that much of an impression, did she?"

I grip two sides of the counter with my hands and tip my head from side to side, trying to downplay my frustration. "Maybe."

He leans into my sight line. "After spending how much time with her?"

I look away. When I turn back, it's with bowed head and hands thrown in midair to display my defeat. "Point made, okay Mr. P.?"

But he's insistent, asking me again how much time we were in one another's company. I can feel his parental stare drilling my temples.

"Thirty minutes, okay? It was thirty *fascinating* minutes. And then she left the flour for me at the marina because she knew I needed it."

"And the note," he adds.

"Yes, and the note. You're really gonna hit this lesson home, aren't ya, Redge?"

"There's your proof," he says, pointing the knife in my direction before setting it aside. "That's all I'm saying." He assembles the booze and tomato juice, then stirs up the pitcher. "I'll tell you where your note is with one condition."

"Name it." *Please don't ask for a bottle of rare Scotch.*

"Ms. Greene may or may not be temporary in Aidan's life. But you have to realize in matters of the heart, three weeks can be like a lifetime. I think I made my point on that. So cut Aidan some slack, okay? Give the girl a chance."

"Yeah, of course," I say. "No disrespect intended. I'm just a little surprised, I guess."

"So were we. But I'd bet you the Garwood and this entire island that he was, too."

"Okay," I nod, "I'm with ya. I have an open mind on the whole subject." I wait, but he says nothing more. "So?" I say, palms up in question.

Where's the damn note?

"Your note is in there," he nods to the pantry. "Check under the quinoa."

"You guys are so cruel, Mr. P. Was that her idea or yours?"

"Hers," he laughs. "She knew you wouldn't check there."

I duck into the pantry, grab the note and exit as he completes his assembly line of salt-rimmed glass tumblers.

"Thanks, Redge."

"You're very welcome, Mr. Oates." He stirs up the pitcher of red liquid, tosses the spoon in the sink, and heads outside with Bloody Marys for a crowd. "See you out there."

I'm in the kitchen alone, breaking out in a cold sweat as I search the drawer next to the fridge for a working pen. After three dead felt tips, I finally score with a mechanical pencil. From the counter by the old wall phone, I grab a notepad with a dive shop logo and plant my ass on a stool at the island, talking to myself as I stare at the first two sentences.

"So if every capitalized letter represents a number, how many total..."

StraNger,

"Two in the first line..."

welComE tO the friendLiest countrY EVAH!

"...eight in the second line," I mutter. "Ten total."

Ho-lee shit.

She did.

I scribble the capitalized letters onto a sheet of paper.

N. C. E. O. L. E. V. A. H.

I tap my screen to wake it up and navigate to the phone keypad.

Six. Two. Three.

"Shit." The stupid screen goes black. I tap it awake again.

Six. Five. Nine. Three. Eight. Two. Four.

I pull up a Canadian search engine, then type the numbers in order. No name comes back associated, but I've confirmed the hunch I initially had last night.

"Ladies and gentleman," I mutter. I rip off the slip of paper and hold it in the air. "We have a cell number."

Hallelujah.

13

Pam

June 10, 2016
Friday, 12:50 p.m.

Bay Falls, Ontario
Canada

At almost one in the afternoon, I'm on my way back from Tim's with my second coffee of the day. I needed the pick-me-up. I was up early this morning after I tossed and turned until three a.m., wondering if the stranger found my note.

Before I drove for my usual caffeine fix at eight a.m., my first stop was the marina. I confirmed the note and the bag of flour were gone, and the SUV he drove last night was parked in the lot.

Sadly, he wasn't in it.

On to Tim's I went, but rather than hit the drive-thru, I went inside. I wasn't expecting to find him pining for me, still sitting there in the corner. *Okay, so maybe I daydreamed about the possibility for like five seconds.* But I knew he wouldn't actually be there, given the SUV was back in Bay Falls.

After last night, I couldn't get the guy out of my head. His tongue-in-cheek nerd shirt, how he radiated knowledge but not in a cocky kind of way. His voice was so sexy. He was confident yet endearing one minute and adorably tentative the next. Despite his good looks, he didn't seem the type that made flirting an art form.

He was just cute and charming without even trying, and I couldn't fight my urge to go back to the one place we'd spent time together. I stared at the cozy chairs by the fireplace like they held a secret, recalling our conversation while waiting for the gazillion people in queue ahead of me. With this distraction, waiting out the Friday morning rush was tolerable.

I arrived home to find Mum still tidying up for our guest. As it turns out, her efforts are beyond necessary. Last night, while I was having coffee with a handsome stranger and hunting down his flour, I replied to Alexis' text without even comprehending what her message had said.

She isn't staying with us this weekend after all.

She is coming up and can't wait to see me (that's the part of her text I did read), but then she said she'd be staying with friends this weekend. While I was out this morning, she called Mum to say she was already on her way to Canada and asked if I could pick her up this afternoon.

The strange part is, as far as I know, Alexis doesn't know anyone else in Canada besides me and my parents. And if she's driving up here now, I don't know why I'd have to pick her up.

Mum wasn't bothered by the change in plans. Alexis will be here for lunch today, allowing time to celebrate with our birthday cake for Ben. I think it's more important to Mum that Alexis and I have the chance to hang out. Plus, Mum always fusses herself into a panic over an overnight guest, so this means the pressure is off.

I'm cruising to pick up my *sistah-in-law* with a second caffeine fix situated in the cup holder. On my second trip to Tim's, I didn't go inside and spend time sulking over a couple of empty chairs. I blazed through the drive-thru and headed for the marina (also for a second time today).

This time, it's not because of my burning and possibly obsessive curiosity about the stranger. I'm going there because that's the address Alexis messaged to me an hour ago. I pull into the marina searching for her, but I don't see her or her convertible.

I also notice the Cadillac SUV is gone. *Sigh.* The handsome stranger is probably on his way back to California.

I exit the Mini and walk around to the passenger side, looking out at the river for boats heading in this direction. A luxury pontoon is crossing the channel toward the shore, but I'm doubtful Alexis is on board. That sucker's a couple hundred grand in American dollars, and I can't imagine any of her friends could afford that ride.

My phone rings to life inside the car, and I open the passenger door to grab for it. My heart races knowing there's a chance the cute stranger may have deciphered my hidden message, but it's my mother.

Dang.

"Mum?"

"Did you pick up Alexis yet?"

"Not yet. I'm here though." I hear the hum of an engine get closer as a boat pulls up, but I can't see it from here. The parking lot sits above the shoreline, so my view is obstructed. "Do you need something?"

"Just making sure you arrived in time. I didn't want you to keep her waiting."

"You worry too much. I was right on time." I turn to the winding, single lane road to my left, but there's no vehicle traffic whatsoever. "Do you know if she's coming by boat or by car?"

"She didn't say, hon. We didn't talk long."

"Wait a sec." I stand on tiptoe and see the fancy pontoon has pulled up here. I'm fairly certain Alexis is the person tying up the front line, but I can't see who the captain is. "I think she's here." She steps away from the boat and waves up at me frantically, and I wave back. "Yep, that's her. Gotta go."

"Drive safely."

"We're ten minutes away. We'll be fine, Mum. Love you." I disconnect and throw my phone into the car before I lock it. I walk a few paces towards the dock just in time to see Alexis in a lip lock with some guy.

Oh boy.

Embarrassed, I turn on my heel and head back to the car. No reason for me to interrupt a moment like that.

And definitely no reason for me to introduce her to Kyle Tremblay.

Looks like my girl's doing just fine on her own.

I'm so nervous when Alexis gets in the car, I spew words nonstop. I have no idea how to address the fact that she was just making out with some dude at the local marina. As of yesterday, I didn't realize she knew anyone else in this entire country, let alone someone in my hometown.

The country radio station plays softly through my car's stereo as I babble on about Carly's birthday night out, what a douche Mick is, how much I miss our mutual friend Charlie and the big dope of a dog that lives with Alexis, the same beast she shared with my brother.

Only minutes in, I talk about how well my third year at OCAD U went. We haven't even made it to the main road yet, but during a pause in my carrying on, I realize Alexis is softly crying.

"Aww, Lex." I pull open my glove box and point out the tissues. "What's up, eh? You all right?"

"Yeah," she sniffles. "I'm so sorry. These are happy tears. I'm so happy to see you, Pam."

"Totes don't believe you." I look over at her. "I mean, I know you're happy to see me, but something more is going on. You feel like talking about it?"

"It's so much." She blows her nose and dabs at her eyes. "I don't want to burden you."

"C'mon, my *sistah*." I smile at her as I turn the radio off. "You know you can tell me anything."

She takes a deep breath and grabs for another tissue. "I sort of met someone."

"Uh yeah," I laugh. As we reach a stop sign and wait for traffic to pass, I take my hands off the wheel to tighten my ponytail. "It sort of looked that way when we left just now."

"This is so awkward."

"Why?" I look over at her. "Because you were married to my brother?"

"Yes," she says, looking out the window. "I don't want to hurt anyone."

"Ben's gone, Alexis. I want you to be happy. So do my parents, and so would he."

"I know." She looks over at me and squeezes my hand. "I still miss him so much."

"Me too. But I also hoped you'd finally start dating. In fact, I was gonna set you up while you were here. But that was before I realized you were here with a guy, obvi."

"Get out," she laughs. "My little *sistah-by-love* was going to try and set *me* up?"

"Was," I say, "but forget it now. I don't think the guy you were kissing would be too happy about that."

"Uh, definitely not," she says, as though it's a huge understatement. "Girl, I've been through so much in the last few weeks. It's been a roller coaster."

"Well, begin at the beginning."

Alexis dives into everything that's been going on in her world, and she's right. It is a lot. Enough that I make the decision not to mention my swoon-worthy encounter with a handsome stranger last night. We've got enough to talk about.

Her new solo law firm almost suffered a disastrous blow when her highest-paying client was taken advantage of by a shady corporation, one that was out to deceive her entire county just to add to its bottom line.

"I almost led him right into their trap," she sighs. "I can't even believe it."

"I take it things have turned around?"

"Thanks to Aidan," she says, a tender smile coming over her. "They're definitely looking up."

"Oh, girrrl!" I reach out to shake her by the shoulder. "I can tell by your tone. That's the guy you were kissing, right?"

"Yes." I look over at her in time to see her face turn red. "My client is his uncle. But I only just found that out. I've been working with Aidan on this new project of his because the Bar Association assigned me to help him. He moved here from California to clean up Lake County."

"The whole county?" I blurt. "That seems...ambitious."

"Well, the City of Stanton and my little town of Mirror Lake, specifically. At least to start with. He's from there originally."

"Yikes," I mumble. "That's still a lot to take on. Ben said the poverty and drug problems in the city are pretty bad. I remember him saying there were parts of Stanton he hoped he'd never be sent to cover on assignment."

"He was right. There are some scary places I wouldn't be comfortable in, even though I'm familiar with the city after the time I spent at Stanton U. Anyway, I met Aidan a few weeks ago, and my world has been turned completely upside down ever since. He knows a lot about me, even about Ben."

"You mean you told him about your relationship?"

She nods.

Whoa. "And?"

"And he's totally fine with it. All of it."

"For reals?"

She nods again. "He's opened up to me a lot about himself, too, which isn't easy for him."

Dang. This is sounding pretty serious. And I can think of one litmus test to confirm very quickly just *how* serious.

"Has Charlie met him?" I ask.

"Oh, yeah."

"And what does he think?"

Her goofy smile returns. "Charlie thinks he's amazing."

"Whoa," I laugh. "Best friend approval." *This is definitely a big deal.*

"I know. I was surprised when Charlie pushed me to dive in headfirst. After Aidan and I started working together, things kind of progressed from there."

"Uh, define progressed," I tease.

She blushes again as she tells me her sexy-time dry spell is over with. "And then some," she laughs.

I ask her to give me some of the juicy details and in her own tasteful way (like any intelligent, self-respecting lawyer would), she drops hints about some of her recent escapades with the new man in her life.

"Damn! My sistah's got it goin' on!" We high five, and I grab for my coffee. "So you said this is a charitable project he's working on. Is he a philanthropist or what? I couldn't really see him very well from up in the parking lot. Is he, like, an older dude?"

"No," she laughs. "He's only a few years older than I am. And you could call him a philanthropist, I guess. He's got his hands in a lot of things."

"Like what?" I ask. "Organized crime?"

"No," she giggles again, nudging my arm. "He's kind of well off. And well-known in the States."

"Like how well off? Are we talking Kardashian famous and Zuckerberg rich?"

"Pretty darn close," she smiles. "And extremely smart, too."

A kilometer passes in silence, and she breaks the quiet to ask me if I'm comfortable with all this.

"He sounds awesome, Lex. Really." I squeeze her shoulder. "You've lived a lifetime since we saw each other last. Shoot, just in the last few weeks by the sounds of it."

"Yeah, that's why I'm kind of screwy. I'm sorry for the emotional outburst."

"Oh, please. We all ride the hot mess express sometimes. I just had to pick up Carly's pieces two nights ago. No worries."

"I've been so looking forward to seeing you."

"Me too," I say, unable to contain my smile. "I just wish you were staying longer."

"Yeah," she sighs. "Was your mom super disappointed?"

"I don't think so. She figured I was going to steal you away anyway, which I was. We could've crashed at Carly's place. She's in Manhattan and headed for Florida on Monday."

"I wish we could have done that," she says, "but Aidan's parents traveled all the way from California to be here."

"So where do they stay?" I sip from my straw again. I'm down to the last drop with only ice left in my cup.

"His parents are hosting us and their guests on this beautiful island. It's somewhere off the main channel." She looks out the window again as we pull onto my street. "We're staying in this adorable little two bedroom cabin. There's a gorgeous main house on the island too. His family calls it The Gables. "

I almost commit the epic sin of spitting out my last sip. I swallow hard.

"Get the frick out," I say, unable to withhold my shock. "The Gables? As in the big white house on Fawn Island?"

"I guess so," she shrugs. "You know I could never find my way around those islands. Ben and I only went out on the river a handful of times."

"Lex, is your boyfriend's last name Pierce?"

"Yeah. How'd you know that?"

I tell Alexis what little I know, how the family used to come up every summer, probably even before I was born.

"Then they just disappeared. Like boom," I say, flicking my fingers out. "Gone. You can't even believe how much I love that house. It's like my ultimate wish for it to be loved again." I leave out the part about trespassing around the island with Dave and Carly the other night.

"I haven't made it through the front door yet, but it looks pretty amazing. The whole island is."

"Well, I don't know much about your man, but I know *of* him. Rumors are crazy about why their family stopped coming here."

"They had a tragedy in their family," she says. "I think it kept them from coming back."

I turn and look at her as we pull in my parents' driveway. "And?"

"Aidan's younger brother," she says. "He was in an accident. He didn't survive."

"Oh God. That's just...wow. That's so sad. Was his brother a child when he passed?"

"Oh no, he had finished college, I think. It's been years since his death. Still, I was worried about coming up here, spending time in a place that Aidan hasn't visited since his brother passed. No one in the family has been back since."

I release a heart-heavy sigh. "Well, I'm glad they're back. Their house is my absolute *fave*. And I hope they fall in love with the islands all over again."

"I know I have," she sighs. "And I've missed you. I wish Ben and I had come up here more often, especially in this weather. It's just stunning."

"Right?" I say, cutting the engine. "It's going to be a gorgeous weather weekend, too. I'd flip to get a tour of that property you're staying in. You've hit the jackpot, *sistah*."

"Why don't you come back with me?" she asks. "Aidan says the more the merrier, and I can actually spend some quality time with you and not disappoint him or his parents."

I have my door open and one foot on the ground when I realize what she's just offered.

"There's plenty of room," she urges. "What do you say?"

What *can* I say?

Holy crap? I'm legit obsessed with that place?

Thanks for making my dreams come true?

I turn and look at her with the cheesiest grin in the history of cheesy grins.

"What do I say?" I climb back into the car, grab her by the shoulders and kiss her on the cheek. "I say *abso-frickin-lutely* yes!"

14

Oates

June 10, 2016
Friday, 12:50 p.m.

Bay Falls, Ontario
Canada

We're on our way to the marina to drop off Alexis. She's headed elsewhere for the afternoon. I enjoyed meeting her, but I'm looking forward to a few hours of guy time. Bonus, it'll just be Aidan and me to greet Nate when he arrives.

"Do we have to go into town to fetch your big surprise?" he asks. "It's gonna be a helluva ride if we do."

"What are you driving now?" My friend has always loved cars. (And boats, and motorcycles. Essentially any mode of transportation to carry him away from his problems, if only briefly.) Given he can afford to drive whatever the hell he wants, it's no shock to me that he takes advantage of it.

"2016 i8."

"A Beemer?" I can't help laughing. "Seems kind of yuppie, even for you."

"It's borrowed, and it's anything but yuppie." He steers the boat to the dock with the same confidence he's always had.

"My surprise will be delivered to us here," I say. "Good thing, too, because it wouldn't fit in that tin can you're borrowing."

"Tin can?" he bristles. He looks to Alexis for confirmation. "It's one fine ass machine, isn't it babe?"

Babe? I look away so he can't see my wide-eyed reaction. *God, it's worse than I thought.*

"Definitely," she says. "Almost as slick as the driver." She's distracted, her gaze fixed uphill toward the parking lot as she ties the bow line. "I see Pam!" She waves frantically, then walks towards the stern as Aidan shuts off the engine.

"Who's Pam?" I'm sitting in the back of the boat as Alexis stands behind me tying up the back line. My head rests on the cushioned sun deck behind me. I'm not in any rush to get up. I'm still beat after my restless night, and Nate's not due here for another half hour.

"She's my sister-in-law."

I jolt upright. "You're married?"

Or does she have a brother who is?

But she doesn't hear me. She's checking the cleat at the front of the boat.

"Was," Aidan says, stepping away from the wheel. "Her husband passed away."

Well, shit.

"Jeez, I'm sorry," I mumble. "I didn't know."

He gives me his typical 'way to go, Oates' look before he steps off the boat. "That's why you should keep your mouth shut, asshat."

"Agreed," I say, saluting his way in affirmation.

Aidan is fidgeting with the boat key, turning it over in his hands until Alexis walks back to us. I catch a look pass between them. He seems uneasy about parting company with her.

"I'm gonna hang here, guys," I say. "My surprise is a half hour out."

"You two should go for a ride or something," she suggests. "I'll see you back here what, about four?"

Aidan agrees reluctantly, and as she heads for shore, he follows. While he sees his sweetheart off, I pull out my phone to text Zach.

> I'm batting zero here.
> Batman. Is. Done-zo.

Dude. I told you.

> The world is doomed.

Gotham will burn. Sorry, man.

Vegas in T-minus eight hours!!
You can still make it back if you
hop a plane now.

> *It's not so bad here. Weather's*
> *good. Beer is chilled. I'll stick*
> *it out.*

What's his girl like?
Supermodel? Royalty?
Tattooed bad girl with a daddy
complex?

> *Triple-threat Lawyer.*
> *Pretty. Funny. Smart.*

Shit. Did you just hear that?

> *Hear what?*

The sound of MML losing half
of everything he owns.

> *Ha! Entirely possible.*
> *He calls her babe.*

No shit?

> *Dead serious.*

Fuck his life. I'll tell Finn we won.

> *Do your worst.*
> *I admit defeat.*

I watch Aidan and Alexis as they take turns talking on his phone. After he disconnects, he kisses her goodbye in a public display of affection worthy of a Nick Sparks movie before Alexis heads up to the parking lot.

My phone pings with another text.

Finn says we expect the bottle
of Scotch by next week.
Distillery will be chosen by
tomorrow. Have fun being a
third wheel.

> *Nate's gonna be here soon. I've*
> *got a fourth.*

Rocket Man cometh? Better let
him know what he's flying into.

> Did. Text him as soon as I met the girl.

At least you two losers can hang together.

> Whatever, dick. Enjoy ogling strippers on the Strip.

You have fun staying single while we mingle.

> If I had any cash left, I'd bet you end up paying to get laid.

I'd stop betting if I was in your Chucks. You already lost once today.

> Fuck off.

Thanks. I will.

> Sorry, I meant fuck off and die.

Don't drown in the river of love sickness out there.

> Noted. Watch out for Toxic Tonyas. (And herpes.)

I check to see if I have any other new messages, excited to see one came in thirty minutes ago.

As soon as I figured out my fascinating mystery girl's code, I programmed her cell number into my phone. I assigned her a simple but suitable moniker, which will have to do until she responds so I can ask her real name. I sent her a message before we left the island and successfully forced myself not to check for her reply every five minutes.

The unread message isn't from her, though. It's from Nate.

Between flights, he responded to my message from this morning that forewarned Aidan's riding a love-induced serotonin high. I laugh out loud at Nate's response — a crap ton of question marks and a *WTF*. As Aidan saunters back up to the boat, I fib to keep my surprise intact.

"What's funny?"

"Ah, nothing. Just Zach being Zach." I look up at my friend and realize how much of a one-eighty he's done since I saw him last.

He's not stressed to the max as he was when his relationship with Stella hit the skids, not haggard like he was in LA last month. He looks healthy and, dare I say, happy. I suppose reeling in someone like the bright and beautiful Ms. Greene would do that for a guy.

That and, if I had to guess at gunpoint, I'd say he's getting laid left, right, and sideways. (Repeatedly.)

But he also looks a little concerned.

"Everything okay?"

"Yeah, great," he says. "Why?" He turns the boat key over and over in his hand again.

"You seemed hesitant about Ms. Greene's departure."

After a long pause, he admits there's been some shit hitting the fan back in Stanton.

"What kind of shit?" I ask.

"Corporate conspiracy, people turning up missing. I'm a little concerned for her safety."

"Jesus. Was she already involved in this when you met her?"

He shakes his head. "A colleague of hers was, and it's a situation I was familiar with before I met her. One she wouldn't have been in, if it hadn't been for me. I'm trying to keep her out of the crossfire, but we're up to our necks in it now."

"Jesus, man. Why didn't you say anything?"

He shakes his head, dismissing my concern. "She's mixed up in it because of the land purchase from my uncle. She's his lawyer."

"Damn." *So that's how they met.* "She seems capable, though. And I'm sure she's fine up here, right? I mean, if it's her in-laws she's hanging with, that seems safe. You're far enough away from this corporate B.S. in Stanton, right?"

"Yeah." He stands on the dock looking up river, contemplative. "It's nothing you need to worry about. The less you know, the better."

"Fair enough, but I'm still wondering why you didn't tell me about *her* before now."

He looks back at me with furrowed brow.

"Were you embarrassed of me or of her?"

"C'mon, man." He puts on his shades and turns away, arms crossed as he eyes a passing jet ski.

"It's a fair question," I say.

"That's a bullshit question."

"One you can't answer?"

He walks back to me. "The answer is I'm not embarrassed either way." He leans his head in the boat and looks back at me, forearms resting on the metal roof. "I wanted to introduce you two, and I wanted it to be a surprise. Are you really giving me shit because I didn't tell you first?"

I shrug. "I'm just surprised you kept it under your hat all this time. It was definitely a surprise, but my kudos to you both. I'm happy for ya, man."

"Not that I need your approval," he says with a tentative smile, "but thanks."

"You're welcome, and you should know my surprise is even more unbelievable than yours. Bigger. Better. Amazing, even."

"Maybe, but you have to admit she's pretty amazing." He can't help his smile from widening into a dopey grin.

"She definitely beats Stella in the sanity and smarts categories, so that's a plus." I pocket my phone and sit forward. "So, when's the wedding?"

"Whoa," he says. "Slow your roll there, brother. We've known each other three weeks." He does a few push-ups using the roof to brace himself, then drums his hands over it.

"Uh huh." He's as blind as a bat trying to fly at noon. Even his father realizes the significance of three weeks' time. I look at my watch, stand up and stretch. "Let's take that ride after all. We've got twenty-five minutes to kill."

I try to move past him, but the fucker's solid and slightly taller than I am. Just standing there he takes up the entire exit.

"What's the hurry?"

"I wanna head over to the next town which takes twelve minutes. We have to get back here by one-thirty."

"What's in Gan? I thought you said the surprise was coming to us."

"It is. But I've got a craving for some coffee. You feel like some coffee?" *Maybe going back there will put a halt to my daydreaming.*

"No, man. I don't."

"Well, I do." He finally lets me pass, and I walk down the dock backwards, nodding towards the parking lot. "Time to blend in with the locals. Maybe get us a double-double. There's a Tim Horton's down the road."

He reaches into the boat, tucks the key away in a hidden compartment and grabs his car keys. "That's our ill-timed Oates," he laughs, smacking the roof as he pushes off and heads in my direction. "Wanting coffee when it's beer-thirty."

I face forward and keep walking, raising an arm high as I flip him the bird.

"It's okay, freshman," he says as he catches up to me. "We can get you a little pick-me-up."

He clicks the fob for the Beemer and the gull-wing doors open. The car is electric blue and, yeah, it's pretty sweet looking — but I'm not about to tell him that.

We climb in and he fires up the machine. "You ready?"

I monkey with the Bluetooth settings and within seconds, my phone is rigged up. Lenny Kravitz blares as he nods in acceptance of my choice. Pierce's taste in music is always on point, an absolute requirement for anyone I choose to spend waking hours with.

"Yeah," I say. "I'm ready."

He cranks the volume even louder, and off we go down the parkway.

We pull into the drive-up line at Tim's and I stare into the restaurant, instantly bummed. She's not staring back at me from the front window. Her car isn't in the lot.

Of course she's not here. It's nearly one-thirty in the afternoon on a Friday.

No one's here.

In truth, I couldn't give a shit about coffee, and a cold beer does sound pretty good. Instead, I order a small iced double-double to save face (and in honor of my Canadian princess). Pierce takes off, driving us back up the parkway at a pretty good clip. I can't admit to him there was a method to my madness, an insane reason for this mission: hoping I'd run into her.

But I do manage to compliment his borrowed ride.

"This thing is pretty hot. Maybe I'll get one."

"You could certainly afford it. Too bad it'd sit and collect dust with as much as you work."

"I've been thinking about cutting back," I shrug. "Hopefully if my app takes off or sells high, I'll have the option."

He looks at me to gauge my sincerity and sees I'm being real. "Life's short, man. I say go for it."

"If I had a hot chick as a distraction, maybe I'd seriously consider it." His grin widens into the 'I'm a lovesick amoeba' version, and I punch him on the arm. "Yep, I knew it."

"You knew what?" He puts on his blinker and pulls in the lot.

"Pierce, you dumb fuck. You're smitten. You're a smitten kitten, bruh."

He laughs, but not in his typical 'Oates, you're so wrong' kind of way. It's more like 'yeah, but so what?'

"Shit, man. I can see it comin' a mile away."

He narrows his eyes at me, back to his wicked serious self. "What do you think you see coming?"

"To put it bluntly? Brother, you're fucked." My phone vibrates and pings from my pocket to indicate an incoming text.

Maybe it's her.

I'm so anxious at the thought that my hands fumble and I drop the phone. I grab it off the spotless black floor mat, then adjust my glasses so I can see.

Two texts!

The first message is from Nate with his ETA (three minutes).

The second message is from Finn with his distillery choice and a website link I can use to place an order for delivery post-haste.

Dammit. Not her.

"I think your surprise is here." Aidan nods his head to the van that pulls in and parks ahead of us.

"Yeah, man!" I pocket my phone as I get out of the car. Pierce opens his door and stands up, shooting me a look over the roof of the Beemer. He's confused as hell, and I'm basking in the moment because, for once, he's the last to know.

I lean up against the car, calm as can be while the shuttle driver steps out. He retrieves a bag from the back of the van, drops it on the pavement, and climbs back into the driver's seat. Nate leans up from the back to tip the guy, then steps out of the sliding door, much to Pierce's amazement.

"Holy fuck," he says as his head jerks back. "You didn't."

"I did indeed, man." I turn to him as I drum roll over the roof of the i8. "Surprise!"

Our mutual friend steps towards us as the shuttle drives off. "Nate Edwards," Pierce mumbles, still in shock. "Ho-lee shit."

Nate's dressed down in jeans and flip flops, but he doesn't look harried by the hours he's spent traveling. He's kind of like Pierce in that way. He always looks good unless there are extraordinary circumstances preventing sleep, hydration, or nutrition. Although with Nate, that sometimes comes with his job.

"Pierce, ya bastard!" He pulls off his shades and tucks them into the collar of his Cal Tech shirt before pulling Aidan into a strapping bro hug. "Did we get ya?" He steps back to size him up, rendering Pierce speechless. "Oates," Nate says, "tell me we got him."

"Look at him," I say. "Dude can't even talk. It was a solid plan, bruh."

"Bring it in, man." Nate throws up his hand to shake mine. "Can't believe you pulled it off." He lets me go and steps away to grab his bag. "God, it's great to be up here."

"What the fuck, guys," Aidan says. "You couldn't tell me we were having this little reunion?"

"I wasn't sure I could make it," Nate says. "It was last minute. You look great, man." He lays a hand on Aidan's shoulder. "I hear you got a woman."

"You'll meet her later." Aidan shoots me his reprimanding glare before his attention is back on Nate. "What the hell are you doing here?"

"I asked Oates if he had the weekend free, turns out he was coming here. Figured I'd join the party. I've gotta be in Florida by Monday."

"I'm honored to host the man on a rare weekend off," Aidan says. "Heading back to Kennedy next week?"

"Yeah." He tosses his bag over his shoulder. "Duty calls."

Nate's definitely the smartest of the three of us. We're used to him being out of touch for months at a time, given most of his contracted jobs are top secret. But when we're hanging out, it's your typical gathering of three college buddies reminiscing and seeing who can best outsmart or insult the other.

"Well," Pierce says, "I'm certainly thrilled as fuck you're here."

Silence falls on us for a second, and I recall what Nate said the other day. The last time the three of us were all together was the funeral for Aidan's brother Thad.

"Guys." After our quiet moment of recognition passes, I clap my hands to reel everyone back in. "We've got a short amount of time to catch up and rage out. Aidan has to be back for his sweetie in," I glance at my watch, "oh, two hours and thirteen minutes. What's first?"

"Let's head back to the Gables for lunch and fishing. We'll rage out later," Aidan promises.

"You're lucky my brain could use some soaking up of nature n' shit," I laugh. "Later, we're partying like it's fuckin' ninety-nine."

After lunch courtesy of Tori, the three of us are on the main dock occupying the Adirondack chairs each with a cold beer and a fishing pole close by. Nate prods Aidan to tell him about Alexis.

"Dude's fucking done for," I say. "*Done-zo.* Toast."

"Gone to the dark side, have ya?" Nate asks.

I'm not surprised by Nate's skepticism. One bad relationship left him bitter right out of grad school, and now he doesn't date. I don't know if he's celibate, but given his work, I wouldn't be surprised if his only outlet is a cold (or longer than usual) shower.

"If you consider happiness the dark side," Aidan says, "then yeah. I guess so."

"Ohh," Nate laughs. "So she makes you *happy*? Oates is right. You're burnt toast, motherfucker."

"Maybe," he says, "but I'm not the only one."

For a split second, panic sets in.

Who the fuck's he talking about?

No one knows about my run-in with the pretty girl in the tiara. And that wouldn't qualify anyway.

Right?

"Who else is drinking the Kool Aid?" I reel in a fish, hoping my tone doesn't convey my unease.

"You guys will never guess in a million years."

I sigh in relief and toss my perch back. *He's definitely talking about someone else.*

Nate takes a swig of his beer. "Cameron Mays."

"What?" I burst into laughter and Aidan joins in. Cameron was the poor bastard Nate pulled his genius pranks on at Cal Tech (including the one with the lawn-mowing robot). "I can't believe you said that with a straight face. That guy's nerdier than I am. He couldn't score with a free hooker."

As our laughter recedes, Aidan says that's not who he's referring to. "Guess again."

"I can only think of one other person we all know who we still have contact with," Nate says. "There's absolutely no way it's him. Hell has not frozen over, and I can tell you for a fact the Earth has not stopped spinning."

And then it hits me.

Aidan's brother befriended a guy by the name of Dimitri when Aidan and I first met. By the end of his short life, Thad considered Dimitri his best friend. Over the years, the four of us hung out on occasion.

To look at them, their friendship seemed unlikely. But Dimitri was a hacker back then and had intelligence and sarcasm in common with Thad. Dimitri fit into our group of nerdy, smart-ass misfits easily.

Chicks ate him up, too, though usually a different kind of chick than the type Aidan and Thad went for. The Pierce men could pass for distant relatives of JFK (without the Beantown accents).

In contrast, everything about Dimitri Floros is dark. He's covered in black tattoos, smokes half a pack a day, and his preferred mode of transportation is an old black Harley he won on a high-stakes bet. His methods were used for good but sometimes they fell outside the law.

Now, he's on the up-and-up. Somewhere outside LA, he manages a Harley dealership by day, and at night works at the tattoo shop he owns two doors down; the same one that's built a rep for catering to the most discerning bikers. Meanwhile, he's refused attention from multiple Hollywood types who think his Sons of Anarchy meets Good Will Hunting story would make a great reality show.

I haven't seen him since Thad's funeral, but every once in awhile Pierce fills me in on how he's doing or we connect remotely to work together on something. Pierce hasn't mentioned him in several months, but he definitely fits Pierce's description as the last guy we'd guess would fall victim to this love bullshit.

"I know who it is."

Pierce looks my way and smiles, realizing I've figured it out.

"I don't believe it." Nate looks at Aidan. "Dimitri?"

Pierce casts again and nods in affirmation, then empties his second beer.

"Holy shit, man." Nate finishes his, too, setting his empty bottle on the dock. "It's an epidemic."

"Nate," I say, "please tell me you can save me from this zombie apocalypse. You got an antidote?"

"No one has an antidote for this," Pierce says. "Once you're tapped, you pegged it exactly right. Toast. Game over."

"Goddamn," I mutter. *Maybe I'm glad I didn't hear back from the princess after all.* "Pierce, can we please get my start-up off the ground before you're too far gone?"

"Deal," he says. "Let's go up to the house now and go over the birth plan for your baby."

I'm on my laptop going over everything Pierce and I have just discussed. As I sit at the kitchen island, Reggie comes in looking for his son.

"I left him in the library," I say. "I think he's still there."

Reggie nods and heads in that direction.

Nate's down at the boathouse getting settled and cleaned up after all his traveling. We're meeting back on the main dock at quarter to four so we can take a quick cruise before we pick up Alexis.

My meeting went well. Pierce's concerns were as I anticipated. My business plan has great bones, but it needs some polishing, and there are a few factors I hadn't considered. On the up side, we could be sitting pretty for Phase Two by next month, after Aidan's first big charity gala back in Lake County is behind him. If that goes well, Phase Three will be a launch no later than the end of August.

I research a couple of companies he told me to keep tabs on, ones that weren't even on my radar as competition.

Tori waltzes in and shakes her head at me. "More work, hmm? Do you ever relax?"

"Just following up on some things your son so wisely pointed out during our meeting."

"I see. And did you find what you were looking for this morning?"

My fingers halt over the keys as I look up. "That was dirty pool, Mamasita."

She winks at me. "Just figured I'd test your resolve, Daryl. Were you able to connect with her again? Reggie said something about you having a way to find her."

I look back at my screen and shake my head and, in the same moment, my phone pings with a text.

I glance down at it.

1 New Message

From: Princess Problem Solver

15

Pam

June 10, 2016
Friday, 3:30 p.m.

Bay Falls, Ontario
Canada

I'm alone in my bedroom and pacing in front of my closet. Panic mode is in full effect.

Within ten minutes of our arrival, Alexis asked my parents if they'd let me tag along with her this weekend. Of course they said yes, without even knowing where she'd be taking me. She didn't go into details about the Pierce family or even reveal that she was seeing someone. She just said she was staying with some friends on a nearby island and left it at that. Given how much they trust her, that's all my parents needed to know before saying they had no concerns.

Not that they'd stop me anyway. *No way am I turning down that invite!*

When it comes to Alexis' love life, I don't think it's my place to tell my parents diddly squat, so I didn't provide more detail either. She managed to find herself a boyfriend (finally), and I'm over the moon happy for her. Given her unorthodox relationship with Ben, the way she suddenly found herself alone at age 29, and her incredibly selfless heart, she deserves the hottest guy on the planet showering her with attention.

By some crazy twist of fate, it looks like the hottest guy on the planet is exactly who roped her in on her first run out of the gate.

Mum pulled Alexis out to the back porch for a hand of rummy, and as soon as she did, I typed her new man's name into a search engine on my phone. The guy is smokin' hot, at least in the gazillion photos that popped up. The list of articles about him was endless. At first scroll, I noticed one about him helping another rich dude fund wells for fresh water in a third world country a few years back, then another about a standing ovation he received as a guest speaker at Yale (which happens to be his grad school alma mater).

So the guy's no slouch, but whether he's good enough for my *sistah* remains to be seen.

If someone had told me Alexis would hook up with the likes of Aidan *frickin'* Pierce, the first born son of the family that owns The Gables, I'd have insisted they were at least out of touch with reality, if not certifiable. Once I found out a few facts about him, I started to wonder if somehow since Carly left for New York, I've been living in an alternate reality.

Alexis is spending the weekend getting to know the Pierce family on that gorgeous island, and she invited me along for the ride. I get to sleep at The Gables, the property I've been dreaming about since I was a kid. I'll be hanging out with my beloved sister-in-law, her new boyfriend, and his super wealthy parents (and probably their uber rich friends).

No biggie, eh?

Pfft. Right.

Never mind having no idea which fork is for the salad at dinner (except I do know, because *Pretty Woman*, obviously), but I have no idea what to wear for such an occasion.

I need my best friend, but I hesitate to interrupt her afternoon in Manhattan. I debate with myself another five minutes in front of an open closet.

It's no use. I must have third party input.

Alexis is still busy visiting with Mum, so I search for my phone to text Carly only to realize I abandoned it in the kitchen when I was helping Dad clean up after dessert.

Crap.

It's after three o'clock. I have less than thirty minutes to figure out what I'm taking so I can deliver Alexis back to the marina on time. I rush out to the kitchen and find Dad busy making two cocktails.

"What's the occasion?" I ask.

"Dunno," he shrugs. "Mum asked me to pour a couple pops and add some rum, so I obliged." He gives me a wink as he puts the liquor back in the cabinet above the refrigerator. "You all packed?"

"Not even close," I laugh. I grab my phone off the counter, kiss him on the cheek, and head back to my room.

We had lunch after we arrived, then celebrated Ben's birthday with my chocolate cake. Carly's recipe didn't disappoint. Before serving it, I pulled the candles out of the package and topped the cake, lost in thought about the moment I first laid eyes on my Perfect Stranger.

Given he hasn't managed to call or text me, I'm considering new names for him.

Either he hadn't cracked my code (Tall, Dark and Dimwitted?), or he didn't have the guts to text me once he figured it out (Prince Petrified). I suppose either way, I'm better off not talking to him again.

I snap a picture of my sad wardrobe with my phone, then tap out a text to Carly about my unbelievable situation and resulting fashion predicament. When I close out of the sent text menu, I notice I have a new message from an unknown number.

I completely missed it with all my excitement after Alexis' invite, and lunch, and cake.

Oh. Holy. Night.

It's gotta be from him.

Please don't be something crass.

I cringe, closing one eye as I open the text.

> *Good afternoon, I'm looking*
> *for Princess Problem Solver, so*
> *I can thank her for saving my*
> *life. Might this be her? (Please*
> *note:*

Seeking Canadian Nerd Princess
spelling with regular dot only.
US imposters spelling with
hearts or circles over the 'I'
need not reply.)
Sincerely,
Stranger With Flour

Before I can figure out what I think of this, Carly's number appears on my screen. I click accept, and she doesn't even give me a chance to say hello.

"What the hell is going on, eh?" she shouts over the noise of clanging pots and pans. "You're going where? And make it fast, I'm on a five second break."

"I don't know what's going on," I laugh. "Alexis is dating the son of the family that owns the Gables. She invited me to hang there for the weekend."

"Holy shitballs! Your sistah got a new mistah?"

"She did."

"Guess that leaves Jay's older brother for you. And that's crazy-amazing you got invited! You're spending the whole weekend over there?"

"Yes, which is exactly why I need to know what to wear around these sophisticated cats. Look at the photo I sent and tell me what to pack."

"I'm thinking your usual sundresses and sandals will be plenty to wow them."

"Doubtful, but probably my only option besides the gown I wore in Ben's wedding. Or the beat up t-shirt and leggings I exercise in."

"Sundresses, sunglasses, and sandals," she insists. "Make sure the sunglasses and your purse are big. Rich people do that. And definitely pack the sky blue dress. No wait, you should wear that now for first impressions."

I scrunch my shoulder to hold the phone to my ear, then pull the recommended dress out of my closet. "Are you totes sure? It's strapless."

"It holds you well," she says. "You'll be stunning. Trust me."

"I do, Carlsbad." I grab for a couple more dresses that hold up without wrinkling and toss them on my bed. "I already took some of your advice."

"What advice?"

"I borrowed your flour and left it for the stranger I met at Metro."

She gasps, apparently more blown away than before. "Get the fuck out. And?"

"He got it along with the note I left with my phone number encrypted in it. I just opened a text from him."

"He must be a little smart at least?" She's eating something, the crunch deafening my ears. "I mean if he figured that out."

"When we had coffee, he claimed he was a nerd. Pretty sure he's hella smart."

"Dammit," she groans. *Crunch. Crunch.* "The second I leave, everything good happens! What did he say? Did he send a dick pic?"

"No!" I laugh. "Just a message. And P.S., gross."

"I know, right? I don't know why guys do that. Not sexy."

"Agreed. Makes me cringe almost as much as your crunching."

"Sorry," she says. "This five seconds is also my late lunch break. And dick pics. *Ugh,*" she goes on, ignoring me. "I mean, *seriously.* What asshole first thought that was a great idea? Like an incredibly dim bulb goes off over his head and he thinks, oh, I know! I'll text her a picture of my junk!"

I laugh as I grab for my Vera Bradley tote off the closet floor and start filling it. "I have no idea, girl. Thank God I've never been in that position."

"If I could track down the first guy that ever did that, I'd make an example out of him. I'd take out a billboard with his dick pic. No!" she says. "Even better. I'd get it on the digital ones in Times Square and plaster the guy's name all over it! Ha!" *Crunch crunch.* "That would serve him right."

"You are terrible."

"Could you imagine if there was such a thing as dick pics when your parents were young? Your mum would literally *die.* Like—"

"God, Carly, that's gross. Just *stop.* Stop *right* there. And anyway, I can't see him doing that. He seems too—"

"Boring?"

"No. Too..." I twirl my hands in the air, searching for words.

"I don't know. Gentlemanly, I guess. Like he holds doors open for ladies and has proper manners."

"Doesn't mean he can't send a picture with his photo-bombing dick and then say 'you're welcome'."

"Good Lord," I laugh. "My gut says that's a no from him. Not this guy."

"Well what *did* he say?" In the background, some guy hollers Carly's name and she tells him to keep his pants on.

"I'll screenshot it to you."

"What are you going to say back?"

"I don't know!" More hollering travels from her work space through the phone. "You should go. I don't want to get you in trouble."

"Ugh, you're right. Please have an amazing time over there and take pictures of that kitchen for me!"

"I will. Love you."

"Love you. Call me when the Fawn Island spell is broken."

I disconnect as I think about what to say back to my Perfect Stranger.

I don't want to ignore him, but I don't want to overthink my response, either. I won't see him again, so what's the point of drawing this out? His message was sweet, but really, it's just a thank you. He's not asking to see me again.

Reception can sometimes be hit or miss away from the mainland, so I don't want to wait until we get to Fawn Island to reply. Alexis needs to be back at the marina in twenty minutes. It takes ten to drive there, and so far the only things in my bag are underwear and a pair of slip-on sneakers.

I compose my message, take a deep breath, and hit send.

> Stranger With Flour, You have reached the correct princess.
> I hope you will put the flour to good use. Since you deciphered my silly code, I have decided to upgrade your status from Stranger to the high honor of Nerd.
> Cheers, Princess

I pull the Mini into the parking area of the marina at exactly four p.m.

Whew.

Given the way I saw Aidan Pierce kiss my *sistah* goodbye (and now fully aware of the influential kinda guy he is), the last thing I want to do is be late bringing her back.

I'm nervous as all get out to meet Mr. Pierce and his parents, and simultaneously, I'm like a kid on Christmas. I'm legit about to step foot on Fawn Island because I was invited. Alexis tells me she confirmed with him by text that I was more than welcome to join her for the weekend.

"I've never met rich people before," I mumble. "Not like these folks." I smooth out my dress and ask Alexis if I look okay.

She responds with her sweet, genuine laugh. "They're totally normal," she says. "I promise." She tells me not to worry as she looks me up and down. "And you look amazing in that dress."

"You don't think the strappy sandals are too much?" I kick a foot out to scrutinize my choice. "I mean, I'm tall enough as it is. I probably should've worn flip flops."

She shakes her head. "The sandals are dressier. And you won't feel out of place around this crew. They're all pretty tall, even Aidan's mom."

"I'm just so *excited*," I say. "I gotta get a grip!"

She comes over and gives my bare shoulders a squeeze. "It's just a weekend with some friends, okay?" She gives me a big sister smile to reassure me. "No biggie."

"Right, no biggie." I exhale a huge breath as Alexis steps a few paces away, looking towards the dock.

"That's them," she says, looking down at the boat that's just pulled up. She stands with her arms crossed, watching whatever is going on when it dawns on me.

Them?

I lock up the Mini, toss my key in my bag, and walk over to join her.

I drop my duffel as I catch sight of her boyfriend stepping off the boat. He's dressed differently than when I saw him earlier. I think he was wearing jeans then.

He's now in sneakers, shorts, and a t-shirt with the sleeves cut off and a washed out beer logo on the front. His aviator shades are hiding his eyes. He ties the bow line, and I can tell from his movements he's hurrying so he can get to his girl.

Another guy on the boat has his eyes closed, his head back while doing absolutely nothing. He's wearing a preppy collared shirt.

And then there's the third guy.

The one who I can't take my eyes off of.

He's tying up the stern line, squatting down, and facing away from me. But there's something about that squat that looks familiar.

That and the ink-black curls hanging to his shoulders. The kicks that, even from here, I can tell are Converse.

Holy crap on a cracker!

This is nuts.

Metro grocery. That's where I've seen all this before. Except this time he's in shorts, so his legs are exposed.

And tan. And muscular.

Sweet Lord!

He stands up and turns our way, but he doesn't see us.

Nevertheless, I'm right. It's him.

"Who is that?" I ask Alexis, trying not to lose my shit.

She looks in the direction of the men. "The guy tying up or the other guy?"

"Not the guy in the salmon colored shirt that stayed on the boat. And Aidan would be the one who was kissing you goodbye, obviously. Who's the other one? He's got glasses."

"Oh, that's Oates," she says matter-of-factly. "Aidan's best friend. I have no idea who the third guy is."

Seriously?

My mystery guy is the best friend of Aidan *frickin'* Pierce.

Mr. Pierce is hustling up the concrete incline as my Perfect Stranger lags several feet behind, his eyes focused on his feet. I turn my attention to Alexis' new boyfriend as he approaches us on a dead run.

"So that's Aidan, huh?"

She nods, a grin plastered on her face like she was just told she won a bazillion dollars.

Seeing him up close, I can't blame her. He's *effing hawt,* and when I can't help blurt "wow" under my breath, she forgives me with a laugh. She must be used to that reaction from any woman who catches sight of him.

Alexis is still giggling when he reaches her and literally sweeps her off her feet. He spins her around like she's the heroine in a Hollywood movie, and I grin ear-to-ear with happiness for her. She so deserves a guy like that. He plants a kiss on her that almost leaves *me* seeing stars, then he whispers something in her ear.

I turn my attention back to the gentleman I've daydreamed about for nearly twenty-four hours and realize he stopped to look at his phone.

He could be reading my text this very second.

Gah!

He pockets his phone and keeps walking, but I notice the corners of his mouth upturn even as he looks at his feet.

Aidan hollers over Alexis' head to his friend, telling him there's an unescorted female who needs a hand down to the boat and that he should hurry up.

Oh, good Lord.

"Hi," Mr. Pierce says to me. He steps forward, offering his hand and a friendly smile. "Aidan Pierce."

"Pam Clayton," I say as we shake. "Good to meet you, Mr. Pierce."

"Please call me Aidan," he says. "Alexis tells me you're off from University for the summer?"

"I am. Just completed my third year at OCAD U."

"Great school," he says. "Toronto, right?"

"Yes." I throw Alexis a look. *How does he know that?* She shrugs at me as if to say this kind of thing happens all the time.

So, he's smart enough to have heard of my school. Friendly. Wealthy. Extremely hot. Definitely hospitable, if he's invited a perfect stranger to stay the weekend with his family, and his best friend.

Lex very well may have hit the jackpot for reals.

I turn away and see the stranger coming up to us with some serious swagger. For whatever reason, he's still paying more attention to the pavement below his feet than anything else. But his guy-on-a-mission gait is on full throttle until he reaches us.

He dials down his confident walk as soon as he gets close to me, then halts in his tracks. His gaze travels from my feet all the way up to my eyes in slow motion, his mouth slightly hanging open. I smile with a knowing grin as we lock eyes.

Watching him realize we're meeting again is a priceless moment I will never forget.

Neither of us can seem to find any words to say.

Alexis saves us by offering proper introductions. "Daryl Oates," she says, "I'd like you to meet my sister-in-law, Pam Clayton. She's going to stay the weekend with us. Pam, this is Aidan's friend, Daryl, also lovingly referred to as Oates."

We just stand there staring at each other with matching grins.

"Pam is heading into her senior year at OCAD U," Aidan says to break the odd silence.

"No kidding?" His eyes don't leave mine. "What are you studying?"

"Digital Futures."

His grin widens in obvious appreciation. "Right this way, mademoiselle." He turns around so we're facing the same direction, grabs my duffel from the pavement, then offers me his right arm. "I'd be glad to escort you to our watercraft."

I laugh at his over the top schmoozing as we walk arm-in-arm down the pavement. Once we're several paces away, he looks behind us.

"What are they doing?" I whisper.

"Commenting about how well we might hit it off," he says. "I guarantee it."

"Do you think we should tell them we've already met?"

"Nah," he says. "No one ever gets one over on the infamous Aidan Pierce, and if we keep this under our hats, that'll make it twice in one day. He had no idea Nate was coming," he says, nodding to the boat.

"Oh, so that's Nate," I say, recalling our chat over coffee at Tim's. "The baker who is definitely not gay."

"The one and only. The flour you delivered was for him." He stops walking before we reach the dock. "But I need to tell you something before he meets you and subsequently tries to hit on you."

"Um," I bite my lip to keep from laughing, "I doubt that will be an issue. But if you think it'll deter him, I'll stick to your advice and throw him off by asking what he does for a living."

"Oh," he says through a good-natured chuckle, "Touché."

"Then I'll ask him if he's gay because I hear he likes to bake."

He throws his head up to the sky as though I've just said something astounding.

"What?" I say, unable to hold back a giggle. "Too far?"

"You're just — I mean, you have the perfect comebacks." He keeps walking and we head for the dock.

"Meh," I shrug. I drop a hand to my side, toying with the fabric of my dress as I walk. "I've had better."

"Like saying you left your proper crown at home?"

"Yeah," I say, "like that."

"And who else would think to encrypt their phone number into a simple greeting *and* save my ass by gifting me the flour I thought would be forever MIA?"

"It was no biggie, really. And that code could be figured out by a ten-year-old, right? Simple. I was just having fun."

As we step onto the dock, he stops short and turns to face me. He says nothing, just looks at me with those intense brown eyes, the same ones that remind me of my favorite root beer candy.

"It's true we're the friendliest country." My shoulders rise and fall as I look down at my feet, avoiding his entrancing stare. "I wanted to be certain someone proved it to you."

He takes a step forward and I look up. He's now within kissing distance.

Crap, now I'm thinking about kissing him!

I don't drink beer (even Mr. Oates knows that about me), but I can tell he's just had one. I don't object to the smell, though. It's not a stale-frat-boy aroma.

It's more like a crisp tropical citrus, and it's mixing with the scent of his cologne.

Maddening, especially combined with his adoring expression.

My pulse is legit racing.

"You're amazing," he finally says. He lifts a hand to brush a hair away from my face. "Never believe otherwise."

"Um," I look down and shake my head to dismiss his compliment. "Thanks." A weird tingling in my chest chases down my body, traveling lower than I expect it to. I clear my throat so my voice will work properly. "Is that what you wanted to tell me, Daryl?"

"No, that was spontaneous. So, Pam," he says, suddenly redirecting his attention to the outside world. He puts one pace between us. "Now that I know your name, the first thing is, thank you for the flour. See our friend Nate over there?" he gestures with a hand towards the boat.

"Yep," I nod. "Nate the Cake Maker."

"Right. Well, he also works for NASA on occasion, and I was fearful for my own safety when I thought I was out of luck on that flour."

"You're welcome," I say with a small curtsy. "Glad to be of service."

"The last thing is, you've just solved a third problem for me, so I *really* owe you now."

"So, more than one cup of coffee?" I ask. "Maybe a week's worth?"

"More," he says. "And probably a whole dozen donuts."

"Let's see. I found and returned your car key, then the flour donation. Now what have I done?"

He drops my bag on the weathered dock, looks up to be sure Alexis and Aidan aren't close enough to overhear, and steps close once more. "I haven't been able to stop thinking about you since you walked out of Timmy Horton's."

Holy crap. His sincerity is slaying me right now.

"And now," his voice drifts off momentarily before he recovers. "Well, now here you are. So thank you, Princess." He claps his hands in a back and forth sweep to indicate that task is all done. "Problem solved." He winks, grabs my bag, and saunters to the boat with that swagger again, leaving me completely dumbfounded.

Did he really just say that?

I'm amazing. He hasn't stopped thinking about me.

Who says crap like that?

Guys that just want to get in my pants, right? Guys that want me to tutor them for free so they can pass their Conceptual Game Design class?

No! Geek Charming Princes, that's who!

"Come aboard and meet First Mate Nate," Daryl says, chuckling at his own rhyme.

"It's your job to untie the boat, Oates." Nate laughs and smacks his friend across the head in brotherly fashion, sending curls flying.

As Daryl brushes by me to tend the lines, chills radiate down my arms.

Wow.

Nate extends his hand to help me on board. "Thank you." I offer him a cordial smile. "Pam Clayton. Nice to meet you."

"Nate Edwards," he says. "Welcome aboard."

God, are all these guys amazing to look at? Carly would keel over. This guy's a looker, too.

"I'd offer you a beverage, but I don't have one. However, I hear there's a killer dinner at The Gables tonight, and we're invited."

"Sounds great."

"I could eat," Daryl says in our direction.

"Me too," Nate smiles. "We haven't eaten since lunch." He makes his way back to his seat and stretches his legs out. "Mama says cocktails are at five sharp. Pierce better hurry the hell up."

Nate's pretty damn good looking. His hair isn't as long as Daryl's, but it's not short either. It's kind of a soft brown, and it's fine and straight. He's wearing the day's scruff on his face, but he's dressed in a preppy shirt, khaki shorts, and boat shoes. Something tells me he's normally close-shaved and the scruff is a middle finger to his daytime work. He's got shades just like Aidan's, but they sit on top of his head, so the sun casts a glow over his eyes which might be hazel, might be blue.

He's wearing a wide grin, almost wicked but without that intention.

Cute as Nate may be, it's Oates I'm stealing longer glances at as he stands by the boat, hollering to Aidan that he better move his ass.

Once on board, Aidan introduces Nate to Alexis and, before he starts up the engine, I learn that Nate, Daryl and Aidan were roommates at Cal Tech when they were undergrads.

Daryl nods in affirmation as we both head for the bow of the boat. "My brothers from other mothers," he says. We sit on the bench seat and he smiles as he drops my bag between our feet.

I smile back, still thrown for a loop that we're suddenly in each other's company again. I look down river toward Carly's place as we head for the main channel. My best friend is never, ever going to believe this curveball Fate's throwing me.

This twist proves Fate's still as drunk and confused as she was yesterday when this dream guy showed up down the aisle from me in Metro. But, at least right now, she's working in my favor. All I wanted was to get near him again and for the next twenty-four to thirty-six hours, I'll have that chance.

Aidan drives us toward Fawn Island as a feeling of anticipation washes over me. Like it or not, Fate's going on a bender, and my gut tells me my only job is to sit back and enjoy the ride.

A rriving at The Gables is as surreal as I expected. The five of us sit on the boat, relaxing and shooting the breeze after we dock at the main slips (the same spot Dave, Carly and I pulled up to incognito two nights ago).

Nate and 'Oates' (as everyone calls him) exchange anecdotes about spending time here during their summer breaks from Cal Tech and beyond. Nate talks about the construction of the cabin Aidan and his brother were gifted as they outgrew staying in the main house with his parents and their guests.

As Aidan tells it, the two-bedroom cabin is called Brat Cottage, a name his parents picked as a tongue-in-cheek tribute to their sons.

"I'm glad to know the actual name of it now," I giggle. "What about the boathouse? Does that have a special name, too?"

"Nope," Aidan says. "We just call it the boathouse. There's only one bedroom up there. It's kind of a cramped space, but good enough for these two shitclowns." He nods to Daryl and Nate.

Alexis laughs. "Nice, babe."

Babe? I grin slyly at Alexis. She's so freakin' happy, and there's absolutely no hiding it.

Aidan suggests we all head up to the main house for cocktail hour with his parents and their friends, and we file off the boat one by one.

I take a deep breath as we walk, inhaling the fresh air and scent of pine. The sun has just dipped below the tree line across the channel, the early summer evening still warm. Fawn Island is left in partial shadow, a surreal glow cast through the trees as the hour turns to five o'clock.

I abandoned my duffel on the boat without thinking, hurrying up the path alongside Alexis. She knows I can't wait to peek inside the main house.

"I gotta snap some pictures of the kitchen for Carly. She's so jealous I'm here without her."

"Go for it," Alexis says. "I'd just keep people out of your photos if you're sharing them on social media."

I shake my head. "I'd never disrespect the Pierce family's privacy like that. Social media is overrated anyway, if you ask me."

"Wholeheartedly agree," she laughs. "Never thought I'd hear that from you, Miss Computer Genius."

I shrug. "I like talking to people in person rather than using a screen as the go-between. Don't get me wrong, I still use it, but...I don't know. I guess I'm kind of old-fashioned when it comes to that stuff in some ways. Or so some of my friends tell me."

"Your parents and brother were a good influence on you," she smiles. "Not a bad thing to live in the moment. And take all the photos you want. I'm sure no one will mind."

"Being here in person is enough to make my day, and the kitchen is all Carly cares about. I think she just wants to see if it's as dreamy as she imagines."

As for me, I'm over the moon hearing people's footsteps across the wide wooden porch, their voices deep in conversation and laughter. *This is what this home deserves.* I'm so giddy my cheeks ache from smiling.

Alexis introduces me to Aidan's parents, who are both welcoming and good-looking (and, just as Lex described, very tall).

"Nice to meet you, Pam," Mr. Pierce says as he hands me a freshly made margarita. "Welcome to Fawn Island."

God, is this my life right now? I smile big as I thank him for his hospitality.

Next we meet and greet the Hamiltons and Reeds, who I learn in conversation are long time friends of the Pierces. They all traveled here from California by plane only yesterday.

"Oh, and Daryl hitched a ride with us, too," Mrs. Hamilton chuckles. "I don't think he was too bothered by us six old timers during the ride, though he had his computer to keep him busy."

And it dawns on me that Mrs. Pierce would be the person who gave him the dating advice not to discuss work when he next met someone. I'm more curious than ever about what he does for a living.

That we've already met and no one here knows it is also making me feel a little naughty, like we've been on some secret mission together.

The two couples seem like very nice, well-to-do people, though I don't learn much upon introductions beyond the fact that they both permanently reside in Manhattan. Mrs. Reed asks me about where I go to school and what I study, then Mrs. Pierce asks what I do in my spare time.

"I tutor over the summer," I say. "Sometimes I'm a server at my aunt's restaurant, if the help at her diner calls out sick. I haven't had much free time until now. I had to double up on some classes after I took time off awhile back."

"Oh?" Mrs. Pierce asks. "How come?"

The Pierces' friends excuse themselves, pulled away by Mr. Pierce to discuss a tour they're taking of the islands tomorrow. This leaves Mrs. Pierce and me in a private moment, which is probably why my glass shakes as I lift it to my lips to take a sip.

Victoria Pierce is sweet as sugar, but she's also direct, classy, and intimidating compared to my mum.

My mother owns more sweatshirts with cats on them than I can count. She considers makeup an unnecessary option, and wears orthopedic shoes no matter where she's headed.

Aidan's mum? Not so much.

Mrs. Pierce is somehow fancy even while dressed down in shorts (which are so white they're almost blinding). She's so, so beautiful, like a leading lady in a black and white movie. She has that regal politeness that some women graciously radiate.

I'm so glad I wore a dress. I'd feel silly meeting her in jeans, even if her friendly demeanor allows me to feel comfortable enough to answer candidly.

"I put my education on hold when my brother passed. My mother insisted."

"I'm so sorry, honey." She lays a hand on my arm. I look down and notice a simple bangle bracelet graces her wrist. She's wearing no other jewelry except a wedding ring and simple diamond earrings. "That's a terrible experience for a young person to have.

When I talked with her earlier, I could see Alexis was so heartbroken to lose your brother."

"I appreciate that, thank you." My eyes well up, but I'm saved the embarrassment of falling tears. "It's getting better. Never easy, but definitely better. I still just really miss him. We all do."

"We lost a son before his time," she sighs. "I understand grief more than I ever hoped to. And I think your mother did right by you, having you take some time off from school. I would've done the same if Aidan had still been an undergrad when Thad died." She takes a sip from her glass. "So, when do you graduate?"

"Next spring," I say, thankful for the subject change. "I'm hoping to study in the States for fourth year at OCAD. It's one of the reasons I chose that school." I notice Mr. Oates looking at me from a few paces away as he talks to Nate. Aidan and Alexis must've wandered off, as I don't see them anywhere.

"That sounds like a wonderful opportunity. What type of work do you hope to do after graduation?"

"That'll depend on how fourth year goes and what business connections I make. I'd like to jump right into the field, but I have the option of grad school, too. I'd love to develop a tool that can analyze medical data, something that could better predict or prevent heart conditions in young people."

"I was in the nursing field for decades," she says with keen interest. "I know so many would benefit from something like that."

"It's a newer interest for me. I'll need more schooling if that's the route I take."

"Oh I'm sure it would take incredible focus and research. But it's noble of you."

"Maybe, but also a little selfish. My brother died from a blood clot in the brain, and I still believe it was a side effect of an undiagnosed heart condition. I'd like to prevent others from suffering the same tragedy our family did."

"Well then, you're doing it for a cause, honey. And I'd say that's definitely a noble path."

Her smile makes me feel proud, and I smile back by way of thanks, too choked up to speak.

"You know, Daryl works in the digital and tech industry. He's done all kinds of things with his career," she says, then leans in closer. "Not that I'm the best one to ask about it. I only figured out how to properly text a few years ago. Just ask him what a fiasco *that* was."

I giggle, unable to help myself from looking in Daryl's direction. And he looks back at me.

"So Mr. Oates is a tech nerd?" *Another tally in the perfect column.*

"Oh yes," she says. "He always has been. He's worked in Silicon Valley for years. Do you have any idea where you'll be studying in the fall?"

"New York, with any luck." My attention is drawn to a loud speed boat zipping through the channel.

"Oh," she mutters, frustrated by the interruption. "That's the one thing I don't recall hearing much of in the past. Those loud boats are obnoxious."

"Boat traffic has definitely increased in the last several years." I look in the distance and heave a sigh, leaning over the porch rail to absorb the view. "I must tell you, Mrs. Pierce, I absolutely love this home of yours. It's always been my absolute favorite around here, even as a little kid. I'm so glad your family is here to enjoy it."

She joins me in looking out over the water. "I adore it, too. Would you like to know how it came to be in our family?"

"Oh my word," I gush. "I would absolutely love to hear that story."

"Let's have a seat then," she says, nodding to the rocking chairs. "I'll tell you all about it."

16

Oates

Friday Night

Fawn Island

Liquor has loosened everyone up except Pam and me. I had one beer to her margarita during cocktail hour, then I noticed she switched to bottled water about the same time I did. I already feel like I'm on some sort of euphoric drug even though I'm fairly sober.

She's fucking *here*. On the same island as me for the next day and a half, at least. I want my wits about me around this girl. I have this inexplicable fear that I'll fuck things up by saying something that's just wrong.

I don't want to blurt that her laugh is more beautiful than last night, prettier than in my memories.

Or how the color blue is jaw dropping on her, especially in the form of that strapless dress.

Or that I wish we were alone on this island right now.

I'm certain Tori's figured out Pam is the girl who gifted Nate's flour and wrote the note. I've noticed her glancing at us every time we interact, which unfortunately has only been in passing. I didn't sit next to her at dinner because I felt like it'd be too obvious.

As badly as I've wanted to, I've had no reason to pull her away and be alone with her.

I exit the bathroom and find Alexis chatting in the kitchen with

Tori, while Aidan is pacing and talking to someone on the phone. There's no one else around, including Pam.

"Where is everyone?"

"I believe the other ladies are relaxing on the porch," Tori says. "Reggie took the guys to the mainland to buy some wood for the firepit and some fresh bait in case you guys want to fish tomorrow."

"Solid plan. The artificial bait we used today didn't result in much of a catch. Where's Nate?"

"I think he was walking Pam down to the boathouse," Alexis says.

Is she fucking with me right now? I can't tell.

The girl dating my best friend has me curious.

I chatted with her a few times before and after dinner and found her extremely likable, but not in a pushover, doormat way. She definitely has a backbone.

During dinner, she told Aidan's father and his friend Mr. Hamilton a joke that was hysterical and borderline crass. Both men laughed at length. But then she hit them with her smarts and spoke about her law career, which I learned is in its infancy. I could tell Pam is wicked proud of her sister-in-law just by the smile on her face.

Despite being a newbie in her field, Alexis answered all the men's questions like a pro. When opportunity presented, she made it clear that back home, she'd already proven herself as capable as any man because situations in her career forced her to.

Somehow, she conveyed this without hitting anyone over the head with it.

As much as she wasn't happy about the boys' club mentality that still exists in her small city, she wasn't irrationally angry about it. She didn't pounce on anyone who opened his mouth to make a counterpoint, including me. She was just being herself. Open and honest, and yeah, as smart as anyone else at the table. (Except Nate, maybe.)

But right now, I think she's fucking with me.

"For real?" I ask. "They went to the boathouse? Together?"

Alexis smiles and pours more wine into her glass. "She wanted to get a glimpse inside, and he was going down there anyway to grab a sweatshirt."

Rat bastard! I step away for three minutes and he's found a way to steal my princess away. Tori looks at me from the corner of her eye, reading me, then looks back at Alexis and smiles.

"I might throw on some jeans," I say.

"Sure," Tori says. Her tone is accusatory, like I'm making an excuse to head in that direction.

Which I am.

"Keeps the bugs away," I say.

"Definitely," Alexis says.

"Yep." I'm already at the front door. "Be right back."

By the time I make it to the boathouse, there's no sign of Pam. Nate stands at the picture window in the living room, hands on hips with earbuds in. He talks into the mic dangling around his neck, then turns to face me.

I throw hands in the air. "Dude. Where is she?"

He puts a finger to his lips to shush me, shrugs, then rifles through his bag. He's carrying on to someone about an impossible timeline and the scope of his next project as I head for the bedroom to find my jeans. I toss my phone on the bed just as it vibrates.

One New Message

From: Princess Pam

I open it to find a text and a picture attachment.

There's about to be a glorious
sunset right here.

The photo is a selfie. Or, half of one. Her features are partially hidden by big sunglasses, and the right half of the photo is focused over her shoulder on the horizon. I recognize the view from the dock at Brat Cottage, looking west through the trees that surround the small bay.

I pull my jeans on in seconds, lace up my sneakers, and salute Nate as I leave the boathouse in search of my princess.

I cross the island paths in a hurry, but stop myself from going to her on a dead run. As I approach the dock and catch sight of her from behind, I halt on the shore several feet from her.

Pam is looking in the direction of the amazing sunset she promised. The water is calm, even in the main channel. No boats are whizzing past at the moment. The sky glows purple, the sun the kind of orangey-red that turns the clouds pink.

None of it is as breathtaking to look at as she is.

She's leaning back on the strength of her wrists, palms flat on the dock. Her legs are stretched out in front of her and crossed at the ankle, her bare feet just hanging off the end of the dock. The fabric of her blue dress cascades over the weathered wood. Her hair falls down her back, sunglasses crowning the top of her head.

She can't see me, but she must sense my presence because she speaks first.

"I thought you'd never get here." She turns her head and smiles at me.

Slayed. Cue the zombie apocalypse music. My grin has to be as goofy as Pierce's was this afternoon.

"I heard something about a glorious sunset about to go down." I take a seat at the end of the dock and dangle my feet over the edge. Rather than scoot forward in a dress, she stands up, walks two steps and sits, her feet dangling next to mine. I notice goosebumps rise up on her arms. "Are you cold? I can grab you a sweatshirt."

She bites her lower lip as her hands grip the edge of the dock. "Not really."

Holy shit is she sexy.

If I'm not careful, I'll be pitching a tent in these jeans right in front of her.

"So, Alexis was married to your brother," I say. "Is it weird for you, ya know, to see her with Pierce?"

"Not so much. I mean, it's different for sure. I've never seen her with anyone but Ben. I'm incredibly happy for her, though. Dating was long overdue. In fact, I was trying to set her up this weekend."

"What?" I laugh. "With who?"

"Oh," she waves a hand in dismissal. "No one. Just some lawyer I know. I tutor his younger brother who's my age."

"I can tell you right now Pierce wouldn't like that."

"So I gather. He seems pretty smitten."

"Yeah," I nod, "I haven't seen Aidan like that oh…" I pretend to consider. "Ever."

She pulls her shades down as the sun sinks and blinds us through a treeless spot on the horizon. "What's he normally like?"

I'm without sunglasses, so I swing around with my back to the water and sit cross-legged, facing the shore. We're not face-to-face, but our hips are inches from touching.

"Pierce is a tough nut to crack. He's usually pretty serious but around her, he's..." I shake my head. "I don't know. He's a different guy."

"You think he really likes her?" Her voice is earnest with concern. "He's not like, using her for something?"

I have to stifle a laugh. "Um, I'd have to guess it's far more than that. Pierce doesn't need anyone for anything. And he'd be the one to offer help before anyone else, whether or not he had the means. He's a stand up guy."

"Does he normally date girls like Alexis?"

"He doesn't really date. I mean, not since we were in college. Except for Stella, but that was different. His thing with her was more about..." I trail off, trying to figure out the best way to describe their odd relationship.

"Sex?"

I turn to her, unable to stop my grimace. "Not so much."

"Okay, so, what was it then? Was he in love with her?"

"I take it you don't read American tabloids."

"Not lately," she kids.

"She caused him nothing but problems. Let's just say it was more like an arrangement than a relationship. She's a hot mess."

"Doesn't sound like you care for her much."

"I don't. I mean, I never spent much time around her, but she was a complication where Pierce thought she'd be a solution. But he does care about her. You know, like as a human being. He's not one for hating on people even if there's due cause."

"I just don't want to see Lex hurt," she says with a sigh. "She's been through enough."

"Trust me, your sister-in-law is in good hands. Er," I pause. "Shit. That sounded perverted."

"Stop," she laughs. Her hand lands on my arm and slides down before she returns it to her lap. "I know what you mean. And I don't mean to doubt your best friend. She's like a big sister to me, that's all."

"I get it. I was concerned when I first met her today, thinking the worst. Like she was just after his money."

"Oh, hell no. Alexis is not like that. She's the least superficial girl you'll ever meet."

"Good," I say. "I'll take you at your word, Princess. We'll just have to let them figure out the rest."

"And that's a relief. Since my brother died, I felt like our roles reversed, like I had to worry about her. She's been so focused on her career, I was afraid she'd burn out."

"Really?" I say. "She seems pretty chill."

"Yeah, she is, but grief does crazy things to people. Overall she is a happy person, especially now. I've never seen her giddy like she is around him. It's adorbs."

"She wasn't like that around your brother?"

"Um, not really. I mean, they were happy, but their relationship was unconventional. I guess maybe like you said Aidan's was with his ex."

Unconventional how? I'm curious but she doesn't elaborate. "Well, I told Pierce today that his goose is pretty well cooked. He's clearly *loco* for her. Nate agreed with me."

"Nate's a funny guy," she says. "He's so serious. But then, you said he bakes?" She says through a giggle. "And just when you least expect it, he comes out with some zinger."

"Right?" I can't help laughing along with her. "He does that. His sense of humor is subtle. He's definitely the most unique guy I've ever met. And his intelligence is dizzying."

"So Nate and Aidan are your ride or die?"

"Yep. My day ones, for sure. Now that Aidan moved to New York, it'll be rare we hang out given I'm in California. And I go years between hanging with Nate 'cause he's just too busy. The three of us used to come up here on summer breaks from Cal Tech."

"Alexis told me the family stopped coming up here after Aidan's brother died. That's who you were talking about last night?"

"Yeah. Kind of a buzzkill topic, huh?"

"Maybe, but such is life. I wasn't planning on losing my 28 year-old brother, but that's the way things went," she shrugs. "I miss him like crazy. That's sort of why I came down here."

"I'm...shit," I mumble. "Did you want to be alone?"

"No," she laughs. "I sent you a text, remember? I was hoping you'd join me."

"Sometimes I'm really bad at reading signals."

"I guess I could've been direct and just said get your ass down here, but I thought that'd be rude."

"A little un-princess like maybe." I wink, then nudge her side. "So, was your brother familiar with this spot?"

She looks down at her lap, then back up at me. "I scattered some of his ashes over there," she nods to the middle of the bay, then leans over to nudge me back. "Talk about a buzzkill."

"I guess he's familiar with it then." *Jesus, Oates. Could you fuck this up any more?*

But her soft laughter echoes around us. "I suppose he is now. So, if you've known Aidan that long, then you know his parents pretty well?"

"Yep. They're like my spare set of rentals. Love them to death."

"I can see why. Mrs. Pierce is just lovely. And so beautiful."

"She is. And I should probably tell you, she knows about our encounter. She's the one who told me about leaving work off the table as a topic when I met a girl. And then she found your note."

"No!" She covers her face in her hands before peeking up at me. "Seriously?"

I nod, unable to stop laughing at her honest, mortified reaction. "It's fine," I say. "Don't worry about it. She stumbled on it in the bottom of the canvas bag, then she hid it from me, just to mess with me."

"Oh my God," she laughs. "I love her even more now."

"Right? Problem was, it dawned on me last night that the first two lines were probably a code to give me your number, but I had no way to get to the note because it was up in the kitchen at the main house, and all the old folks had gone to bed. As it turned out, I wouldn't have found it anyway because she hid it under the quinoa in the pantry."

"Get. Out," she says. "She's hysterical!"

"Hysterical like a fox. I had to pry the note's location out of Reggie because the two of them were in cahoots."

"Oh, crap!" she says, her eyes opening wide. "He knows, too?"

"Yeah, but it's totally cool. As long as we get one over on Pierce, I'm happy."

She looks apprehensive, but finally lets out a relaxed sigh. "That explains why I didn't hear from you sooner. I was starting to wonder if you weren't as bright as you let on. You think they'll tell anyone? Like Alexis?"

I shake my head. "If I asked, she'd take it to the grave and make Reggie swear to it, too. Tori's amazing. She was just chatting it up with your big sis in the kitchen when I walked out. Alexis told me Nate whisked you off, and I figured he'd taken the chance to hit on you. I practically ran for the boathouse."

"You came after me?" She lays a hand over her heart. "I'm so flattered."

"Nah," I shrug. "Just wanted to change into jeans."

"Right." Her expression indicates she's not buying my excuse. "Well, I did walk out with Nate. I wanted to see the inside of the boathouse in person, and he offered. But to be honest, you disappeared, and I sort of thought that's where you were."

I just look at her, happy to know she was looking for me, too.

"Then he took a phone call as we walked, and I remembered I left my bag on the boat, so we split up. I was heading for the main dock, then the path just kind of called me over this way."

"I'm sorry if I interrupted a solemn moment," I say.

"No, it wasn't really like that. I mean, yeah, this place is special to me. But Ben and I also used to dock here and sneak around the little island." She nods up to Brat Cottage. "We peeked in the boathouse once. Never had the courage to go up to the porch and the main house, though."

"Kind of a rebel, are you?"

She blushes. "Um, not really. Just uber curious. I have loved this island for what seems like forever."

"Well, you're welcome here any time," I say. "From here on out. I'll show you around the whole place if you want."

"I'd so love that." Her appreciative smile reaches her brown eyes. "My friend Carly will flip when she sees the pics I took of the kitchen after dinner."

"Ah yes, the chef headed to Florida that was making sure I didn't murder you last night. Does she know we've crossed paths again?"

"Not yet. I told her you figured out my code. She thinks you're a superior geek."

"Uh, I prefer superior nerd please, Princess."

"Done and done."

I find the courage to look her in the eyes, hoping she can't read me. I feel like this is a moment, and I don't want to blow it. Her chest rises and falls as her breathing shifts, and I can't help admire what I'm seeing.

She's wearing the same delicate necklace as last night.

Still not even a bit of cleavage showing, just her bare neck and shoulders.

Fuck me.

Does she know how badly I want to kiss her?

"Oates!"

A long moment passes as our eyes are locked onto each other. When I finally look away toward the shore, I see Nate hollering to me, hands cupped around his mouth. "Redge is back with firewood. Come up here and help a brother out!"

Foiled again.

"Shall we?" I spring to my feet and reach my hand down to her. "We'll grab your bag, start tonight's tour with you watching me carry wood to the firepit."

"Absolutely," she grins as she stands up, "I'm all in."

This night could not be more perfect.

The five of us are gathered down on the brick patio by the water while the elders are up on the porch. Our Adirondack chairs are arranged in a circle around the cement firepit that Aidan and his brother built one summer. The discussion has turned to music — one of my favorite topics.

My best friend is relaxed, more than I've witnessed since we were broke freshmen with nothing but time on our hands and big plans rattling around in our heads. And who would've thought Nate would be a fifth wheel? I'll get to brag to the twins.

But the cherry on top is Pam Clayton.

Instead of walking around in my subconscious thoughts, my gorgeous brunette princess is seated next to me, and now I have a real name to go with her phone number.

This girl throws me for a loop at every turn.

Her pretty attire didn't stop her from volunteering to help carry firewood up from the main dock, but Nate and I insisted it wasn't necessary. She reluctantly agreed, but grabbed her bag instead, demonstrating that this princess is *not* prissy. Now she takes the initiative to grab for a log and toss it into the dwindling fire.

She's about to sit back down when she lets out an adorable (and extremely loud) squeal. She freezes, and I look up to see a spider crawling on her bare arm.

"I got it." I remove the creature and hurl it over the granite cliff. "Are spiders your only weakness?"

"The bugger scared me," she says, trying to laugh even as she pants from panic. Her right hand grasps at her necklace. "Shoot."

Nate is in hysterics. Pierce is amused too, but Alexis is sympathetic, even if she is grinning. "I'd have screamed even louder, girl. I hate spiders."

"No worries, Princess." I lean over to her. "I'd be happy to help you out any time."

Countless times, if it allowed me to touch her again. Her skin is the softest I've ever laid a finger on.

As I learn more about her, I realize she's more my type than any girl I've met. More than any Tantalizing Tina, Co-Worker Carolyn or Friendly Jenny the Barista could ever be, even if you combined them all.

Even more than any woman I could dream up and design into reality.

And in true craptastic fashion in the World of Oates, she lives not only on the opposite coast, but in another country.

Fucking awesome.

Our discussion is back on topic, and Alexis and I go back and forth about Paul Simon versus Paul McCartney. Before I can blast her for being of the opinion that the Beatle is the lesser talent, she explains that her father — who passed away in recent years — is the reason for her preference because he shared his love for Simon and Garfunkel with her.

"Well I'm not arguing with that," I say. "I concede, madame." I stand up and bow at the waist to admit my defeat, then sit again.

"Good," she says. "And I'd think someone named after an eighties rock duo would have done so long ago."

"You told her?" I pick up my empty plastic cup, crush it and huff it Pierce's way. "Damn, man. Way to throw a brother under the bus."

"Relax," he laughs. He catches my only ammo and tosses it into the fire. "I didn't tell her anything. But you just confirmed it for her, shit for brains."

Damn. I sure as hell did.

"Who were you named after?" Pam asks.

"It isn't the exact same name," Alexis says. "How did you end up with it, Mr. Oates?"

"Yes, okay? I admit it. My mother was a diehard eighties music *fah-naa-tic.* My dad's last name is Oates. And she loved Hall and Oates. End of story."

Pam's still unsure.

"Daryl Hall and John Oates," Alexis says. "They had a lot of hits in the eighties."

"Right," Pam says. "I know the group. Guess I didn't make the connection."

Nate busts into "Rich Girl", and I wish I had another cup to throw at him.

"I know that song," she says. "Do they also sing the song from *Flashdance?*"

Aidan confirms, but he's wrong.

"No, you're thinking of "Maneater"," I say to correct him. But I'm looking at Pam's cute smile, unable to take my eyes off her. "The song from *Flashdance* was "Maniac" and that was Michael Sembello."

"Okay, him I've never heard of," Pam whispers.

"'Maniac', 'Maneater'," Aidan says. "I knew it was one of those."

As he sets down his empty glass of whiskey, I can tell he's pretty lit, at least for him. He isn't out of his own control because Pierce refuses to cross that threshold. But he's definitely chilled out.

"We used to play "Maniac" in volleyball warm-ups," Pam says. "Still, that's so cool. I'm not named after anyone famous."

"It's not so bad, I guess." Her smile is a reward that makes it seem like less of a curse, at least. "I've taken my share of razzing about it in the past." I nod to Pierce.

"Once," he says in defense. "When you first told me."

"Your mother didn't want to take it all the way and name you John Oates?" Alexis asks. "Why'd she use Daryl instead?"

"My grandfather — that is, my mom's father — was John, and he was kind of a bastard. So she decided on the next best thing."

"That is cool," Alexis says. She offers me a warm smile.

A moment of silence comes over us, and Pierce asks if we should call it a night. I glance at my watch to see it's only ten p.m. I look up at him, wondering why the hell he's cutting our time short. Then Alexis pipes up that she's kind of tired, too, and it dawns on me that he's taking a woman to bed with him.

Duh, Oates.

"Actually, I've been up twenty-four solid," Nate chimes in. "Point me to my bed, and we shall reconvene this round table tomorrow night."

"You and Oates in the boathouse, as always," Aidan says. "Alexis and I in Brat Cottage. Pam," he nods up to the main house, "would you feel comfortable sleeping in a guest room up there?"

"Really?" I expect she'll be as disappointed as I am to turn in already, but instead she's squealing with delight as her eyes fly open wide. "Mr. Pierce," she says in teasing, "you, kind sir, have just made my freakin' year."

"You can go through the front door and head upstairs, then make a right. It's the third door on the right. Mom can show you if you're not sure."

"Mamasita's visiting with the elders. I can show her," I offer.

He gives me a briefly suspicious look, then nods. "Don't let him bore you to tears telling stories," Aidan says to Pam. "See you guys at breakfast."

Alexis hugs Pam good night before throwing me a pointed finger in a big sister, 'you'd better behave' fashion. I nod in understanding, and after we say our goodbyes, she takes off down the path with Aidan.

"Am I assigned to the pull-out couch?" Nate asks.

"Dude, you can take the bed. You've been traveling all day. I'll take the couch."

"Thanks." He smacks me on the back. "You're such an upstanding guy, Oates."

"You're welcome, asshat. I'll be right down, soon as I show

Pam to her room. And shut the door so I don't have to listen to your snoring."

"I don't snore," he says.

"Let's just acknowledge you might and play it safe, okay?"

"Whatever, bro. Good night, Pam." He nods to her and makes his way towards the boathouse, leaving us alone.

Finally.

17

Pam

Friday Night

Fawn Island

As Alexis hugs me good night, I try to quiet the butterfly wings fluttering in my stomach.

I've just been invited to sleep up in the main house. At *The* Gables. On Fawn Island. I never thought this bucket list item had a snowball's chance to be marked off.

Even better, I'm about to be left alone with my incredibly handsome Perfect Stranger. *Finally.*

"Are you good with this?" Alexis whispers in my ear.

I nod enthusiastically into her shoulder and whisper back I'm better than good.

She releases me and steps back, a knowing grin coming over her. "See you in the morning. Love you." She nods Daryl's way. "Good night, Mr. Oates."

"Good night, mademoiselle." He stands up in a gesture of politeness and does his over-the-top bow in her direction.

Nate talks to Daryl about their designated sleeping arrangements as I watch Alexis and Aidan walk arm in arm away from me. They head for the footbridge leading to the cottage until he stops abruptly, sweeps her up, and throws her over his shoulder.

She protests briefly before losing herself to a giggle that echoes around the whole island.

I heave a sigh of happiness for her as Nate's voice calls my attention.

"Good night, Pam."

"Oh, good night, Nate." I smile as he starts away from the patio. "See you tomorrow." With his back to me, he throws up a hand to wave and takes the other path, downhill to the boathouse.

I look to my right. Daryl's now standing two steps away from me, also watching his friend walk away. He reaches for my hand and gives it a squeeze.

Alone at last.

"Hey, Princess, you tired?"

"No." I smile in the darkness. The fire has died down, no longer providing much heat or light. I'm still wearing my sundress and my shoulders are bare, leaving me chilled.

But *tired*? No. I'm definitely not tired.

"Good," he says, "because I have an idea."

My heart speeds up to rabbit pace. "Okay." I secretly hope it involves him kissing me. He's still holding my hand, looking straight ahead.

"Didn't you say you like fishing?"

"I did." I turn my head to look at him. It's too dark for me to see his expression, but fishing is definitely not what I was expecting him to suggest. "Is that really what you hand in mind?"

"Let's put it this way." He looks at his feet for a moment before he lets my hand go, steps in front of me, and stares me straight in the eye. He raises a hand to my face, his fingers tracing my hairline, his thumb gently grazing my cheek. "It's the only thing that comes to mind that isn't R-rated, thereby landing me on the shit list of Pierce and Ms. Greene."

My head falls back, my eyes closing as I soak up the sensation just from his touch. Everything in me feels like it's running on extra cylinders.

My heart, my mind, my lady parts.

Holy. Shitballs.

This guy is making everything in me *zing*. And all he did was touch my head. As his hand falls away, I shake my head and open my eyes.

"Fishing," I say, trying to steady my voice. "Sounds good." I look past him up to the main house. "I'm kind of cold though. I think I'll go up and change into some jeans."

"Good idea." Now that he's facing me, the glow from the dying fire illuminates his face. He's grinning from ear to ear. "We can't have a princess shivering in the chilly night air."

My face contorts with a sarcastic smirk. "Funny."

"I hear there's fresh bait," he says. "I'll meet you down at the main dock?"

"Sure. Probably safer to steer clear of the bay by Brat Cottage. The lovebirds headed that way."

"Uh, yeah," he smiles. "I'm not about to intrude on that." He steps away and I turn my head to watch him go. He stops to look back at me. "Pam?"

I inhale a deep breath. My head is swerved in his direction, but my body is rooted to the spot where his touch made me feel this crazy cocktail of euphoria and aching arousal.

"Yeah?" I ask over my shoulder.

"Hurry."

"Okay," I say. My cheeks ache from grinning. "I will."

I head up to the house, realizing the 'adults' must have gone inside. Perhaps they've even gone to bed. My bag is no longer on the porch, but as I reach the front door, I can see it laying at the foot of the stairs in the foyer. I open the screen door only for it to echo through the silent evening with a loud creak. Inside, the house is quiet and still, and I'm afraid I've disturbed everyone upstairs who may be trying to sleep.

"Come on up, honey," Mrs. Pierce calls softly. I look to the top of the stairs and see her standing there, still fully dressed.

"Has everyone gone to bed?" I whisper.

"Oh no, they're in the library for a nightcap. It was getting too chilly outside for Mrs. Hamilton. Bring your bag and I'll show you to your room."

I climb the stairs, still in delighted shock that I'm staying in this house. The wooden banister is curved and painted a shiny black to match the stair treads. The black contrasts with the white risers and spindles of the railing. As I reach Aidan's mom at the top, I look down and realize the intended design. The foyer is tiled in large, black and white squares in a checkerboard pattern, complementing the grand staircase.

"Mrs. Pierce, this place is just...it's crazy. That floor. And that staircase! All I can say is wow."

"Thank you, honey. It is quite beautiful."

"Did you design it yourself?"

"Not entirely." She guides me down the long hall to the right until we reach the third door, the one Aidan mentioned would lead to my room. "We hired a designer to help keep the formality and tradition of the original home, had contractors update things to suit our family's needs. But yes," she says, "I picked the black and white for the stairs and the entry all those years ago, and I still love it. I didn't want it to go out of style in twenty years."

"It's to die for," I sigh. "You have excellent taste."

"I appreciate that. And might I say, I think your taste is lovely, too."

She opens the door and lets me into a cozy bedroom with a four-poster bed. A carved cherry fireplace is tucked in one corner. The windows must overlook the river, but all I can see is darkness through the open curtains. A doorway to the left leads to an en suite bathroom, which I'd guess is the result of a remodel given the age of the home.

I set my bag on an upholstered side chair and look her way. "My taste?" I ask. "How's that?"

She smiles warmly. "Mr. Oates is a wonderful guy. I understand you two have taken a liking to each other."

My cheeks immediately flush.

"It's okay, honey." She lays a reassuring hand on my shoulder. "Your secret's safe with me, and not much of one anyway. But I'll share a secret with you, if you'd like to make it even."

Whew. I drop my shoulders in relief and smile. "Um, sure."

"I've known him since he was a teenager, and he is the most genuine soul you'll ever meet. You've nothing to worry about around him."

"My gut instinct was the same, but I totally appreciate the confirmation. Thank you, Mrs. Pierce."

"Please feel free to call me Tori. Now, I'm going down to say good night to everyone. There are extra blankets in the wardrobe, and please just come get me if you need absolutely anything. Our room is down the hall, it's a left from the top of the stairs and then another left, to the front of the house. Okay?"

"Okay," I say. "Got it."

"And if you're going back out, please dress warmly."

"Yeah, um—" I stall a moment, but I don't want to be dishonest. "I think I'm going to fish with Daryl for a little bit before I turn in. I'm kind of wide awake."

"Oh, it's a great night for fishing. You can go down the back stairs and out that door, if you like. It's a right down this hallway here." She gestures behind her. "Then you won't disturb anyone when you come back in."

"I'll do that." I can't stop grinning at Tori Pierce, who's officially the coolest mom ever.

"Have fun, honey." She winks, then closes the door and leaves me.

"Holy shit," Daryl blurts. "Really?"

We sit in a couple of canvas camping chairs we dragged up to the end of the dock. He hands me one of two fishing poles and sets a Styrofoam container of fresh worms wriggling in dirt on the dock between us.

My new (and might I add, extremely hot) fishing buddy is shocked that he doesn't have to bait a hook for me.

"Really," I say. "I've got it." I cast my baited line into the water.

"So spiders petrify you, but worms are okay?"

"Guess so," I say. "You've discovered my weak spot when it comes to creepy crawly things. So, tell me more about Mr. Oates. What are you afraid of?" I keep my eyes on the dark water, hoping it will help him talk freely. I can tell he's more nervous now than on our coffee date. I'm not sure if it's because we're now entirely alone or because of the scenario we've found ourselves in — knowing my sister-in-law is dating his best friend. For whatever reason, he's been quieter since we came down here.

"Nothing comes to mind, really. At one time, I was a major hypochondriac. So I guess fear of illness and disease maybe."

I look at him quizzically, unable to picture that. "You're serious?"

"Briefly, but yeah. I took this course to study rare and infectious diseases, and it included a lab requirement. I was convinced some samples were being stored in the lab. For almost a year, I was paranoid any time I so much as sneezed funny. I was constantly running to the campus infirmary."

"I can't picture that. You really thought you were exposed to something terrible?"

"In retrospect, no. The chick that worked at the infirmary was cute, and I was crushing on her, which was an internal fact that took me awhile to realize. I was seventeen and totally not the ladies man I am now." He winks, and I giggle. "Then, over one school break while I was hanging at Aidan's, I was convinced I was coming down with something awful I'd just studied. I don't even recall what it was, but Tori looked me over. She's a nurse, or was then. She's retired now."

"And?"

"And she told me I was breaking out in hives, but it wasn't from a disease or an allergic reaction. It turned out to be stress-related."

"Aww," I sigh. "That's terrible."

He shrugs. "My classes were tough that year. I was in an accelerated program, I was chosen for an internship at a huge tech company, and I didn't think I was ready. With all the pressure, my mind was just finding any excuse to run away and focus on something else, and it affected my body, too."

"So what did you do?"

"Realized after talking to her that there was absolutely nothing wrong with me, and Aidan gave me the kick in the ass I needed to get my head right. I rearranged some classes, put one off until the following year, and psyched myself up to dive into that internship, which everyone in my class would've killed for. I nailed it. Never had a medical issue again," he says, knocking a knuckle on the dock.

"Wait, what was that?" I say through my laughter. "Did you just knock on wood?"

"Um, yeah. Guess I did."

"And here I thought you were laughing at me last night."

He looks at me with a questioning glance.

"You know, when we parted ways at Tim's and I told you not to say it out loud that we wouldn't see each other again."

"Guess it worked," he says. "Cause here we are. I'm superstitious too sometimes, usually without even realizing it. Kind of like my mom."

"I just got picked on for that. Carly's friend Dave was mocking me for always trying to look on the bright side yet also being superstitious. I told him not to toast with water because it's bad luck."

"I've never heard that one."

"Yep. Mum always told me that. Dad did too."

"So, this guy gave you grief over that?" He sets his pole down and looks at me intently. "I think that's a silly thing to pick on someone about."

"Oh, he wasn't really picking on me, like not in a rude way or around other people. He was more pointing it out as an odd combination. Dave's a trip. Picture James Cordon but funnier. And gay."

He laughs, seeming satisfied with my explanation. It's adorable that he cared how someone who's a stranger to him might have treated me. *Or maybe it reveals more about him because he was picked on?* Regardless, he's making me swoon, and he doesn't even realize it.

"I'll concede to your friend's friend on that point," he says. "It is odd. I'm still not sure how someone educated well enough in human biology and chemical processes in the brain could ever knock on wood thinking it will prevent a God damn thing. But alas, I just did it."

We both laugh. "Right? I find it fascinating what our brains are capable of, whether it's to our benefit or detriment."

"Truth. What else would you like to know, Princess?" He pops open a small cooler and grabs a beer, skittering away from topics of vulnerabilities. "Help yourself," he says. "I put some hard lemonades in there. Or there's bottled water, too."

"Thanks." I grab for a spiked lemonade and set it on the dock. "Tell me anything. As long as it's not about what you do for a living because that's *totally* lame."

He laughs again, this time more relaxed. My reminder of last night is just the icebreaker we needed. He tells me about his parents and the sister he first mentioned over coffee.

"So you're like, normal then?" I ask. "No islands or yachts or mansions in your family's list of assets? No criminal, serial killer history?"

"Totally normal. My mom's a retired teacher and my dad was a math professor at Cal Tech. I guess my sister is the only weird one."

"Weird how?" I open my lemonade and take a sip. And another. It tastes better than I thought it would.

"Meh," he shrugs. "I guess maybe weird isn't a good way to put it. She's just kind of the black sheep. She's a great kid, but she's kind of flighty."

"Kid?" I ask. "How old is she?"

"Um...shit." He clams up, and I turn to look at him. "She's close to your age. I guess kid isn't a good word either."

Now I'm the one laughing. "She's your baby sister, and you've probably always thought of her as a kid. I'm not insulted."

He shakes his head and looks to the sky, then back at me as though I've said something mind boggling.

"What's that look for?"

"She's twenty-five, so she's older than you by what, almost four years?"

"I guess. Your point?"

"You're far more mature than she is, just based on your capability to make that statement. Add in your behavior the last two days, you'd easily pass for having five years on her."

"Well, thank you. I think. But there's probably some reasons to validate our differences."

"Really?" he asks. "I'd love to hear your theory."

"Well," I sip once more and clear my throat, "when I lost Ben, it sort of turned everything upside down for me. I had my college career all wrapped up in a package that I just had to unwrap, one year at a time, layer by layer. I'd study in the States my fourth year and decide where to go from there. But when we lost him, I just..." I shake my head as I reel in my empty line and recast. "It had me seeing things in a different way than most of my peers."

"I suppose that makes sense. I know Aidan was devastated

when he lost Thad. It wrecked him. And it ultimately got him on the path that led him to New York."

"A loss like that is life altering. I kept thinking about how we just never know. I didn't start partying hard or doing anything crazy. I had a bit of an experimental phase, I guess. But mostly, his passing just had me rethinking everything. Mum insisted I take a short break from school, but then I dove back in more focused than ever. From the time I was in elementary school, I couldn't wait to get out of here and see the world, and those flames were fanned to the point of an inferno when Ben died."

"So you worked harder than ever to get where you are."

"I did. My parents knew I wouldn't do well sitting in a classroom for an entire four years. They loved that I chose OCAD, so I could get into the field that much sooner and have a chance to travel, too. They wanted me to see it through. They just didn't want me to attempt it while I was dealing with fresh grief."

"They sound pretty awesome," he says, "and hella-supportive."

"They're amazing like that," I say proudly. "And that's why I'm going to New York next semester. I want to be able to support them, if they ever need me. If I get into one of the programs I applied for, I'll still be close enough that I can come home on a random weekend or for longer breaks." I sip more lemonade. "Do you get along with your sister?"

"We're not really close." He casts his line out again. "I mean, don't get me wrong, I love my sister. It's just, she's sort of a nomad. She's not decided on a career path or finished any schooling beyond her high school degree. She's started a shit ton of stuff, but she never finishes. She doesn't keep a steady job. She doesn't reach out to me much, so I just kind of let her be. Support her if I can."

"So, she doesn't have a direction yet at twenty-five. That's okay with you, right?"

"Oh, yeah. I don't blame her for not knowing where she's headed yet. Shit, I don't even know what I want to do half the time. Pierce is helping me develop this app. That's part of the reason I'm here this weekend. We went over it today. But it scares the hell out of me to think about actually launching it."

"What kind of app?"

"Music sharing. My platform would allow indie artists to have more control over their offerings and make themselves more money. It also suggests new music for the user with a better success rate than anything out there now."

"That is so cool. I love music. That was a great influence my brother had on me."

"I love it too, for sure. But various kinds depending on mood, task, whatever."

"Okay, here's a question." I set down my fishing rod and grab my lemonade. "What's the one genre you could forever live without, if you absolutely had to?"

"That's an easy one for me. Disco music," he says. "Definitely don't need that."

"Aww, really?" I say through a cheesy grin. "No "Stayin' Alive" for you?"

"No thanks," he grimaces.

"Okay, well I'd have to agree. I do like some music from that time period, but disco? Not so much."

"See?" he says. "That's what makes the app fun to work on. I was tired of people complaining about how off the mark their recommends were. If you like a Simon and Garfunkel song from 1970, doesn't mean you want to hear K.C. and The Sunshine Band." He swigs from his bottle and sets it down.

"Totally. Just because I like one nineties alternative song doesn't mean I'll like them all."

"Exactly. So that, plus I wanted to give people an interface where they can easily share music, but the artist still gets compensated, so they can keep making music. Maybe even throw in a feature where the artist can interact with the user, which makes the consumer feel recognized."

"Which encourages them to buy and share more music and so on."

"Precisely," he says.

"That would be amazing. Are you going to do that?"

"I was, but that idea got pushed to the side with the advancements in social media apps. You can Tweet something to your favorite artist if you want, and they just might share it or write back. So, in a way, that already exists."

"Mm, I see your point."

"I'm hopeful the app will be my ticket to a nest egg as is. That's the real goal. I'd like to have a job that's a little less structured, not stuck in the rat race forever. I admire what Pierce does, helping people. It'd be nice to serve more causes with my capabilities, not just run someone else's dreams up the flagpole of success."

"Well, it all sounds amazing to me. I'd love to hear more about your development and launch. I'm a tech geek," I shrug. "Most people think that's boring. Not the people in my classes, but Carly definitely does. And some of our mutual friends."

"Been there," he smiles. He tugs on his line as it pulls taught, but then all tension goes out when he reels in an empty hook. He baits his line again.

"While Carly was scoping out boys in grade twelve, I was in grade nine and focused on Isaac Asimov books and conquering all the levels of Super Mario Brothers."

"That's awesome. So Nintendo is your favorite gaming system?"

"Not necessarily. I liked the Sega console for..." I trail off, interrupting my own thoughts. "I know!"

He looks at me funny.

"I know where I've heard that song by Hall and Oates! "Maneater" is in Grand Theft Auto!" I say. "I knew I'd heard it before."

His smile lights up his eyes, then quickly dissipates. "You like Grand Theft Auto?"

"Um, yeah. Is that a bad thing?"

He shakes his head. "I don't think your nerdity is boring, Pam. I've been writing code since I was twelve. I think it's a huge turn on."

"You're just saying that to get in my pants," I giggle.

"Uh," he sputters, almost choking either on his own saliva or his beer. "No, I'm not. But you're the first girl to suggest that might work." He turns away for a second, and I could swear he mumbles something like 'so hot'. "Anyway, back to my sister," he says with a good natured laugh.

"Right, your sister." Except now I can't stop thinking about him saying I turn him on.

Get a grip, girl. I turn back to the river and set down my almost empty lemonade. Now I'm buzzing, and if I'm honest, so is everything below my waist.

"The problem is my parents are always giving me shit over Annie's behavior, as though I have control over the choices she makes. They had me chase her down in Europe one summer to drag her ass back home."

"Ah, gotcha." I reel in my line which is without any reward, then cast it out again with my worm still on the hook. "That does sound frustrating."

"It's like, sorry guys, but I learned about her latest bonehead move when you did. And nothing I could say or do would change her mind anyway."

"Are your parents really strict? Or, were they when you were growing up?"

"Nah, I wouldn't say strict. They were sort of this weird combination of hippie and conservative. My mom was all peace and love, yet she was overly cautious. My dad was always the level-headed one, but he's also more relaxed than Mom. He can hang with anyone. We exchange music and movies all the time. Sometimes books, too."

"He sounds awesome. My dad's more of the strong, silent type."

"Nothing wrong with that," he says. "And my dad's cool vibe surprises people because he taught at the college level. Most of my friends growing up assumed he'd be totally nerdy or impossible to relate to."

"Aww," I say. "Nerds always get a bad rap."

"Not according to my mom. She always says she fell in love with his reliable nature, said he kept her grounded."

I tilt my head, considering. "Sounds like maybe you're more like your mom than you thought? If you're knocking wood while hoping for something less structured as a profession?"

"Now wouldn't that be something," he laughs. "Please, let's *never* tell her. She would hound me if she thought I was straying from reliable nerd to nomadic gypsy like Annie."

"Deal," I say. "Your parents sound like a case of opposites attract."

"Mm," he says, sipping his beer. "My dad's father was a lawyer, and eventually a Judge here in New York. But Gramps passed away in the seventies, and Dad moved to California after his undergrad years to go to Stanford. He met my mom, and they settled down. Mom was a kindergarten teacher when she had me and retired after she had my sister."

"That's so sweet," I sigh. "An American love story."

"Well yeah, but once they got into their routine, I think they both sort of forgot what a free spirit my mom used to be. Annie seems to be just like her. But it still drives both my now-settled parents batshit crazy that my sister has no direction. Meanwhile, I've always been the one scheduled to the nth degree and on the fast track to a career."

"Mrs. Pierce mentioned that. And you said you went to Cal Tech?"

"Yeah, as an undergrad. At the tender age of fifteen."

"Holy shit," I blurt. "I couldn't imagine going to college at fifteen."

"It kind of threw me into some social situations I wasn't prepared for, but Pierce had my back. And Nate, too. I probably wouldn't have gone if my father wasn't a professor there. But I lived on campus like any other freshman. I wasn't treated any differently because he worked there."

"Maybe, but it definitely explains why you're so close with Aidan and Nate. And why you were stressed to the max by seventeen."

"Yep. The guys were there for me before I was successful at anything and vice versa. In fact, Pierce got me thinking about the job I'm in now. Never would've considered it if it wasn't for him."

"What job's that?"

"I'm a VP at Soft-Cell." He shrugs, like it's no big deal. "Engineering."

"That's um," I clear my throat. Sip my drink. Set it down. "That's awesome."

And it's a big deal to me!

Everyone studying in my field knows about Soft-Cell. They're a huge company that was started by one of the masterminds in the business of cell technology. If my classmates knew I was sitting next to someone at the VP level *right now*, they'd be blowing up my phone with questions to ask him.

Things like what makes a Canadian student's application for an internship stand out in a crowd?

I can't even count the number of students trying to break into Silicon Valley for their internship next semester. Soft-Cell is high on their list of requested companies to intern with, unless by some chance they decide to shoot for the moon and apply with *the* man, Bryson Chalmers.

That's a pipe dream application, of course. Students do it just to say they did, realizing it's near impossible to land an internship with him. If I wasn't so fixated on New York as my choice next year, I'd consider the pipe dream app myself, even fully aware we'd all have a better shot interning for the Pentagon.

So yeah, I don't want to gush over Daryl, even though he's just unveiled another layer of awesomeness.

Even though his humble grin has me swooning *again*.

As a grown-ass man, he's no doubt earned his place in California, and his nonchalance about his accomplishment is warranted. He's just one of many talented people out there doing his thing. To him, it really is no big deal.

So I won't make it one.

I change the subject.

"I'm glad you keep insisting Pierce is a good guy. If he breaks my sister's heart, he'll have to answer to me," I kid.

He sets his fishing pole aside again, rests his hand on his knee while he cocks an elbow. "Can I level with you about Pierce?"

"Please do." He seems serious, and I'm fearful for a moment.

Does he secretly think Aidan is an asshole?

"Aidan had kind of a rough start in life." He takes another sip from his bottle, his expression full of concern. "He and his brother went from chaos in their youth to a stable home when Tori and Reggie moved them to California. Then ten years ago, his brother's death totally wrecked him. So you should know he never takes normalcy for granted. That's why he shunned attention from the moment he became extremely successful. He likes his private life private."

"I appreciate you sharing that. And Alexis is a private person, too. She wouldn't want to be put on display. I wasn't really aware of how successful he is," I admit, "until I Googled him. He's next level."

"True, but all the attention he gets has never been something he wanted. He thinks of it as a necessary evil. He'd rather just be a fly on the wall, go on about his business. Do some good for the world behind the scenes." He settles in his chair again and picks up his pole to cast further out.

"Sounds like he and Alexis have a lot in common. And speaking of leveling with each other?" I wait for him to look at me. "Tori admitted to me that she knew about our coffee date."

"Did she sing my praises or tell you to run?"

"Let's say she confirmed my gut instinct," I say without looking at him. "And, bee-tee-dubs, she's the coolest and prettiest mama I've ever met."

"Right?" he laughs. "I've always loved having her and Redge as my back-up set of rentals. They're so chill."

"That Mrs. Hamilton is quite a looker, too," I comment. "My mum is probably older than those ladies by a few years. I was sort of a surprise baby after my parents had Ben nine years before, and Mum's not what I'd call a fashion plate. I love her to pieces, but she's never been the person I went to for advice about beauty trends."

"So who was your fashion consultant, then?" he asks. "Because whoever it is does a damn fine job. I'd also like to know who Princess Pam's day one is."

"My best friend Carly, for sure. She's all that and more."

"Yeah?"

"Definitely. We sort of learned the clothes and makeup stuff on our own. Not that she needs it. She's a knockout. But her mum passed when she was little, and she was raised by a single dad. So it was something we kind of figured out together. But yeah, she could've been an actress. Or a champion figure skater like her mom, if she wasn't such a klutz."

"Did you know Mrs. Hamilton used to be an actress in B-movies?"

"Get out," I say. "That's so cool! Was she in anything I would've seen?"

"Doubtful. I think it was before our time."

"What kind of films?"

"I'm not exactly sure. I just know Mr. Hamilton used to direct, and she was in a few of them. That's how they met."

"Wow," I say. "I had no idea. I'm a huge fan of romantic movies, especially old ones. And eighties movies, too. Then again, I'm not really a film buff. If she was in obscure movies from way back, I wouldn't recognize her."

"Okay, here's a question for you. What's the romantic eighties movie you've watched the most, like over and over again?"

"Well, if we're talking just eighties movies, it'd be a tie."

"Between?"

"Ferris Bueller's Day Off and *Goonies."*

"I knew I liked you," he kids. "Epic films. But not romantic ones."

"True." I sip my drink. "That's an easy answer too, but I can't."

His eyebrows raise. "Why the hell not?"

"Because it's embarrassing. It's not even my favorite, really. It's Carly's. But I know for a fact it's the one I've watched the most."

He looks at me in earnest. "Earlier you had to point out you'd scattered the ashes of your dearly departed sibling in the waters we were sitting in front of, all because of an ill-timed question I asked. I think it's your turn to be embarrassed, Princess."

"Okay," I sigh. "So, it's not my *favorite* romantic movie of all time, but I do love it and like I said, my BFF is ga-ga over it. It's um—"

"C'mon," he says to encourage me. "I promise not to laugh."

"Okay, okay. It's *Cocktail."*

"With Tom Cruise as the bartender?"

I nod profusely, my head buried in my hands.

"Wait, doesn't one of the main characters kill himself at the end of that movie?"

"Um, yeah," I laugh. "He does."

"That's not how I'd define a romantic movie."

"Shakespeare might."

"Oh," he says, pointing a finger at me. "Ya got me there, Princess."

"Totes kidding," I say. "That part is awful. But the way the hero fights for the heroine, even though it's Tom Cruise, who is not my favorite. And...hey, it's got a killer soundtrack, okay?" I squeak out a nervous laugh. "Carly's nuts for Tom Cruise. It's either him or the Hawthorne Brothers."

"Wait, who?"

"Oh, no one," I say, waving a hand in the air. "Just some guys she used to watch cook on YouTube. They're from California, and they cook pancakes shirtless from time to time."

"Yeah," he says with a devilish grin. "I've heard of them. I was just surprised you had, too."

"Well I don't, like, watch them religiously. But yeah, I've seen their show. Do you like to cook?"

I'm not sure how to read his expression. I can't figure out why else he'd watch that channel, unless he was gay, which he told me last night he's not. And the way he's looking at me tells me he's *definitely* not. I drink some more, surprised when I notice my bottle of twisted lemonade is nearly empty.

"Sadly, I don't cook," he says flatly. "But yeah, they do. And let me tell ya, they can make a mess when they do it. They're my roommates."

I throw a hand to my mouth, swallowing so hard it makes my throat hurt. "Get. The frick. Out. *Seriously?*"

He laughs. "Seriously. We just bought a house together in Palo Alto, so we could be closer to work."

"Carly is going to crap her pants if I tell her this! She's made me watch their videos over and over again."

"As much as *Cocktail?*"

"More." I raise my bottle in affirmation and polish it off. This is a total mind-blowing revelation.

"And how do you feel about the guys?"

I tilt my chin down, my expression utter confusion. "How do you mean?"

"Like, do they seem your type?"

"Um, no. Not at all. I mean, they're good looking guys but...wait, let me guess. Did one of them steal a girl from you?"

"No," he shakes his head, swigs from his beer and sets it beneath his chair. "Nothing like that. We've got a strong bro-code. Chicks typically flock to them first, but our tastes are different."

I lay a hand on his arm. "Well, I know what it's like to have a best friend who snags attention from every member of the opposite sex that walks by. I don't resent her for it. I'm sure you don't resent that you have roommates who do the same, even if they're double the distraction. But I know how it is."

Rather than simply agree or ignore what I've said, he slays me yet again.

"I can't see anyone passing by you, at least not without doing a double take."

Shit! Here come those zingers again. My skin tingles despite the fact that I have on a light sweatshirt over my tank top.

"That's..." I mutter. "I mean, I don't see what you see. Dave tried to tell me the other night that my celebrity look-alike is Emmy Rossum," I scoff. "So see, he wasn't only *not* picking on me for my superstitious whims, but he was also filling my head with nonsensical compliments."

"I think he's right," he says matter-of-factly. "Although not the version of her in that cable show where she's poor and sleeping with a heroin addict. More like when she was on the cover of *Self*, except your skin is darker."

I look at him, flabbergasted. "I take it you're a fan of hers?"

"You could say that. I mean, I'm not obsessed. But yeah, I think she's a spectacular looking female. And I see the resemblance."

"Well, I don't see it," I shake my head in dismissal and shrug. "I'm just me."

He reels in his line again and gets up, taking both our poles and setting them out of the way on the dock. He turns his chair so he's facing me and sits.

"And who *is* Pam Clayton?" he asks.

His eyes are trained on me with the same intensity as last night when he held the door for me as I left Tim's. I'm back in that core-stirring moment — scared I'd never lay eyes on him again, thrilled thinking just *maybe* he'd kiss me.

All the feels are back.

"C'mon," he urges. "It's your turn, Princess."

Without the alcoholic beverage I've just consumed and my earlier margarita, I wouldn't be as forthcoming as I'm about to be. I take a deep breath before I answer.

"I'm the girl who tutored guys in algebra, not the one they sported wood over. I'm the one whose French-Indian heritage gave her a great complexion and skin that tans beautifully, but in the same shot graced me with a figure resembling guys that play American football."

He chuckles at the way I just described myself, despite the fact that it's all true.

"That's funny?" I ask, slightly wounded.

"Not funny 'ha-ha', but funny, yeah. I'm gonna have to object. First part of your statements are facts, maybe. But every qualifier following them is false."

I smile and shake my head. "You don't have to be so polite. I know who I am, Daryl, and I'm okay with it."

"Politeness aside then, I can tell you for a fact I'm proving the second half of your first statement wrong this very minute."

My eyes go wide. *Sweet baby Jesus.* So he's...like, *right now?*

And he nods. He looks at me through those sexy black frames with those stunning brown eyes, and *he freaking nods!* He's agreeing with my *thoughts.*

"If you were tutoring me right now, I'd need my textbook to hide it. Thankfully, politeness back on the table, I'm sitting far enough away it's not a problem."

Holy...so *yeah*...he's hard, and he just let me know it.

Even through my jeans, I can feel it. I'm wet.

"And as far as your figure," he concludes, "I'm going to guess you've never watched the NFL because our football players look nothing like you do."

Eff my life.

I want him to kiss me *so* badly.

He leans in, the scent of campfire mixing with an intoxicating cologne. Or is it a soap of some sort?

Cripes girl, shut off your freakin' brain!

I will him to come closer, praying he'll finally do it.

Why doesn't he just do it?

Does he think I'll smack him? That I don't want it?

He can't think that. This guy *knows* what's going on in my head. He just proved it to me.

"Pam?" he whispers.

"Yeah." A sigh escapes me as he puts a hand behind my head.

"You are stunning." He runs his thumb across my lips. "Would you mind if I—"

His phone rings to cut through the silence and break our moment. He drops his hand from behind my head and hangs his head in defeat, his hair falling forward as the ring echoes around us.

Gah! Damn you, Fate!

But in the moment, I can't take it anymore. I flip Fate the middle finger, and for once in my life, decide to forget about ill-timed interruptions and just do it.

I'm going to take what I want.

My hands grab for him, my fingers roam the back of his head.

The feel of his soft curls between my fingers is heaven. The phone continues ringing as he looks at me...

...and grabs me back, his hand cradling my head.

I let go of him, dropping my hands in my lap as he comes at me.

He's sweet at first, almost tentative as we feel each other out. His lips are gloriously full, not like the thin bird lips of the last guy I can remember kissing.

And they're *so* freaking soft.

I doubt he's shaved since he's been here, but nothing tickles. I trace fingertips down his jawline and, sure enough, even his facial hair is soft.

Everything about the first few seconds of our kiss is gentle. But then he traces a finger down the back of my neck, only to slide his flat palm back up and tug gently on my hair.

He pulls again, enough that my head falls back, and he goes for my neck.

Oh. My. *God.*

The scent of him surrounds me, my fingers roaming his hair again. I tug, lifting his head up to me so I can kiss him more, over-taken with some crazy lust that tells me I need his lips on mine again *pronto.*

He complies. This time, there's nothing gentle about it.

Neither of us is holding back.

The taste of beer migrates from his tongue to mine as he parts my lips to dive in, and I moan in appreciation. Just as I have the thought that I could kiss him all night and be completely satisfied, he pulls back slightly, breaking the kiss to rest his forehead on mine. He doesn't release the gentle grip his right hand has on the nape of my neck.

As much as I feel like time stopped, our first kiss lasted mere seconds. His phone is still ringing.

"Hot damn," he mutters.

"Um, do you think you should answer?" But the phone goes quiet.

He grins wickedly and his lips find mine again, greedy this time. Every last molecule of my being springs to life, electrified by kissing him.

We're interrupted by more ringing.

"Fuck." He leans back, pulls his phone out to silence it, then sets it in his lap.

I clear my throat, searching for my voice and hoping it's not the biggest turn off ever. "Maybe it's important?"

"Entirely possible, though honestly I could not care less." He leans forward, nips at my lips again, kisses my cheek. He moves my hair so he can graze the sensitive spot beneath my ear, his lips still wet from kissing me.

Holy. Bananas. Daryl Oates is one *effing amazing* kisser.

"Please," I whisper, "please don't stop."

"God, Pam," he moans. "I don't want to. But let me tell you what's going to happen." His lips graze my earlobe as he talks softly in my ear. "You're going to walk away now, and I'm going to say good night while I watch you walk up to the house. I'll get up and put away the worms, only *after* you're a good fifty paces away."

I giggle — until another soft kiss lands on my neck. Another moan comes out. His lips on mine stop the noise, then his head rests on mine again.

"Then, I'm going to walk very uncomfortably across the island to the boathouse where I'll lie awake on the pull-out couch and re-play this moment in my head until dawn."

I'm amused at his admission. But also...but *also*?

Also, I'm completely freaking awestruck.

I'm high on the way just *kissing* him has made my body react. I've never felt so riled up for a guy.

And I desperately want to do it again.

"Are you sure?" The need in my voice is unrecognizable to me.

He nods, pulls me closer to lay a sweet kiss on my lips, then abruptly leans back in his chair. He grabs for another beer from the cooler and tugs at the knees of his jeans, pulling them forward. "Yeah," he says with a sort of frustrated grunt.

"What if that's not what I want?" I can't look at him as I ask the question. My eyes are fixed on the spot where my jeans meet my naked ankle, then on the stripe of teal that slashes through the dull-gray of my sneakers.

He's the first guy who not only moved the needle, but blew it clean off with all the power of hurricane force winds.

And what if he doesn't want me?

"Pam," he says, calling for my attention. I look up at him. "It's not what I want, either."

Oh. I give a slight nod of understanding.

"But if I do what I want," he adds, "we're both gonna be in hot water." He raises his beer bottle at me.

Well, damn.

Did he just friend-zone me all because of my relationship to Alexis? Or because of his with Aidan?

I blow out my frustration with an exaggerated exhale, sighing up at the blackness. Clouds are rolling in, a first quarter moon about to disappear along with the stars that were visible an hour ago.

And the sky about sums up what's just happened.

We've thrown a blanket over a fire to put it out. No sliver of moonlight left. No shooting stars of epic, next level sexcapades on the agenda for this girl tonight.

Okay, so it'd be the first time I'd *ever* get to describe my drab and abbreviated sex life as a next-level-sexcapade. Until now, it's been a grope, grunt and grind with young guys who have as much experience as me and last eight minutes or less. And at that, there's only been three.

But I just *know* that's not what it would be with Daryl Oates.

It would be like nothing else I've ever experienced.

An epic, earth-shattering, life altering sexcapade.

I know that's how it would be because just kissing him has caused me to need a long, cold shower or, if I was home, a reach over to the nightstand drawer. But now, I can only assume how it would've been. If I'm reading signals right, he does not intend to take this any further than the dreamy make-out *sesh* that just came to a screeching halt.

I place my empty in the cooler, then get up and walk a few paces down the dock. As I turn back to him, his phone rings for a third time.

He makes no move to answer it.

"Good night, Mister Oates."

"Good night," he says, shooing me away with a wave of his hand. Just as I think he's completely blowing me off, his sweet words drift over the water and reach me at the shore. "Sleep well, Princess."

18

Oates

Friday Night

Fawn Island

Before Pam makes it to the guest bedroom upstairs, I send her three text messages.

The first apologized if I was too forward, though I can confidently assume from her body's reaction she was more than receptive to what just happened.

She confirms that not only did she think I wasn't too forward, but she wishes I'd kissed her sooner. What's more, she wished I had *not* put on the brakes. After I adjust my pants for the umpteenth time since being up close and personal with my princess, I send her a second text, apologizing for the phone interruption.

If I had half a brain while I was around her, I would've turned the damn thing off the second we sat down. But when she's near me, my mind goes haywire — like I've tripped a breaker, zapping all power to cognitive thought.

This isn't my usual thing, like the slightly uncomfortable short circuit I get around girls if they compliment me or pay me some attention. On the contrary, she hasn't openly swooned over me. I can tell she admires what she sees, but the connection between us is far deeper.

Chemical. Mental. Almost spiritual?

Or as spiritual as a guy who *isn't* spiritual can get.

Add all that up, plus the way she just *listens* (and looks at me, and responds intelligently, and listens again). It's a formula resulting in my synapses rapid firing, *pop pop pop*, while all the blood rushes to my dick.

With her, it's all just *different*. Like no other code I've had to decipher, no other problem I've had to dissect to get to the root of it.

She's different.

Another text response comes saying she understands about the phone calls and hopes she didn't keep me from responding to an emergency. My third and final message of the night explains that it wasn't an emergency. It was my flaky sister the first time, followed up by two calls from my parents who don't realize I'm not currently in the same time zone they are.

I never had a chance to tell them about this weekend getaway.

I add a 'good night' sign off to message three, along with a link to the first song that came to mind as I watched her beautiful form saunter up the path and back to the house. It's Johnny Mellencamp's "Ain't Even Done With The Night", of course. Because that rock n' roll icon hit the nail on the head with that song.

I sure as hell didn't want to be done with this night.

I call into my voicemail and listen to two messages from my dad conveying my parents' annoyance about my sister's latest news. Mom and Dad were just informed Annie's left Arizona (again) to move to New York City (again).

I wasn't aware of the fact, either. But Annie does what Annie wants. They aren't going to get much sympathy from me.

The timestamp indicates my sister's call came first, but she didn't leave a voicemail. She sent a text warning me that Mom and Dad would be calling, thanking me for the beautiful picture from the Thousand Islands, and scolding me for not telling her I'd be in Canada this weekend.

I respond with my typical big brother snark-casm.

> Hope you're happy and
> comfortable in NEW YORK.
> YOU didn't tell ME you
> were MOVING. I'm just here
> visiting with Pierce and

> *working for the weekend.*
> *Just invited here 2 DAYS ago.*

Her response comes immediately.

> *Gah! You're with Aidan? How is*
> *that handsome stud?!*

> *Smitten and now severely*
> *committed to a new &*
> *incredibly normal woman.*
> *Sorry, sis.*

> *What?! Damn! I didn't even*
> *know he was on the market!*
> *Still, happy for him. Anyone is*
> *better than Stella.*

> *Agreed. And his status with*
> *New Girl is on the QT. TELL NO*
> *ONE. Going to bed now. Catch*
> *up when I'm back home.*

> *Okay, brother. I'd avoid Doc and*
> *Penny for awhile. They're in a*
> *tizzy after I told them I'm back*
> *in the Big Apple.*

I laugh out loud. When Mom and Dad are on a tear about her choices, she always refers to them by their first names, even when face to face with them.

> *Doc left two messages already.*
> *I'll settle them down tomorrow.*

> *(eye roll emoji) Thanks, bro.*
> *You're the best!!*

She follows up with more emojis. The first is a heart, then a bunch of kiss faces. I shake my head. Ironic, given that's exactly what little sister interrupted tonight.

Some damn fine kissing.

I put the fishing gear and camp chairs away and cross the island paths to head for bed. I know I'll be lying awake thinking about Pam for at least an hour, if not until dawn as promised. As I reach the iron steps leading up to the second floor of the boathouse, my phone vibrates with a text.

One new message

From: Princess Pam
I open it, unable to stop my perma-grin.

*Thank you for the song. Getting
sleepy. Here's one back for you.
This song was playing in my
earbuds when I first saw you!
Good night, Mr. Oates.*

I click the link to a YouTube video for Ry Cooder's cover version of Elvis' "All Shook Up" from the *Cocktail* soundtrack.

That's definitely what I am.

All shook up.

To the bone.

After traveling and staying up late (twice) obsessing about Pam, my mind finally relaxed from sheer exhaustion, and I drifted off to sleep before 12:30. It didn't hurt knowing we were passing out on the same island. At least come morning, I knew I'd see her again.

I wake up on the pull out couch and realize it's just dawn. Though I'm feeling rested and energetic, I've only slept for five hours. I can hear Nate snoring, even through the closed bedroom door.

I head downstairs to shower on the dock. I set my glasses on the ledge of the chest-high shower wall and discard my boxers, lathering up as thoughts of Pam come to mind. And from there, I can't help it. I feel like a teenager again. I can't remember the last time I felt so pent up, in need of a release if only to clear my mind, because I need a woman.

Not just any pre-categorized, run-of-the-mill girl the twins have labeled with unfortunate accuracy.

Nope.

I need *her*. Her words are rattling around inside my head, and I'm physically aroused just at the recollection of kissing her, from her warm mouth to her sweet scent, the one that overwhelmed me as my lips grazed her neck, behind her ear…

Jesus Christ on a skateboard.

Warm water cascades over me as I lean up against the teak shower surround, head resting on my forearm while I shudder in release. I rinse off and turn off the water, shaking out my wet head as I hear Nate's signature loud whistle from upstairs. The only other person I know who whistles that loudly is Aidan's mom, but I know it's not her.

Thank God.

"Oates, you up?!" he shouts. "Let's take a sunrise cruise!"

"Coming," I shout.

And I let a juvenile laugh escape me, because yeah.

I so did.

J̲ust after six a.m., Nate and I cruise the channel in silence, the only sound the noise of the Whaler engine. We pass a few early risers in kayaks along the shoreline and one pontoon on open water as we cross the channel. It's super quiet on the river this early.

Nate comments about the summer we spent chasing a group of girls who were camping at one of the sites nearby. He points to the shore as we drive past and gives it a salute. We continue on, then slow our roll through more secluded spots, past some camps we're familiar with from back in the day. The rest of the ride passes in comfortable silence.

I'm driving, so on our way back to Fawn Island, I cut two close circles around the now abandoned island where I lost my virginity, throwing up a peace sign as we pass (to thank the Universe, or God, or the girl herself, Jessica James, because that was a pretty epic turn of events).

Halfway through my second pass, the pleasant memory delivers me a sock in the gut.

What if Pam's never had sex?

She's only twenty-one. A self-professed nerd. It's entirely possible, dare I say likely.

I can't be responsible for deflowering that gorgeous girl.

It definitely wouldn't happen on the weekend I've just met her, on this island where I have to worry about who's nearby and might interrupt. My thoughts skid into how amazing I'd want to make that experience for her, how much time I'd take to make sure everything was just right for my princess.

And now my thoughts raise the issue I cured with my shower, excitement rearing its horny head again.

Down, boy.

If something is about to happen between us, I'll have to ask her about this. In fact, I might have to ask her before we get anywhere near each other again. I don't want to ask her over a text, but I've got to know. I'm not sure I want to embarrass us both by asking her in person, but there really isn't another respectful way to go about it.

If I'm interested in Pam, I'd be a concern to Alexis (maybe Aidan, too). Long distance romances don't typically have a snowball's chance of avoiding heartbreak. But to have that risk *and* take her sacred virgin status? Be the first guy she's ever been with?

That's a double hit of no-can-do.

If she's never done the deed, I'll have to forget about ever laying a hand on her. Forget how *right* she feels. It can't happen. I just have to psych myself up into believing it's the only option.

This is no problemo, Oates. You can do this!

It's Saturday morning. We'll be parting ways tomorrow, and I'll probably never see her again, unless or until Pierce marries her sister-in-law. Then they'll have a bunch of babies, and Pam and I can swoon over them like a proper aunt and uncle, and I'll ask her to pass the potatoes during the few holiday dinners we might see each other.

Just have to ignore my rampant thoughts for thirty hours or at least keep them to myself.

No sweat.

No way in hell can you hold out, sucker!

I ignore my subconscious.

This is how it has to be.

Pam Clayton is off limits.

Not just because disappointing Aidan and his new sweetie puts an epic fear in me, but because if she's a virgin, I'd forever be her first. And statistically, it's unlikely I'd ever be her last.

I'm not sure I want that as a reality.

Our chemistry is too off the charts for me to lie and say I *don't* want to have sex with her. She'd see right through that. I've never been able to fib well, never mind pull off a straight up charade like that. But the bigger problem is, this feels like *more*.

More than my dopamine levels skyrocketing. More than a triple release of a shit ton of endorphins.

As comfortable as I feel around her, it's like our connection is deeper. Like it's happened before. In a past life, or an alternate universe.

That's some heavy shit, Oates. Slow your roll!

That's crazy-ass, emotion-led thinking with no scientific basis.

And she's off limits!

But what if she's not a virgin?

I'm incredibly flustered. I have to find out.

Now.

I throw the gear shift to full throttle and in less than ten minutes, we're back at the boathouse dock.

Nate ties up the lines. "Thanks for the cruise, boss. I'm gonna shower before breakfast."

"Solid plan," I say. "I'll go wake up First Musketeer."

I hop off the boat and walk up to a thicket of trees, scouring the granite and dirt floor. I rake my foot over needles to uncover some pine cones and, once I've gathered enough of them, toss my stash into the Whaler. I do a drive-by of Brat Cottage, hollering up at Aidan's window.

"Wake up in there! You two lovebirds gonna sleep the day away?"

I buzz by the point the cottage sits on, tossing some ammo at the window of Aidan's old bedroom. The curtains part as Alexis eventually appears, curious about the ruckus. Her silhouette is wrapped up in a bed sheet as she waves to me, then ducks at pine cone number six. I drive by the point twice more, heaving more ammo at the other window of the bedroom, then head back to the boathouse as my phone buzzes in the pocket of my shorts.

One new message

From: Princess Pam

I fumble to open it.

> *Hey, keep it down. Some of us*
> *were up late!*

> *So sorry, Your Highness. Are you*
> *decent? I'd love to take you for*
> *a ride.*

So I don't sound like a complete pervert, I quickly delete the last word then type "boat ride". Her response comes immediately.

> *Yes. Where to?*

> *Not far, I think we're due up*

*there for breakfast soon. I've
got the Whaler over at the
boathouse dock now. Pick you
up on the main dock?*

*No, it's ok. Stay there. I'll be
right down.*

As I watch her walk down the dock, my princess is more of a breath of fresh air than the actual fresh air. She's wearing a t-shirt that says 'But First, Coffee', and the same pair of jeans and sneakers from last night. A sweatshirt is tied around her waist.

I grin as she approaches. "Hey," I say. "Sleep well?"

"Too well," she says with a warm smile. "Eventually."

"I hear that. I passed out within thirty minutes."

"I think it was one a.m., but once I was out, I was *out*. I forgot where I was until I woke up to the sound of you cruising around. And I had some really crazy dreams."

"Oh yeah?" I lean in to kiss her cheek, but she suddenly seems tentative. "Shit, I'm—" I run a hand through my hair, rub the back of my neck as my elbow points awkwardly to the sky. *Now this feeling I'm used to.* "Sorry. That was presumptuous."

She touches my arm, sending a shock of electricity directly to my chest. "No, it's just um, I didn't get a chance to shower yet. I'm sure I smell like yesterday's laundry." She looks away, then back at the boat. "I was going to, but I didn't want to waste any time getting to you before everyone else was awake. The house is still eerily silent."

My lips curve into a grin, and I pull her closer. "It's all good, Princess. You still smell as amazing as you did mere hours ago." Not a lie. She smells like shampoo and campfire and outdoors. I kiss the top of her head and wrap her up in a brief hug, then help her step down into the Whaler. "Let's go for a ride."

19

Pam

Saturday Morning

Fawn Island

We zip across the channel from Fawn Island in the direction of Lily Bay. I'm next to Daryl on the small bench seat, thankful for my sweatshirt given the breeze.

"You know this area?" he asks.

I let a nod be my answer until he reaches the small bay cocooned by a semicircle of small islands.

"It's a popular fishing spot," I say once the engine quiets, "and the cottage that used to be there was a regular stop for my parents and their friends. The Santini family used to summer here and throw some pretty wild parties." I gesture to where a cottage used to span two of the larger islands where there's now a gap, the view now open to the main channel.

There are no other boats around, except those in the distance tied up at their respective docks. The mainland is only fifty meters away. Massive homes are perched on a cliff of granite overlooking the river as we drift below them. Elaborate stairways of metal or wood lead down from each owner's property to their respective docks.

"I love those places," I say, nodding up to a cluster of three gorgeous properties. "Not as much as The Gables, but they're quite impressive. I used to sit on the point over there while my parents were here hanging out with friends. I'd stare up at the one made of stone and make up stories about who lived there."

He follows my gaze. "I always liked that one, too," he smiles. "We used to fish here once in awhile." He nods to a buoy bobbing in the middle of the bay, surrounded by a green blanket of lily pads. "I don't remember that, though."

"Mm, the Santinis put it there so fishing boats would have a place to tie off. Years ago when their private parties were constantly disturbed, it kept people from driving further into the bay to anchor. The cottage was damaged by flooding and had to be torn down last year."

He looks wistfully at the hole in the horizon. "That's sad."

"Yeah," I sigh. "Mum was so bummed. The Santinis hadn't come up in a couple years, but this place was such a treasure. Some fishermen used to drive right up and park at their floating docks, even if there was an island full of people mingling about."

"That's gutsy. So your parents knew the owners?"

"Oh, yes. I've witnessed the party intrusions with my own eyes."

"Were they American assholes?" He shakes his head. "Some people have no manners."

"No, usually they were Canadians who'd been tipping a few. They'd end up joining the party and forget about fishing."

He laughs. "Further proof. You *are* the friendliest country."

"Yep." I nod to the buoy. "Go ahead and tie off."

He maneuvers the boat and ties a line onto the hook. As he leans out of the boat, his t-shirt rides up and I can't help admiring his exposed skin. He's *so* tan.

And muscular.

Even his lower back has muscles.

Is it hot out here?

I take off my sweatshirt and toss it on the seat ahead of us. The sun must be warming me now that we're still.

Right.

We're floating in the middle of the bay, surrounded by the horseshoe of islands, trees draping over us like a canopy. "This truly is one of the prettiest spots on the river."

"Agreed," he says. But he's not looking at our surroundings. I can feel his gaze on me.

Our phones sound off simultaneously. I read a text from Alexis letting me know breakfast is bacon and eggs, and it's ready anytime we are.

Thank goodness. I'm starving. "I hear breakfast is ready?"

"Yeah," he says, "Aidan just messaged me." He fiddles with the boat key dangling in his lap, then removes his glasses and cleans them in a hurry. I can't tell if he's nervous or ticked about another interruption.

"We can head back," I say. "Maybe we'll get a chance for another ride later."

He throws his left leg over the bench, straddling the seat as he grabs for my hand. Chills rush through me, same as they've done every time he touches me. I am fascinated by the way my body reacts to him.

"Pam." He says it quietly, then looks off towards the bare spot in the horizon

I squeeze his hand once.

"I have to ask you something."

"Anything," I say. "Shoot."

His head is down, staring at the seat we share. His curls are still damp at the bottom, and it's all I can do not to run my fingers through his hair. *God, this guy!* How can anyone be so sweet and incredibly sexy at the same time?

"It's kind of personal." He looks up and locks eyes with me. "I don't want to embarrass you, but there's something about you I've gotta know."

"For you?" I shrug, trying to downplay the severity of his tone. "I'm an open book. As long as you don't share the royal secrets with the tabloids, this princess will tell you whatever you want to know."

"Okay, here goes." He draws a breath and holds it in, even as he blurts his question at breakneck speed. "Are you a virgin?" Even as he squints waiting for my reaction, he exhales a huge sigh of relief that the question is out there.

It's sweet he's curious and adorable how he had to work himself up to ask me, but my dominant emotion is amusement.

I mean, *that's* what he's all worked up over?

I've had guys at school ask me this in a casual debate about the scientific studies of love and sex, knowing someone who feels they've been in love or who is sexually active is going to have a different argument than a virgin. How can we understand one another's reactions to such research without knowing the status of the person interpreting it?

I burst into a giggle, a hand up in the air to indicate an apology for my reaction.

He laughs at himself. "I know," he sighs. "God, that was lame."

"Sorry," I finally manage. "I mean really, I'm *so* sorry. I'm not laughing at you. I'm just...you seemed so concerned. I thought it was something serious."

"I didn't want to ask. But I guess in a way, it is kind of serious. For me. If that's your status, I can't...I mean..." His posture changes, his shoulders sinking as he mumbles *shit* under his breath. He drops both hands in his lap. "I totally know how to fuck up a moment."

"It's okay." I nudge him with my right shoulder. "I understand why you're asking."

He sits up straight, a hand on his knee. "Yeah?"

"If things went the way I think we both wanted them to last night, you're probably wondering if it would've been a first for me. I get that."

"Yes," he says in relief, "exactly." He looks down at his Converse, then back up at me. "I don't need Alexis ready to murder me. Then Aidan would make *sure* to murder me just for pissing off his girl. And all because I'd done that to you. Or, I mean, with you..." he trails off. "*Fuck.* This is not coming out the way I intended."

"How about we don't complicate things?"

He looks at me curiously.

"I enjoy being around you, that's no secret. Everyone currently staying on Fawn Island knows it. And yes, I'm insanely attracted to you," I say. "But tomorrow, we part company and will probably never see each other again, at least until Alexis and Aidan's wedding. And the next time will be when they surprise us with a set of twins that we get to buy super cute outfits for."

"A wedding and twins?" he laughs. "You've thought about this?"

"Oh, yeah. I can't wait to be an aunt. It wasn't in the cards for me to be an aunt before. But Alexis and Aidan are going to be married, and they'll have twins. One boy and one girl."

"Their names being?" he asks, testing to see how deep my theory goes.

"That's easy. Julie and Jake."

"You're so crazy," he laughs. "I can't believe you have names for their non-existent children. But you're probably not wrong about that direction. They seem pretty head over heels."

"Then someday, you and I meet up to take Jules and little Jakie to the amusement park until they eat too much cotton candy and puke, at which point we'll drop them off to their parents and run for the hills. And we'll forever escape changing dirty diapers. We'll be the cool aunt and uncle, the ones who are always up-to-date on the latest trends."

"But we'll make sure they're educated in old school video games and records, too," he adds.

"Absolutely. We'll teach them how to code and how to crash the website of their rival school."

He's laughing but also looking at me with obvious disbelief, like he's just seen a unicorn having tea with a leprechaun. I keep talking.

"Let's just enjoy the next thirty hours, and whatever happens, happens. We make our own rules and alter them to fit as needed, just like the game we played when we met. Okay?"

"How do you do that?" he asks.

"Do what?"

"I did not want to have this conversation, like at all. And you just pulled a Jenga on me. Collapsed the tower. Flipped the game table upside down, and now what's coming out of your mouth is exactly what I've been thinking."

"Oh, that," I say, waving a dismissive hand. "I can read minds."

He scolds me with a sarcastic smirk.

"Yeah, I've just had it patented. You'll get the technology in the States soon," I tease. "You know, once your slow moving government has approved it."

His smirk turns to an adorable grin, and I wink at him.

"Uh, there's one last issue to address," he says. "Are you or aren't you?"

I blush but answer candidly. "Um, I'm not."

He turns away to do one of those mutters under his breath. I think this time it's 'thank God'. He gets up to untie the boat, then seats himself behind the wheel again. He starts the engine as I add, "Ironically, it happened after one of the parties I went to here with my parents."

He whips his head to me and shuts the engine off. "That's hella ironic."

"Right? But sadly, it wasn't anything to write home about."

"No, huh?"

"I snuck off with a guy I'd known for years, and he absolved me of my innocence. I suffered the same fate most girls do in their late teens."

He raises an eyebrow, unsure what I mean.

"Awkward sex that begins on a twin bed in the guy's childhood bedroom and ends in under ten minutes."

He laughs, shaking his head. "That's terrible."

"I completely agree."

"Can I ask if that was that the only time? Or has it gotten better for you?"

"All improvements have been self-taught." I exaggerate a proper tone, as though I'm a real princess. "But I did have two other brief relationships that resulted in coitus. Would you like to know the gentlemen's names?"

"No." His expression is serious. "Just their current addresses will do."

My amusement turns quickly to confusion.

"I'll be sending them each a letter telling them what fools they were," he says, "because they shall never again have the privilege of courting Princess Pam."

Insta-panty-melting-swoon.

I'm done.

"But this begs another question," I say. "I take it you're also not a virgin, Mister Oates?"

He starts up the engine again and cocks his head at me, his smile becoming a wickedly delicious grin.

Apparently not.

By the afternoon, I can tell our early morning chat has reassured my gorgeous Geek Charming. He seems more relaxed than he was on the boat this morning. Meanwhile, my nerves are partying like rock stars in my gut. During breakfast, while Nate and Daryl scarfed down three plates of food, I barely ate.

I am falling hard for this guy.

He's smart.

And not just 'regular' smart.

I dare say the boy is a genius.

I listened from the opposite end of the breakfast table while he and Nate talked about a problem at one of Nate's job sites two projects ago. Daryl insisted he could've solved it in three less steps. Then the guys debated the likelihood of an asteroid hitting Earth in 2135.

I followed some of it, but some was over my head. Then Aidan and Daryl had to gang up on Nate when he wouldn't admit their valid counterpoints, which led to them busting on him about when his cake-making skills will be on display for all of us.

But it isn't just Daryl's intelligence.

It's the way he looks at me. The way he laughs, always with his guard down and unapologetically himself.

It's the way he hesitated to agree when asked to go for a quick spin in the Whaler with the guys.

He looked at me before answering, an unvocalized ask whether I was okay with it. We made a tentative plan that we'd fill up two coffee mugs after breakfast and head back to the main docks for a little more fishing and a lot more talking.

I smile at him, hoping he'll understand I'm absolutely fine if we don't follow through on that plan. He hasn't spent time with both of his best friends in years, and I'd never want him to miss out on that.

I clear my dishes to the kitchen. As I thank Aidan's parents for a delicious meal, I hear Daryl tell Aidan a quick ride sounds fun. I smile to myself as I head for the stairs, knowing he got my message.

As I reach the foyer, I feel a hand on my shoulder. He spins me around, smiling as he takes one more step to close the gap between us.

We're facing each other, his left shoulder touching my left shoulder as we look past one another. My view is of the kitchen. I'm thankful Alexis is chatting up Tori as she walks to the refrigerator. She's not looking this way to see the giddy expression on my face.

"So sorry," he says. At his tone, my insides to melt like an ice sculpture in spring. His voice is soft in my ear. "I promise I'll be right back, then we'll do some more fishing. Maybe even catch us something this time."

"It's all good, I'll see you when you get back. I'm gonna grab a shower."

"Um, yeah." He looks away and clears his throat. "Thanks for that image."

I raise my eyebrows in confusion.

"I'm on the verge of needing a textbook right about now."

Oh.

He sways toward the screen door to put some space between us, then leans back into my shoulder and whispers, "See you soon, Princess."

I move toward the stairs wearing a goofy smile, but he grabs my hand to pull me back to him. He gives my knuckles a chaste kiss, then exits swiftly through the screen door.

I sigh as the door smacks shut.

Tori shouts from the kitchen. "Don't slam the door!"

He turns back, only sharing with me his look of regret. "Sorry, Mama!"

And he's gone.

B y the afternoon, I'm back in Daryl's company. We're on the dock again, soaking up the warmth of the early summer sun in our canvas chairs. He has more luck than last night, already catching three fish to my one.

We've talked (and talked) for nearly two hours. We've covered a variety of topics from how he met the Hawthorne twins (a charity trivia event where they paid him to join their team because they knew after meeting him, he'd only decimate them as an opponent), to brainstorming crazy ideas for my future and how I might satisfy my craving for travel and still earn a living.

He's currently distracted by incoming messages on his phone and apologizes while he takes time to respond, leaving me lost in thought about my conversation with Alexis this morning.

After breakfast and parting ways with Daryl, I'd practically floated upstairs. I hopped in the shower and...

Well, yeah. I went *there*.

I couldn't help it. Just thinking of the guy currently seated next to me had me hot and bothered. When my thoughts drifted to the way he kissed me last night, it was enough to encourage a ramp up to a pretty mind-blowing orgasm.

I stepped out feeling relaxed and satisfied, inhaling fresh air from an open window in the bathroom.

And the *bathroom*. Lord, have mercy. That in itself was breathtaking enough to inspire a girl to ecstasy. Modern, electric fireplace in the middle of a floor to ceiling wall to separate the vanity from a to-die-for clawfoot tub. Carrera marble everywhere. Shiny silver fixtures. Incredibly fluffy towels softer than cashmere.

The room was heaven.

I was dressed, standing before the mirror drying my wet mop of hair when Alexis wandered in for a girls' chat.

She vocalized that she saw Daryl staring at me over breakfast. Given her observations and my shower excitement five minutes before, I blushed and breezed through our conversation like a giddy teenager.

The tables turned when the subject of my brother came up. I could sense her guilt for being happy, and I wasn't about to have that.

I told her how ecstatic I am for her. That Ben would be happy for her. That he knew he'd never give her the kind of relationship she seems to have found with Aidan, despite how much he loved her.

And who are any of us to stop true love anyway?

A few tears fell, we laughed, we hugged it out, and she went off to find Aidan while I met up with Mr. Oates on the dock.

And now, I've missed what he just said. A hand on my wrist brings me back. "You need help reeling that in, Princess?"

I realize then what's happening with my line, but I'm too late. The tension goes out of my pole and I pull up the line with an empty hook. No fish, no worm.

"Dang."

"You were zoned out there," he says. "What's going on in that pretty head?"

I grin like a total goofball. "Just a conversation I had with Alexis before you guys got back."

"Uh oh," he says. "Sounds serious." He gets up and returns his pole to the cabinet near the dock. "I think I need to get off my ass for a minute. Pierce jumped some wakes and bounced us all over hell in the Whaler. You want to keep fishing?"

"Actually, you can take mine, too." He does, and I stand up and stretch. I'm wearing another dress today, and while I feel like I'm overdressed for a casual day hanging out on the island, I know I'll be glad for it later.

Tori and Reggie have taken off for the day in their wooden boat, aptly named the Victoria. All the Pierces' friends are out today, too. I'm told the plan is for all of us to gather here for dinner, and another couple is coming to join us.

Rumor has it they're the couple who readied everything for the Pierces' arrival. They're locals and probably the same people Dave, Carly and I hid from the other night when we were snooping around. I expect dinner will be casual, but also the 'main event' of the weekend with uber wealthy people. I'm glad I'll be dressed for it.

"Hey, have you ever been up there?" He nods to a high spot on the east end of the island, off to our left. A gazebo sits on the point looking out over the water, but it's surrounded by trees.

"To be honest, I've been by this island a thousand times, and I've never noticed it before."

"Yeah, it's kind of a hidden gem. Used to be one of our spots to escape the rentals," he laughs. "Come on, I'll walk you up there. The view is amazing."

We start up a lesser worn path as he takes my hand, which is becoming like second nature.

"So tell me what had you so distracted," he says. "I'm curious if Alexis was warning you off me."

"Not at all. She did say she noticed you looking at me during breakfast," I say, my face flushing.

He laughs. "I guess I should've kept my eyes on my plate."

"Kind of difficult given how high it was piled with food."

"Point made," he says. "I'm a growing boy." He pats his incredibly flat stomach. "And my appetite is always double up here."

"I've heard a lot of people say that when they visit the river."

"It's the fresh air," he says with a wink. "So she didn't tell you that all boys are evil?"

"No," I laugh. "Our chat was more about her than me."

"Yeah?"

We arrive at the gazebo and there are no words. He's right about the view. You can see all the way to the bridge that spans the main channel and terminates on the Canadian mainland.

"*Wow.*"

"Right?" We're standing in the middle of the structure, the rustic pine floor dusty beneath our feet. I walk to the railing and lean forward. It's a straight drop to the water. "Careful of that railing," he says. "I'm not sure how secure it is after all these years."

I turn to look at him. His hair is blowing in a breeze that seems stronger up here. He's just standing there in his Chucks and board shorts and a ridiculous blue t-shirt that softens his dark brown eyes. It says 'Beer Thirty', and 'beer' is spelled out in digital clock letters.

I'd laugh, except I already did when I first saw the shirt this morning.

Right now, I'm overcome with emotion just looking at him. Goosebumps raise on my shoulders, and a weird sensation spreads through me, like I want to laugh and cry at the same time.

"I need to tell you something," I blurt.

He tilts his head, his brow furrowed for a split second. "Okay," he finally says. His smile is reassuring. "Tell me something."

"My sister-in-law was feeling a sort of 'survivor's guilt' this morning, I think because she's happy with Aidan after losing my brother." I raise a sandaled foot and glide it down the back of my opposite calf. I take the hair band off my wrist and tie up my hair, take a deep breath. "You can probably imagine what I mean."

"Maybe," he says. "I'd imagine it's a terrible feeling. If she's happy, she should be able to just ride the wave."

I want to explain to him just why my sister-in-law has these hang-ups. I know she's already told Aidan.

"You don't have to say anymore," he says, reading my thoughts again. He wraps me up in a hug. "It's girl talk, I get it. I was asking to satisfy my own curiosity, or I guess my own paranoia. I don't need to go around pissing off New York lawyers."

"Trust me, she digs you. It's just, um..." I exhale a long breath. "Remember how I said last night that my brother's relationship with Alexis was unconventional?"

He nods into my shoulder.

"And today I mentioned they never had children in their plans?"

He releases me from our embrace and steps back. "Yeah, I remember. I didn't want to push you on it. Figured it's not really my business."

"Well, they loved each other," I sigh, "but they weren't really *in* love."

He's transfixed, waiting for what I'll say next.

"They met in college, and my brother...well, first the two of them hit it off in the friend zone. Like, they were inseparable, especially when he first moved to the States. Then some things kind of went off the rails."

"They had a falling out?"

I shake my head. "No, just as far as his options of staying in the States. She married him so he could get citizenship and work in broadcasting in New York."

He's stunned into silence, blown away by the revelation. "Wow," he finally says. "That's a lot to do for someone. I totally admire her generosity right now. And they never got caught? I mean, no authority ever suspected—"

"Nope. In their personal lives, everyone knew how much they cared for each other. People just assumed they'd been dating and this was the normal progression of things. But that wasn't actually the case."

"Well, that's nothing to be concerned with. It was their—"

"He was gay," I blurt, interrupting him. "My brother wasn't interested in women."

His eyebrows shoot up, eyes wide as he nods, adding an 'ah' of understanding.

"Does that weird you out?"

And he laughs, genuinely laughs, as though I'm being ridiculous to even think that.

"Not at all. I mean, it's a revelation, for sure. But no, it's not an issue for me. I take it he wasn't out, then?"

I shake my head. "Just with Alexis and me, and one guy he

briefly dated. No one else knew. Not my parents, no one. He was never ready, I guess."

"I can't imagine having to hide who you are from the world," he says. He steps to the railing, looking out to the bridge. "Life is so short. Seems a waste to expend so much energy denying who we are."

"I agree." I turn back to the water, stepping over to join him. "We never pushed him on it. They had sort of an open marriage. Ben could see someone if he felt so inclined and so could Alexis."

"I take it she didn't," he says.

"Never. She never had the time. She worked her ass off to open up her law office after her dad died."

"That's right," he says. "I'd forgotten she lost her dad, too."

My nod is solemn thinking of how much heartbreak Lex has suffered in the last five years.

"Jesus. That chica's been through some shit."

"She has," I say quietly. "But she's so strong. Like, the strongest girl I know. She dove into school after losing her father and into the new practice after losing Ben. She just didn't date. So to see her so happy with Aidan..." I trail off.

"I get it," he says. "I think it's a big deal for both of them. Aidan's not opened up to anyone really. Not ever that I know of. So you think maybe Ben just didn't want to open himself up to whatever he thought would come his way if people knew?"

"I think so. I figured if he didn't want anyone to know, it was his choice. He met someone in New York City on assignment, and that's the only person he ever really dated, as far as I know. But they weren't in a committed thing."

"No?"

"I think if circumstances were different, they might've been. But my brother was living in Stanton with Alexis, reporting for Channel 8, and playing the role of a husband. Charlie, that's our friend's name," I explain, "is openly gay. He was living in Manhattan, and it just didn't make sense long term. They hadn't spoken for awhile when my brother died."

"Dang," he says solemnly.

I go on. "Charlie came to the funeral, though. Alexis and I knew who Charlie was. She'd gone with Ben on assignment a couple times, so the three of them would pal around together. Eventually, he ended up really close with Alexis. He moved up to Stanton after Ben died and sort of picked up her pieces. She'd have been lost without him."

He smiles. "So they're like BFFs now?"

"Yes. In fact, she tells me she has Charlie's approval of Aidan, so that says a lot."

"Wow. Sounds like Charlie's got good instincts then."

"From what I know, he does. I've only had the privilege of hanging out with him a couple times, but we keep in touch by text. He's amazing. He also works for Lex as her paralegal."

"That's so cool. I bet she kind of feels like Ben's still around that way, too."

"Maybe to a degree. But he's also damn good at his job. He's funny and charming. He sort of looks like Taye Diggs, but his skin is a little bit lighter."

"Like, how much lighter? Meaning he's not black?"

"No," I say through my laughter. "He is. It's just...well here, I'll just show you." I pull up the same photo I showed Dave two nights ago. "See?"

"Well, shit. Remind me never to piss him off. I don't care if he's black or as blue as a Smurf. He looks *strong.*"

I laugh. "He is built. He loves the gym. It's an outlet for him. He sometimes sends me motivational memes 'cause he knows I hate to work out. Or he'll send me a picture of some guy he saw in tight bike shorts and make me guess if he's gay or straight."

He laughs, then a moment of quiet passes before he wraps an arm around my waist. "Thanks for trusting me with all that."

I nod. I've never felt this way around another person in such a short time. But with Daryl everything just seems natural.

"I didn't want you to find out from someone else," I say. "I think Aidan might know the truth, and if he ever said something—"

"He wouldn't." He crooks his finger and gently turns my face to his. A look of concern washes over him as he reads me. He swipes at the single tear that's forming in the corner of my eye. I'm not sure if it's there from laughing or from raw emotion thinking about Ben.

"But if he did," I say pointedly, "I didn't want you thinking I was embarrassed of my brother or his relationship with Alexis, thinking that's why I didn't mention it. I love them both, and I'm proud of them both."

"I'd never think that." He pulls me to him, his arms surrounding me in a bear hug.

"Good," I smile into his shoulder, a sigh of relief escaping. "Thank you for listening."

"This conversation stays between us," he says. "Swear. And if you ever wanna talk about it, don't hesitate." He pulls back from our embrace and throws his glasses up on his head. He glides a hand behind my ear, a thumb across my top lip, and then he kisses me.

I know he means it to be tender, a sweet gesture to let me know he truly cares.

But that's not how my body is responding.

Heat radiates below my waist, and my lady parts are literally pulsing with excitement. The breeze compounds matters as chills chase up and down my bare arms.

Holy. Moly.

His tongue slides into my mouth, and I'm becoming deliriously horny.

No two ways about it.

Horny. That's the word.

"Daryl," I whisper.

"Mm," he moans.

"Tell me about your app."

He stops kissing me, but his lips are still dancing over mine, then moving lower, down to my neck. "Now?"

"Yes," I breathe. "Right now."

His lips are back at the spot beneath my left ear that drives me absolutely mad, even as he tugs at my hair to spike the thrill.

"Why?" he whispers.

"Because if you don't hit me with some facts, I'm going to tackle you right here. In broad daylight on this filthy floor." As his lips move down to my collarbone, I can feel them curve into a wicked smile. He traces over the sensitive skin above my cleavage with a fingertip and my breath hitches. "If I wreck this dress, I'm showing up to dinner naked tonight."

That little gem of a statement has him groaning in appreciation.

And then I'm thrown into a tailspin.

I want him.

I tilt his chin back up and crush my lips on his, then break our kiss to gently bite his bottom lip. When I pull back, he hugs me again, this time tightly enough that I can feel exactly how his body is responding to this moment. Our waists are aligned so the bulge in his jeans hits me perfectly.

"You're killing me, Princess," he mumbles. He moves his hand to his jeans and adjusts himself.

I apologize through my laughter. "Right back 'atcha." I don't want him to think I'm intentionally teasing. I'm one-thousand-percent certain I want to sleep with him. The fact that it can't happen — at least not right *now* — is no picnic for me either.

We're pulled further out of our moment by Nate's sudden hollering. His voice comes from the direction of the sun deck where I last saw Alexis and Aidan relaxing in lounge chairs. He's calling our names at an incredibly high volume, saying something about jumping.

"Oh man," he says, obviously understanding whatever Nate's carrying on about. He steps back, then playfully leans into me with his shoulder. "Come on, Princess. Shit's about to get real."

20

Oates

Saturday Afternoon

Fawn Island

I take Pam's hand and lead her down the path away from the gazebo, skidding downhill as we get to the bottom. We run past the main docks and up another path to get to the south side of the island. Nate's hollering has come from the sun deck off the enclosed three-season room.

I know exactly what's about to happen and wouldn't miss it for the world.

First, it's the only activity currently available to me that will kill this raging hard on because hours alone with this beautiful girl is not in the realm of possibility right now. Second, someone's been challenged by someone else, and I can't wait to see who's walking the plank.

"What's going on?" Pam asks me. "Why are we running?"

"Someone's gonna jump off the deck."

She slows up behind me, still holding my hand. I turn and see the confusion in her solemn brown eyes. "You'll see," I tell her. "It's all good. C'mon, your highness." I give her a reassuring smile, she smiles back, and we continue on to arrive at the deck, both slightly winded from rushing up here.

"What's going on?" she asks Aidan. "Daryl said someone's gonna jump off the deck?"

We both look to Alexis, who is absolutely petrified. I tamp down my smirk, realizing just who started this dare.

She's scared now, but she'll love it in the end.

"No," Alexis says to Aidan, her jaw firmly set. "No. Fucking. Way."

"Oh yes, baby," he says.

Nate and I give each other the look, and we strip off our shirts as Aidan speaks to my girl.

"Pam," he says. He hands her his phone. "Please run in for some towels, then down to the lower dock to take some pictures of my baby jumping."

Pam looks to Alexis, who is shaking her head, panic-stricken as a live chicken at a barbecue.

"Um, somehow I don't think she's going to go along with that," Pam says. "Do you know how cold that water is?"

I sure as hell do. For me, it's going to be a good cure for the insanely hot moment with Pam that extinguished far too quickly thanks to these shitclowns.

"Sixty degrees, tops," Aidan says as he stares down Alexis. When Pam doesn't move, he redirects his attention to her, throwing out the clipped tone he usually saves for rogue employees. "Go," he says, "or she's going to freeze down there without a towel."

Pam looks my way and I give her a reassuring nod. "It's okay," I mouth. "I promise."

She ducks into the house in a hurry while Alexis bargains with Aidan, but he's not having it. She argues that it's fifty feet to the water, and Nate corrects her that it's indeed less than twenty.

This is true.

And I know from personal experience it's safe. We've jumped off this deck multiple times.

For Nate, it's even less of a deal. His sport in college was swimming, as with all of us, but his preferred event was diving. To him, this is child's play.

I can see why Alexis is afraid, though. It's a big leap.

Pam hollers up to us. "I'm ready!"

I move to the left and look down at her, giving her a goofy wave.

She looks nervous, so I blow her a kiss, which gets her laughing. *Good.* I smile and step back, satisfied. I don't like seeing her worried.

I stand with hands on hips as I wait to see who's going to do the honors of going first.

"It's really no big deal, Lex," Nate says. "I'll show you how it's done."

And we have a winner!

"Do it up, bruh." I fist bump Nate, then he saunters to the far edge of the deck where the railing's missing. He turns his back to the water, does a killer backflip, then forms himself into a perfect dive. He gracefully cuts through the water with minimal splash, but I give him shit anyway. "I give it an eight," I holler down through cupped hands.

He raises a middle finger at me, then swims the short distance to the ladder and climbs up to the dock as Pam holds out a towel for him. Alexis spouts further objections to her beloved, now realizing that Nate was highly qualified for the jump.

"Hey, *chica*," I reassure her. "I'm not a professional diver, but I see my lady down there waiting, and I'm going for it." I take a few long strides backwards as the two lovebirds move aside, then run for it. As I form the requisite cannonball the guys would expect, I shout to Pam that I'm coming for my princess.

I hit the water and realize that yeah, this was exactly the adrenaline rush I needed. The water is freezing. It allows my body a moment to recoup, at least until we can be alone again.

I swim to the dock, smiling as I climb up and see the look of concern on her face. She hands me a towel, then her eyes travel from my neck down. "Um," she says. She shakes her head as though she's trying to shake off thoughts, too. "You're okay?"

I take the towel and dry my face. "Perfect," I wink. "Just what I needed."

"Right?" Nate pipes up. "I forgot what an awesome feeling that is. The water here is just...ahh!" He grunts. "So *fucking* refreshing."

He steps to his left toward the end of the dock, looking up to see if Aidan is going to jump. I nudge closer to Pam and whisper in her ear. "Next time, you should do it, too," I whisper. "Nothing like it."

"No thanks," she says. "I don't do cold water."

I shake my head near her like I'm a golden retriever coming in from the rain. "No?" I tease. "You don't like that?"

She giggles, grabs me around the waist and pulls me close for mere seconds. She rakes her right hand through my soaking hair, tugging until my ear is close to her lips. "I might," she says. Then whispers, "if we were both topless."

And then she hip-checks me to push me away, as though she's said absolutely nothing of significance.

I wrap my towel around my waist. Nate's already done the same so my move isn't obvious, but I curse at myself internally for my lack of control. There goes all my blood from one head to the other.

We all look up to Alexis, wondering if she's going to do this.

"Let 'er rip, tater chip!" I holler.

"No way!" she calls back.

And then it happens.

Either she got ballsy, or Aidan made the choice for her. They're both off the deck and falling over the water. He lets her go around halfway down, and she cannonballs into the water like I did.

"Pfft," I lean over to Pam, "at least she could come up with her own style."

"Hey, she did it," she says as she elbows me. "That's the important thing. My *sistah* is petrified of heights."

"Definitely an accomplishment then," I say. "Props to her." As Alexis emerges to the surface, Aidan takes longer. She's furiously searching for him even as Nate's doing his loud whistle and we're all cheering. I'm amazed that Lex took the leap and have to admit I'm kinda proud of Ms. Conservative Lawyer.

Aidan appears and she wraps her arms around him as he swims to the dock with her, then lifts her up so she can grab the ladder. Nate offers a hand, and Pam wraps her shivering sister-in-law in one of the oversized towels.

"I can't believe you did it, Lex," Pam says, taking her by shoulders. "That. Was. Awesome!"

Alexis smiles through chattering teeth.

"Yeah, chica!" I say on my approach, then offer her a fist bump.

She hits me back and smiles. "Thanks."

Nate offers his congrats next. "Nothing like taking that first leap. Want to do it again?"

"No. *Way*," she says through her shivering. "Thanks for the offer, though."

Aidan thanks Pam for the towel and makes quick work of drying. "Hot tub, guys?"

"Damn. Now that I'd love to do," Pam says, "but I don't have a suit."

My eyes divert to Pam's, and my grin turns mischievous. I know all she said is 'I don't have a suit', but my mind hears it more like, *'I'd be naked'*.

Having her naked in a hot tub?

Fuck me.

Or her.

Jesus, Oates. Quit that.

Alexis makes a remark that suits were not necessary for jumping off the deck either, given none of us is wearing one.

I tell Pam she can borrow one of my t-shirts and throw an arm around her. "We'll stop up in the boathouse. The hot tub's over there anyway."

Nate takes off ahead of us, and Aidan promises they'll be right along, which I don't believe for a second. They'll head for Brat Cottage, and we'll be lucky if they show up for dinner.

"Holy crap," Pam mutters. "I can't believe I'm going to set foot in here."

"It's no biggie," I shrug.

"Is to me," she whispers.

We arrive on the landing at the top of the stairs, about to go into the boathouse when Nate exits in swim trunks with his wet shorts in hand.

"I'm gonna head down." He opens the screen door to us, hangs his wet shorts over the railing, and takes the steps two at a time. "Hurry up!" He shouts as he reaches the bottom. "After this, it's cocktail hour!"

I turn to her. "Ready?"

She nods.

"Are you okay?"

"Just memories," she says with a shy smile. "I'm good."

I give her hand a squeeze. "I gotcha, Princess."

We walk into the living room, and she inhales deeply. "Wow," she says. "It smells awesome in here."

"It's probably those." I nod to the lilacs on the table. "So what's your preference?" I ask. "I can grab you a t-shirt, a pair of shorts?"

"I think I'm good," she says. "Why don't you change and I'll wait here?" She wanders over to the kitchen sink, looking out the window.

"I don't need to change if we're heading for the hot tub. Are you sure you're okay?" I lean on the counter, hands gripping the worn laminate. "I feel like you're not telling me something."

She looks down at her hands as she rests them on the lip of the stainless sink, then toys with her bracelet. Her gaze shifts up to the big house.

"I'm not really comfortable in a bathing suit, especially with a smart, handsome guy and his best friend who I'm totally crushing on."

"Okay, that cannot be. You're crushing on Nate?"

She lets go a soft laugh. "Definitely. I was hoping you could put in a good word for me." She looks to me and winks, then turns her gaze back to the window.

I want to get closer to her, but I keep my distance. She needs to know my words actually mean something. They're not being said because I want to lay her down as soon as humanly possible.

Even though that's true.

I whisper her name to get her attention and she turns to me. "Do you remember what I said to you before we left the marina yesterday?"

Her eyebrows draw together as she thinks. "Um, not specifically. You said a few things."

"I told you that you're amazing and to never believe otherwise. I knew it in that moment, and I know it even more now."

She looks away, her expression soft and shy.

"You're believing otherwise right now, and I won't have it. What makes you so sure you're not everything I'm telling you?"

She doesn't answer, but I can tell she wants to. She doesn't want to close down.

She's just scared.

As scared as Alexis was to jump off that deck.

"Don't even look at me to answer. Just look straight at that window, like it's an open portal into another dimension. All those bullshit reasons are going to fly out of your mouth right now. Send them into that universe where they will disappear forever. Pretend you're in some forcefield where I can't hear anything you say."

"But you *can* hear me."

"That's why you have to pretend," I tease her. "Go on, try it."

She looks at me, then trains her gaze through the window again.

"Please," I insist. "Blurt whatever reasons pop in your head why you're not God damn gorgeous."

"Okay, fine. I'm too tall."

"Keep going. Close your eyes this time."

"Um," she stalls a minute, closes her eyes, then, "my hips are too wide."

Good God. Her hips are perfect in my mind. It baffles me she'd think otherwise. "Is that all?"

I stare at her, watching her unburden herself with these admissions. *My thighs are too big. My shoulders are too broad. I'm a nerd. My feet are bigger than most girls.* Her shoulders finally relax after the last one.

"And what do all these alleged flaws mean to you?" I ask.

She heaves a deep sigh. "They mean I'm not feminine. Not sexy, even when I feel like I want to be."

Bingo. There's the issue.

"Pam, look at me." She does, and I stare right into those innocent baby browns. Maybe she's not a virgin, but she's fragile where it counts — her ego. "You want to know the only thing I don't find incredibly sexy about you?"

She hesitates, then nods.

"That you lack confidence about your beauty because you base it on the standards of someone else."

"You're just saying that to get in my pants," she kids.

"See?" I say through a broad smile. "Your sense of humor is killer. You're using it as a deflection tool in this instance, but it's still killer." I move around the peninsula that separates the kitchen from the living area and stand behind her, gently resting my hands on her shoulders. "Remember how you lit up when we talked about getting the feather in Super Mario Brothers Three or how fired up you got when we talked about Elon Musk's unauthorized biography?"

She cracks a smile. "Yeah."

"Your confidence when we talk about stuff like that is the same confidence you should have about your body. You are not overweight, or unhealthy, or unattractive. So you don't look like a Barbie doll?" I turn my voice to a whisper in her ear. "And by the way, thank God for that."

"But that's what guys want," she says quietly. "They want a sexy blonde who doesn't wear a size nine shoe."

"My ass, love."

Whoa.

The term of endearment was a blurt, but one that felt uncommonly *comfortable* coming out.

I keep going, trying to hit home my point while I have her undivided attention. She's gone completely quiet and still.

"I don't want some specific type of girl because I've been socially programmed to believe that's what I want. I know what I like and what I don't. And no guys *I* know want a stick figure with boobs and no personality. Do we all have different tastes? Sure. But beauty standards do not equal beauty. That eye of the beholder thing is fact."

She acknowledges with a slight nod, and I take one step closer, thankful she isn't looking at me with the truth bomb I'm about to drop.

"You think a guy like me feels confident a hundred percent of the time around guys like Nate and Aidan?"

She turns her head, her gaze drawn to my hand on her bare shoulder as she speaks. "You should be."

"Please," I scoff. "Around them it was like I was wearing chick repellent. It was never me the ladies went after." She turns around and looks up with sympathy in her eyes. "That is, until I changed one thing several years back."

"What's that?"

"How I felt about *me*. I figured out what I brought to the table and capitalized on it. Anything I was unsure of, I improved on. After college, I kept working out. Took advantage of my company's gym and lifted so I could build some confidence that I was strong enough to lift more than a pencil. Once I believed in myself — and sidebar, I know this sounds like some Tony Robbins shit, but that mother fucker is aces in my book."

"I love him," she says. "My brother used to listen to him."

"Your brother was a smart guy. Anyway, once I had that confidence, it didn't matter how big my arms were or that I prefer glasses over contacts. Chicks were suddenly on me like white on rice."

"Seriously?"

"Not even exaggerating. It was like a light bulb turned on, and the ladies were my moths."

"So you get hit on a lot?" She seems slightly disappointed.

I look at her sternly. "That's not what I meant. My fair share, sure. Point is, where before it never happened, suddenly it did. And if you try telling me you never get hit on, I'll call you out. 'Cause I know that's bullshit, too."

She shrugs. "My share too, I guess. More since college."

"See? And that's because not only are you stunning, but you do have some confidence. It's just not consistent like it should be. Now, there's a fine line between confident bachelor and cocky bastard, but I came from the other side of the fence, where lonely nerds hang out," I pause, *"alone."*

We both laugh.

"So, I guess I'm lucky that way," I say. "I've always known where that ceiling is, and I don't try blasting through it. I'm just happy being me. And you need to be more confident being you."

"You are actually quite cocky," she says through a smirk. "You certainly put on some swagger when Alexis introduced us in the parking lot."

"But that's a total act. I'm expected to be a goofball sometimes, and I don't mind that. It's part of who I am, and it's a great way to break tension. It's also what Aidan expects, and I couldn't let on that we'd already met. At least not without asking you if you were okay with that."

She looks at me and sighs again, and I'm trying not to stare as her chest rises and falls.

How does she not know how gorgeous she is?

"Let me put it to you another way." I hop up on the counter to sit, then pull her away from the sink to stand between my legs. "I understand if you're uncomfortable baring certain body parts. I'm not pushing you on that." She looks up, her face flushed as I stroke her hair. *God, this girl.* "But my next request is for you to show up for a private hot tub party in your underwear. That thought is giving me like, my third — possibly fourth — chubby of the day, and it's not even three o'clock in the afternoon."

"Oh. My. *Gawd*," she giggles, the pretty sound echoing through the rooms. It must be the best sound this place has ever heard. "Way to lighten the moment."

"You're welcome."

"I have an idea," she says, "instead of the hot tub."

I push her hair away and smile down at her. "What's that, Princess?"

"You could show me the bedroom."

Holy. Fuck.

Did she just suggest—

Yes, you dumbass. She did.

And you have no condoms.

Stupid. Stupid. Stupid.

I hear Nate's incredibly loud whistle at the bottom of the stairs, then the sound of his footsteps as Pam steps away from me. From where I sit perched on the counter, I turn around and glare at him as he enters the room.

"Dude."

He holds up his phone. "I need to get online. Can I borrow your laptop?"

"Yeah, it's on the coffee table." I turn back to Pam, even though I'm still talking to him. "No more hot tub for you?"

"No, I've gotta check in with my team real quick. Where's the WiFi signal strongest?"

A mischievous look comes over me. "Up in the main house," I say. "Definitely."

"Great, I can kill two birds." He runs for the bedroom and comes out fully dressed in what feels like mere seconds. He throws his swim trunks outside before coming back for my laptop. "Gotta get my cake made and put out this fire with work. See ya."

He attaches earbuds to his phone, pockets it in his flannel shirt, and takes off.

"So, what do you think?" she asks once we're alone. "You wanna give me a tour?"

"I think, as much as I'd love to show you the tiny ass bedroom and demonstrate exactly how small that bed is," I adjust myself and swallow hard, "I'm completely unprepared to, how shall I put this?" I hop off the counter, trying to keep my wits about me. "I guess you could say I'm unprepared to show you the bedroom responsibly without a way to guarantee we don't create cousins for little Jakie and his twin sister."

"Julie," she says. She smiles in understanding as her hands lay gently across my bare chest, no doubt able to feel how fast my freaking heart's beating.

It's killing me to say no to her.

"Well then," she says, moving her hands to my shoulders as she taps her fingers. "What should we do?"

"I'm going to dry off and get changed, and you can fire up the TV over there," I nod to the living room behind me. "Then, I'm kicking your ass as a cartoon hedgehog."

She laughs then, seeming a little relieved. "You're *so* on, Mister Oates. But you're also gonna be sorry because it's me who's gonna kick *your* ass."

I laugh as I make my way to the bedroom because that much I'm certain of.

I'm already damn sorry.

Sorry I didn't say yes and drag her off to the bedroom with me.

An hour later, I'm glad we decided not to jump into bed together because we've been interrupted by a text from Pierce. He's summoned us up to the main house. Yeah, it was an irritating interruption. But an hour wouldn't have been enough time anyway.

Not with her.

And not for that.

We walk arm in arm up to the main house. Pierce has declared our group will prepare tonight's meal. I've been tasked with marinating enough chicken for the entire Canadian Coast Guard.

The elders of our island crew are due back at five-thirty for drinks, and we'll all break bread around seven. The Lonergans (the River Rat couple who prepped everything for the Pierce fam in a hurry) are also joining us. Pierce wants his parents and their guests able to enjoy a good time without having to do any work, and of course we agreed it's the least we can do.

On our walk up to the house I replay our last hour alone in my head. My girl slayed at Sonic while we traded stories about fights with our respective siblings. She was the brains behind conquering video games in her house, just like I was in mine. For our siblings, games were a way to pass time; something they played and walked away from when they got bored. For Pam and me, it was a puzzle to solve as quickly as we could, a skill to master with precision before the next new game came out.

She made good on her threat, too. She did kick my ass. We took turns advancing the little blue bugger through levels. I'd brushed up on my skills as recently as Thursday night and she hadn't played in years, but she was the one who took him the distance.

In my defense, sometimes I screwed up because I was concentrating on not tackling her.

Pam Clayton is legit everything I ever wished for in a girl, even as a young dude sitting in front of that old console television.

Suddenly I had a sexy brunette on the beat-up leather sofa, her long legs stretched to the coffee table and crossed at the ankle, punctuated with naked feet. (I don't give a shit what she says, her feet are gorgeous.) The soft pink dress she wears is like a bonus — like my drab, long-ago dreams were dusted off and turned into lucid, Technicolor ones. The dress also solidifies the nickname 'Princess', so much that it will forever stick.

The kicker is, it's more than her looks.

It's the giddy laugh she releases when I take the controls and cause our hedgehog his unfortunate demise, even though it's her fault. (Because she's *hella-distracting*.)

It's her scent that I'm becoming addicted to because it just means *her*. It means she's close enough for me breathe in.

It's the way she just gets me, despite our difference in age. She often acts older than the twins. And the girl was able to carry on a conversation about the guy who invented the addicting game we were in the midst of playing. (Yuji Naka, if anyone asks. And yep, she knew that.)

In fact, she admitted she once wrote a report about the algorithm Naka created for his original tech demo, the one that ultimately led to Sonic's creation. She told me she did the report in high school for extra credit even though she didn't *need* extra credit, because she already had perfect grades.

This girl is my long-ago fantasy come to life.

I'm now basting skewered shrimp in the kitchen of the main house while she's out on the porch putting together a plate of appetizers, and I can't stop grinning, even though she's not near me.

It's official. I've become the newest zombie recruit.

I toss the prepped chicken and shrimp back in the fridge and pop my second beer of the evening while Nate voraciously mixes the batter for his cake from his spot at the kitchen island.

"All set there, Betty Crocker?"

"You bet, Fuckerberg."

Alexis is standing across from him near the prep sink washing veggies for a salad. Aidan exits the pantry with an oversized pot.

"Everything's lubed up and back in the fridge," I tell them. "I'm gonna go help your sister-from-another-mister, Lex."

"You do that," she says, winking at me. She carries on, searching drawers for a sharp knife.

"Yeah," Nate jeers, "you do that, Romeo."

"Thanks, I will." On my way by, I stick a finger in his cake batter and swipe it across his forehead.

"Fucker," he mumbles. He stops mixing to reach for a hand towel. "Payback's a bitch."

"Hey Nate," I call on my way to the porch. "Don't forget to preheat the oven."

21

Pam

Saturday Evening

Fawn Island

"Get. The. Fuck. *Outta here!*" Carly screams into my earbuds. "Are you kidding me?"

"I'm not." I'm on the porch putting together three trays of various cheeses and crackers and fruits while Carly carries on. It's after four in the afternoon, and she called me on one of her five-second breaks. I just explained to her that Daryl's with me.

On Fawn Island.

Oh, and that he's Aidan's best friend.

And the Hawthorne Brothers' only roommate.

She's been freaking out for three minutes.

"I can't even believe this is your life right now," she finally says. "Will you get to meet them?"

"Get real, Carly. They live in California. But he drops their names every once in awhile, usually in conversation about business or some crazy bro-story. He's only known them a few years. They just bought a house together."

"Holy shit, girl. I'm so pissed I'm not there!"

"You would *love* it. It's been a blast."

"Those pics of that kitchen. *Oh-em-gee*. To die for."

"Right? Aidan's other friend is super smart and funny. You'd like him. He's baking a cake in there. And," I say, turning my voice to a whisper, "he's pretty hot, too. His name is Nate."

"Send me a pic! I've got major FOMO, girl. What about the hot nerd?" she asks. "Did you screw him yet?"

"*No!*" I whisper in scolding.

"What the hell are you waiting for? You *so* want to."

I giggle. "Yeah," I say, "I totally do. He's an amazing kisser."

"Yeah, girl. Get some." Through the sound of clanging dishes, I hear a deep male voice call for her. "I gotta go. This guy thinks he's Gordon fucking Ramsay. He'll crucify me if I'm not back there in two shakes."

As she's saying this, I hear the squeak of the screen door, and I turn to see Daryl coming out to the porch. I turn back to the table where I'm prepping food so I can discreetly say goodbye.

"I gotta go, too," I say. "Chat later. Love you."

"Love you more," she says. "And p.s."

"What?"

"Tonight's your last chance to jump on his ass. You better do it and tell me all about it tomorrow."

She disconnects before I can respond. I immediately text her a GIF of a girl telling her friend to shut up. She sends back a middle finger emoji, and I laugh to myself as I discard my earbuds and set the phone down. I finish plating the last of the crackers before turning around to Daryl. "Ta-dah!" I say, holding up one of the trays.

But wouldn't you know, he's on the phone.

I'm such a moron! No doubt whoever he's talking to heard me. I do a one-eighty back to the table as I shake my head, completely mortified. Then hands gently land on my bare shoulders and those familiar chills are back. His touch is possessive, but in an endearing way.

Like a guy would do to his steady girlfriend.

Which *should* seem odd to me, but it isn't. It feels completely natural. Like us being an *us* is totally routine, even though it's new and extraordinary at the same time.

"So you didn't go to Vegas?" he says into the microphone dangling around his neck. His hands graze along my shoulders and down my arms, barely touching my skin. My head's out of my control as it bobs to the left. His lips trace behind my ear, then trail down to my right shoulder. "Mm hmm," he says.

Oh good God, whoever you are on the phone with, please let that person keep talking.

Don't stop doing that.

"Um, sure," he says. He abruptly leans away. "One sec."

He plants a kiss on my shoulder that leaves me shivering, then shifts his stance behind me. He wraps his left arm around my waist, his right outstretched on my right side, closing me in as he holds the phone away and points the screen at us.

"Hit that button," he says. "They want to video chat."

"They?" I turn and whisper into his shoulder.

"It's the twins. Tap the green phone."

I do. A guy appears on the screen while a live image of Daryl and me shows in the upper corner. Carly may literally die when I tell her about this.

And p.s., we look pretty good together.

The top of my head falls just below his nose. My hair is tied back in a ponytail, and I'm still in my pink dress, so I'm semi-presentable. We're both smiling like goofballs.

Pretty happy goofballs.

"Now hit the amplify button," he says, "so we're on speaker."

I reluctantly tap the button.

The guy on the screen is not looking at the camera. He's staring at something else that we can't see.

"Zach, this is Pam. Pam, Zach Hawthorne."

He leans closer to see us, and I give a pathetic wave.

"Well, hello," he says, suddenly giving us his undivided attention. "Where'd you come from, and what's your sign?"

Bah! This guy. I'm used to seeing the fabulous Mr. Hawthorne from farther away with no shirt, but even close up, Zach's as handsome as he is in the cooking videos. He's wearing a t-shirt, but I can only see him from the collar up. I play along with his teasing.

"Uh, I come from Canada," I say, "and my sign is 'stop'."

"Oh, you're sassy," Zach says. "I like that."

I nudge Daryl with an elbow, trying not to laugh.

"She has her moments," Daryl says, pulling me in tighter. The closeness is wreaking havoc on my body, but also my heart. It's clear he's unafraid to demonstrate we've become pretty friendly, even in front of his roommate. "So why'd you guys bail on Vegas?"

"Meh." Zach has turned his attention back to whatever's distracting him. "Just didn't feel like it. Yesterday was brutal for Finn with work. And as it turns out, I have a date on Sunday night. Woken-baked this morning. Brunch with parents tomorrow for our mandatory birthday celebration so we can get that out of the way."

He leans away from the screen, then comes back surrounded by a cloud of smoke as Paul Simon's voice floats to us through the speaker.

"Nice," Daryl says. "I hope you opened the windows."

"It's a vape," Zach says through a tightly held breath. He exhales another puff of smoke. "There's no smell. It's a mellow buzz kinda day. We were even productive enough to go for a run this morning."

"Yeah, and I had to nag him just to keep a ten-minute mile," Finn hollers from the background. "He kept stopping to look up at the clouds."

"Come look," Zach shouts to the air behind him. "Oates has a date."

The volume of the music in the background drastically lowers. I blush as Finn comes to the screen, albeit not as up close as Zach was.

"Hey," he says, "I'm Finn."

"Hi, Finn. I'm Pam."

"Good to know you, Pam. Is Oates behaving himself?"

"So far," I shrug, "unfortunately."

Finn turns to his brother. "Ooh, she's sassy."

I burst out laughing then look back at Daryl who gives me a look that says 'told you'.

Oh, they're twins all right.

"Hang on a sec, guys." Finn puts the phone down, and we're staring at a ceiling fan in a very bright room. The California sun casts between shadows as the blades spin.

"I'm getting dizzy," Daryl shouts at the camera. "Hurry up. This is costing me."

Someone props the camera up and walks away, and now we can see both guys sitting on the floor. They're leaning against a coffee table, their legs outstretched as they stare at a movie-theater sized flat screen surrounded by bookcases.

"That's your house?" I ask.

"Yep. Home sweet home. That's our media room," he whispers. Then louder to his roommates, "What are you guys playing?"

"Call of Duty," Finn says.

"We're kicking the ass of some twelve-year-old from North Dakota," Zach adds.

"You guys would appreciate this. We dug up a relic today," Daryl says. "Pam kicked my ass at Sonic."

"That's awesome," Finn says. He elbows his brother. "We should totally dust off the old Sega. Haven't played that in forever." He puts down his controller and swaps it for an extremely large spoon, lifting it to his mouth. The spoon clangs into the bowl as he picks the controller up again, and the sound of his crunching radiates through the speaker.

"What are you guys eating?" Daryl asks over my shoulder. "Is that cereal?"

Munch, munch, munch. "Yeah," Finn says. "Cap'n Crunch. So?"

"What flavor?" I ask.

"Peanut butter," Zach shouts towards the camera, though his yelling is unnecessary.

"Obviously," Finn says.

"Is there any other kind?" I giggle. "Peanut butter is the bomb. My brother turned me on to it when he lived in the States."

Zach responds with an agreeing grunt. Finn comments "I *like* her," as though I can't hear him.

"Those aren't cereal bowls," Daryl says. "And that spoon is as big as a shovel. You guys look like Neanderthals."

The guys look towards the camera in unison, then down at their laps.

This is a revelation.

"Shit," Finn says. He inspects his lap more closely. "What'd you do, brother?" He elbows his twin as he examines his utensil. "I didn't even realize what you handed me. Dude," he scolds further, "these are our best batter bowls."

"And that's a serving spoon," Daryl adds through a good-natured laugh. "You guys, those bowls could hold an entire box of cereal."

"They *are* holding an entire box of cereal," Zach says. *Munch. Munch.* "And a quart of organic whole milk."

"Because only organic milk is good enough for the Cap'n?" Finn says with a smirk. "You're such an idiot, Zach. Oates is right. This must look super obnoxious to that sassy girl."

I giggle as I grab for Daryl's arm and coax him to draw the screen closer. He's right. They're eating out of metal bowls similar to the huge one Nate hauled out to mix up his cake batter.

"Fuck do I care?" Zach says as he shrugs. He sets his bowl aside and picks up his controller. "Saves us a trip back to the kitchen to fill up tiny bowls three times. You ask me, it's genius. Now watch me send this kid cryin' to his mama."

"Dude, we're not even playing him anymore. We're playing each other."

"Fuck." He drops his controller and digs into his cereal again. "Really?" *Crunch, crunch.* "Am I winning?"

"Holy shit," Daryl says. "You guys haven't been this high in awhile. This is how you're spending your birthday, huh?"

"Yes," Finn confirms. "We decided to time-travel back to our twenties. You objecting?"

"Not at all," he says. "Go nuts. Just don't cook while you're stoned and burn the place down."

"Worry not, Oates," Zach says. "We promise to be responsible Hawthorne men at all times."

"Happy Birthday, guys," I say through my giggle. "I'm going to duck out of this convo before *ish* gets real."

Daryl pulls me tighter and whispers in my ear. "Don't take off. I'm about to hang up."

"Nice meeting you," Finn says to me.

"Yeah, laters," Zach says. He comes closer to the camera again, but this time he holds it far enough away so I can read his shirt.

'Not Tonight Ladies. I'm Just Here To Get Drunk'

I burst into another giggle, laughing so hard I'm nearly folded in half. This guy's a trip. It's even funnier that he's wearing the shirt while high as a kite in his own home, where it appears there are no ladies to fend off.

"Pam, that is a beautiful laugh," he says to me.

"Uh, thanks." I nod to his image on the screen. "I was caught off guard with your shirt."

"All the chicks are. Works every time," he says, tapping alongside his forehead. "Reverse psychology."

"We're gonna jet now," Daryl interrupts. He shakes his head to me by way of apology for his friend. "Uber if you're going out," he says to Zach.

"Yes, dear," he jokes. "See you when you get back."

"You got it."

"And don't forget to wrap it, young man." Zach's voice drops an octave for a solid dad impression as he shakes a finger at the screen. "Safety first. We don't need a Baby Oates running around here mucking up our new digs."

Bah! This guy. I raise the back of my wrist to my eyes, dabbing away tears from my laughter.

"Christ," Daryl bristles. "Bye, Zach." He deflects his embarrassment and before he disconnects, lifts his beer in a toast. "Happy 30th, you crazy fuckers."

This night has been absolutely perfect.

The dinner we put on was *ah-mazing*.

I learned Aidan has a signature dish in his repertoire, which apparently was news to Alexis, too. (Who knew rich guys can cook?) He said he learned the technique while in Italy one summer. Daryl declared his friend's potatoes were not to be missed because they're 'crazy-sexy-good'. Though the ingredients were simple — fresh basil, olive oil, and salt on boiled red potatoes — Daryl was right. They were *so* good.

Nate served his 'Best Fucking Cake You Will Ever Fucking Taste' which he did not name out loud in front of our more distinguished company of couples (the Reeds, Hamiltons, Lonergans, and of course our hosts, Tori and Reggie).

But the cake's moniker was a brag well-earned. It was the best cake I've *ever* tasted. (Which I will never admit to Carly.)

I noticed Aidan didn't partake, but Lex told me he eats clean and is all about avoiding sweets. Pretty obvious given his physique. (I mean, c'mon. There was no *way* I could avoid noticing his body when the guys jumped shirtless off the deck this afternoon. Lucky us, Lex and I were surrounded by attractive men who are nothing short of ripped.)

We ladies cleaned up the kitchen while the men dispersed, then I took off with Daryl for a quick stroll up to the gazebo before completing our stated purpose of departure — grabbing more firewood from the main dock.

The few minutes we stole were more perfect than dinner, despite the fact that I admitted to him out loud how much I've become addicted to kissing him. The glass of Riesling I drank with our meal was probably the reason for that candid moment. But he smiled even as he was kissing me, then threw me for a loop when he told me he felt the same.

We returned to the stone patio to get a fire going while the older clan settled upstairs on the porch.

Aidan and Nate just joined us. Each of us settles into the same seats as last night, while Lex is up in the kitchen with Tori. They were deep in a bottle of red wine and conversation the last any of us saw them.

"So what shall we play tonight, Oates?" Nate asks. The guys set up two small Bluetooth speakers between them. "Something chill?"

"Play some Miles," Aidan says. "Let's talk about your research, Oates. Did you look into those companies I told you about?"

"Sure did, bruh," Daryl says. "You were on point."

"How close are they?"

"Pretty damn," he sighs. "But I think we can squeak by. If we launch in August like we planned, there's no way they can beat that. And they haven't thought out their market. We know who we're going after."

"Who's your target market?" I ask.

"College students," he smirks. "Gorgeous ones. You want to be in our beta program?"

I laugh while shooting him a look for being a wise ass. "So your thinking is to launch when classes begin again?"

He nods. "And hopefully have it take off as the must-have new app on every campus in the country."

"Are you going to be ready that quickly?" I ask. "That's two months away."

"I hope so." He looks Aidan's way, then back at me. "But if not, we're kind of screwed. There's competition on my heels."

"Including that asshole Chalmers," Aidan mutters. "You need to watch him."

"Already on it. I've got eyes and ears there."

Wait, what? These guys *know* Bryson Chalmers?

And Aidan saw fit to call him an asshole.

Interesting.

Conversation continues about tech market trends, and Nate pipes in about what he's seeing in his fields of practice — engineering and neuroscience.

That's when I realize just how out of my league I am.

I'm smart, sure. A total geek. But listening to these guys is like trying to follow a conversation among three legit Einsteins. They're getting into some pretty elaborate concepts, so I observe and listen, staying quiet until Daryl pipes up.

"Sorry, Princess," he laughs. "Guess we geeked out there for a minute."

"It's fine," I say with a smile. It's fascinating to me, and it's a way to learn what makes Mr. Oates tick.

Nate chimes in to ask me questions about what I study and where, and we get into a discussion about me going to the States in the fall.

"New York's a great choice," he says, "though California's probably a better location to apply your studies in the field."

"I'd like to be close to my parents," I say. "Since my brother died, I'm all they've got, really. Except for my crazy aunt. But she owns a restaurant on the river, so she's typically in her own world. Not that I'd be coming home a lot, but if anything ever came up with them, I could be there in a short car trip from Central New York or a quick flight from Manhattan."

"I think Alexis' alma mater has some programs if I'm not mistaken?" Aidan asks. "You ever look into Stanton U?"

"Yep," I smile proudly. "I was sure to apply there. I was considering Brockton State, too. Alexis was an undergrad there when she met my brother."

"I'm aware," he says. "Didn't realize they offered anything in the way of Digital Futures, though."

"In the past they haven't. They're beginning a new program in January 2017, but I didn't want to wait so I ruled it out. I busted my ass over summer session 2015 after I took a semester off."

Daryl discreetly squeezes my knee, knowing exactly the reason for my hiatus from school was Ben's passing.

"So you'll graduate on time then?" Nate says.

"Yes."

"That's some dedication. Good for you. What's after that?"

"Honestly," I say, "I'm not sure. I don't know if I want to do a masters program or dive into a career immediately."

"You'll figure it out this year," Nate says. "And in the meantime, write it down."

"Write what down?" I ask.

"Where you want to go, what you want to do once you graduate."

"It'll help you decide," Daryl says. "It helped us."

"We're all a bunch of nerds who make lists and set goals constantly," Aidan qualifies. "Definitely a good idea to write down your goals. Otherwise, it's easy to get lost."

Silence settles over us as whatever playlist Nate picked comes to a halt. Daryl puts on some Dave Matthews as Alexis saunters down the stone path to join us. Nate comments that it's about time she got down here, which prompts me to check my phone for the time.

It's just eleven.

Crap.

In a mere hour, we're clocking over to the day I have to say goodbye to Mister Oates, which absolutely sucks. Right now, the only goal I can see worthy of writing down is to spend more time with him.

And that just isn't in the cards.

Thirty minutes later, I'm ready to admit I'm falling head first for one Mr. Daryl Oates.

The jerk can sing.

And I don't mean he might sing some okay notes in the shower. Not like your best friend belting out a so-so Madonna interpretation while drunk in the 24-hour convenience mart as you dance nearby.

More like, he's musically *on point.*

He's rapped to Macklemore and DJ Khaled and sung back-up

parts in *tune*, mirroring the original artist. He's now chugging a bottle of water after he ran out of breath.

Nate has a pretty smooth voice, too. Aidan even chimes in on "All I Do Is Win". His rap is more of a lip sync, but it's still pretty hysterical — and he nails every word, even without vocalizing.

My cheeks hurt from smiling for the millionth time this weekend, and my gut hurts from laughing. These guys are so much fun, and they share such a camaraderie I feel honored to witness.

I also can't believe Mr. Oates had this crooner trick up his sleeve. Color me incredibly impressed.

And incredibly stimulated.

I suggest to Alexis that she give the guys a run for their money and sing the Norah Jones tune my brother always loved to hear. She politely declines.

"Come on," I say. "Your voice is boss. Show these clowns up."

After the guys encourage her, she reluctantly agrees. She leans over to Daryl and tells him what she wants to sing, and he pulls up a karaoke version of "One Flight Down" for her. Aidan calls up to his parents. Their crew was enthralled with the guys' earlier performance and managed crowd participation from the porch a couple of songs ago.

But it's clear he wants his parents to be down here, close enough to hear Alexis up close and personal because he knows they're in for a treat. She shoots him a look that says, *'really'?*

I know she prefers singing to crowded barrooms of rowdy drunks with her friend Harry's band or at the occasional karaoke joint. Sometimes she'd grace us with something if my brother was playing acoustic in their living room. But sober, captive audiences are not her thing.

This always struck me as a huge bummer because she's amazing.

She sings the song with her usual grace, and halfway through I can tell she's feeling it and not giving a shit who's listening. At the end, we all cheer like mad. She freaking killed it. Aidan's mom lets out this deafening whistle of approval, and I laugh all over again at that unexpected talent.

"Yeah, Mrs. Pierce," I say in her direction. "Definitely the coolest mama," I lean over and say to Daryl. "I love her."

He nods and grins at me, and we both stand up. He congratulates Alexis with a fist bump and an explosion. "Killer set o' pipes, chica."

"I told you she can sing. You're welcome," I say to him.

"I would've hated missing out on that," Daryl turns and says to me. "Thanks for encouraging her, Princess."

Alexis grins at us.

Daryl turns and ropes me in with just a stare. Suddenly, it's like there's no one else on the planet besides us. "What about you?" he asks. "You hiding a beautiful voice behind that smile?"

Holy. Shit. My panties are practically stuck to my thigh. I swear, if he stares at me like that one second longer…

"Afraid not," I manage.

I so want to rip his glasses off and climb him.

What the hell's wrong with me?

I clear my throat and go for humor instead. "My brother had the musical talent in our family. But I can keep up on the dance floor like no one's *biz-nass.*" I demonstrate with a little head tilt and swerving motion with my hands while I swing my hips back and forth.

I think I hear him grunt an 'mm' under his breath, but we both ignore it. "I'd love to test that claim." He grins, again looking at me like he's a bear and I'm a delicious picnic basket full of food.

Oh God.

We step away from the crowd of 'grown-ups' who gather to say good night to Alexis and Aidan.

"Would you wanna ditch this party with me?" he asks once we're alone.

I nod so enthusiastically my head may fall clean off.

He says good night to Reggie, and I grab my phone from my chair. It's quarter to twelve.

I'm overcome with emotion.

I'm only hours away from leaving this place.

From leaving him.

Aidan pulls Daryl aside as Tori comes over to chat with me.

"Your room's okay?" she asks.

"Oh yes, lovely," I say. "Thank you so much."

"Anytime, Pam. Truly." She kisses both cheeks, then holds me by the shoulders, her arms extended. "Make sure you stay warm if you're going to be outside. I'll see you in the morning." She smiles and gives me a strong squeeze. "Good night, honey."

She heads up the path to the main house with Reggie. Nate's ahead of them, declaring he's having a nightcap before he heads to bed. He has to leave tomorrow morning.

And I'll probably be dropped off at the mainland with him rather than make Aidan take two trips. I'm not sure what time the Pierce family is leaving, but I know from what I overheard at dinner that Daryl is flying home with them tomorrow. The Pierces' friends live in Manhattan, so they made their own travel plans back to New York, departing by eleven tomorrow morning.

Alexis blows me a kiss as she and Aidan head for Brat Cottage which once again leaves Daryl and me at the firepit.

Alone.

22

Oates

Saturday Night

Fawn Island

"Hey Princess, you tired?" She's seated across from me in the chair Aidan occupied earlier in the night.

"Not in the slightest."

"You feel like fishing tonight?"

"No."

I look up at her pretty face in the firelight. "Me either."

I've never wanted a girl so badly in my life.

She gets up and wanders over to me. My eyes are on the swing of her dress as the skirt part flows back and forth. She halts in front of my knees, and I look up at her, literally in agony.

I've run through eight scenarios of how and where I can take her, but as I pan out each one, none affords a stop off for condoms because we're on a fucking island. They also end in disaster by way of embarrassment (for being caught) or because they're far too primitive (like up against the nearest tree), thereby discounting my feelings for her.

Yeah, I broke a cardinal Hawthorne rule.

I caught feels *already*.

No fucking doubt in my head.

Which means I won't have sex with her just anywhere or just for the sake of it, not that I've ever been the type to do that anyway.

"I have an idea," she says. She rests hands on my shoulders and eases me forward, the top of my head resting at her chest. Then she completely chills me out by dragging her fingers through my hair.

"Whatever it is, I hope it does not involve anyone but us."

"Just us," she says quietly. "But the idea is a little out there."

I pull back and look up at her. "I'm all ears."

"Do you think anyone would notice if we took off for awhile?"

"You mean like," I pause, "left the island?"

She nods.

"Notice or care?"

She considers a moment. "Both."

I think about it.

For all of two seconds.

"I say we're adults and that's a solid plan, Princess. Let's go."

Within twenty minutes, we're in her car. I'm impressed with the futuristic feel of her Mini Cooper, and even more with the way she drives a stick shift like a pro. We haven't stopped talking and laughing like teenagers who've just escaped their parents' supervision for the first time.

That's how she makes me feel — absolutely silly, lost in the moment, and not giving a shit about the outside world.

After she made the suggestion to leave, she hustled upstairs while I ran down to the boathouse and grabbed the keys to the Whaler. She changed into jeans and grabbed her car keys, and we met at the dock and took off for the lot where her Mini was parked.

Now, she's driving us to her best friend's apartment.

Her best friend's *empty* apartment.

I suggested we stop somewhere because, again, shitty timing for me to be without condoms. But she told me not to worry about it.

I'm not sure if that means we have two different ideas for this outing. I'm trying to shake off the excitement of getting her naked as soon as we get there, just in case that's not the plan.

If she wanted to sit up all night talking or playing Super Mario Three, I'd be down with that.

Just not quite as excited.

We pull down a long gravel driveway and she shuts off the car, silencing "All Over You" by Live.

I glance out the window. The surroundings are desolate. We're barely ten minutes from the Town Dock and this is like another world. We've gone rural, more fields around us than buildings. In fact, there's not another house in sight. The river is to the south, just across the road.

"That was a good tune," I say. She agrees as I turn from the window in time to see her pull out her phone and check something. "Um, if you're not comfortable, we can just head back."

"This place is like my second home," she says. "I'm totally comfortable. My parents live three minutes down the road. I was just checking the time. It's almost 12:30 now. If we're back on the island before dawn, no one's the wiser. Hopefully. Agree?"

I nod. I like this take-charge version of my Princess. And by her logic, I have at least three hours alone with her.

"C'mon," she says, nodding to what must be her friend's apartment above a two-car garage. "No one is here, not even Carly's dad." She nods to our left, to a small A-frame house. "He's with her in New York."

She exits the car, and I follow her up steps that remind me of the climb to the boathouse. A wide metal staircase is attached to the side of the structure, and she pulls a key from under the mat on the landing to let us in.

"That would never fly in California," I say with a nervous laugh. "At home, even our security systems have security systems."

For the first time, she doesn't laugh at one of my wisecracks, and she doesn't give me a chance to try again with something less lame. The second the door closes, she's on me.

I don't have to wonder anymore. We were on the same page the whole time.

She doesn't turn on any lights. We're kissing in the dark, and we almost trip over a recliner as she tugs me further into the apartment.

I don't want to stop kissing her, but I have to.

Before I *can't* stop, a conversation is in order.

"Whoa." I grab her by the shoulders, resting my forehead on hers. "Pam, are you sure you want to do this?"

She nods. "Don't you?"

"That's the most ridiculous question I will *ever* be asked." I lay soft kisses on top of her head, lower my voice to a whisper in her ear as I wrap her up in my arms. "What I don't want is for you to have regrets. Or think this was my goal from the moment we met. I'm not like that."

"I know, and I'm not that kind of girl." She pulls back, throws her arms around my neck, and devours my mouth.

Well, okay then.

"I still don't have any condoms," I say when she pauses for a breath.

"That's what best friends are for." *More kissing.* "C'mon, the bedroom's this way." She takes my hand and leads me down a short hallway.

"I suddenly feel like a piece of meat here."

That engages her brakes. She stops dead in the hallway and turns to face me. "Seriously?"

"Um, at least half-serious, yeah."

She takes a deep breath, turns her back to the wall, and leans up against it. It's still dark, but my eyes have adjusted enough that I realize she's desperate to slow her roll.

"Can I be honest with you?" she finally says.

I tilt my head, totally confused. "Have you not already been honest?"

"No. I mean yes, I have been."

I stand there with arms crossed over my chest. "Please, go ahead."

"I have never wanted anything more in my life. However, if you don't feel right about it, we can stop."

Feel right?

Nothing's ever felt *more* right. For me anyway.

I want to have her underneath me. And not because it's been awhile or because she makes my dick twitch just walking by me with that yummy scent.

Her hair smells like this crazy mix of fresh baked cookies and suntan lotion. I don't know how, but it does. Her shampoo's probably infused with a love potion made by a gypsy woman here in the backwoods of Canada.

It's the most intoxicating scent, not one a person could easily recreate.

It's as unique as she is.

I don't want *any* girl. No 'Crazy Carolyns' or 'Vanilla Blondes' will ever compare to this girl.

The girl who is petrified of spiders but not worms. The girl who keeps an Asshole List. The girl who giggles uncontrollably at the same funny shit that I do. The girl who seems to just *get* me and is comfortable being as dorky or awkward as I can be.

The same one who lights up a room when she walks in it and brightens even more when she sees me.

"I realize we may never see each other again, Daryl," she carries on, "but this…" She heaves a sigh and comes towards me. She kisses me gently, but as she wraps a leg around my waist and grinds on my dick—

Sweet mother of God. *She is soaking wet.* I can feel it, even through her jeans. She stops kissing me, but doesn't break from her Dirty-Dancing style pose.

"*This* has never happened to me before. Not from kissing someone. Not from just looking at someone. You've had me shaken up since the moment you squatted in front of that spice rack in Metro, Mister Oates. And I'd love to see where that road leads, even if it's only for a few hours." She exhales with an adorable sigh and buries her head in my chest. "Even if it's never again."

I smile down at her in the darkness, surprised at her candor, at how badly she's been craving the same thing I have. From the first moment I saw her, in a grocery store that carries more kinds of maple syrup than any hundred consumers will ever need, I knew something about her was different.

Which is mind-blowing to a nerd who always suffers from poor timing, never thinking to give Fate a chance.

"So?" she asks, a hint of frustration expressed at my lack of response. "What's it going to be, Mister Oates? You in or out?"

"In," I mutter. I lean into her with a soft kiss, my hand behind her head. I pull her hair and expose her neck for the pleasure of my tongue as she moans in acceptance. "I'm definitely in."

23

Pam

June 12, 2016
Sunday, 12:40 a.m.

Bay Falls, Ontario
Canada

Finally.

I'm alone with my Geek Charming, no one around for miles. I have the only guy who's ever ignited my mind and electrified my emotions all to myself.

The only guy who's ever tuned up my body like *this*.

I'm not a complete dud on the sexual scale! Who knew? I always felt like I was Veruca Salt in Dahl's *Charlie and the Chocolate Factory*, going down the garbage chute as a 'bad egg'.

Not because I was a spoiled brat, but more like a spoiled *egg*, because no one ever made me feel the way I was supposed to feel. I've never experienced an eagerness the way other girls claimed they did.

I sure as hell get it now. I just needed the right guy to turn me into a 'good' egg. Daryl Oates is the catalyst for my inner sex kitten to break free. When we weren't laughing or talking during our short trek here, all I could fixate on was my desire to see him naked.

And freaking jump on him.

We're in Carly's bedroom, which is a bit of a mess. I strip him of his shirt in a hurry, and suddenly I don't care about the mess.

Holy crap on a cracker.

This boy is built.

I knew he had some pipes on him. The few times we've hugged or he's pulled me in tight, I could feel some serious pecs beneath a shirt just loose enough to hide them.

But *Jesus*.

He's also sporting some wicked toned abs, and they feel amazing under my hands. When he jumped off the deck today, I only managed a few quick peeks. I couldn't have anyone see me gawking at him.

We almost trip trying to make a break for the bed, so I kick a few random things out of our path — a hair straightener I know is broken, two mismatched flip flops, a discarded outfit of Carly's not suitable for Florida, a fuzzy gray throw that slipped off the bed.

I look at the floor and suddenly feel his gaze on me. "What?" I look up, my smile coy against my will.

"Nothing." But I catch a glimpse of his amused grin before it disappears.

"Okay." I throw a hand on my right hip as it juts out, matching my accusatory tone. "What's so funny?"

"You are."

"Why?"

"Because five seconds ago you were a raging firestorm, and now you're caught up in what's on the floor while I'm feeling quite the opposite?"

His grin is adorable right now. I can't even be mad that he's sort of picking on me. I laugh out loud because he's totally right. I don't know why I'm suddenly housekeeping.

"Listen," he says. "I need to make one thing clear before we do this." I look up at him, and he slays me with the severity of his expression. Whatever he's about to say is important to him.

"I'm listening."

"You can change your mind. At any time. I'm not going to pressure you, no matter what stage we get to in this room. I follow your lead. Clear?"

I nod, fully understanding, though it wasn't a concern to me.

My instinct tells me he'd never make me do something I didn't want to do.

But I am suddenly nervous.

Not because I'm having second thoughts about the act itself. I know exactly where there's a ten pack of condoms in this room, so that's not a concern. But it dawns on me he probably expects to see me naked.

Fair is fair.

This will be a true test of bravery. At my insistence, no guy has ever seen me completely naked.

"We can go back to the island whenever you're ready. Okay?"

I sigh as I slide one foot across the floor in a final swipe, giving us a path to the queen size bed, which is actually tidy. The duvet is neatly tucked beneath one extra large pillow and several smaller decorative ones. This is the irony of Carly. You can't get to the bed, but it's perfectly made.

"Just to clarify, I'm not changing my mind. I'm not having seconds thoughts about you." I kick off my sandals and sit on the bed, knees drawn up to my chin as I stare at my bare feet. "I just don't want to disappoint you."

He throws his head back in frustration as he paces through the open door of the bedroom and back in. By the fourth pass, I laugh at him. "You're going to wear a hole in the hardwoods."

He stops in the doorway, his dark curls falling around his face. He rests an arm above his head, leaning into the door jamb. "I don't think you're ready."

"Oh, I'm totally ready."

"Physically, yes. Mentally, I'm not sure."

"Um, are you really saying this right now? Because I *am* an adult woman who is capable of making her own decisions."

"Shit," he shakes his head, again frustrated. "I'm not trying to insult you." He comes and sits next to me and takes my hand. "I'm sorry, that came out wrong. And awkward. Sometimes...okay, a lot of times...I don't say the right thing."

"I told you this is not a first for me. Why would you think I'm not ready?"

"But it is a first in some ways," he corrects. "You just said so in the hallway. And I'd be lying if I said I wasn't right there with you. I feel like I'm about to become addicted to something, like I'm going to get that first taste, only to be taunted forever because after that, it'll be just out of reach."

"I think I know what you mean." I scoot backwards toward the pillows, laying back with an arm draped over my forehead. "You think this was a mistake."

He doesn't say anything. I squint, opening one eye just in time to see him shake his head. He finally speaks, his words directed at the closet door ahead of him.

"That's not what I mean at all. What I mean is, much like you, I've never felt this kind of connection with another person."

Whoa.

My heart rate triples at his admission.

"You're the reward. The cookie in the jar that's marked off limits, Princess." He turns his head toward me, chin dropped to his left shoulder. "What's your favorite cookie?" he asks. "One they only make here and not in the States."

"Um," I smile at his sidebar and think on my answer, "Dare Maple Leafs."

"You're absolutely sure?" he says. "Like, that's the cookie you'd fall apart over if it no longer existed?"

"Hands down."

"I've never even heard of those."

"It's like an Oreo, but in the shape of a Maple Leaf. And it has a maple-flavored center. And a vanilla cookie."

"In other words, nothing like an Oreo," he chuckles.

I laugh.

"Okay," he says, "we'll go with it. So, you're like the only Dare Maple Leaf left because the factory's about to close. Forever. Trudeau has started a national campaign to save these cookies, just to prevent riots. Normally calm, uber-friendly Canadians are picketing they're so pissed about it."

He turns away and leans forward, forearms resting on his thighs as he rants. "So, I'm in Canada, and, call it God or Fate or whomever, but some greater force wants to prove to me how exquisite this cookie is. What an experience it is just to get one lick. It's the *best* cookie there may *ever* be, and never mind comparing it to other cookies — especially those nasty Oreos — because there's no need. I already know Maple Leafs are unique to my palette," he turns to me and grins, "because it says so right on the box."

"It does, huh?"

"Indeed. But," he holds up a finger, "there's one catch. It's the only one left because, as you might recall, the ol' folks at Dare are closing up shop for good. So what is this Maple Leaf cookie to me, then?"

I crawl over to him on my knees, hovering over his naked back. I lay a soft kiss on his shoulder as I wait for him to finish his point.

"I'll tell you what it is," he says. "It's a trap in jar. That cookie doesn't exist except on this rare, alternate universe island."

"Fantasy Island?" I ask, gently biting his shoulder so I don't giggle.

"No. Royal Canadian Island, thank you very much. Which, to get specific, is off Cookie Jar Point. In Maple Leaf Bay. And it's ruled by a hella-hot princess."

"Oh jeez," I say through my now permanent grin. "That's almost worse than me picking out names for Alexis and Aidan's non-existent twins."

"Just hear me out, Princess." He turns away again and hangs his head, as though he's truly distraught and working through a life-shattering problem. "So now, if I give in and sample this last sweet treasure in existence, it's going to be the one cookie I'll have no choice but to compare others to. Quite possibly for the rest of my life, given how amazing these Maple Leafs are. I mean, c'mon," he shrugs. "People are picketing."

I kiss the spot where I just grazed my teeth, lay another on his opposite shoulder.

"Every time I bite into a chocolate chip or a perfectly lovely oatmeal cookie, I'll always be thinking, 'damn, that sure was great, but it doesn't beat that sweet Canadian Maple Leaf I once had. It's a cryin' shame they're gone forever.'"

"Oatmeal cookies are not lovely," I tease, "unless they have chocolate chips instead of raisins."

"Right?" He huffs as I raise up on my knees so I'm tall enough to rub his shoulders. "And further," he adds, his voice softer now, "raisins should be banned from everything. Wrinkly, dead grapes should never jump out and surprise you like that."

"Agreed," I whisper. "Nasty little things."

His phone is sticking up out of his back pocket. I hand it to him, then run my hands over his back, reveling in touching his skin. It's incredibly smooth. I trail his shoulders with my fingertips, then start kneading. For a split second, his head falls to the side in relaxation.

"Hey, Oates," I tease in a whisper.

"Yes, Princess."

"You should stop talking now and just sample the damn cookie." I lift his hair off the back of his neck and kiss him there, soaking up the combination of smells — coconut shampoo, sunblock, and pure masculinity.

Ah-mazing.

I feel brave without him looking at me. I remove my sweatshirt and tank top. A strapless bra, jeans, and a tiny pair of underwear is all that's left. I toss both shirts past him with a flourish, and we both watch as they land in the hallway.

He laughs as he stands up to set his phone aside, then stands in front of me. He eyes me with adoration as he cradles my head in his hands.

Whoa.

I can't catch my breath with that intense look. I feel like I'm about to bust over the cups of this bra.

Entirely possible with my chest heaving in such wild anticipation.

He leans away from me, searches the bedside lamp for a switch and clicks it on, then grabs for his phone again.

"You're calling someone?" I say softly. "You want to phone a friend?"

"Zach's right, you are sassy." He kisses me so fiercely my clit is pulsing, and I'm right back to where I started in the hallway.

Soaking wet and ready to pounce on him.

Then he stops.

"What are you doing?" I say.

"Music is a must." He pulls up something and lets it play. In the small bedroom, it sounds decent for only coming through the phone, though not very loud. "Do you have a..."

"Yep," I say before he can finish.

I run to the kitchen, holding my chest so I don't flop out of a bra that's useless on a dead run. I grab a wide-mouth glass from the cupboard and run back to the bedroom.

I feel like the clock is ticking down on our time together.

When I return the room is dark except for the light from his phone.

I hand him the glass and he props the phone in it to amplify the music. He sets it on the nightstand along with his neatly folded glasses as I climb back on the bed, propped up on my knees and facing the open doorway. Without looking, he gently kicks the door shut behind him.

He stands in front of me, all taut muscles and quick breaths, looking like he wants to sin. He grabs for the belt loops of my jeans and tugs me to him.

Yee-haw. Just that possessive gesture is a freaking rush with him.

Though I've seen him do it many times this weekend, any adjustment to his pants at the crotch would do him absolutely no good right now. There is nothing to make that predicament go away except a climax or a swift kick in the groin.

He starts kissing me as Phil Collins' "In The Air Tonight" echoes through the room, and that's it.

I'm totally gone.

Toast.

I *love* this freaking song.

My thighs are soaked again, and, modesty be damned, I can't wait to get these jeans off.

I figure he's reading my mind again because he undoes the button. But then he unzips *incredibly* slowly. I'm amped up, ready for him to use both hands and shimmy the jeans off my hips. Instead, he kisses me sweetly and whispers that I need to have patience.

"If this is the only Maple Leaf I'm ever going to get, I'm going to take that *Dare*," he teases with his play on words. He lays a kiss on my left shoulder, another at my clavicle. "And I'm going to savor this." He sucks my earlobe, then whispers, "*Every. Single. Lick.*" He traces kisses along the top of my bra. "This may be the only time I'll ever make love to royalty."

I giggle as he kisses my neck, even as I swoon at his words.

No guy has ever said he's about to 'make love' to me.

He glides his right hand over my breasts and yanks down the cups of my bra. My giggling halts when he touches my bare skin.

His palm moves down my belly into my underwear.

He's using two fingers inside me and a talented thumb on my clit. I'm already seeing stars. His left arm wraps around my back, pulling me into his chest while his left hand glides up the back of my head.

Ho-lee shit.

"Don't come," he whispers in my ear. "Not yet."

I wait a moment, then nod.

Don't come. Check.

Oh, but sweet Lord, I *want* to freaking come.

He's good at this.

He changes technique, and I feel like I'm on the verge of crossing a line I've never crossed before. Two fingers move together like he's saying 'come hither', while his thumb works in circles. His tongue dives in my mouth with greed; the kind I've never elicited from a guy before.

And then, ever so slowly, right when I'm on the edge, he quits one technique at a time.

First his fingers leave me empty and throbbing, then his thumb is gone, leaving my clit lonely as it pulses. He uses both hands to grab the sides of my jeans, doing the two-fisted shimmy I hoped for in the beginning.

In retrospect, I'm glad I didn't miss out on that first exercise in patience.

"I can't believe how wet you are," he says, his lips dancing over mine. "It's fucking awesome."

"Mm-hmm," I moan. "All your fault." My jeans are pulled down to the knees, the fabric gathered on the bed. I still kneel on the edge.

"I wanna taste you now," he says, his breath shallow.

Another moan escapes me, but I can't get out the words dancing in my head.

Hellz yeah.

"Okay?" He wraps his arms around my back, gliding fingertips along my spine. He unclasps my bra with impressive speed, then rubs the sensitive skin beneath it, loosening up every muscle in my body.

I breathe out a *yes*.

He tosses my bra aside and leans away as he cups my breasts in his hands. "That is some creamy filling," he grins. His mouth dives onto my left breast, just as the crescendo of Phil's infamous song resonates through the room — the part everyone waits for from the first notes of this tune.

The drums pound through my ears, amplifying the eager feeling coursing through me.

"Patience," he whispers onto my skin, and my nipples go from slightly erect to almost painfully hard. His mouth covers one, then the other. He nips with gentle bites over my bare breasts, sucks on my nipples.

"Holy *shit*," I blurt. "I feel like I could come."

"My God, you are just revved. Try to relax." He stops his assault and cradles my head again, laying a gentle kiss on my lips. "You have to slow your roll, or you're going to rob me of savoring the last amazing cookie on Earth. There's no way I'm getting you to multiples right out of the gate. You'd need practice. If you're going to be a one and done in the big-oh department, we're going to take it slow."

"Can't we jump to an advanced class?" I kiss him back, then lean up to his ear. "I'm a fast learner. Like you said, this might be our only shot at this."

He considers me a minute, and instead of talking me out of it, a wicked grin comes over him, like he's been hiding this alpha thing under his 'Oates' persona, much like his ripped body is tucked away under his t-shirts.

He tugs on my hair in that way that drives me crazy, leaving my neck open to the will of his lips. But this time as he glides his lips from behind my ear to my breasts, his left hand slides past my navel.

Three very effective fingers work some magic, and I'm not sure what I blurt next. They aren't words, but they're not coherent sounds either. I have to force myself not to come as he sucks hard on my right nipple and drives into me harder with his triple threat.

"*Don't stop.*"

But he does, almost immediately.

He pulls his fingers out of me, but before I object, I'm rewarded with his glorious head of hair in front of my hips. My hands dive in and rake his curls on top of his head, keeping them out of his way.

I throw my head back with a deep moan as his fingers spread me wide. His tongue enters me, greedier than it was when he kissed me.

Motherfu...damn! My boy's good at this, too!

Within thirty seconds of his mouth's handiwork on everything from my clit south, I'm on the verge of convulsing. Then he adds his fingers to the mix again, driving in and out. One long suck on my clit and those stars I saw earlier come back brighter than before, only for each of them to burst into a million tiny ones.

An orgasm like I've never experienced slams through me. My legs quake, barely holding me up.

"*Holy crap,*" I huff, fisting his hair tighter. "Stop a second. I can't..."

His teeth graze my naked right hip and I giggle, tickled by the sensation as I quiver from the inside out.

"You asked for it," he laughs. "Welcome to the advanced class. That could be the first of many, if you can handle it."

"*Gah,* I can't even."

"Lay back," he insists, his voice soft.

"Gladly." I collapse backwards on the bed. He tugs my jeans at the ankles, sliding them all the way off, right along with my underwear.

I'm completely exposed.

"My God," he whispers.

"What?" I lean up on my elbows.

"I can't take my eyes off you. And before you crack a joke — yes, I can still see without my glasses. You're just gorgeous."

Well, crap. I actually was holding out hope his vision might be too blurred to see me very clearly. I roll over on my stomach and groan into the pillow.

"Why are you hiding?" he whispers, gliding a hand over my behind. "Where's that sassy princess that was here a minute ago?"

I turn my head to him. "You don't have to flatter me. I'm already going to sleep with you."

"Pam, good God. Did someone tease you incessantly when you were younger? How could you think these are empty words?" He pries me over onto my back. "That was the single hottest moment

I've ever had going down on a girl — sorry, adult *woman*," he emphasizes.

I know we've been over this once already, just today in the boat-house. I don't want him to think I'm constantly begging for affirmation. I'm truly not, and I do have *some* self esteem.

"I'm not trying to fish for compliments. Like I said at the island, I just don't see what you see. I see something that isn't perfect. A body I sometimes wish was different because I feel like it's not going to be desirable based on certain standards. I guess it's a leftover from high school."

"Well, I don't wish you were different. Not in any single aspect. And it shouldn't matter what people look like." He hops off the bed, strips down to nothing, and stands there. "Look," he says.

I do. He is *effing hawt*. Definitely the best looking guy that's ever laid a hand on me.

"Oh, I am looking," I tease. He's not quite as hard as he was a few minutes ago, but he's definitely not flaccid, either. My Geek Charming is well hung (and not to an intimidating degree, thank goodness).

"What you see in front of you is not perfection."

"Could've fooled me," I mutter. "I think you're perfect."

"Ah," he says, correcting me, "perfection doesn't exist."

He walks back to the bed, completely confident in his bareness as he army-crawls across the duvet until he's above me. His strong arms surround me as he holds himself up in a plank position and stares into my eyes.

"When I tell you you're beautiful, you're gonna believe me. Your curves are *so* goddamn sexy." He glides a hand around my breast, down my side to grab me by the hip and wrap my leg around him. "But it's so much more than that."

"Sure it is," I kid him.

"Stop," he says, his voice stern. "I'm being serious, Pam."

I brace myself for whatever is coming next, because I can tell by his tone that yeah, he's damn serious.

"What I see is beautiful, but when I say that, I'm also telling you what I want to *feel*. It's not about what other people consider beautiful or perfect. It's about what I know will feel good underneath *me*. You're the girl — the *soul* — I want to feel. You're beautiful because of what's in here," he gently taps my breastbone with his index finger. *"That's* what makes you fucking amazing and gives you beauty."

He trails kisses on my chest where he's just tapped me, then looks up at me again.

"I'm just another lucky bastard who's stumbled on a Maple Leaf Cookie, and yeah, I see the beautiful paper she's wrapped in like everyone else." He releases my leg, then nudges both of them apart with his knee. "But it's what's inside that makes it epic and awesome. Especially because what's inside this particular wrapper is *so* rare. It's not just the last cookie. It's a *special edition.*"

Eff my life.

Call. This. Game.

I'm a swooning loon.

My emotions are bursting as he lowers himself, his head falling between my legs.

He kisses every inch of both inner thighs, inhales at my wet center as he tongues me. He sucks on my clit with ferocity, just for a split second, then traces his tongue all the way up, over my right breast, along the curve between my neck and shoulder. "Here," he breathes. "I'll prove it. You are incredibly sweet."

And he kisses me.

Not harshly. Not with forceful tongue shoved down my throat.

Just a gentle kiss that leaves my own wetness traced across my lips.

"Lick," he whispers.

I swipe my tongue across my lips and as he watches, a low moan hums in his throat. He's hovering again, our skin barely touching, but my entire body is just buzzing, wanting him *closer.*

"I wanna feel you underneath me now." He nuzzles my neck, behind my ear. "Are you ready?"

I nod eagerly. I'm chills all over after what he just said to me, knowing it's not some lame bullshit a guy says to get a quickie in the backseat of his parents' SUV.

Everything he's said — and what we've said to each other — is real.

The music coming from his phone adds to our moment. I've

never heard the song, but the female singer has serious soul. It's an R & B jam about finding the love of your life and letting it burn.

"Nightstand," I say, my voice raspy. "Over there."

He slides open the drawer and I lean up to reach for the box stashed in the back. I pull out a foil pack and hand it to him, then reposition myself beneath him. His knees rest on either side of my thighs.

"You're sure?" He pauses before he tears open the package.

"Now?" I breathe. "More sure than I am of my own name."

He smiles, then makes quick work of wrapping himself. He hovers again, this time positioning his hardness between my legs. But he doesn't enter me yet. He looks at me with that intensity, then moves my ponytail off my shoulder, just so he can lay a kiss there.

"Your name is Princess," he whispers. "Princess of Maple Leaf Cookies." He breaks into a sly grin.

And then he slips in, and I exhale a huge sigh of contentment.

He kisses me even as he braces himself above me, gliding in and out. He takes a breather and lowers himself with his arms, moaning into my shoulder. "Even that wet, you're tight as hell. Am I hurting you?"

"No," I breathe. "Not at all."

And he's not. This feels better than any sex I've ever had. I'm not sure if it's because he's already made me come once, or if it's just being this close to him, but it's definitely all new to me.

Surreal even.

He slides an arm under the back of my thigh, lifting my leg higher to give him better access. I run my hands along his chest, and his eyes don't leave mine as he moves.

I pant as he starts to thrust faster, hitting deeper each time.

Those stars are creeping into my head again and I close my eyes, feeling like I'm going to explode.

"Yes," I breathe. "Don't stop."

He doesn't.

I open my eyes and see him head back, completely lost in the feeling of burying himself in me. It's freaking awesome. "Can you come?"

"All you, Princess." He looks down at me. "Royalty first."

Not that I can admit it in this particular moment, but I've never had an orgasm in this position. Nor have I ever had a guy truly *care* if I have one. I felt like I was on the cusp for a second, but it's gone now. And I don't want to disappoint him.

"I did already, remember?"

He stops, wipes at his brow with his forearm and slides out. "I told you, first of multiple." He kisses my neck, nuzzles into my shoulder. "If you're up for it."

"It's your turn," I say. "It's only fair."

"Yeah, um..." He flops onto his back. "Ironically, it's hard to make it rain if I'm wearing a raincoat."

"Ah," I say, unable to withhold a goofy grin. "Well, that sucks."

"There's ways around it. I mean, I can work around it. Not that we have to have sex without it. I just wanna be up front with you, so you're not expecting miracles."

I giggle as he goes on.

"Condoms sort of prevent sensation for a guy. For me, it's a barrier that's hard to, you know, *overcome*."

"Oh, good one," I say with a grin. "And I guess I could admit something, too. There's no way I'm having another 'big oh' in missionary position."

"Challenge accepted," he laughs. "But not tonight." He reaches an arm out for me. "Come here."

I move closer to him, thankful to give my heart rate a rest. "So now what?" I ask. "I've never done the no condom thing."

"And I'd never ask you to."

We're lying on our backs, and I'm cradled in his right arm as we take turns talking up at the ceiling.

"I am on the pill, but um..." I bite my lower lip, then ask if he remembers the guy he saw me talking to in Metro.

"You mean the one who manhandled you? Yeah," he grunts, his tone disapproving. "I'm not a fan."

"Neither am I. Carly had to be tested because she found out he was also a player off the ice. On the road any girl with a vagina and a pulse fit the bill. Thank God, Carly's fine. But the thought is scary. Sometimes I wonder if we ever really know people, even people we trust."

"Mm," he says, then grabs for my hand. "I know we agreed not to worry about what comes after tonight, but I hope you know I'd never be dishonest with you. Awkward and ridiculous, maybe. But never dishonest."

"Stop," I giggle. "I don't think you're awkward. And you're funny. That's not the same as ridiculous."

"You're entitled to your opinion, your highness. But what happened to your friend..." His voice falls for a moment and he props himself up on his elbow, just staring at me. He trails the back of his left hand along my cheekbone. "I could never do that to someone I care about. And just so we're clear, I never have."

I. Can't. Even!

Emotions bubble up and fizz like a shaken tonic. Two parts sweeping adoration, one part aphrodisiac.

"Um, yeah," I finally say. "I couldn't either. I just broke things off if I felt it wasn't right, which was always. I've never been with anyone long enough to trust that it'd be safe to try that. As much as I wanted to, it just hasn't been an option."

"So, real feel is something you've never experienced?"

"I've never dated anyone on a long-term basis. So, no. Never."

He sucks in a breath of hesitation, then admits he hasn't either.

Whoa. What? He's got nine years on me. I'd never have expected that we had this in common.

"Seriously?" I say. "Not with any long-term girlfriend?"

"Long term dating material's never materialized for me, Princess."

I'm on the side of the bed closest to the door, near the nightstand. He asks me to grab his phone and glasses. I furrow my brows in question but do as I'm asked.

He settles his hair away from his face and puts on his black frames, swiping through his phone until he finds what he wants to show me. "Here," he says. "Official proof from my M.D. I'm totally clean."

"Okay, that's a first," I laugh. But sure enough, his latest exam results are right there. "No guy has ever shown me that."

"What a coincidence. I've never offered to show anyone before."

I scroll through the report. "Ooh," I seethe through my teeth in exaggeration, "but I do see another problem."

"What?" he grabs the phone back from me.

"It says your LDLs are at borderline unhealthy levels. I'm afraid I can't see you again."

He scolds me as though I've just offended him on the deepest possible level. "It most certainly does *not* say that."

"You're high risk, Mister Oates. I'm afraid I just can't go through with this. A girl's gotta draw the line somewhere."

He reaches over me, returning the phone to the glass as Atlanta Rhythm Section's "I Am So Into You" begins.

This song is in one of my saved playlists somewhere. I'd forgotten how much I love it.

"Listen, Princess Sassy." He lays next to me again, leans over and gives my left nipple one long, glorious suck.

Wow.

"*Mm*," I say. "What?"

"I'm just sharing this with you, so you know my history," he says. "That way, if you get a wild hair up your ass to sleep with a puck-pusher next week, and he leaves you broken hearted and diseased, you'll know there's no way that disease came from me." He pauses, then adds, "And, ya know. If that was ever a first we want to experience together — sometime in the future — now you know I'm clean."

"Oh yeah?"

He shrugs. "I'd be game."

"But I'd need updated medical records if we're talking about future sexcapades. If we aren't using that information now, it renders it somewhat useless."

"That is true. That would be a shame."

"A waste of information," I say with a *tsk*. "I should probably share with you that, as I said, I'm on the pill, but I'm also clean. Though I don't have my medical records on hand to prove it. So I guess we'd have to wait for that."

"Interesting." His breathing shifts. "I do trust you implicitly, though. What've you got to lose? It's your last night in existence, my tasty Maple Leaf. You've got no reason to lie."

"True. Also interesting is I know where I am in my cycle. There's absolutely no way I could be impregnated right now."

"Yeah?"

"Biologically impossible."

"No shit." He sets his glasses back on the nightstand. "So, what you're saying is—"

"I think what I'm saying is, I'm tired of saying," I breathe. "I'm suddenly more in a doing mood."

I reach for him, gently stroking until he's fully erect again. And then I peel the condom off, leaving him exposed to my bare hand. I toss the condom towards the opposite nightstand, then stroke him some more.

He moans my name, then asks if I'm sure.

"I want to experience that first with someone who makes me feel what you do," I whisper. "I want it with you."

He gently removes my hand from his erection, then rolls onto his side so we're face to face. He glides fingertips up and down my arm, then along my side over my hip bone, eliciting goosebumps from my breasts to my bare butt.

"Cold?" he asks. "You want to get under the blanket?"

"No," I say. "I'm just—"

"Nervous?"

"More like nervous-*excited.*"

He pulls me closer, kissing me, letting me get the feel of his naked body against mine.

Physically, the feeling is crazy-awesome. But something twinges in my chest. I don't recognize the ache as familiar, but I know what it stems from.

It's an honest longing for this moment to go on forever.

Somehow a condom was preventing this connection between us, which totally sucks. There's no way I'm making a habit of this with anyone else, and I may never see Daryl again.

But right now, I'm with my 'Oates', my Geek Charming. The guy Fate has thrown into my life for this one glorious weekend, and I want him inside me with absolutely nothing between us. Not space, not air, and definitely not a piece of rubber.

Our kissing is intense. He rolls over onto his back and guides me on top. I'm sitting astride his thighs in all my glory, covering up nothing.

A first for this 'good girl' who's dreaded bathing suit season since grade nine.

I throw hands to my face and shut my eyes. I can't help it. I'm playing the childhood game, believing if I can't see him, he can't see me.

He gently pulls my hands away and leans up, our bare chests touching as he reaches around to release my hair from its low ponytail. He tosses the hair elastic aside and fans my hair out around my shoulders, then lays flat on his back again.

He stares up at me like he's at a barn sale and has just stumbled across the original Mona Lisa.

"Gorgeous," he says, his hands gliding over the tops of my thighs. "You *are* amazing, Pam. I told you a shit ton of times now, and you just keep giving me more proof. Never believe otherwise. Not anymore."

I nod.

"Listen to these lyrics," he says. "I put this song on repeat for a reason."

I do as he asks, moved as much by the sensual mood of the old song as I am by the lyrics about how into me he is. He's right, the song's on a continuous loop, a reminder about how much I'm driving him crazy.

I need this to happen.

Like now.

"Ready?" he asks.

"*Mm,*" I moan. "*So* ready."

He lifts me up by my hips and slides me onto his hardness, and the feeling is incredible.

Holy shit, it's *ah-mazing.*

I have no words.

We're both moaning. He's wet, and thick, and this feels a thousand times better than it did with him wrapped.

"*God, that's awesome.*"

"You feel so, *so* good," he says. He lifts me up then guides me back down hard and runs his hands along my outer thighs before resting them at my hips.

I grunt in acceptance. "Again," I breathe.

He complies once, then again.

Once we've found a rhythm, I'm lost in the moment, uncaring how I might look. This feels better than *anything.*

"Jesus, you're tight." He moans my name, along with an 'ah, fuck'. "I'm close, love."

I quickly nod, grab for his wrists and move his hands off my hips, then release them on either side of his head. I sit up straight, my back set in perfect posture. I lift myself up gently, then ease back down.

And that feels *so* good, too. He must agree because every time I slide back down, he gasps along with me.

He reaches for my hands with his, our fingers intertwined. He gyrates underneath me, then pulls me forward, my belly taut, my hair falling around us. He releases my hands so I can brace myself on the bed as he cups both of my breasts, pushing them together, thumbing over my nipples.

"You can come now, Princess," he breathes into my chest. "I can feel you. You're there." His lips graze my flesh, his tongue flat against my left nipple. Then he gently sucks.

And I'm gone.

Over the edge I go, tumbling into another mind-blowing orgasm as he hits that deep spot, this time skin to skin. As I climax, he rolls us, scooping me over to my back with ease. He lifts my left leg so it's cradled in his right arm like before, leaving me spread wide for him.

I swear I'm having an out-of-body experience. I can see him from above, watching him make love to me. I can see the muscles in his back and shoulders flexing as he slides in and out of me, then hear myself moaning in what I decide on the spot must be ecstasy.

Is this a dream?

He thrusts a few more times. A masculine groan escapes him that's so freaking sexy it makes my insides clench.

That's when I feel it, and I know this is happening for real.

Warmth spreads through me as he comes. He collapses on me as I'm filled with his release. He's breathing hard as he removes his arm to release my thigh. I wrap both my legs around his waist and he cradles me, his heart rapidly beating against me.

"*Holy shit.* That's...you just..." He pants some more, his breathing trying to catch up with his thoughts. "*Pam, you feel incredible.*"

He's still above me, his forearms surrounding my back as hands grip my shoulders from underneath. He's ever so slowly relaxing. There's no measurable amount of space between us as he rocks me back and forth and kisses everything above my neck.

My closed eyes. The tiny diamond studs in each earlobe. My

forehead where it meets my hairline, despite the fact it's slick from sweat.

"See? Told you," he whispers in my ear. "Officially the most glorious sex ever. You okay, Princess?"

All I can utter is a lame '*mm-hmm*'.

Even though I agree with him a thousand times over.

Even though I'm more than okay.

I'm practically levitating.

Finally, I vocalize a coherent thought. "You like Dare Maple Leafs, eh?"

"Mm," he grunts, working his hips to demonstrate his enthusiasm. "This is Daryl Oates for Dare Maple Leafs," he says with a smirk. "Officially *the* best cookie on the planet."

"I hear they have a new tagline, too," I giggle. "Now with more creamy filling."

A laugh rumbles deep in his throat. "Another good one from my sassy girl." He lifts his head to eye me. "Future 'sexcapades'?" he says. "That was clever, too."

"Mm, you can borrow it," I say with an easy smile. I'm suddenly drowsy.

I touch his face with both hands, my fingertips tracing his strong jawline and the surprisingly soft black scruff he's grown in the last two days. He looks different without his glasses on. "I like seeing your eyes this way."

"Anything for you, Highness." He kisses me sweetly, and I release a sigh.

He may be right about his new addiction, how sucky it is to crave something he can't count on having outside of this moment.

But the reverse is also true. For me, all future cookies will be compared to this one.

To *this* moment.

One I never want to end.

24

Oates

June 12, 2016
Sunday, 3:00 a.m.

Bay Falls, Ontario
Canada

"Wake up, Princess."

I glide a hand across her shoulder, slide her hair away, and kiss the back of her neck.

"Mm," she moans, then stretches out like a cat.

Like a very sexy cat.

"No," she says. "Don't want to."

"We have to go, love. We need to make it back to the island before daylight."

Her eyes snap open and she darts up, wrapping her arms around her chest either out of modesty, or because she's cold.

"Shit! I fell asleep?"

She did. I slid out of her, leaving us both a soaking wet mess. But she rolled over, curled into a ball, and passed out. I grabbed the soft blanket off the floor, covered her up and gave her fifteen minutes to sleep, while I laid next to her in my boxers and tried to relax.

Impossible, of course. I used the bathroom and got dressed. I queued up some Miles Davis on the phone. I thought about checking email, but who could give a shit about that?

"I let you pass out for a few minutes," I say. "You're fine."

Indeed, she is more than fine.

Everything about tonight was *exceptional*. Exquisite. Perfection when perfection didn't exist before. Only during this crazy weekend.

Making love to her is something I'll never forget, just as I predicted.

I mean yeah, it was fucking amazing. Her luscious curves, how sweet she tastes, the sound of her moans…

Fuck me. *Ah-mazing.*

But also unforgettable because I want *more.*

More cookies.

I'm the God damn Cookie Monster from *Sesame Street,* and I gotta have those cookies.

Dare Maple Leafs for breakfast, lunch, and dinner. Any chance I get.

But right now, I'm putting my impulses on ignore. I need to get her back to Fawn Island before someone realizes we're gone and calls in the Mounties.

"Okay," she says, rubbing her eyes. "I'm up, I'm up."

"If you keep doing that," I nod to her bare tits bouncing as she gets off the bed, "I'm going to be up, too."

She throws my pants at me. "Aren't you sassy after sex."

"I guess I am," I smirk. "Must've rubbed off from you."

I make no move to get dressed. I just watch her put her clothes on, in awe of her.

"Daryl, we gotta go, yes?" She grabs for her tank top and throws it over her head. "Aren't you coming?"

I break into a grin. "Did. You should've been there. It was awesome."

She laughs, climbing back on the bed as she leans down to kiss me. "Oh, I was there. It was awesome, and I remember because I totally need a shower, if you get my drift."

I grab behind her head and give her a deep kiss, then sit up. "I have a great idea then. Let's get back to the boathouse."

"I'll have to sneak back up to my room," she sighs, getting off the bed. She grabs her sweatshirt off the floor, then searches for her hair thingie. "Oh shit!" She grabs for the half-used condom and makes her way back to the door. "Gotta get rid of this."

She heads for the bathroom, and she's gone for a few minutes. I tidy up the bed as best I can while navigating the messes on the floor, grab my phone, and wander out to the living room to wait by the door.

"You think anyone will hear me come in the main house?" she asks when she emerges. She shrugs into her sweatshirt. "I'd be mortified."

"I have a better idea," I smile. "Do you have any extra clothes here? So you can get re-dressed without going up there?"

She tilts her head. "Actually yeah, I think I do."

She runs for her friend's room, then comes back with a small tote bag. "I always leave stuff behind that Carly washes and hangs onto for me. But we don't have time for me to shower. We should get back."

I wrap her up in my arms and kiss the top of her head. "Trust me, Princess. I've got a plan you're going to love."

"*Oh-my-Gawd*," she says with a sigh. "This is so freaking awesome. It must be even better in the daylight."

"It is," I say, loud enough so she can hear me.

She's under the hot running water of the shower on the boat-house dock, soaping up.

I showed her how the controls work and turned on the water to warm it for her first, so she wouldn't have to stand there naked and cold. I let her keep her modesty, undressing and showering in privacy while I stand with my back to the opposite side of the shower wall. I lean against it and stare up at the lamppost that casts a dull orange light over us.

It won't be dark much longer. It's nearly four in the morning.

She shuts the water off, and I reach around the wall and hand her a huge towel.

"God, even these towels are awesome," she sighs. She steps out with it wrapped tightly around her, her soaking wet hair clinging to her shoulders.

She is the most beautiful person I've ever beheld. Legit. Can't even get a breath.

She steps towards me. "I'm kinda cold now."

I shake off my thoughts. "Yeah, let's get you dressed." I rest hands on her shoulders and march her around to the boathouse steps.

"Up there?" she asks. "What about Nate?"

"He's out cold, I'm sure. And he took the bedroom. We're just going up so you can use the bathroom to get dressed."

I throw her bag over my shoulder and lead her up the steps. As soon as we enter, we can hear Nate sawing logs.

She giggles softly. "Wow," she whispers, "he does snore."

"Don't I know it. Go ahead and get dressed and meet me downstairs."

She gives me a look that says *huh?*

"Trust me. I've got a comfy spot in mind, and no one will be the wiser. Use the side door behind the steps." I head for the bedroom, hoping not to wake Nate.

He rolls over as I access the closet for a couple of blankets, but he doesn't wake up. On the bright side, his position shift causes his snoring to stop. We'd probably hear that through the floorboards he's do damn loud.

As I come out, Pam stops me, standing in the bathroom doorway, still wearing only a towel.

"Be right down," she whispers. She kisses me sweetly, then closes the door.

I run downstairs and flick on a dim bulb at the back of the boathouse, searching for the huge striped hammock that used to be here. I find one, but it's definitely not the same hammock from ten or more years ago. Looks like someone's upgraded it for rental guests.

I hang it on the hooks over the middle slip, pleased to see this one's even bigger than the last one, if memory serves. Plenty of room for two people to crash and listen to the sound of the river flowing beneath us. The hammock is easily accessed from the dock that runs along the back wall. No dangers of falling into the water, unless you're trying to navigate the contraption drunk, maybe.

Pam comes in the door with a towel wrapped around her head. She looks comfy dressed in a pair of yoga pants and her coffee t-shirt from earlier.

"Wow," she mutters. "That hammock's gotta provide an amazing view of the main channel with the doors up."

"Right?" I grab for the blankets I pilfered from upstairs. "I'd open the doors if I wasn't afraid of waking Nate. Climb in, Princess." I reach for the hammock and offer a hand so she can have leverage to sit, her feet still touching the dock below. "This probably works best if we both lean back together," I say as I sit next to her. "Ready?"

"Yeah," she grins. "Ready."

We stretch out lengthwise with feet facing the back wall, our heads towards the bay doors. We're on our backs, staring up at the ceiling beams and the metal chains used to pull boats. She snuggles under the blankets and I grab for her hand.

"Comfy?"

"Totally," she says. "Except now I'm wide awake."

"Yeah, I think I'm beyond tired. Like that stage where you're all dopey and hungry because it's so late."

"And giddy because you're on a sugar high from Maple Leaf cookies."

"Oh," I say, shaking my head in amazement, "don't even get me started. Those things need a warning label."

"So do the actual cookies," she laughs. "They really are good. Do you think Alexis will figure out we left?"

I shrug. "They may have heard us take off in the boat, or even come back. But there's nothing saying we can't take a boat ride. Maybe you were showing me around the islands."

"I don't care if she knows eventually, but I think we can keep it to ourselves for now. I don't want her thinking I'd just go off and sleep with any guy I've just met."

I lift her hand to my lips and kiss her knuckles one at a time. "No one would ever think that about you."

I feel the shrug of her shoulder.

"Hey," I say. I tilt her chin so she'll look at me. "I'm fine with however you want to play this. I feel like it's our business, but as long as you and I are always on the same page, I don't really care what's said or what details remain left out. If you'd rather be up front with her, then tell her. I don't want you to be forced into lying."

"I'd look at it more like downplaying our adventure from sexcapade to—"

I raise one eyebrow. "Fishing?"

"No," she laughs, "but maybe I'll phrase it that we spent the evening right here. That we stayed up all night and talked and talked and talked."

"Well, in the interest of making that a true statement, let me ask you something I've just gotta know."

"Anything," she says.

"What fueled your interest in eighties music?"

She giggles, one of my now-favorite sounds echoing over the water. "Oh that," she says. "I thought you were going to ask something serious."

"This *is* serious." I push up my frames. "I mean, if you had a distaste for the fresh jams of that decade, that'd be my cue to exit this highway. A guy's gotta draw the line somewhere," I tease, throwing her words back at her.

She removes her towel from around her hair, twists it up, and snaps my bare leg with it.

"Damn," I say as I elbow her. "That's some talent there. You been hanging around locker rooms with those hockey players?"

"No, with my volleyball teammates," she says. "Could you hang that up, please? I'm done with it."

"As you wish, Highness." She elbows me back before I climb out of our cocoon to place her wet towel on a nearby hook.

"I heard that," she says. *"The Princess Bride."*

I look back at her in shock. "You know it?"

She nods. "If he were still alive, you could thank my brother for my love of everything that existed before I was born."

"Yeah? That's quite a legacy he left for you."

"Yeah, except he had exposure to all the cool things first."

"Lucky he shared it with you. My sister and I weren't really that close. But my Dad was a pretty hip college professor."

"My parents are kind of square when it comes to other stuff, but they do have good taste in music. We were introduced to tons of it growing up. Ben played the guitar, and so did my dad before his arthritis stopped him."

"That's so cool," I say as I climb back in the hammock. "My dad didn't play an instrument. Mom liked piano, but she says she had to quit when she was a kid because her parents couldn't afford it anymore. She had four sisters, so it wasn't in the cards."

"Wow, that's a big family."

"Sadly, I'm not really close with them because Mom isn't either. My parents raised us in California, and her sisters all lived in other parts of the country. My dad only had one brother who died a few years ago. Aidan's family has been like my extended clan."

She looks at me and smiles. "I'd say that makes you pretty lucky."

"Absolutely."

"Okay, my turn now," she says. She shimmies to her side. "Tell me about the last girl you dated."

"Ugh," I groan. "No one wants to hear about that nut job."

"Oh? She was a little cray? Did she go all Glenn Close on your ass?"

"See?" I shake my head. "Most girls have no idea what that reference means. Shit, even some people my age don't."

"What?" she gasps. "Who doesn't know *Fatal Attraction*? That movie was the bomb."

I lean over to face her. "Obviously you're just trying to get in my pants."

She lets out a louder giggle, and I 'shh' her.

"Oops," she whispers. She stifles her laughter with a cupped hand.

In the same moment, Nate's snoring returns. We try not to carry on with laughter, but it's pointless. We're both cracking up.

"C'mon," she says once she catches her breath. "You can't lead off with 'my ex is a nut job' and stop there."

"She was just a piece of work. Hard to describe."

"Try," she says. "What'd she look like?"

"Hideous. She had a hump on her back. A big wart on her nose. In just the right lighting, she looked a bit green."

"Stop," she says with a huge grin. She lays a hand on my chest. "Be honest."

"I don't remember what she looked like."

"Was it that long ago?"

"No, it was a few months ago. And it only lasted a few months."

"Okay, so start with why you dated her to begin with. I'm curious how any girl would not want to just snap you up and be with you forevs," she sighs. "You're pretty amazing. At least as good as an Oreo."

"Well, shucks." *God, this girl.* "All right, so I'll tell you the story of Crazy Carolyn, my last crash and burn relationship. You ready?"

She nods quietly but with intended enthusiasm.

"So, once upon a time, I met this chick at work. I thought she was pretty, I guess. Kinda. Not really. But she was a little smart. She was assigned to work for my team, but this was after she'd already expressed an interest in going out some time. So we did."

"And?"

"And, we never agreed on anything. She hated the movies I liked, the music I liked, the foods I liked. And I completely ignored all of these red flags for the first month, because she'd disguise her disdain and say shit like, 'oh, eighties music? That's *cute*', and then she'd change the music to suit her taste."

"To what?"

"To some indie band that sucked, but she knew the drummer once, so she insisted they were the next Matchbox Twenty."

"As if," she says. "That's impossible."

"Exactly. I mean, I love indie music. But she seemed drawn to bands who were indie simply because they suck ass. She may have been hard of hearing. I'm not really sure."

"Ugh," Pam smiles, laughing again as she lets out a *tsk*. "She sounds mean. And it seems all her taste was in her mouth."

"That's a fact."

"So then what?"

"Eventually, it got to the point where, instead of just being polite about our different tastes, she was flat out condescending."

"Like a straight up 'I'm better than you' snob?" she asks.

"Kind of, yeah."

"Was she fantastically rich or something?"

"Her family does have money, but that's no surprise where I live. Lots of people do."

She toys with the threads on the fuzzy green blanket. "I can imagine. That's not something I'm familiar with."

I shrug. "Money isn't a big deal to me the way it is to some. I find people are either assholes or they're not, despite how much cash they have. But before long, it became apparent she was indeed an asshole. Then she pulled some serious shit, and now I loathe her. The End." I kiss her temple. "Sweet dreams, Princess."

I pretend to turn over and sleep, and she taps me on the shoulder.

"So, if I'm you're favorite cookie, she's like..."

"Asparagus," I say with disgust. "She's like nasty-ass asparagus with frizzy hair stuck to a completely pin-straight body with absolutely nothing interesting about her. You have to dump something on her to make her interesting. Like a vat of butter. Or some Hollandaise sauce."

She laughs. "I do like butter."

"So do I, but she'd probably find a way to ruin that, too."

"What'd she do that was so terrible? You know, so I don't make the same mistake. Did she boil your pet rabbit?"

"No," I laugh. "Just work shit. She tried to sabotage someone on my team. It was a nightmare."

"That's low. Was this because you tried to break up with her?"

"No, actually. That was the weird thing. At work, we behaved professionally. Nothing inappropriate in that environment ever went down."

"No snacking on asparagus in the break room?" she asks.

"Ick, God no," I grimace. "Sex with her was—"

"That bad, eh?"

"Clinical," I say. *Which is the God's honest truth.* "Soft-Cell is pretty strict about that. But the problem was she came after my ideas, though it had nothing to do with Soft-Cell."

Her expression changes to shock. "Your app?"

I nod. "When I found out, we were already over, but I confronted her. She denied it, then tried to sabotage a fellow team member and make it look like he was the culprit, which is when I realized she wasn't nearly as smart as I thought, and a total whackadoo."

"Seriously?"

"Oh, yeah. If you ever decide you want to go into this field and work in a place like that?" I shake my head. "I'm telling you, prepare yourself. You come to me, or Pierce, or someone you trust. Because people are brutal. I didn't even realize her attempt to hack my shit until after I broke up with her. She'd done it while we were dating. Thank God, she failed. I was mortified that I didn't find it sooner. Felt like I was losing my edge."

"Sheesh. So why did you end it then, if you didn't know until later? Or were you dumped after she tried to get into your laptop's pants and couldn't get what she wanted?"

I'm amazed. She has me smiling even as I'm telling her about this regretful experience.

"No, it was me that ended it. I'd decided to buy the place in Palo with the twins, but I was second guessing every decision I made. It was around the time I clocked over to thirty and that likely had something to do with my hesitancy. We're eating Chinese food one night, which I detest and she loves. It was my birthday, and I didn't feel like arguing with her over where to get dinner."

"Unfortunately, I'm gonna have to side with your crazy ex on this one. Chinese food is aces."

I feign shock. "I knew it."

"What?"

"I knew you had to be flawed *somehow*." She smiles and grants me the sound of her sexy giggle again.

"That's okay," she says. "I can see a love of Chinese food being a flaw. It isn't exactly healthy."

"No, no," I say, palms up. "You go ahead with your General Barf Chicken, Princess. I'll stick to my Mexican food."

"Um, Taco Bell is *not* better than Chinese food."

"That's true, but I wouldn't eat there, either. I'm talking fresh ingredients for South of the Border dishes, not drive-thru. Though I do need my occasional In 'N Out fix."

"*Love* burgers. Never been to an In 'N Out, though. And your ex sounds awful. Who doesn't pamper their man with what he wants for dinner on his own birthday?"

"I know, right?" I scoff. "She should go on your Asshole List. Post-haste."

"So what happened during dinner?"

"I made an off the cuff remark about moving to the East Coast someday, maybe giving up my line of work to do something more meaningful, and she went *apeshit*. It wasn't even a declaration, the way I said it. I was just spitballing ideas, and this girl, who really had no ties to me whatsoever, completely lost it."

"So she wasn't that involved in your life? Hadn't met your Mum and Dad?"

"Nope. I never had any ambition to introduce her to anyone. The twins only met her once. Or actually, I think it was just Finn."

"What was her objection to your ambitions?"

"She said what a waste of talent that would be, to move away from the Valley. That California was the only place for someone like me, the only location where real capital could be earned and invested. That it'd be a loss to the tech community."

"Huh," she says. "That sounds like a compliment, really."

"You'd think so. Yet somehow, she managed to make me seem inferior. Like she's complimenting me for my talent and in the same breath, calling me an idiot. Hard to explain unless you know her, I guess. But she rattled all this off in her usual asshole way, eyes bugging out and all. That's just when it clicked for me. *Adios*, Crazy Carolyn."

"Wow. That's more like a Kamikaze mission into a mountainside than your run-of-the-mill crash and burn."

"Yep. I broke it off that night, and then found out later about her shenanigans and suspected thievery attempt, which she never did admit to. But she was shit canned not long after."

"They caught her?"

"No, her firing had nothing to do with me. My app's not part of my work at Soft-Cell, and I kept it under wraps that she tried to pin it on a co-worker. There was no problem at the company, because it was a private matter between me and her."

"And that poor unsuspecting dude she tried to throw under the bus."

"Well, yeah. But I worked it out with him. I never knew why she left, and I wasn't about to get involved. It came down from the top. Security escorted her ass out of the building that fateful day, and I did not object. Actually, no one did. I don't think anyone was fond of her."

"That totally sucks. I'm sorry you went through that."

"I could've avoided it if I'd been paying attention. I kind of dated her on autopilot. If I'd put her through my first test of dating, it never would've happened that way."

"Oh yeah?" she asks. "What test is that?"

"I can't tell you."

"C'mon," she says. "I think we're past keeping secrets. Don't you?"

"Yeah," I manage as she shifts next to me. The movement is enough to make me wish I could make love to her in this hammock as properly as in a bed. It doesn't seem like a feasible option, so I clear my throat to summon back my voice. "Okay, so usually if I date someone — especially if it's like a blind date — I have a sure-fire way to know if I'd like to ask her for a second date."

"Oh, do tell."

"First, I insist on taking her to a nice restaurant."

"Paper napkins or linen?"

"Linen is better, but it could be either. As long as it's one where we have to order from waitstaff."

"Got it," she says. "Then what?"

"Then, I arrive early, send her a screenshot of the menu and ask her what she might want to order, then ask what she'd like to drink so I can have it waiting."

"That seems like a nice thing to do. I'm not sure how it helps you figure out a girl, though."

"Because I haven't told you the best part yet, sassypants. Patience, dear." I give her a chaste kiss. "So, she tells me her cocktail order, and I intentionally order it wrong."

She's baffled. "So if I want a mojito, you're gonna go and order me a margarita?"

"Because there's a method to my madness, sweetheart."

"And that would be...?"

"When she arrives and the drink is wrong, I can tell just about everything I need to know on the spot. Does she get pissed, does she put on a fake smile, is she far too accepting? Or does she march back to the bar and yell at the bartender?"

"No way," she says. "Did someone actually do that?"

"Yep. You'd be surprised what you can find out with this simple experiment."

"Huh," she says. "Maybe someday I'll try that."

A brief (if unreasonable) pang of jealousy races through me. Temporary as this euphoria with Pam may be, I don't want to think about her having to feel out the intentions of another guy. I continue with my explanation.

"If that goes well and she handles it smoothly, occasionally I'll take it a step further and say I've got to use the bathroom, then ask the kitchen to change something about the meal she ordered and see how she handles that. Sometimes, that proves even more telling.

If she's treating the waitstaff like crap, chances are I'm not going to get away with accidentally leaving my dirty underwear on the floor someday."

"Okay, maybe. But there are holes in your theory. Circumstances could change the outcome," she says. "What if your date had a really terrible day? Like, she got shit canned from Soft-Cell, and the month before that, this incredibly handsome guy with gorgeous black curls and glasses dumped her ass? That could definitely have a girl throwing daggers at the waitress who screwed up her vegan order by delivering a hamburger. Or brought her a glass of Malbec when all she was craving was a beer."

"Ah," I say, a pointed finger in the air, "that's just it. It's all about how you handle yourself under pressure. Would you flip out at someone just because you were having a bad day?"

"I..." She sighs. "No. I don't think I would."

"There ya go."

"I tend to be pretty compassionate for other people, even if something doesn't go my way. I'll give my two cents if someone is messing with me, like on a personal level."

"Like if it's an event worthy of adding them to your Asshole List?"

"Precisely. But I tend to think out consequences before I react. And P.S., you did not screw up the coffee I ordered on Thursday night. Did you ever think to?"

I look away, seriously pondering. She's absolutely right. I didn't.

"Honestly, I was so bowled over, it did not occur to me. Plus I figured, you know, royalty deserves proper treatment. And P.S. back 'atcha, I like that you're not a doormat."

"Carly says she loves that about me, too. But she also says if I *was* a doormat, it would say 'Welcome', because I'm always so nice."

"That's my Princess. Always welcoming people to her kingdom."

She beams at me. "So that's your big secret, huh?"

"That's it. The one and only."

"My brother always told me to watch out for guys like you," she kids. "Guys with *secrets*."

"Tell me about Ben."

She's taken aback.

"Anything," I add. "Tell me something you miss about him."

"Oh, a thousand tiny little things," she sighs. "His laugh. His jokes. Kicking his ass at Scrabble."

"You like Scrabble?" I say. "Me too."

"Right?" she says. "When *Words With Friends* became a thing, I had to discipline myself not to play it 24-7."

"I kicked myself for not inventing it."

She giggles. "Me too. And we used to play Scrabble with my Gram. My mum's mother. She passed about two years before my brother did."

"I'm sorry, that's—" I stall. "Well, no two ways about it. That kinda blows."

"True, but she lived into her nineties. Said she was ready to go to God, if he'd just have the good mind to show up."

"She sounds sassy, too."

"Oh, she was. Sometimes I make myself feel better thinking she wanted Ben with her, so they could play games and try on her crazy hats together. I used to watch them do that when I was a kid."

"That's a nice thought," he says. "Is your family religious? Like Gram's up in Heaven playing Scrabble with God?"

She laughs softly. "Not at all. We went to church school as kids, but beyond that, my parents just figured we'd make our own way. They were not churchgoers. Ben wasn't concerned about fitting religion into his life. Maybe that's part of the reason he hid who he was, though, because of what he learned as a kid. I never asked him."

"What else do you miss?"

"Definitely the hugs he used to give me. When we were younger, we behaved like normal siblings who sometimes fought," she says. "He was older, and I could be a nuisance."

"Little sisters are like that," I say with a wink.

"Once he left for college, I think he — or actually both of us — realized how much we truly got along. After he moved to New York, he always gave me those super-long hugs when we parted ways, the kind where you just know how much the other person loves you or misses you. That's what I miss most."

And that's it.

The soft, sad expression on her face. The look in her eyes as she's saying this.

I'm a fully converted zombie, and this moment seals my fate.

Done-zo.
Head over heels.
This is my girl.

"That's why I miss Alexis, too," she adds. "And Charlie. I really hope I can have them in my life more when I get to New York. They keep my brother's memory closer, but they're awesome in their own right. Alexis' practicality and no B.S. attitude and her strength. God, she's amazing."

"Agreed. From what I know, anyway."

"And Charlie," she laughs. "He's just witty and crazy, and he gives the best fashion advice. If Carly's not available, I always message him for opinions. He and Lex are the kind of friends you hope for, ya know? The kind you can pick up with after not seeing each other and it just doesn't matter. You're thick as thieves again."

"That's how Aidan and Nate are for me. The twins, too. They're not day ones, but they probably would've been if I met them sooner."

"They're a trip," she says. "That thing with the cereal bowls was hysterical."

"Oh shit, that was the least of their antics. One time, Zach was so high on a strain of pot he'd never tried, and we were at this fancy fundraiser his parents were throwing. He showed up between the cocktail hour and dinner, so there was no food set out, and as he put it, he was *motherfungry.*"

"That sounds serious."

"Serious enough he went to his brother's car, scoured the trunk and found a huge container of those crunchy cheese balls left over from a tailgate party the week before."

"Did he bring them in and pig out?"

"Nope. Sat in the car and ate the entire tub of them by himself in less than ten minutes. He rejoined us inside for the black-tie event and planted himself at the table for a sit-down meal, orange-stained fingers and all."

"Oh my *God,*" she laughs.

"It was funny, until he ran out and puked behind a dumpster just as the rest of us were digging into our salmon."

"Stop," she says. "He did not."

"It's true. Every word."

"Holy cow. Are they total waste cases? They've never seemed high in their cooking videos."

"Definitely not. They are really productive, go-get-em guys, though they can be juvenile sometimes. Well, mostly Zach. But they don't really party like that now. What you saw earlier tonight was their reckoning with turning thirty."

"Ah," she says. "Makes sense. Sort of a quarter-life crisis."

I nod. "Another time back in the day, they went to make themselves cereal — and I can't remember now which of them did it, 'cause I wasn't there — but one of them put the milk away in the cupboard instead of the fridge and didn't find it until the next day."

"Ugh," she grimaces. "Who found it?"

"The other twin," I smirk. "This was in their townhouse before we bought our current house. The kicker was, the A/C was on the fritz, so not only was the milk unrefrigerated, but it was like a thousand degrees while they were gone all day. By the time they found it, it was totally rancid."

"Gross."

"You said it."

She lets out a huge yawn, and then I'm doing the same.

"You should sleep, Princess. How about if I set my alarm for three hours, so we can be up by seven?"

"Perfect. Then I'm going to sleep from the moment I get home straight through to Monday."

"Are you comfortable?"

She scoots down an inch, burying her head in my chest. "Completely."

I pull my phone from my pocket. "Music?"

"Mm-hmm," she says. "Can you play that song from earlier?"

"Which one?"

"R and B jam," she says quietly. "You know, the one you played when you were sampling Maple Leaf cookies."

"Cookie *singular*," I correct. "There's only one left, you know. They're very rare."

"Mm," she smiles. "That's what I meant. The last cookie."

Fuck yeah, I know the song. I pull up Jazmine Sullivan's "Let It Burn", which better win a damn Grammy, if anyone on that committee knows their ass from a whole note.

As the song reaches the second chorus, she's out like a light. And I'm not far behind.

25

Pam

June 12, 2016
Sunday, 7:00 a.m.

Fawn Island

I wake up alone in the hammock, snuggled under the blankets. I don't know how he managed to crawl out without me noticing, but he damn sure did.

"Good morning."

"Hey," I say. "Where are you?"

His voice comes from behind me. "Over here, in the corner."

I roll over onto my stomach and see he's standing by the overhead doors.

"Time to get up, sleepyhead." He doesn't have a gravelly morning voice. It sounds like he's been up for a bit. My chin rests on crossed arms as I grin over at him. He looks freshly showered, wearing different shorts and a plain blue t-shirt. "You ready for daylight?"

"What time is it?"

"Just seven."

I look at him pointedly. "Did you sleep?"

"Solid two point five," he says. "You wanna see the view?"

"Sure," I say. "Go for it."

He lifts open the left bay door, letting the morning come in. The sun is behind us to the east, but the channel before us is sunlit, the waters calm. He walks around the decking to the hammock and offers to help me out.

I stand up and nod to the view. "That's gorgeous."

"Agreed." He wraps his arms around me from behind, his chin resting on my shoulder. "Would you like me to escort you so you can sneak into your room upstairs, or...?"

I consider it a minute, and figure at this point, what's it matter? I'll never see the other couples again, and Tori already knows about Daryl and me. It's likely no one else but Alexis would notice, and if she's not up yet, there's nothing to worry about.

"I'm totally comfortable going up to the house for breakfast together." I pull a hair elastic from my bra and tie my freshly washed mane into a top knot.

"Look at you with the tricks upon tricks up your sleeve. Beautiful right out of bed, even when the bed's a hammock." He pulls me in and kisses my forehead. "If you're okay with us appearing together this morning, so am I. And I guarantee Redge has coffee on." He takes my hand and we exit the boathouse. "Let's go, Princess."

We get up to the porch to find a lot of folks are already up, based on the musical laughter coming through the open windows. Tori greets us in the foyer as she talks to her son, telling him he should already know the answer when he asks what's for breakfast.

"It's always pancakes on Sundays, Mamasita," Daryl says. "Everyone knows that."

Tori grins at the three of us, then heads towards the kitchen.

"I'm starving," I mutter. "Where's Alexis?"

"Still sleeping," Aidan says. "Can you go wake her?"

I blurt out 'sure', probably a bit too eager. If she's sleeping, she has no idea what shenanigans I've been up to. Running down there will be the perfect chance to talk to her in private.

I bravely lean up to kiss my guy on the cheek, then waltz out of The Gables with confidence. I'm wide awake without consuming a single drop of coffee and euphoric to a degree I've never been before.

When I get to Brat Cottage, I'm drawn in by the modest details of the cabin. It's more like the boathouse than the main house. It's not decorated in fancy finishes, but built to suit a couple of young guys who were here for an escape, uncaring about creature comforts like fancy drapes and tile floors.

I walk into a small kitchen to see an old-fashioned gas stove, probably a relic saved from the main house. To the left, a dining room with huge windows overlooks the river. The cabin sits on a cliff of granite, on a point closer to the water than the main house.

To the right are two bedrooms with a shared bathroom between them. I hear the shower running.

"Lex?" I call.

"C'mon back," she hollers.

I hear the water turn off as I stand outside the bathroom door. "Aidan asked me to come wake you up."

"Oh, I'm up," she says. "I wish he hadn't left me like that. I feel like a jerk for oversleeping."

"I think people are just coming around. I hear pancakes are on the menu, but I haven't been inside yet."

"Wait, what?" I hear the shower curtain jerk open. "Open the door this minute."

I do, finding her standing there much like I was mere hours ago on the dock. Her hair is wet and she's wrapped in a towel.

"You haven't been *in* the house yet? Didn't you sleep in your room last night?"

I bite my lower lip. I'm not sure what to say, but I don't want to lie. "Um, no."

She cocks her head. "Pam, did he put moves on you?"

I shake my head. "No, it was nothing like that."

"Oh, good," she says in relief.

Quite the opposite, actually. *It was all my idea.*

She steps over the high-sided tub and stands on the bath mat. "So what, did you guys sit around the fire all night?"

"No, not for much longer after you left." *Truth.*

"Okay, then what?" She exits the bathroom and goes to what I presume is Aidan's bedroom. "I'm gonna shut the door, but I can still hear. Talk, girlfriend."

"Um, he showed me the boathouse," I say to the closed door.

Truth, just with parts omitted.

"I thought you played video games up there earlier in the day?" she asks.

"We did. This time he showed me underneath the boathouse. The bays where you can store or pull boats. But the slips are empty. And there's this hammock..."

She opens the door, dressed in capris and a bra. Totes fine, because we've never been that modest around each other.

But obviously, she wants to know more.

"And?"

"And..." I heave a little sigh. "And we just stayed up till the wee hours and talked and talked."

"So...you like him?"

Whew. We've skimmed over the sexy part of the timeline. I get to the heart of the matter, which is exactly why I raced down here. I need her sisterly input.

"I do, yes. Like, really, *really*, like him, Lex." I flop back on the bed in dramatic fashion. "I'm so screwed."

"Oh honey, you're not screwed." She lotions up her top half and throws on a pretty fitted tee in a flattering plum color.

"Cute shirt."

"Thanks. Now tell me what you like about him. Maybe we can sort this out," she grins. "Find some kind of flaw that will change your mind."

"That's hopeless. I've been over it repeatedly since I met him. Other than the fact that he lives a bazillion miles away, he's perfect."

She towel dries her hair.

"No one is perfect," she says. "And I really like him, too. I like him *for* you. But the distance is another story."

"Exactly."

She moves to the bathroom to hang up her towel and comes back in a hurry. "Tell me what you like about him specifically."

"He's sweet. And kind. Funny. A total geek, like me. He's a gentleman. We dig the same things."

"Such as?"

"Everything. There's pretty much nothing we don't find common ground on."

"There must be something."

"Well, I don't drink beer and he does. And I like Chinese food, and he doesn't."

She laughs. "Okay, so not deal breakers, obviously."

"Nope. And he loves his parents, and he looks out for his sister, even though he declares she's a pain in the ass. He listens when I talk. And he asks me things that no guy ever has. He's just... Lex, I can't even explain it." I stand up, hands waving as I talk, pacing like I'm a detective trying to solve a mystery. "I've spent the weekend on an island with the most amazing guy I could ever find," I sigh. "And the short of it is, it's highly unlikely I'll ever see him again."

"Aww, sweetie." She wraps me up in a hug, then pulls back to rest her palms on my shoulders. "Listen. You do you, and let it play out. You never know. Maybe Fate's got different plans."

"Fate is a fickle bitch in my world," I insist. "You know this about me."

"Well, I believe there's a reason you found him. And he is Aidan's best friend, so I know he's not disappearing from my life. Which means he won't be disappearing from yours. Not that easily."

"True," I smile. "Thanks for the pep talk. And by the way, I've heard nothing but good things about your man. I'm so happy for you, Lex."

She releases a sigh far more lovesick than mine. "Thanks, girl. Now go on up and get your coffee fix. I know you're jonesing. I just have to dry my hair and I'll be up."

"God, yes. *Coffee*. And please," I say, throwing up praying hands as I exit the bedroom, "please, let there be more of that amazing bacon."

When I reach the kitchen, I let an eager Aidan know that his girl is on her way up. Sadly, there's no bacon today like there was yesterday. But breakfast does smell great. Aidan mentions they'll be taking Nate over to the mainland after breakfast so he can catch his ride to the airport by nine a.m.

Less than two hours from now.

"Did you want to come over with us?" Aidan asks. "Or we can drop you over there later. It's totally up to you."

"Um, I don't want to have you make a special trip."

"Lex and I won't leave for a bit yet. We have an easy drive. It's fine if you want to stay a little longer."

But is it?

Should I really put off the inevitable? As much as I want to stay on this island with Daryl forever, this is it. Today is goodbye, and despite Alexis' reassurance, suddenly this departure is hitting me like a ton of bricks.

"What time are you leaving?" I ask.

"Probably around one," Aidan says. "After lunch."

Shit. That seals my fate.

I'm supposed to meet Jay this afternoon to outline his prep material for the summer. We also need to solidify our schedule that's set to begin in two weeks. I can't pin him down on that unless he's looking at me because the kid is a freaking spaz.

I cast a glance in Daryl's direction, memorizing the features of the guy I was happily underneath just hours ago. He's standing only steps away, pretending to listen to Reggie and Nate converse about something, but he's looking straight at me, waiting to see how I'm going to answer.

"Um, yeah, I can go back with Nate. I've got an appointment for my tutoring student this afternoon I can't miss. Let me just get my stuff together now so I'll be ready."

As heartbroken and unprepared as I am to leave, I won't have Nate missing his ride because of me. I head away from the kitchen, on the verge of tears. Staying an extra hour or two would do nothing to improve things, either. In this moment, no amount of time feels like enough.

That's the heart-wrenching ache of it.

I walk to the foyer and Daryl follows. I feel his familiar touch on my bare arm when he reaches me, realizing that I've left my sweatshirt in the boathouse along with the little tote I brought over at three a.m.

He wraps me in a hug and I bury my head, unable to look up at him.

"Get your stuff together," he whispers. "Use the back door and meet me down on the dock. Breakfast isn't for another twenty minutes or more. I'll tell Aidan we're fishing one last time. Okay?"

I say nothing, unable to get any words out.

"Nod once if you're in agreement."

I do.

"I'll go get the stuff you left at the boathouse and meet you down there."

I shake my head no.

"No, you don't want your stuff? I don't mind running up there if…"

"I don't need it," I manage. "Just meet me on the dock."

He releases me, and I walk upstairs without looking back.

In the second floor bedroom of the main house, I gather all my stuff, then wash my face in the bathroom. I'd choked back my emotional outburst, but make-up is definitely necessary. I swap my 'But First, Coffee' tee and yoga pants for the blue dress I wore on Friday, which I'd hung neatly in the wardrobe that first night.

I'm as ready to say goodbye as I can be.

I grab my bag and exit the back of the house. When I reach the main docks, Daryl isn't here yet. I throw my bag onto the bench seat of the pontoon, assuming that's what we'll be riding back to shore in. I turn and stare up at the back side of the grand house, then up the path to admire the little gazebo, the one I never knew was there until he took me to it.

I'll never look at this place the same way again.

I walk to the end of the dock and turn my attention to the water, looking in the direction of the bridge. I know it's out there, though it can only be fully seen from the gazebo or some of the upstairs windows. I can see the traffic driving over it, but the top of the enormous structure is out of sight, seeming just out of reach.

Like Mr. Oates will be all too soon.

It's his eyes I feel on me first, his gaze landing on my shoulders. I turn my head to the left. Out of the corner of my eye, I see the soles of his Converse meet the dock. He's a few paces behind me carrying something, but I turn back to the river before I can make out what it is.

I can't look at him. I'll totally lose it.

"Where's your bag?" He doesn't come up behind me as I predict he will.

"There," I say, nodding to the boat.

He walks over to the middle dock where the boat is parked. I hear the unzipping of my bag, then he comes back to stand behind me, his hands on my shoulders.

"Are you okay?"

"Yeah, totes fine," I say. "You?"

"About as fine as you are," he says. "Pam, I know this isn't easy, but don't fall apart on me. I can't leave my Princess if she's sad."

I turn around, somehow keeping my tears held in, even as he's looking at me like this is killing him, too.

God, is it?

If that's the case, it's only going to make matters worse.

He swipes a thumb across my cheek, catching the one tear that's just escaped.

"I cannot possibly express to you how much I've enjoyed this," he says. "I know that sounds totally lame, and I'm not trying to be a dick, like saying I won't ever talk to you again. In fact, you can expect a text from me before you sit down in the Mini. And I'm going to need your email address."

I manage a chuckle. "So you can add me to your app's pilot program?"

"This is no time for sass, Princess." He takes both of my hands in his, looking at me with that *I'll-slay-you* intensity. "I need you to know, I have never had an experience like this. And no matter what happens, I know I won't have it again. Ever."

I'm stunned into silence.

"But I need your permission — that is, I need you to understand — why I can't drop you off when Nate goes."

"I…" I swallow the lump in my throat. "Okay."

"I don't want to watch you go. It's like you said in Timmy Horton's that night. It's just…it's better not to say it out loud. Let's just spend the last hour of our time together the same way we've spent the last two days, okay?"

He kisses me, and I'm lost in the feel of his lips on mine, legit panicked that I won't ever get to feel it again.

"Okay," I finally say.

"Now tell me what you'd like me to do with your stuff," he gestures with a nod behind him, "because I left it up in the boathouse like you told me."

"Right," I say, pulling myself together. "So, whatever you find just put it on the boathouse dock before you leave today. I'll use Carly's boat to come back for it once everyone is gone."

"You can drive a boat?" he asks. "Alone?"

"Um," I scrunch up my face in confusion. "Yeah. So?"

"Fuck my life." He pulls me into a tightly wrapped hug, the long kind where no one's letting go, even after a solid minute.

The kind that lets me know it with certainty.

This *is* killing him, too.

"Why do you have to be so fucking amazing?" he whispers.

One of Dave's humorous lines pops in my head.

"It's the least I can do, and what I'm best at," I say through tears.

I can feel him smiling, and I lean back to see it before I kiss his cheek. "I don't mind coming back. I think I'll wander around the island for a bit. It's a special place for me anyway, and now that I have Tori's permission, and I'm sure no one will be here this afternoon—"

"Dear God," he interrupts, "that's a crushing thought."

"What?"

He runs hands up and down my arms. "My Maple Leaf Cookie Princess sashaying her beautiful hips around this island, sad and alone. It's like a ghost story." He takes a deep breath, squinting with one eye as he exhales, like he's about to ask something he's not sure he wants the answer to. "Are you going to be sad?"

"Yes, Mister Oates." I look up at him, more tears falling in a free dive down my cheeks. I put my hands in his curls, thankful I remembered to do that one last time as I press my forehead against his. "To put it bluntly, I'll be freaking devastated."

26

Oates

June 12, 2016
Sunday, 8:54 a.m.

Bay Falls, Canada

I'm currently in socks because I had to leave my Chucks on the porch. They got filthy when Pam and I bagged our fishing ruse. Instead, we crossed the island and spent the time in the little bay by Brat Cottage, where her brother's ashes had been scattered. We skipped some rocks from the mucky shore, laughing and talking until we reached an impasse. A long moment of quiet settled over us, and I couldn't take it anymore.

I just grabbed her and held onto her.

I knew Tori would kill me if I came into the main house for breakfast wearing my filthy kicks. Pam was able to avoid any muck, of course. That's what princesses are good at — staying proper and pretty.

We're now in the kitchen cleaning up after Nate's made us all pancakes. The Pierce's friends — all three couples — departed moments ago. The Hamiltons and Reeds are bugging out for Manhattan by plane from an airport an hour away, and the Lonergans dropped them at the marina to meet their ride before heading home.

Nate and Pam are hitching a ride to the mainland with Aidan and Alexis post-haste. I can't bear to go with them.

I already did my thing with Nate, told him see ya next time. That wasn't extremely hard, but difficult enough. We bro-hugged and said we'd stay in touch before he headed to the boathouse to grab his shit.

Pam is pretty wrecked about leaving, and yeah, I admitted it to her before breakfast.

I'm wrecked, too.

I've already played out ten scenarios in my head of how I could stay longer, the when and how of seeing her again. Meeting in the middle. Taking more time off work. Flying her to California.

But that's not in the cards *today*.

The 'now' of her departure, knowing I'll be flying away from this little paradise of ours, with no plan to see her again because there just wasn't a proper time or place to discuss it. That's what's killing me.

In fact, there's a dark cloud over this kitchen right now, because no one currently standing in this room wants to go back to reality. It's palpable.

I don't want my time with Pam to end on a sour note. A grin comes over me as I think of the only thing I know that will cheer her up and simultaneously bring back the good old days for Aidan and his parents, too.

I cue up my man Frank's "At Long Last Love", which was one of Aidan's brother's favorites. I grab for a wooden spoon from the island and pretend to croon it out like Thad would do, gliding around in my stocking feet. My Tom Cruise imitation from *Risky Business* is on point as ever, and bonus — it's a wink and a nod to Pam's best friend Carly, the Tom Cruise *fah-naaatic*. Mama lets out one of her loud whistles.

"Sinatra Sundays," I say to Aidan as I drop the spoon back in its home. "I didn't forget."

He smirks in amusement, nodding to acknowledge my tribute to his brother.

I move to Pam, catching her off guard when I offer my hand. She takes it and grants me a deep curtsy, then I pull her into a slow dance around the kitchen island.

Here in the room where I first bartered with Reggie, telling

316 • M.J. WOODS

him I just had to have the slip of paper with my Canadian Princess' phone number on it.

And look at us now.

I twirl her around, unable to take my eyes off of her. Everything falls away but the music, everyone falls away but her.

She's smiling up at me, as euphoric to be lost in this moment as I am. Her brag last night around the fire was no joke. She's an amazing dancer, following my lead like we've done this a hundred times before. As the song ends, I spin her out, then pull her in tight, her back to my front with my arms wrapped around her waist, my lips hovering over her ear.

"This is Daryl for Dare Maple Leafs," I whisper in an announcer voice. "Best. Goddamn. Cookie. *Ever.*"

She tilts her head back further, a soft laugh leaving her as she leans into my shoulder and I sway us along with the music.

"Hey, Pam," I say, my voice still low.

"Mm," she turns so only I can hear. "What, Mister Oates?"

"Screw the warning label. One's not enough, and I just got word. The factory is staying open."

27

Pam

June 12, 2016
Sunday, 8:00 p.m.

Bay Falls, Canada

Daryl was true to his word.

Before I even planted my butt in the Mini, I had a text from him asking for my email address, which I replied to immediately. The second one from him read:

This island sucks without you.

I smiled wistfully and typed back.

Canada will suck worse without you.

Alexis again tried cheering me up when we hugged goodbye standing next to my car. She made the argument that with modern technology, Daryl and I could really 'see' each other whenever we'd like. But I admitted flat out that wasn't the same as having him in person.

That's what I want, and it's just not in the cards.

So I went on about my day, because what else could I do?

I went to Tim's and had coffee, but I was too sad to go in and lay eyes on the spot where we first started getting to know each other.

I went home and prepped the materials for my tutoring session with Jay Tremblay.

When I couldn't shake off my sad thoughts, I went to Carly's and cleaned her entire apartment. (Except the bedroom, because I couldn't bring myself to go in there.)

I suffered through my meeting with Jay on his parents' back deck while he was distracted by his phone every five minutes. Pissed, I finally grabbed it from him and withheld it until we finished plotting out our study goals for the summer. We scheduled which days we'd meet, putting them in his phone calendar (with reminders).

The kid is already a pain in my butt. He may be my age, but even on a good day he behaves like he's still in grade nine. Thankfully, this will be the last summer I have to suffer him.

I've still not heard from my advisor, and my brain's gone crazy wondering why. I finally broke down and emailed Fedders as soon as I left Jay's parents' house. I had to send something out into the Universe to figure out why I hadn't heard from him.

By then it was four in the afternoon, and I didn't want to go home and socialize with Mum and Dad. I wanted to be back in the place where I spent the most intimate moments of my weekend with Daryl Oates.

The most intimate moments of my *life*.

The best seconds of time I've ever spent with anyone.

I impulsively drove back to Carly's, knowing no one would be there. Her flight leaves for Florida tomorrow, and her dad is driving his rental car home after he puts her on the plane.

I let myself in, curled up on her bed and sobbed. The combo of my crushing sadness and an entire weekend of too little sleep brought me to the point of exhaustion, and I passed out.

I wake up to my phone ringing from the nightstand and look at the display, blurry-eyed and groggy. It's eight in the evening.

Before I left the island, Daryl shared the "Let It Burn" song with me — the one we made love to — and I assigned it to him as a ringtone. The song now bounces off Carly's bare walls, leaving me all mixed up.

I'm elated he's calling, but thinking of the last time I heard these powerful lyrics echo in here, while I was naked and completely high on him...

I clear my throat to choke back tears. "Hello?"

"Hey, Princess."

Gawd.

His *voice.*

Is it possible to miss his voice to the point of aching?

Already?

"You there?"

"I'm here," I manage.

"You all right?"

"Um, yeah. Totes fine. You arrive in California?"

"Totes did," he says. "Where are you?"

"I just woke up in Carly's bed."

He grunts. "You're killing me, Princess."

I can't find words.

"Tell me you're okay."

"I'm good," I say. "Really. How was your flight?"

"I composed an email to this amazing girl I met in Canada, then I slept the entire plane ride. I was exhausted. Tori probably thinks I have mono or something."

"Impossible," I say through a quiet laugh. "I've seen your medical records."

"True enough." I hear him take a deep breath. "I wanted you to know I made it home safely."

"I'm glad you're safe. What's in the email?"

"You'll have to check it and see."

We both fall silent for a moment. Just like when Alexis reintroduced us to each other at the town dock, neither of us knows what to say.

"Listen, love, I have to get ready for my week. I've been off work for five days straight and it's going to be a bitch diving back in. Can I call you later?"

"It's already after eight here," I say. "I've gotta get home. Probably grab a bite and go to bed myself. I passed out for a few hours, but I'm still run ragged."

"Ah right, time difference now. I honestly forgot. Or," he sighs, "or maybe I'm subconsciously blocking it out."

"I hear you."

"Did you go get your bag yet? I left it outside the boathouse."

Shit. I'd completely forgotten. "Um, no. I will though."

"Don't leave it too long. The critters will get into it."

"Good point. Maybe I'll run over there now. I haven't even unpacked. My other duffel is still in the Mini."

"You haven't unpacked?"

"No, why?"

"I put something in your bag. If you didn't unpack, you didn't find it yet."

That's right, he did! "What was it, exactly?"

"You'll see. I'll let you go for now. Message me when you get back from the island so I know you made it safely, being you're alone? It's dark there now, right?"

"Not for about forty-five minutes. But I will. Message you, I mean."

"Okay, love. Talk soon."

"Okay," I sigh. "Bye, now."

"Not goodbye."

"You're a superstitious nut," I say through a half-smile.

"Um, hey pot, have ya met kettle?"

My giggle is back. "You want me to knock on wood, too?"

"Wouldn't hurt."

"See you later, Mister Oates. I'll message you soon."

"Night, Princess."

Twenty minutes later, I tie up Carly's boat at the dock on Fawn Island. I'm lost in thought, wondering if there are any other knee-weakening surprises left for me here. I pawed through my duffel in Carly's driveway to find what my gorgeous geek had tucked away for me.

His 'Talk Nerdy to Me' tee.

With one fell swoop, he gifted me his sexy scent, his silly nerd charm, and something of his I could look at, run my hands over, cuddle up with.

It's going under my pillow as soon as I get home.

The next gift was the email in my inbox with a playlist. I didn't even look at the songs. I just downloaded them and cued them up. It's over two hours of music, so his song selections are still blasting in my earbuds right now.

I grab my little tote off the dock near the boathouse. It feels incredibly heavy for the few items I left behind. I look through it to find my unmentionables and my jeans, but no sweatshirt. Instead, there's a note attached to what remains of Carly's canister of flour.

No wonder the bag's heavy.

I stand on the quiet island alone, laughing out loud as I open the note.

Princess,

I'm holding onto your OCAD U sweatshirt.

The ransom is an unlimited supply of Dare Maple Leaf cookies, because I was right. They should've come with a warning label.

One will not suffice.

I'm returning this gift of flour to you, so you can reopen the factory immediately. Get baking.

Miss you already.

-D

As Lenny Kravitz's "Again" comes up on the playlist, I read his note over and over again. I'm not laughing anymore.

I'm an emotional wreck.

A Rubik's Cube utterly out of order.

But I'm a new version of the game, one that's unable to be solved because it's been cursed by Fate. Every emotion is here to play, each represented by the scattered rainbow of colors, a jumble of everything from euphoria to utter sorrow.

Under normal circumstances, it would take me only minutes to make the puzzle cube right again.

But now, I just can't.

I'm filled with this longing for him, a need for him to just *be* here, standing next to me again. Not for any other purpose than to look in his eyes, or have him take my hand, or call me Princess in the vicinity of my ear.

I don't know if this weekend led me to love, or lust, or something 'meant to be'.

I don't really care about assigning it a definition.

All I know is I've never felt such an ache that someone so amazing came into my life, only to disappear.

Six Days Later...

28

Pam

June 17, 2016
Friday, 8:00 p.m.

Bay Falls, Canada

"Delivery guy just left," Daryl says. I hear the closing of his front door.

"I just got the notification you signed for it." Before I can ask if he's opening my surprise, I hear the cardboard box being cut open.

"Aww, babe. You didn't. This is amazing." I hear the brown paper I gently tucked around four boxes of cookies rustling in the background. "You totally shouldn't have."

"I had to thank you somehow," I say as he tears the foil open. "P.S., they're best with milk."

"I don't have time for that. If I don't run to my room with these, the twins will confiscate them. It looks like a Cheech-n-Chong movie set out on the back patio."

"They're at it again, hmm?"

"Well, Zach is. Finn's not partaking. Some intern in Zach's office told him he looked familiar today, so he's baking his troubles away."

"Um...I don't get it."

"She asked if it was possible he graduated high school with her brother because she thought he looked like one of his classmates."

"That's not so bad."

"Her brother is forty."

"*Ouch.*"

"Yeah. He came home a little hurt."

I hear the familiar quiet as he closes the door to his room. We've talked every day since he left, and our routine is for him to retreat there for privacy and say goodnight to me. Usually I'm in bed and he's just finished dinner, but it's Friday and we're talking earlier than our usual time. I'm meeting Dave for a drink in an hour.

"Are we alone now?"

"Mm," he says. *Crunch, crunch.* "Holy shit. These *are* awesome."

"Told you. Four boxes going to be enough?"

"Unh-uh," he mumbles. "No way. Always want more. So tell me where you guys are going again?"

"Duke and Earl's. Just for one. Dave wants to celebrate his break-through. The owners have decided to give him a chance to shake things up for Sunday brunch at Layla's."

"That's awesome."

Over the last six days, we've talked about everything under the sun. The friends in our respective worlds are as familiar as our own now. Carly asks me over text every day how my Nerd Prince is doing.

And he's doing *awesome*, by me anyway.

We've laughed to the point of tears and fallen asleep together.

We also had some mind-blowing sexy times, mostly thanks to the supersonic vibrator I received in the mail on Tuesday.

My current apparatus wouldn't prepare me enough for the next time we see each other, or so Daryl insisted. I haven't objected to the practice. (Especially while he's talking sexy to me, his voice smooth in my earbuds as I pant under the covers at Carly's apartment.) Since the place sits empty and her dad's on the road all week, I've spent a few nights there.

My gift of Dare Maple Leaf cookies is a thank you to my Mister Oates, who has earned every right to be called Mister "O" now, even if I only call him that it in my head.

"I'm gonna get some dinner, now that I've had dessert. I'll call you around eleven your time?"

"Perfect."

"You staying at Carly's?"

"That's the plan."

"Good," he says. "I plan on taking advantage of that."

"I hope so. I'll be ready."

"Mm, good." *More crunching.* "Talk soon, love."

"Okay." I start to say bye, then correct myself before he can scold me. "Later, Mister Oates."

Two days later, I lounge on the dock on Fawn Island, the one by the little bay near Brat Cottage. It's two in the afternoon. I confirmed with Mrs. Lonergan via text message that no one is renting The Gables this week. The last party moved out by eleven this morning and the grounds are all mine.

I was told where there's a spare key to the cottage, if I want to stay here. There was no need in my mind. I just want to spend the beautiful, warm Sunday afternoon outside in complete peace and quiet.

I'll soak up the sun then take my iced coffee and my copy of *The Notebook* up to the porch. It's the latest read Daryl recommended to me.

Yeah. He *so* did.

Because he's read it, and believes it's even better than the movie.

My guy reads books. All kinds of books.

This is his latest recommend, which is swoon-worthy for obvious reasons.

I'm *done-zo*, as he'd say.

As much as I miss him, we seem to have fallen into a comfortable pattern of continuous contact that almost makes the ache bearable.

He's home in California, hard at work on his day off trying to hurry forward on Phase Two of his app plans. I'm relaxing in an effort to turn off the nagging feeling in my gut. I still haven't received a reply to my email from Fedders.

This long wait to hear about my final year plans is unusual for any student. I confirmed as much by asking some of my friends. So, I left a phone message with Fedders' office on Friday, just before Daryl called to tell me his shipment of cookies had arrived intact.

It's now Sunday and still nothing.

My phone trills from the corner of my beach towel and I grab for it, hopeful that my advisor is calling with some answers.

But no.

It's my aunt.

"Hello?"

"Pam, honey, how are you?"

"Soaking up rays on Fawn Island, Aunt Lil. Couldn't be better."

"Oh, I hate to bother you on your well-deserved down time!"

"You're fine," I insist. "What's up?"

"Patty called in sick again. Can you cover her shift at three?"

"Be happy to. I'll head your way in a few," I say. "I could use the extra money."

"Thank you, honey. You're a lifesaver."

"That's me," I say cheerfully. *Princess Problem Solver.* "See you soon."

Sunday night, I end up back at my parents' house. It's after ten p.m.

I came home after closing at nine, watched thirty minutes of mindless television with Mum, and headed to my room. Daryl will be calling soon, but right now I need a shower as badly as my grease-stained clothes do.

I return to my bedroom after showering and starting up laundry to find my phone lit up with notifications.

Two voicemails.

The first is from Aidan. He wants to talk with me about a surprise for Alexis, one he wants to pull off two days from now, on Tuesday the twenty-first. Since it's top secret, he says not to return his call now. He'll reach out to me in the morning.

The other call is from my advisor.

Fedders is returning my call from Friday, and needs to speak with me immediately. He's sorry it's so late.

But he wants me in Toronto *tomorrow.*

To see him in person.

Shit.

29

Oates

June 20, 2016
Monday, 10:00 a.m.

Palo Alto, California

I fire up a motivating playlist and cover my head with earphones. I need to get back on task. I can't get my girl off my mind and I'm supposed to be working. We talked during my drive in this morning, while she traveled the three plus hours to Toronto for a meeting with her advisor.

Technically, our conversation wound up as *sexting*. Never thought I'd see the day where I'd talk dirty to a hella-hot Canadian princess via talk-to-text, but it's now a fact of my very happy life. With the too many miles between us, we've taken messaging to a new level of sinning. (At least compared to most polite Canadian college students, if I had to guess.)

Sometimes we're both alone, sometimes one or both of us is in public. Our respective locations aside, it never fails to be a sexier exchange than most conversations I've experienced with other chicks in person.

Today, the sexy talk also served as a distraction.

She knows I'm torn up about the looming demise of my music app dreams, which became likely as of yesterday. I haven't broken the news to Pierce yet.

Meanwhile, she's on her way to campus to discuss her fourth year. Last night, I asked why she had to appear in person for the conversation. She said she wasn't really sure and changed the subject. When I brought it up today, she again steered us in another direction. Our messages also took my mind off the fact that I can't be in Central New York tomorrow to support her during what I'm sure will be a happy yet incredibly emotional occasion.

As is typical, Pierce has pulled out all the stops for his own birthday. For years, he's deflected his feelings and memories by refusing any kind of celebration for himself. Instead, he honors his brother's memory in some epic way. An unsuspecting friend from Thad's past who's fallen on hard times will find himself with a significant windfall, or Pierce might travel to a place he and Thad once visited together and make a hefty donation to a lesser-known yet worthy cause.

This year, he switched things up entirely and in a weird way, Pam will be one of the beneficiaries. Pierce is going overboard with charity, but this time he's created the cause. He's planning to honor Pam's brother, Ben Clayton — the same guy who used to be married to his girlfriend.

That's how Pierce rolls. He doesn't feel threatened by the ghost of Alexis Greene's dead husband. He's already won Alexis over by being himself, and he's giving back — honoring someone who was important to her — because that's just who he is.

My brother-from-another always brings that confident game because he feels threatened by nothing and no one.

Except for the tattooed psycho he has me tracking down.

I guess when a shit storm of epic proportions reigns down on him, a guy's allowed to feel a little concerned, grasp at a few straws. With wealth and influence like Pierce has, enemies are inevitable — as inevitable as calling on your best friends for help.

Earlier this week, his building and Alexis' home (not to mention her dog) were attacked by the crazy fucker I've been tasked with finding.

Pierce makes it a point to avoid this kind of violence at all costs. Unfortunately, greed is as powerful now — even in the backwoods of Lake County, New York — as it was in Rome during the days of

Caesar. The bastard father of his ex-girlfriend is wreaking havoc at his whim, calling on lowlifes to do his bidding.

The bitch of it is, I haven't been allowed to breathe a word of all this trouble to Pam, which leaves me feeling horrible. I intend to correct this with Pierce as soon as things calm down, make sure he understands Pam and I are involved and I won't leave her out of the loop in the future.

At the same time, Pam told me she hasn't felt ready to share with Alexis that we've been in constant contact, so I don't want to share too much until Pam gives the green light. Because my conversations with Pierce have been monopolized by his crazy circumstances in New York, I've been able to avoid the topic.

Last night, I reached a dead end tracking the criminal scum he asked me to find. I have to pass off all details — including the new information I was able to uncover — to Dimitri Floros, another long time friend of ours. I'm confident his hacker past will allow him to get what we're after.

My playlist rolls over to "Everything Remains Raw" by Busta Rhymes, the volume cranked. I don't hear my co-worker Jordan knock, or step into my office. I jump as he taps my shoulder.

"Damn, son." Jordan steps back, hands raised in apology for startling the shit out of me.

"Sorry." I pull my headphones off and toss them on the desk. "I was buried in this project and some *supah-sweet* rhymes. 'Sup?"

"There's someone downstairs asking to see you."

My expression shifts to confusion. "Seriously?"

He looks out my door to make sure no one's passing by, then turns back to me. "It's a chick."

"Shit." I stand up as my gaze darts in all directions. "Is it Crazy Carolyn?"

"No way, dude," he says. "Security would never let her past the gate."

I look out the window and scan the parking lot for Carolyn's car just to be sure.

No late model, Gloss Black Mercedes is circling the lot.

Whew.

I turn back to Jordan. "Front Desk Cindy says this lady is older," he adds. "Professional and shit."

Jordan's surname is Wong. He looks like he could be a side-kick in Kal Penn's next movie. He legally changed his name to Jordan because his given name is too difficult for most people to pronounce. My fellow geek dresses like he's an extra on Magnum P.I. — Hawaiian shirts, jeans, white sneakers. As office neighbors go, he's cool. He's not a too-loud gum chewer or close-up spit-talker, and he sticks to a strong bro-code even in our competitive field.

"Why didn't she just call my desk?"

"She *did.*" He nods to my headphones. "You didn't hear it. She finally got wise and called my extension. I told her you'd be right down."

"I'm on it. Sorry for the interruption, man." I thank him and leave my office.

"Bring back an energy drink from vending," he shouts on his way back to his desk. "I need more caffeine to make it to lunch!"

I throw a thumbs up over my head and take the elevator down from the fourth floor, apprehensive as I approach the front desk. I have no idea who could be here to see me. I know it's not my mom. She and Dad are in Arizona trying to settle the drama my sister left behind when she left her former landlord in the lurch and moved across the country on a whim.

"Ah, here he is," Cindy says. "Mr. Oates, Mrs. Jessica Fletcher is here to see you."

I stifle a laugh, recalling my mother's obsession with Murder She Wrote. "Like, the mystery writer from Cabot Cove?" I ask. "Are you here looking for a suspect, ma'am?"

Mrs. Fletcher is not amused. She looks ticked, either that she's been kept waiting or at my ill-timed wisecrack. Welcome to the World of Oates, Mrs. F. *Open mouth, insert foot.* I clear my throat to recover my sincerity.

"So sorry," I say, "I thought perhaps my incredibly juvenile roommates put you up to this."

"I've just come from a meeting with Mr. Caruthers." I notice she drops the 'er' in Caruthers in favor of an 'uh'.

"Gerry Caruthers?"

My boss?

"That's correct. He thought now would be a good time for me to introduce myself. He had to press on to his next meeting."

The woman tries to wrestle her New York accent into submission, but I pick up on her slightly nasal tone, the way she draws out 'thought'. To me, her accent is endearing. She's the epitome of the five boroughs, reminding me of my recent trip to the East Coast. No one I visited speaks the way she does, but still. This woman stands out among the California vibe at Soft-Cell as much as Pam would with her friendly Canadian mannerisms.

Ah, Pam.

Shit.

Focus, Oates!

"I can certainly spare a few minutes," I say, "if you're sure it's me you'd like to see."

Mrs. Fletcher tightens her grip on her big black purse as she considers me. She looks nothing like Angela Lansbury. She's petite, her hair cut short to frame her face and dyed an unnatural orangey-red. She wears black glasses that are round like mine, but much larger. I don't think her pantsuit was sewn in this decade, but the puffy white shirt beneath is one even Jerry Seinfeld would envy.

"You're certain you're Daryl Oates?" She looks me up and down as though I'm not what she expected.

I feel embarrassed to be dressed down in jeans and Chucks today. We don't have a dress code, but Mrs. Fletcher is someone I'd be more comfortable meeting if I was wearing a suit. She's a no-nonsense, get down to business (and-bring-me-a-double-espresso!) kinda gal. And I don't need to go pissing off personal friends or business associates of the owner of this company.

I mix professionalism with some charm and hope to hell it works.

"I am the one and only Daryl Oates," I say, "at least at Soft-Cell. I apologize, but I didn't receive anything from Mr. Caruthers telling me about a meeting. What may I do for you, Mrs. Fletcher?" I drop my shoulder and narrow my eyes, radiating an exaggerated Double-Oh-Seven vibe. "If that is your real name."

Her expression softens as she extends her hand to shake mine, her grip firm as she looks me in the eye.

"Jessica Carolli Fletcher." She emphasizes Carolli, but all my ears focus on is the way she pronounces her last name as 'Fletchuh'.

"Pleased to meet you," I say.

"As you can probably tell," she adds, "I'm not from Maine."

I smile, and she responds with half a smirk. She does have a sense of humor, even if it's stocked in short supply.

"I'm thrilled to finally meet you, Mr. Oates." Her lips curve into a full smile. "It's been a long time coming."

After lunch, I take the elevator to the top floor of the building. I've been summoned by my boss, and I hope I haven't sweat through my shirt on the ride up here.

Gerry Caruthers looks up at me through his drug store specs. He sits behind his desk in a black ergonomic chair, his fingers hovering over a sleek laptop.

"Come on in, Daryl."

I discern nothing from his customary informal tone. Caruthers' usual poker face is in place.

The top of his desk is tidy. The thin wooden legs of the antique are pin-straight and marred with scuffs. There's nothing ornate about the relic, but it's definitely the oldest thing on Soft-Cell's entire campus. The desk screams of Gerry: simple, sturdy, and functional. As the story goes, when he took over ten years ago, it was the one thing he insisted on bringing with him.

Here on the fifth floor, foot traffic is less than the floors below. Only three offices are up here, the ones set aside for the highest of the higher-ups. Still, I'm thankful as Caruthers hits the button to frost the windows for privacy, then asks me to shut the door. There are a couple of conference rooms up here, too, and anyone might happen by. I prefer none of my colleagues overhear this conversation.

It's possible I'm about to get shit-canned for conversing with a head hunter.

"I understand you met with Jessica earlier." He gestures for me to sit down.

Shit, is he mad? I still can't tell. I try not to cringe as I answer. "I did."

Silence.

Nearly a full ten seconds of it.

"So," he finally says.

But that's all he says. He's distracted, staring at his screen.

Come the fuck on, Gerry! I'm getting an ulcer over here.

"When shall we select your replacement and begin their training? I'd like you to be involved with the transition, if you're amenable to that." He rifles through his desk drawer for a pen, then makes notes on the pad of paper on his desk. "Where are we now, June already?" He shakes his head. "God, every year time seems to go by faster."

He goes on before I can open my mouth to blurt that I have no idea what the hell he's talking about.

"We can start our search by end of next week and have your choice settled in before September. You think that's enough time? Jessica didn't specify a start date when we spoke. She was beat, I guess her first flight from Albany to Chicago was delayed. I don't think she's slept in the last 24 hours."

"I hadn't made up my mind to go anywhere, Gerry."

He drops his pen and looks up. "Are you being a wise ass, Mr. Oates?"

"Definitely not. No disrespect intended." A wave of embarrassment washes over me. Gerry's a laid back boss. He saves addressing me as 'mister' for the occasions I fuck up. Admittedly it's rare, but I always feel like a fifth grader being sent to the principal's office when it does happen. "I just, uh... wasn't sure how much Mrs. Fletcher told you. I'd never make a decision without talking with you first."

"I hope I didn't make a mistake here." He gently closes his laptop and pushes the notepad aside, arms folded on the desk as he leans forward. "I didn't give your name to Jessica only for you to be slow in accepting the opportunity. Did she invite you to New York? Discuss getting a feel for the work ahead, the benefits?"

"We talked some, yes. But I didn't give her an answer. I need to meet with HR about my contract here. The only reason I met with her this morning was because she said she'd just left a meeting with you, so..."

He interrupts me. "Horseshit, Daryl. Contracts aside, you know how I run things. Common sense trumps all in any company I'll ever run. If there's no room for that, there's no room for me."

This is the steadfast, no-nonsense guy who hired me. When Pierce recommended I look into the opening at Soft-Cell three years ago, Gerry Caruthers' approach to running the company was the reason I considered it at all. He's never been corporate-minded, at least not to the extent that the bottom line is more important than his employees.

"I appreciate that, Gerry. I just didn't want to explore an opportunity without your input. Soft-Cell's been good to me. I wouldn't leave you in the lurch."

"I'd sooner say that's what my brother did," he mutters. "Up and dies trying to hike to Everest Base Camp and leaves me his fancy company. I was perfectly happy teaching in Oregon."

"He'd be proud of what Soft-Cell's grown into," I say. "You've accomplished a lot."

"Oh, no doubt in my mind he'd be happy. Hell, maybe even impressed. But that's not what we're talking about here." He removes his cheaters and lays them on the desk. "He wouldn't agree with me hanging onto an employee — one who I know is talented beyond most of his peers — only to watch him toil away his whole life here. Lucky you came to us, but we both know this position was beneath your skill level. We were your escape route from Bryson Chalmers' egomania and shady...well, you're already aware of exactly what goes on there."

As I open my mouth to respond, Caruthers raises a hand.

"I'd have done the same, son. I know you were on the right side of that mess. There's no need to rehash it. But when I ran into Mrs. Fletcher at a fundraiser a couple years ago — you know, one of those black tie functions where I want to leave as soon as I get there?"

I nod. Gerry hates any social aspect of this business. Schmoozing, as he calls it, has always been something he avoids.

"She was the only interesting person I found to talk to. In the whole room, Daryl."

"She must've stood out in that crowd," I say with a half-hearted laugh. "She's New York through and through."

"She sure is. From Long Island, originally. Anyway, a colleague introduced us near the buffet, which led to a longer conversation in the bar over a couple of very dry martinis. She let slip her tentative plans with the State University system, specifically that she was just waiting for funding approval to make a go of it. I dropped your name to her as having great potential."

"I'm honored," I say. "Truly."

"You'd only been here a year then, but you'd already turned the department around, brought forward the innovation that led to your VP promotion. She approached me the following year, asking me to remind her of the name I mentioned to her that night. I made my recommend official and told her you were the best I had."

"And that's why you're getting rid of me?" I say with a smirk.

"No, I'm getting rid of you because an opportunity like this means your talents will further the entire field. Her team's been on the look-out for candidates for some time."

"I appreciate your confidence in me, Gerry. And I did tell Mrs. Fletcher I'd consider it. Encouraging new blood to enter our field is a great motivator for me."

"My point exactly. We're not talking about you leaving my company to cushion another's bottom line. You can help create a learning environment that may result in some serious advancements. A place where young minds can be plucked from obscurity. Those kids will have a chance to excel, to trounce the half-assed ideas Chalmers thinks up while taking a shit."

I laugh. "That's certainly possible."

"It's only possible if those kids are given a place to study that's worthy of their brainpower. The East Coast is a ripe, untapped resource. Education is the key, Daryl. You know this is my firm belief."

"And I agree," I say. "A hundred percent."

"Yet you hesitate. For God's sake," he says, leaning back in his chair, "why aren't you packing already?"

I shrug. "I've spent more time in this building in the last three years than anywhere else. I've been in California all my life." I clear my throat, glance at the commercial gray carpet under my feet. "Leaving for the East Coast is admittedly—"

"Frightening?"

"Intense." I pull off my glasses and clean the lenses with my shirt.

"You're meant for bigger, Daryl. I'm not about to stand in your way. In fact," he says, opening his laptop again, "I'm going to push you out of your own way. You'll go to New York as soon as possible. That leaves just one question remaining. Then we can both get back to work."

I look up. *What else is there?* He's already decided I'm giving this a go, whether or not I feel like I'm the man for the job. "What question's that?"

"Will you help train your damn replacement or not?"

My mouth curves as the tension in my shoulders eases. "Of course," I say. "If this pans out, I'd be glad to."

"It's going to pan out, Daryl. Your promising future will lead to many more promising futures. You'll prevent us from losing a new generation of New York students to other fields. There's just one other thing you cannot lose."

"What's that?" I ask, eyebrows raised.

"Focus." He puts his glasses back on and stares at me. "Never lose focus on where you're headed. Or just as importantly, on your 'why'. You remember that, keep it up here," he says, pointing to his temple, "and you'll do just fine."

After work, I pull in to Rosita's to meet the twins for our usual cure for the Monday blahs — tacos. We're stopping at a different bar to check out trivia afterward because Finn insists we avoid the Wednesday game at The Tap Room.

Turns out his recent flavor of the week (Chocolate Brunette, a/k/a Random Rachel the math teacher), frequents that pub. After hooking up with her a couple of weeks ago, he ran into her there last week. She's not stalking him, he says.

She was there with another dude.

Now he just wants to avoid another awkward run-in.

I snag the last parking spot behind the restaurant and wander in to find the guys have already ordered. Zach nods to me from a booth they scored in the front corner.

"You're late," he says.

"Thanks, bruh. Owe you one."

"What you owe me is twenty bucks and change."

I reach for my wallet, but he stops me.

"I'll let it slide, given we scored the Scotch times two after your Canadian vacation."

"The second bottle was all Pierce," I say. "He insisted you guys get a consolation prize slash birthday gift after I bailed on Vegas."

"Which led to you becoming pussy-whipped in one weekend," Finn says. He raises his margarita, then takes a swig.

"You guys blew off Vegas anyway," I dig, returning his gesture with my beer bottle. "And fuck off. I like being whipped."

"No fighting, children," Zach says. "We need to get our heads on straight. I hear competition is pretty intense at Gina's Table."

Finn looks to his twin as though he's lost his mind. "We're not jumping in the game," he says, "just scoping things out. I've gotta turn in early."

Zach shrugs. "We'll see."

"Same goes for me," I say. My intro to Mrs. Fletcher today has taken over all my brain power, anyway. I want the twins' opinion on the offer she presented. As Zach polishes off his second taco, I broach the subject.

"I had an interesting meeting today," I start. "One of Caruthers' colleagues showed up at Soft-Cell."

Finn raises a brow. "Who?"

"She's from New York."

"From what company?" Zach asks with a mouth full of food.

"Not a company." I sip some water then grab for a chip. "She's with New York's State University System."

"Yeah?" Finn says. "What'd she want with you?"

"She made me a job offer."

"You already have a job," Zach says after an extremely loud belch.

"Excuse you." Finn throws an elbow to his brother's ribs. "You think Caruthers knows?"

"He's the one who recommended me. The way he tells it, he gave me the nod two years ago."

"What's the job?" Zach asks.

"They're looking for someone to implement a new curriculum for future students looking to study in my field."

"What school?" they say in unison.

"Not for one school," I say. "The whole system. State-wide."

Zach's eyes go big. "No shit."

"They currently offer job-specific programs, but only on a few campuses," I say. "Tech is an underserved field in New York, at least outside the Big Apple. They've had a hard time keeping up, given the speed the industry advances."

"You could say they're a decade or two late to the party," Finn says.

"This Mrs. Fletcher claims the State realizes this. They want new program offerings to compete with private schools back East, but they also hope to rival programs on a national level. Attracting more paying students is the goal, obviously."

The guys are quiet for a moment, considering.

"I would hope they know the amount of work that lies ahead," I add. "They'll have to expand existing programs to every campus."

Finn beats me to the point. "And create a lot more that don't currently exist. That's quite an undertaking. Is there a demand for it?"

"According to their research, there's a need."

Zach laughs. "What about the shitty weather? Have they figured out how to make it stop snowing for eight months of the year so people might go there to study in the first place?"

"Hey, some people dig the snow." *So what if I have no idea whether I'm one of them?*

"What's the curriculum they're proposing?" Finn asks.

"Programming. Integrated Tech. Cyber security. The list goes on. They want to compete with the likes of Cal Tech."

"And they think you're the man to make it happen, huh?" Zach says.

Finn comes to my defense. "No doubt he could be. It's not a one-man job, though. Would you have to travel the entire state?"

"On occasion. I'd be overseeing the course expansion and curriculum development along with a team of people while finishing my doctorate."

"That's a nice perk," he says. "Smart to have that done."

"It's more like a requirement with them, but yeah. It makes the offer more attractive."

"Who else is on their radar?" Zach asks. "Anyone you know?"

"So far, they've only got one other guy's yes. Terry something or other. I didn't recognize his name. The rest have been approached but not responded yet."

"That's important information," Finn says. "You end up with a team of boobs, it's all gonna be on your plate."

Zach chimes in. "Or on your head if they fuck up."

"That's part of my hesitation. This lady was familiar with my career, and Caruthers sang my praises. I'm sure they've researched all of us, but I have no idea who else is being offered positions."

Finn grumbles. "Chances are you know them."

"Exactly. That's a risk," I shrug. "The position would go beyond implementing the programs, though. Once each phase is complete — which they think will take a few years — I move closer to the cherry on top."

The guys lift their brows in unison.

"I have the option to teach."

"Dude," Zach says.

"Whatever program I choose in the expanded department. And," I add, "at whichever New York campus I want."

Zach stares in disbelief. "Anywhere?"

"Anywhere they have a campus."

Finn just nods. He knows this is a golden opportunity.

"So what's next?" Zach says.

"They want to fly me to New York to meet with the higher-ups and get a feel for what I'd be tasked with. Talk about compensation, benefits, *etcetera-etcetera*," I say with an exaggerated pompous tone.

Finn's smug grin has me laughing. He knows I could never imagine this chance would fall in my lap. I show up for work with enthusiasm, though maybe more or less depending on the project. I always pull my weight. But I'm not the guy who dreamed of climbing the corporate ladder to become the head cheese.

I never finished my path to become an academic, either. As much as my dad hoped I'd carry on the tradition after he retired from Cal Tech, I gave up on pursuing my doctorate when I took the job at Soft-Cell.

"Your dad is going to keel when he hears this news," Finn says.

"Right?" I dip a chip into our shared guacamole. "I really thought Soft-Cell would be it through retirement. He probably did, too."

Zach tilts the neck of his beer bottle at me. "I would've banked on it. We know your sister wouldn't continue the academia bloodline. She never finished that community college program in Arizona."

"Meh," I say. "It isn't her thing."

"Well, you can carry the torch now. Professor Oates, Two-Point-Oh," Zach says. "Now nerdier, and with more hair."

"Funny." I flip him the bird. "Attracting the interest of a whole new generation of geeks like me, though?" I swig my beer and smile. "That's something I can get behind."

"Make sure your app plans don't conflict with their offer," Finn adds. "Did you untangle that mess yet?"

"Hell no," I sigh. "Pretty sure Chalmers has won that race."

"You want me to check in with my contact on the inside?" he asks.

"Nah," I say, "don't bother. I'm behind the eight ball with the marketing. There's just no way to pull off an August release like I wanted to. Chalmers is going to take the lead with his shitty version, and that'll be that."

"Can't Pierce help?" Zach says.

"He's up to his eyeballs. Gala prep for July Fourth weekend, trying to get his Center off the ground. I'm on my own at the moment."

I leave out the details of the nefarious character Pierce has been faced with. His misfortune isn't something I can disclose. Besides Pierces' right-hand men, only Dimitri Floros and I know, and we were brought in only because Pierce needed help tracking down the bastard who broke in.

I'm not sure how much Alexis knows, and Pam's going to flip out when she finds out that her sister-in-law has been through all this. If she becomes aware that I knew first, I'm not sure we'll even be on speaking terms.

I shake off my thoughts.

"You've had this app in your back pocket forever," Zach says. "Don't just quit, dude."

"If I didn't have regular work, I'd be severely depressed about it. Its demise is inevitable. Meant to be, maybe. It's barely on life support at this point, and this offer from New York makes it easier to pull the plug. Letting Pierce down is the shitty part."

"Hey, with this job, you'd end up closer to him. And to your Canadian princess," Zach says.

I start to say Pam hasn't been a consideration in this regard, but Finn interrupts by holding up a hand. "Don't even try to play us like that hasn't crossed your mind."

My mouth snaps closed. *Yeah, of course it has.* Even if Pam was living in Canada next year, we'd be within driving distance of each other with me in New York. But she'll be studying in New York for her final undergrad year, whether it's downstate or with a University near her sister-in-law.

If I take this job offer, we'd be that much closer — geographically speaking.

My mind has been in turmoil all afternoon about the pressure this would put on such a new relationship. I don't want her to think I'd make a career decision based on an intimate connection that's less than thirty days old, because I wouldn't.

Even if that connection is incredibly intense.

Unique.

Mind-blowing.

I can't deny the idea of living in the same state as Pam is a draw. I've spoken to her daily since we met, and our conversations never disappoint. They're always the best part of my day.

But I won't admit any of this out loud, especially to these two bozos.

"Even if you don't say yes, this is a hella sweet deal for you," Zach says. "Soak up all the freebies you can. These head hunter types usually have big expense accounts. Was she hot?"

"Maybe. If you're into sixty-something redheads who talk like Marisa Tomei in *My Cousin Vinny* and look like Annie Potts in the original *Ghostbusters*."

"Um, nah I'm good." Zach's cheeks meet his eyes, his cringe becoming a full-body shudder. "Probably for the best, though. No mixing business with pleasure."

I polish off my taco, wipe my mouth with a paper napkin, and throw it at him.

"So what's next?" Finn asks.

"Meet with Mrs. Fletcher tomorrow about possible travel plans, then Caruthers again next week about my replacement search if that trip goes well. At first, I wasn't sure he'd be keen on all this. I thought it was some kind of test of my loyalty to Soft-Cell."

"Then you'd have failed," Zach says before laughing his head off.

Finn interrupts, insisting Caruthers wouldn't do that. "Our company's had enough dealings with him. You already earned his trust three years ago when he hired you."

"And I repay him by leaving?"

Finn shakes his head. "I get you not wanting to bail, but Soft-Cell is healthy with or without your daily presence. Agree?"

"I suppose," I say. "Thanks for making me feel valued, bro."

"Point is," Finn says after downing his drink, "I'd throat punch you if you didn't consider an offer from the university system of an entire state with the academic cred you already have. Cred that's been lying around dormant for years. Cred that could bump up your pay and set you up for a sweet retirement a helluva lot sooner than if you kept running the rat race, especially when we all know how short this life is, and..."

"Yeah," I cut him off and give him the okay signal with my right hand. "Got it, oh philosophical twin. No need for the diatribe."

"I'm just saying, only an idiot would say no without finding out more. You have your out on the house equity, if your maybe turns into 'goodbye California'." He gestures with his thumb. "Even if it leaves me stuck with this asshole."

"You'd be fine in that big house, especially with my bedroom empty," I say as we pretend to ignore Zach's presence. "You'd have an extra room to escape from him."

"Putting up with his shit by myself — yet again — was my biggest fear," Finn says. "You were supposed to stick around to run interference. At least until this dope marries the first Vanilla Honey that holds his interest longer than ninety days."

Zach punches his brother's arm. Finn retaliates by stealing Zach's last taco.

"Give that back, fucker."

Finn ignores him and dives into the stolen goods.

"Whatever," Zach scoffs. "My roommate status doesn't seem to bother you when I make half the mortgage payment."

"Or when you shared a womb," I offer.

Zach's face screws up in disgust. "Don't talk about our mother's uterus."

"Second that," Finn says. "Ever again."

My phone vibrates with a text from Pam. I'm distracted while Finn carries on.

"Oates," Zach says, clapping his hands in front of my face, "are you listening to my brother's sound advice?"

"No, sorry." I take off my glasses and rub my eyes. "What'd ya say?"

Finn stares me down. "For once, your timing is on point. Get your ass to New York and meet those university suits," he says. "*Pronto.*"

30

Pam

June 20, 2016
Monday, 12:00 p.m.

Toronto, Canada

"Thanks for coming by on such short notice." Fedders gets up from his chair and moves around his desk, stopping at his printer on the other side of the small room. "I wasn't sure you'd be able to get out here so fast."

I've already declined a donut, a cup of coffee, and a glass of water.

I just want him to get to the damn point.

"No problem," I say. "I'm glad it worked out. You caught me before I leave to visit my sister-in-law tomorrow."

Now why am I here?!

Edwin Fedders has been distracted since I arrived. He also hasn't behaved in his typical scatter-brained manner.

This is the guy who once lost his keys and made an entire class of students scour the path from his car to his office in a mad search for them. It was the dead of winter, and his wife was in labor with their third child. Meanwhile, the keys were in his office the whole time, hiding in the pocket of his suit coat which he'd completely forgotten he'd worn that day.

He's customarily panicked about something he's lost or a deadline he forgot about, so it's not unusual to see him run around in a tizzy. Yet today, he seems incredibly calm. Something tells me that's a bad thing, at least for someone.

"So how are you planning to spend the summer?" he asks as he sits again. "You tutoring Jay Tremblay?"

"I am. But you didn't ask me to drive all the way out here to talk about that."

"No, you're right." He sets down his red pen, leaning back in his leather office chair with an expression that concerns me. "I'm glad we could get to this now."

"It's no trouble."

Well, it sort of *is*, but no need to split hairs. I'll have spent six hours in a car today, only to spend another four plus tomorrow riding to and from New York with Mum and Dad.

But, whatever. This is my future. I had nothing better to do than mope around anyway, unless I was in my happy place while talking to Daryl as I'd been on the drive here.

Fedders is silent, hunting and pecking keys on his laptop.

"Please just tell me, Mr. Fedders. Am I short a credit or something?"

"No, Pam." He closes his Mac and looks up at me. "I have to apologize because this is entirely my fault."

"What's your fault?"

"The program that you chose for final year in the States."

No.

Oh, please God, no.

My only ticket out of here.

"I… did I not make it in?"

"Don't be ridiculous. You had the third highest average in your entire class."

Whew.

"Okay," I say as I lean back, more relaxed now. "Then what? What's your fault?"

"I submitted your paperwork to the wrong program. Or rather, the wrong location."

Wait, what?

"Excuse me?" Thankfully, ingrained politeness conveys with my words.

"You got in, of course. I had no doubts you could have your pick of internships and complete your fourth year at any of the locations we offer placement in."

"But?"

"But as it turns out, I accidentally submitted your paperwork to the California programs."

"You mean in addition to New York?"

"Unfortunately, no." He leans forward, hands clasped over his large-print paper calendar covered in coffee stains, his tone solemn. "I'm so sorry, Pam. I tried to get you into New York once I realized my error — that's why it took me so long to get back with you — but there's no room. Every program we offer in New York is full."

Shit!

"It's possible you can transfer there in January if someone leaves the program after fall semester. But I wanted to tell you in person that New York is not an option for you. At least not this fall, for the first half of your fourth year."

"I see." I choke back tears, doing my best to ignore the lump in my throat. "But California? I can go there?"

"Yes. It fits with your thesis proposal, and by the way, the program chair is quite impressed with you. By August, you can be kicking back in the Golden State and flying through your last two semesters under palm trees and tournefortia. I know it's not New York, but—"

"It's just so far away from my parents. I didn't want to be too far, especially now that my brother—"

"I know," he gestures with palms up. "I hear you. I explained your situation to the program chair in New York. If any spots become available, you're first on the list. She was sorry she couldn't do more, but our hands are tied."

My face turns sullen against my will.

"Hey, you never know," he says. "Someone may change their plans by August and leave an open spot for you."

I swallow hard, trying not to be ungrateful though the rug has just been ripped out from under me. "Where would I be, exactly? In California?"

He flips through some paperwork attached to a clipboard. "You have a choice between Silicon Valley and San Francisco. Right now, I only need a confirmation that you're accepting California as your location for the year of study. We can give you some additional time to make the choice on which location and affiliate school."

My stomach flips.

Either way, that lands me pretty close to Daryl.

I have no idea if my heart is ready for that.

Or how he'd feel about it.

I wasn't sure what would happen in this meeting, but my worst fears paled in comparison to this. Still, I didn't share my concerns with Daryl last night or this morning, knowing he'd had a crap day yesterday. Phase Two for his music app plan is falling apart thanks to Bryson Chalmers, and Daryl's hopes for a flawless launch have been bleak since he left here. I didn't want to burden him further.

And now, how can I tell him I may end up in California? I don't want him to think I rearranged my whole life to be closer to him. Talk about stalker.

I can't help wonder what it would be like to live out there, be closer to him...

...but what if my parents need me?

I'd never get to visit Carly, either. Visiting her in Florida was a possibility with a quick, inexpensive flight from Central New York or Manhattan. I could even drive to see her if I had a long break.

I'd also have to let go the idea of seeing more of Lex and our friend Charlie.

There's no way I'd see any of them very often over the course of my fourth year, if at all.

If I'm learning my field and making contacts in California, a career might present itself out there. Statistically, the likelihood of me coming back here would be far less.

"I feel absolutely terrible about this," Fedders says, diverting me from my thoughts. "Ask my wife. I found out New York was out for you last week, and I haven't had a decent night's sleep since. She says I keep her up more than our toddler."

"It's okay, Mr. Fedders." I manage a smile.

"No, it isn't. " His voice is stern as if scolding himself. "It's a mistake on my part and I can't tell you how thankful I am that you're not shouting at me right now. I've only had this happen once before, and that didn't go so well. At least, at the time."

Say what?

"May I ask with whom? Like, was it an epic fail in the end?"

"You tell me. Her name is Helena Horowitz."

My eyes go wide. "The founder of HHIS?"

"That's her. Still get a Christmas card from her every year."

"But you screwed up—er, I mean, she didn't end up where she thought she would?"

"That's fair." He laughs genuinely, putting a palm up once again. "That's exactly what I did. I screwed up. But clearly, things turned out all right."

"I'll say. She's her own multi-national conglomerate."

'HHIS' is Helena Horowitz Identity Security, the highest standard for identity theft prevention and recovery. Everyone in the digital world knows who Helena Horowitz is, if not the whole world.

Her self-designed logo is internationally recognized. It's a cartoon of her own profile in black shadow, her petite frame punctuated with heels on her feet and a beret on her head. In the image, her right hand is upturned and holding a skinny cigarette, conjuring images of a 1960s Paris model.

Nothing of a reminder for identity security, the early critics said. But her idea proved genius, if unorthodox. Her logo is what made her recognizable from day one, even before she built up her business and proved herself as the best in her field.

"She may be her own brand now, but she has a temper. At least, she did eight years ago. She was so angry when I sent her to California, she hacked into my system and caused me havoc for the entire summer leading up to it."

"Wow," I mutter. "Remind me not to look her up if I go to California."

"I couldn't blame her then. I really messed up her plans. She was engaged to a guy who ran a marketing firm in New York, and she wanted to be near him. But, maybe it was for the best, eh?"

"I suppose," I sigh. "She may never have found the success she has now if not for that mix-up."

"Now that's the way to look on the bright side. She realized the same, once thanked me by sending an entire season of front row theater tickets. Turns out her fiancé was an embezzling pariah, and she was grateful my mistake kept her from going through with her marriage."

I just sit there and nod, stunned.

"So," he says, clapping his hands with renewed enthusiasm. "This means you have a decision. You can stay here for your last year, if you want to. You'd have your choice of internships here in Toronto, of course."

"California is still a great opportunity, Mr. Fedders. You know I want to be in the States."

"Fair enough. Do you want to talk with your parents first?"

"I—yes, I suppose. You're certain this is my only option?"

"I'm afraid so, Pam. Unless you want to take the semester off and try for the New York program at Brockton State. But, as you know, that doesn't begin until January of 2017."

"Which puts my graduation off a full semester."

And renders the time I spent busting my ass to graduate with my original class a complete waste.

No, thanks.

"I don't want to wait until January. I'd love to be in New York, especially at Brockton State. That's my brother's alma mater, and close to my sister-in-law. But I need to finish on time. It's an important goal for me."

A promise I made to honor Ben's memory.

"Okay, here's the deal then. You take this form out to the waiting area," he says as he looks up at the clock on the wall. "I have to meet with another student briefly. Then come back in, and we'll talk some more before my next appointment. Keep in mind, I've got to get back to the chair of the California programs one week from today. That's all the additional time I can offer. If it's a yes to studying in the States, you'll have through mid-July to decide on which program in California you'd like to enter. The program chair extended you that courtesy given the situation."

"I can definitely decide on Toronto or California by next week."

That's about all I'm sure of right now.

As much as I love Mum and Dad and my university, no fiber of my being wants to stay here.

But the one person who has turned my world upside down for the last two weeks is in California. Just thinking of Daryl Oates leaves me quivery, unsure what the hell is the right choice. I can't make this decision based on where he is, even if he's the best guy I'll ever meet.

I've worked too hard for this.

I head out to the waiting room with the stupid clipboard and the form Fedders gave me. If I want to be in this program, all I have to do is sign it. I plunk down in a chair and, with a shaky hand, immediately sign my name. As another student comes in and sits across from me, I toy with the paper, flicking the corner of the form.

That's when I realize there are stickers plastered all over the clipboard, probably thanks to one of Fedders' kids. The stickers are incredibly familiar.

Glittery red maple leafs — the coveted prize from a box of Dare Maple Leaf cookies.

The rare holiday edition.

I shake my head in disbelief, knowing this little sign from the Universe may as well be blinking up at me in pink neon.

I remove the form, fold it up, and tuck it away in my bag.

Fate's left me in a state of flux, and I'm in no position to rush into a decision right now.

There's someone I need to talk to first.

Music Playlist for

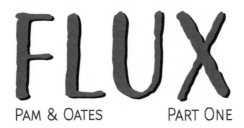

PAM & OATES   PART ONE

Beauty And A Beat - Justin Bieber featuring Nicki Minaj
Since U Been Gone - Kelly Clarkson
Stop Draggin' My Heart Around - Stevie Nicks & Tom Petty
All Shook Up - Ry Cooder
Power of Love - Huey Lewis and The News
Ain't Even Done With the Night - John Mellencamp
One Flight Down - Norah Jones
All Over You - Live
In the Air Tonight - Phil Collins
So Into You - Atlanta Rhythm Section
Let It Burn - Jazmine Sullivan
At Long Last Love - Frank Sinatra
Again - Lenny Kravitz
Everything Remains Raw - Busta Rhymes

Author Biography

M.J. Woods lives in Central New York with her family and her Bernese Mountain Dog. She has worked in the legal field of a small town for twenty-five years and often draws from these experiences in her writing.

Her first novel "Balance" (Book One of The Amped Series trilogy) garnered glowing reviews from fans as well as Foreword Clarion and Readers' Favorite. In 2018, "Balance" was awarded a Silver Medal by Readers' Favorite in the Romance-Suspense category.

M.J. is a member of the Central New York Romance Writers and the Romance Writers of America.

To find out more about the author including
upcoming releases, giveaways and other news, visit
www.mjwoodsbooks.com

Also by M.J. Woods

The Amped Series Trilogy
"Balance" (Book One)
"Sway" (Book Two)
"Fall" (Book Three)

Made in the USA
Middletown, DE
08 April 2020

88443699R00215